Blind Eye

William Malmborg

Darker Dreams Media
Chicago, IL

Darker Dreams Media
Chicago, IL
www.darkerdreamsmedia.com

Publisher's Note: This is a work of fiction. Names, characters, places, and incidents are a product of the author's imagination. Locales and public names are sometimes used for atmospheric purposes. Any resemblance to actual people, living or dead, or to businesses, companies, events, institutions, or locales is completely coincidental.

Book Layout & Design ©2013 - BookDesignTemplates.com

Blind Eye/ William Malmborg. -- 1st ed.
ISBN 978-0-9962831-1-3

Dedicated to Aynne Malmborg

"Punishing the prostitute promotes the rape of all women. When prostitution is a crime, the message conveyed is that women who are sexual are "bad", and therefore legitimate victims of sexual assault. Sex becomes a weapon to be used by men."

- Margo St. James

"Prohibition will work great injury to the cause of temperance. It is a species of intemperance within itself, for it goes beyond the bounds of reason in that it attempts to control a man's appetite by legislation, and makes a crime out of things that are not crimes. A Prohibition law strikes a blow at the very principles upon which our government was founded."

- Abraham Lincoln

Thursday

October, 24 2013

1

Alan Miller was sitting on the toilet in the tiny basement bathroom, a hand pressed into his right side, eyes closed, when he heard the familiar musical tune start to echo from his bedroom.

Oh god, he thought while yawning. *Already?*

The music stopped thirty seconds later.

Alan slowly stood up, checked the toilet for blood, saw nothing unusual, cleaned himself off, flushed, and headed back to his bedroom to disable his alarm before it could start playing again. Once that was done, he went upstairs to the kitchen to get the coffee started and then went back downstairs to shower while it brewed, a debate on whether or not to shave that morning ending without the razor being unsheathed.

The hot spray felt good on his body, and had it not been for the waiting coffee that he desperately craved, he would have stood under it for twenty minutes, his skin turning bright red as the heated water pounded his tired flesh. Instead, he began the necessary cleansing routine, his hand cutting the spray off at the six-minute mark.

His mother was sitting at the kitchen table when he returned a few minutes later, a large pink ARMY MOM cup before her.

"Good morning," she said, a yawn punctuating her statement.

"Morning," he said while pouring a few ounces of half-and-half into his ALAN cup. From there, he headed to the coffee pot.

"Rough night?" she asked.

"What makes you think that?" He eased the coffee from the carafe into his cup so he wouldn't splash the cream everywhere and watched as the two liquids swirled together.

"Heard the toilet flushing several times."

"Oh." He grabbed a spoon, stirred the mixture, and then took a seat at the table across from her. "Sorry."

"Was it bad?" she asked.

"What can I say? *Same shit, different day.*"

"No, that isn't right."

"What isn't right?" He sipped the coffee and winced as it scalded his tongue, the creamer having done little to cool it down.

"*Different shit, different day* would be more accurate."

He smiled. "You're right." He blew on the coffee and then added, "It woke me up at three, and then…well, you know how it is." For two hours he had gone back and forth, the diarrhea seeming to always have one last *hurrah* every time he thought he was finished and tried to crawl back into bed, the time left for sleeping quickly disappearing as five o'clock loomed closer and closer.

"Have you talked to the doctor about—" she started.

"Mom, not now."

"It just seems like it's happening more and—"

"MOM! *PLEASE!*" he snapped, and then, more calmly, "I really don't want to get into this again right now."

"Okay. Just promise me you won't wait too long if it really starts to become a problem."

"You know I won't let that happen," Alan said. "And remember, the diarrhea is just a result of the surgery and not a sign of coming out of remission, and if I do come out of remission again, I'll know what's going on this time around and nip it in the butt before it gets really bad." Memories of the sudden back pain that had begun a little over a year ago filled his head. At first, he had just thought the pain was a result of the strenuous training he had gone through before heading to Afghanistan, and then continued due to the living conditions they faced once they were finally there. But then the pain had shifted, and the thick brown urine had appeared. He stopped the memories and added, "Please, try not to worry so much, okay?"

"Try not to worry?" she said. "I'm a mother. That's like telling a fish not to spend so much time in the water."

Alan sighed.

"So, what do you want for breakfast? I could make you some eggs, or maybe French toast, or we could even go out somewhere since it's still early, maybe Butterfield's or Seven Dwarfs or—"

His stomach clenched. "I really can't think of food right now."

"You sure?"

"Yes."

"How about some cinnamon toast or just a waffle or two?"

"Mom, stop!"

"But you don't want to go to class hungry, do you?"

"Mom!"

"And you probably should buffer that coffee with something. I talked to some friends that have IBS, and they said drinking coffee—"

"I don't have IBS!" he snapped.

"Alan—"

"Just stop, okay," he said. "It's bad enough I've been up

since three running back and forth to the bathroom. I don't need you pestering me too." With that he stood up, coffee in hand, and headed down into his bedroom.

2

I'M SORRY, his mother texted a few minutes later. And then, when he didn't answer right away, I KNOW IT'S NOT IBS AND SHOULD STOP COMPARING THE TWO.

Alan shook his head, replied with an IT'S OKAY, and then set the phone down so he could check his email before going to his *Memoirs* project, where he would attempt to add a few pages before leaving for class at seven thirty.

Inbox (3)

He clicked on the (3) and waited for everything to load.

Remove ten pounds from your colon!

(Um, just did.)

MESSAGE MARKED AS SPAM

Check out my webcam!

(And all the viruses you can send me.)

MESSAGE MARKED AS SPAM

Long time, no talk

(More like long time, NEVER talk…)

His finger hesitated on the spam button as his eyes realized there was a name next to the email.

Stacy Collins.

Holy shit!

Could it really be Stacy, or is it just a coincidence?

The possibility of it being a coincidence was almost nonexistent, given that a name only appeared with the email if he had physically added it to his contacts at some point.

He clicked the email.

Hey Alan, thanks for letting me know you were back home, you jerk. Okay, just kidding. Seriously though, when did you get back and why so early? You weren't shot again, were you? I looked all over your blog to see if you'd written about it, but you never did. What's the deal? Too traumatic? Talk about cliché. Anyway, I'd love to hear from you, so give me a call or drop me an email. Best, Stacy.

A phone number followed along with a PS that read: *Accept my friend request already so I can start FB stalking you!!!*

Alan stared at the message for a long time, an image of him and Stacy in bed together refusing to leave his head. Nothing bad had happened between them, the understanding that it was going to be a short-lived affair accepted from the start, but that didn't make his decision on what to do next any easier. In a way, it probably made it harder because there was nothing to base the next step on. If things had ended badly, he could just ignore her. If they had ended really well and he craved more, he could jump all over it. Instead, things had just been, well…two adults seeing each other who had no ability to attach any strings to the situation whatsoever.

You don't have to reply right away, he finally told himself. *That's the beauty of email.*

Unfortunately, that meant he would spend the next five hours thinking about it, his mind unable to focus on anything but the time the two had shared together.

3

Stacy Collins read through the final paragraph of her article on a local family in Wheaton that was trying to keep their tree house, one that the father and two sons had built in their backyard without a city permit and thereby in violation of several building codes, and groaned at how stale the writing was, her mind wishing she could put words on paper (the screen) that would entice the readers into action. She wanted them to throw down the pages (slam shut the laptop or push away from the desk) with a sense of anger, their voices ready to symbolically eviscerate all those who would attempt to pull down the wooden structure. It wouldn't happen, however. Even if she had been allowed to keep the section that linked the police and city officials with the members of Hitler's Nazi party, the words "we're just following orders" providing the necessary connection, she knew most would be indifferent. People just wouldn't care. Hell, she didn't care. It wasn't her yard, or her family, or her tree house, and the readers would feel the same way.

But it is what they want you to write, the bill-conscious portion of her mind said, *what they're paying you to write.*

Of course she had suggested another direction for the story, one which could have spawned a regular column on how the father-son activities of yesteryear were slowly dying out, but the editor had said no and just wanted the bare bones of what was unfolding. The problem with this, the one that she was conscious of throughout the writing process, was that anyone could have reported and written about it. Her name wouldn't be important. Even a high school English teacher couldn't infuse a sense of style or importance into the sentences.

Which is why people so often turn to the talking head news programs, the frustrated side said. *They crave personality over substance.*

And you crave food and a roof over your head, so finish the damn read-through, take out any last bit of fluff you know they will make you take out anyway, and send it along.

Stacy nodded, as if the bill-conscious part of her brain needed a visual acknowledgment, and finished it. Once that was complete, she headed into her kitchen to pour another cup of coffee and then went back to her office / dining room to make sure the email didn't bounce back.

Inbox (0)

She refreshed it to see if anything changed, but nothing new had come through. From there she opened a separate project file, one which she had been working freelance on for a while now but still didn't have enough information to fully write out, and started to read through a few things while trying to come up with another angle to investigate.

Her phone buzzed.

Stacy looked down at the number illuminated on the screen, her eyes expecting to see the familiar digits of her editor's cell phone. No recognition followed. It was local though, so she picked it up.

"Hello?"

"Stacy?" a voice asked.

"Yes?" she said.

"Long time, no talk."

"What..." she started, and then it clicked. "Alan? Alan Miller?"

"Yep," Alan said. "I just got your email."

"Wow," Stacy said. Silently she added, *I didn't think you'd actually get in touch.* Out loud, "That was fast."

"Yeah...so, what's up?"

"Nothing really, just working on an article."

"Ah, still writing for the *Wheaton Sun*?"

"Yes and no. I'm a stringer now."

"A what?"

Stacy laughed. "A stringer. It's just another way of saying freelancer, only all the different editors will send me story topics and events they want me to cover, how many words they want it to be, and what they will pay if I complete it."

"Oh, you get to pick and choose," Alan said. "Sweet deal."

"Yeah." *If they'd send me enough topics where I could afford to let some go, that is.*

"No more being forced to go interview a boring soldier on leave from Iraq whose only claim to local fame was that he had no idea what he wanted to do with life and joined the army, right?"

"Boring is hardly the word I'd use…well…for the interview part of our time together at least." She couldn't help but let out a chuckle at this.

"Nice," Alan said, his own laugh echoing. "Time has obviously eroded away your memory, so I think a refresher is needed."

"Oh, is that so? Well then, how does drinks early this evening sound, possibly followed by dinner if I don't find you too boring?"

"Sounds good to me," Alan said.

Silence settled.

"Um, did you have a specific place in mind?"

"How about our old hookup place, say five o'clock?" Stacy suggested.

"Alfie's?" Alan said. "My god, is that place still there?"

"Um, yeah. How long have you been home?" She had a pretty good idea, given the sudden consistency of his blog updates that had begun in July, but couldn't picture him being in town all this time and not knowing that Alfie's was still around.

"Since May."

"May! And you mean to tell me you haven't been to Alfie's at all—it's like five minutes from your house."

"True, but believe it or not I haven't really had a need to go over to that part of Roosevelt since I've been back, so…"

Stacy waited, but nothing else followed. Whatever excitement had started to build between the two, excitement that could probably have allowed them to talk for hours if allowed to continue, faded, and with it their call came to an end.

With the silence came concern that their time together now wouldn't be the same as it had been before, that "before" being something Stacy had pretty much been missing since the two had gone their separate ways in early 2008.

But isn't that always the case? she asked herself. *Doesn't the past always seem better than it really was and make you wish you could keep reliving it rather than moving forward? Hell, next year you may be looking back at this moment with nostalgia and wishing you could relive it and everything that follows for the next few weeks.*

Next year.

Whenever she contemplated the following year, she always saw herself as having finally broken into the big leagues with her writing, her name in high demand with editors, given its potential to sell papers.

For eight years she had been doing this, the sought-after and hoped-for breakthrough never occurring.

This time it will be different, though, she told herself. *This time you've gotten hold of a real story that needs telling.*

Such thoughts weren't uncommon whenever she found herself working a story outside of the suggested (demanded) topics that were sent to her, but this time it felt different. This time it felt real.

And you have no idea how to proceed with it.

Her phone buzzed.

She looked at the number, and though it was one she recognized, she didn't answer the phone. *You'll get your money when I get some money.*

Speaking of which…

She refreshed her email screen to see if the editor at the paper had replied. If he had, and if he liked what he saw, then a check would be on its way. If not, well…he would like it eventually once all his suggestions were added, following which she would get paid, eventually. She just hoped it was sooner rather than later.

A new email was waiting, but it was just letting her know that Alan had accepted her friend request on Facebook.

Alan closed the phone and thought about the consequences of his agreement to meet Stacy, his mind unsure how to feel about the situation. Fear was present, though it wasn't the typical fear one probably felt in the hours leading up to a date-like engagement with a girl. Instead, his was based on the concern that he would hurt her, his lack of interest in any type of romantic entanglements putting a quick end to any hope she might have of going beyond the casual-sex-focused state of the relationship they'd had back in 2008. This wasn't to say he wouldn't be interested in revisiting some of the activities the two had done back then, just that he wouldn't want it to lead to anything serious.

Which it will, he told himself. *Even if she says it won't.*

This was something he had learned about women yet, thankfully, had never had the displeasure of experiencing firsthand. Instead, all his knowledge came from fellow soldiers who had met girls that wanted nothing more than to be "friends with benefits" while the soldier was stateside, and then wives once the deployment orders arrived.

But maybe Stacy won't be like that. Maybe she really does just want to meet for old times' sake and have a little fun in bed from time to time as a distraction from the seriousness of life.

Stacy was different from most of the women he had met during his lifetime. She was also really tough and determined, her eyes often set on a goal that she would do anything to achieve. Back then, it had been becoming a world-renowned journalist, one who was known to take on any assignment no matter the risks involved. She also seemed the type that would push others out of the way in order to achieve this recognition, which had once caused him to make a verbal comparison between her and Gale Weathers from the *Scream* movies. It had been spoken as a joke, one of those light-hearted after-sex comments, but had sparked a pretty serious discussion on how women in her field had to be just like Gale

Weathers—bitchy and ruthless—to get the respect they deserved and the success they desired.

Well, Alan had said in reply, *just stay away from reporting on teen slasher situations and you should do okay.* Again, the statement had been meant as a joke, something to ease them away from the serious conversation that was brewing, but she managed to weave it into the point she was making and told him she would love to get involved in a situation like that. *The story I could write afterward would be priceless,* she said. *And if I get cut at some point during the bloody climax of events, even better, because I could have photos of me taken while in the hospital recovering, my fingers dancing away on a laptop that is sitting next to my tray of disgusting hospital food.*

The comment had sparked a memory of beating an insurgent to death with the butt of his rifle while going house to house in a suburb of Baghdad. It was a disturbing memory, though not one that he regretted because it had been a necessary moment. He also wasn't haunted by it, as some would be, though he did occasionally have nightmares about the situation—anyone who had watched an enemy come at them with the barrel of an AK-47 pointed at their chest would have nightmares from time to time.

Shit, that was seven years ago next month, he realized. Even more amazing was that it had been twelve years since he had made the decision to join the military, the thought process having begun shortly after watching the towers fall on September 11.

He stared at the mental calendar for nearly ten minutes, his inner eye slowly turning the pages until he reached the present day. Once there, he turned on the TV and went to AMC, his mind reminding him that horror movies would be playing every hour until Halloween—his first Halloween at home since 2001.

Still have to go get all the necessary supplies for your display.

Halloween was the following Thursday. On Saturday he planned on setting up a horrifying display at the front door, one that was sure to scare away all but the bravest of the brave when it came to the trick-or-treaters that showed up. It was a moment he had been looking forward to since coming home. Actually the entire holiday season—which in his eyes went from Halloween to New Year's Day—was something he had been looking forward to and excited about since realizing he would be home for it all.

Of course his birthday, which had been in September, had been like a prequel to the holiday season. His mother, equally excited that he would be home, had gone all out in celebrating. A month later, he still couldn't believe how many gifts she had given him, or the amount of work that had gone into decorating the upstairs of the house with streamers and balloons—all while he was at class.

On screen, the commercials that had been playing ever since he turned the channel to AMC finally ended, and he watched as a girl screamed while being chased by the white-masked Michael Myers. Ten years earlier, he would have known within seconds which of the sequels the scene was a part of, but now he was unsure. *Four, Five,* or *Curse* was the best he could do, though he eliminated *Curse* fairly quickly since that was one he had watched frequently during his high school days, his favorites back then being the original *Halloween, Halloween II,* and *Halloween: The Curse of Michael Myers.* All the others had been lacking, in his opinion, though were still fun to watch as the Halloween season settled in.

5

"Yes! YES! OH GOD! *YES! YES! YES!*"

Amanda didn't even think about the words, or how they sounded, as she faked the moment of orgasm, the routine so commonplace that she could probably do it in her sleep if needed—*wonder if that kink is out there.*

Beneath her, the man grunted, his sweaty body straining

against the bed as a very real orgasm erupted from within, her insides feeling the sudden warmth as semen filled the tip of the condom.

"YES! GIVE IT TO ME!" she cried.

"Uh! Uh! Uh!" was his only reply, followed by a quick, "Okay, *okay*, STOP!" His hands going up to grab her, stopping her steady, well-practiced thrusts. "PLEASE!"

Amanda giggled while complying, a silent sigh of relief flowing throughout her body as she rolled off and snuggled up against him in the bed, a hand settling upon his chest. She then trailed the hand down to his groin, fingers lightly touching the thumping penis, another giggle echoing. "Looks like someone is all worn out," she said.

"Yes," he sighed, voice strained. "Completely."

Good, because I got homework to do, her mind said, dreading the math problems that awaited her on the text next week.

"Thought I was going to explode so many times," he added.

Amanda smiled. "I think that's the longest I've ever kept you going." Though indifferent to the man, she felt pride at what she had achieved, her skill with her own body having kept him on the edge for a full forty minutes. "Must've felt good to finally release."

"Good doesn't even begin to describe it," he said. "You completely drained me."

"Did I?" she asked, a playful ring in her voice. "Let's see." Before he knew it, she had his penis in her hand, fingers squeezing to see if anything else spurted into the condom.

"Gahhhh!" he cried, the organ still overly sensitive from the orgasm.

She laughed and then gently pulled the condom free, the weight it now carried a testament to just how much semen had built up and burst free from within him.

Glad he doesn't want me to swallow it.

Some of her clients did, an odd sense of pleasure arriving within them from seeing her squeezing all the fluid from the condom into her mouth, almost as if it were the last remnants from one of those freeze pop things. Swallowing semen itself wasn't something that got to her, her mouth having become accustomed to the varying tastes many years ago, but taking it from a condom...that was just gross.

"Was it good for you?" he asked after a few minutes, body still sprawled on the bed.

"Fantastic," she lied. "I don't know what it is, but your penis has this ability to hit the magic button over and over again."

He grinned.

"Wish every man was like you," she added.

"Hmm, maybe I should get a discount," he teased.

"I would if I could, but you know I'm not in charge of that." She sighed. "And before you bring it up, you know I'm not allowed to see anyone outside of the service."

"I know, I know. We are, but alas, two lovers trapped within a system that we cannot escape from." He smiled. "So tragic."

She smiled back. "So romantic."

He kissed her.

What a tool, she thought. *No wonder his wife isn't giving it to* him.

6

Wary about the possible consequences of having food within his damaged digestive track, Alan forced his body to endure his growing hunger as the afternoon hours ticked by, his mind knowing that such discomfort now was better than the agony and embarrassment that could follow later.

Especially if she wants to go back to her place afterward...

A tingle of excitement appeared within his groin at the thought, one that he normally would have appeased with a trip into his bedroom, a special folder on his laptop containing dozens upon dozens of videos that would help bring about the desired conclusion. This time, however, he left the tingle alone, past experience having taught him that while enjoyable, the release he would bring about now would be nothing compared to the one he would experience later, one that would be even more pleasurable if he denied himself until then.

So now what?

No answer followed, at least not one that was appealing, so he ended up staying by the TV in the family room, eyes watching, but not really processing, an entry in the *Hellraiser* series.

You should be studying, he told himself, the movie breaking for some commercials. *That history test is going to kick your butt if you don't.*

As truthful as the inner words were, they did little to inspire him; therefore he spent most of the afternoon watching horror movies on AMC, the only break in that arriving when he dozed off for forty-five minutes.

A female scream from the movie pulled him back, the cry momentarily bringing about a visual of a bloodied mother discovering her child among the torn bodies of a crowded market car-bomb blast. It wasn't a flashback, just a memory, one that he would have preferred to stay buried within his mind.

A yawn followed, the unexpected nap having alerted him to how exhausted he actually was after this morning's gastrological disturbances.

You should go catch another hour, he told himself. *Get all rested for tonight.*

Instead, he headed into the kitchen to make some tea, the leaves he decided upon being from his Glenburn Estate tin, which, in his opinion, was one of the finest first-flush Darjeeling teas one could find.

Once ready, he continued to watch TV, but this time with his laptop on the couch alongside him, a half-assed attempt at adding some pages to his memoir project taking place.

7

Deciding what to wear became quite the ordeal as the time of the get-together with Alan neared, the question of what exactly would unfold and what direction she wanted the evening to take getting the better of Stacy.

Do you want sex?

The question was important because if she wanted it, she would get it. Of this she was certain. Equally certain, she wanted sex, but did she really want it with him tonight?

Yes, but...

Nothing followed, and it was because of this that she was having such difficulty, the idea that she might simply want sex for the sake of sex hard for her to accept.

You do want to spend time with Alan too... a part of her mind countered. After all, if she simply wanted sex and had no qualms about going out to get it, she could have been doing that daily. With Alan, however, it was something more. At least it had been back in 2008.

Five years.

Not only had a lot of time passed since they last saw each other, but a lot had happened during that time, especially with him. And if her theory on his having been discharged from the military was correct, something that she hadn't been able to confirm through his blog posts or Facebook statuses, then something really big and monumental had happened, because he had planned on being a career soldier. The question was, *what had it been? And had it changed him to the point where she wouldn't like spending time with the person he had become?*

You won't know until you see him, so why worry about it?

The thought did little to ease her concern.

And she still didn't know what to wear.

8

Amanda arrived home just as her roommate Emily was descending the stairs, a look of aggravation plastered across her face.

"You're late!" Emily snapped.

"So? I had to stop by the store to get more coffee creamer."

"And Dick Blick?" She glared. "I didn't know more art supplies were on the list too."

"I just needed a new sketch pad and some pencils. It took five minutes, tops." *Well, more like fifteen, but who gives a fuck?*

Emily sighed while shaking her head and then sat down to pull her boots on, skirt rising to reveal garters attached to her stockings, something Amanda hadn't noticed she was wearing until that moment.

"Do you have a scene tonight?" Amanda asked.

"No, a study date, and now I'm probably going to be late since you had the car."

"A study date?" Amanda questioned.

"Yes, a study date!" She stood up and held out her hand. "Keys, please!"

Amanda handed them over, tongue held despite her desire to call *bullshit* on the study date. Emily had a scene. It was obvious. Equally obvious was the reason she wouldn't admit it. She was moonlighting, getting cash on the side, which was totally forbidden.

And she thinks I don't know.

This irked Amanda, though she wasn't sure why. Maybe because it felt as if Emily wasn't giving her enough credit, thinking that a simple "study date" statement was enough to pull the wool over her eyes.

But she knows me better than to think that.

So maybe it really is a study date.

But why the short skirt, stockings, and garters?

And why a study date?

At no point during the semester had Amanda ever seen Emily studying. She also had never seen her doing homework nor heard her talk about what was going on in her classes or how she was doing in them. All this had led Amanda to believe Emily didn't really care.

But maybe she does…

If so, it would totally paint the girl in a new light, her original opinion that Emily was a lost cause proven incorrect. That said, becoming motivated was easy, maintaining it over a long period of time…not so much.

"So when will you be back?" Amanda asked.

"Fucked if I know," Emily replied.

Fucked being the key word? she silently asked. Out loud, "Okay, well, *have fun.*"

"Yep, thanks." Emily reached for the door but then stopped and said, "Oh, by the way. Got a new girl moving in tomorrow. Nikki…Vicky…something like that." She waved a hand. "Anyway, figured you'd want to know. Not sure when exactly they're bringing her over, but it will probably be in the afternoon. You have class in the morning?"

"No, just the schoolgirl guy."

"Oh, nice. He's fun."

"Yeah."

"Okay, well see you later."

Amanda nodded and then, once Emily was beyond the door, made sure the main lock and deadbolt were secure. From there, she went to the kitchen screen door, which, naturally, wasn't locked, and threw that latch as well.

One day... Amanda started, an image of someone in dark clothing and a ski mask opening the door filling her mind's eye. The big letters of a newspaper headline followed, ones that spelled out: TWO COLLEGE STUDENTS RAPED AND MURDERED, TIES TO PROSTITUTION SUSPECTED.

Wait, make it three students.

The thought shifted her focus, questions about what the new girl would be like echoing from every corner of her brain. Speculation was all that followed, speculation that pretty much created a clone of Emily.

They'll probably be best friends and always gang up on me when I have a different opinion or thought on something.

Such was life.

No matter what situation she found herself in, she always was the odd one out. It never failed. Even in her classes, despite appearing to be a standard student, she could tell everyone knew she was different. Something about her just projected it. She didn't know why.

A heavy sigh left her lips, one that was meant to clear her mind. It worked, and five minutes later she found herself sitting on the couch in the family room, math book open, a study guide before her, TV clicker put out of reach so she didn't give in to temptation.

9

Alan was a bit early to Alfie's, his mind and body unable to take waiting at home any longer. Of course, arriving early didn't speed things up at all, but mentally it seemed to pass the time faster, mostly because he spent a good chunk of it observing the place, his eyes trying to figure out if anything beyond the waitstaff had changed.

"Is it just like you remember?" a familiar female voice asked.

Alan shifted himself in the seat and stood up. "It is, except the red highlights," he said with a smile, a bit of hesitation hitting before he opened his arms for a hug. "It's so good to see you," he added as their bodies connected.

"It's good to see you too," she said, arms squeezing him closer even though they were already touching, his chest actually feeling a tingle where her boobs pressed into him. "I can't believe it's been five years."

"Me either," he said.

The hug broke.

Silence settled.

Then, after nearly thirty seconds, "Do I really look the same to you?"

"Aside from the hair, which has totally changed, you really do."

She blushed. "If you saw me standing next to myself from five years ago, you'd probably not even realize we were the same person and be like, 'Who is this hag?' or something."

He shook his head. "If one of us was not to recognize the other, it would have been *you* not recognizing *me*, but you did, so all is well." His mother hadn't, not when he came out of the terminal at O'Hare last May, the hundred-plus pounds he had lost since the last time she had seen him causing her to gasp. Thankfully, he had managed to regain about twenty pounds since then, his face looking full once more as opposed to bony, which was probably why Stacy didn't say anything. Sweaters had a way of hiding how skinny one actually was.

The waitress, who was running the entire bar area, came up to them and asked if she could get Stacy anything.

"Um…" She looked at Alan and his drink. "…what's that?"

"Just a Coke," he said. "I actually don't drink anymore—ever."

"Really?"

"Really."

"Well, I hope you don't mind if I do."

"Not at all," Alan said. "Order anything you like, my treat."

She did just that and, once the beer was in front of her, asked, "Should we go get a table?"

"We can do that," Alan said. "You want one of the ones in here or an actual table in the main area?"

"Um…whichever you want," she said.

"Okay." Less than two minutes later, they were at a table in the far room, her beer already half gone and his Coke needing a re-fill.

"So," he said while looking around a bit, eyes noting that nothing had changed within the room at all, "how are you?"

"I'm good," she said. "How are you?"

"I'm good, too."

"That's good." She took a sip.

Silence settled once more, both of them looking at each other, then away from each other when their eyes met, and then back at each other.

"So…" Stacy said. "Five years."

"Yeah. Hard to believe, right? That's longer than the time one spends in high school."

"Wow, you're right." She shook her head. "Shit, that makes it seem even longer now." She sighed. "Honestly, though, it doesn't feel that long, at least it didn't when I sent you that message."

He sipped his Coke and then looked around for the wait-ress.

"It probably felt longer to you," she noted. "You know, be-ing overseas and all."

"It's weird. Being overseas, it didn't feel like a long stretch of time, but rather several moments of time clumped together, some of which were filled with longing and despair, only not like during my very first deployment way back in 2003." He thought for a moment, trying to figure out how to explain things. "During that first tour, and the second, there would be weeks when all I could do was think about home, and I wanted nothing more than to will myself there. Other times, days would come and go without much thought, and I'd suddenly realize that I hadn't thought about home for two or three weeks."

"And it wasn't like that in Afghanistan?" she asked.

"Afghanistan was different. I also wasn't there very long, at least, not like I was in Iraq."

"How come?"

"Well, for starters, after passing selection I spent nearly two years doing nothing but training."

"Two years?" She lifted her glass to signal the waitress. "Fuck, I thought the twelve weeks of basic was tough, so two years…shit."

"Well, it wasn't all running and push-ups and being broken down. A lot of it was classroom instruction, learning languages and getting educated on the social and economic structures of the region for deployment. Actually, that was the toughest for me. I've never been good at learning languages. Totally failed Spanish in high school. But after a while, things clicked."

The waitress finally arrived at their table. "Sorry about that. No one told me I had another table. What can I get for you?"

They both got new drinks but decided to wait a bit before placing an order for food.

"So after two years you finally made it into…what was it you always talked about wanting to get into?" Stacy asked.

"Delta Force," he said.

"And you did it," she said.

"No, didn't make it that high."

"But you passed everything?"

"Oh, I made it into Special Forces and was part of a team, but getting into Delta Force, well, that's even more advanced and selective." *I could have though*, he silently added. *If I hadn't gotten sick...*

Obviously, even if he hadn't been struck down by his own immune system, there was no guarantee of achieving that goal, but even so, a part of him just knew he could have done it if given the chance.

"And..." she pressed.

"And what?" he asked, even though he knew exactly where this was going.

"Why didn't you make it? What happened? You were supposed to be a career soldier, yet now here you are, living with your mother, writing a blog and posting on Facebook, which tells me you're no longer in the military, especially Special Forces, because I'm pretty sure they would not like you doing such a thing."

"You're right, they wouldn't," he said and then looked up as the waitress slowly approached, hesitation evident, as she didn't want to disrupt them.

"Are you two ready to order?"

Alan looked at Stacy, who nodded.

They both ordered cheeseburgers, cooked medium, hers with everything, his with nothing but the cheese.

"So what happened?" Stacy asked.

"Crohn's disease," Alan said.

"What?"

"Crohn's disease," he repeated.

"Is that the one that makes you shit all the time?" she asked. "I think I've seen commercials for it."

"Yeah, that's the one, only shitting all the time is a poor way to describe it because it sounds like an annoyance rather than a legitimate disease that can kill you, which is what it almost did to me."

"Seriously?"

"Yeah. Put a hole in my small bowel, one that opened up into my bladder, causing massive infections and quite a bit of pain."

"Holy fuck, I didn't know that. When did that happen?"

"About a year and a half ago. Started as simple back pain that just got worse and worse until I was nearly bedridden, and then it became groin pain, and then, well, one day I felt a pop between my legs during a briefing and suddenly had to piss like a racehorse, only it wasn't..." He thought about the brown gritty sludge-like fluid that had come out. "...probably not something you want to hear about before eating, actually."

"I can handle it. What happened?"

"Well, let's just say that the stuff that was supposed to go out the back door began to go out the front door."

"Seriously?"

"Yep. It's called a fistula. I developed one between my small bowel and bladder. Basically, it was the result of my immune system suddenly attacking a small area of my intestine. Eventually that caused a hole that opened up into the bladder."

"Why?"

"No one knows. Apparently, it's a disease you're born with. Doctors don't know why the disease will become active all of a sudden. For most with it, it happens in their early twenties. Mine waited a bit longer." He shrugged. "After that, I had surgery that removed the damaged bowel and part of the bladder, and even though the disease seems to be in remission once again, I can't be an active-duty soldier, especially not Special Forces, so, well, I took a medical discharge."

"Wow. I'm really sorry to hear that."

Alan nodded.

10

Though Amanda had just gone shopping that afternoon, nothing within the refrigerator appealed to her, which was why she found herself contemplating a quick walk down to Chipotle for a pork burrito. While thinking about this, she headed into the bathroom to check the scale, concern about her weight getting the better of her.

Fuck! Fuck! Fuck!

Chipotle was off the table. In fact, eating anything that evening would be a mistake, given what the scale had just displayed.

Unfortunately, such resolve didn't nullify the hunger she felt, hunger that seemed to be intensifying with each passing second. It wasn't fair.

Equally puzzling was the steady increase in weight these last few weeks. Sex was supposed to burn calories, and she had it almost every day, sometimes twice a day if the client desired and had booked a large chunk of time, yet here she was, looking at a scale that showed her weighing more than she had ever weighed before.

You're eating a lot more now.

It was the only answer.

And you aren't really having that much sex. At least not when one compared it to the amount she had been having last year at this time, or really at any point during her late teens and early twenties. In those days, the number of men that fucked her in a day was greater than what she saw in a week while working here, which probably played a huge part in keeping her weight down.

Plus there was never anything good to eat.

Here, there were too many good things to eat, the options making it difficult to decide. Case in point, last year at this time, she would never have stood staring into the fridge for so long, the simple fact of being able to go to the fridge and take something making her grab the first edible thing she came across.

So, what, you want to go back to that?

The answer was a solid NO, yet at the same time she did think that maybe having a few more clients might be a good idea. Unfortunately, she didn't know if the boss would allow such a thing, which was weird. With other pimps, the standard mode of operation seemed to be to see just how many dicks could get off inside her in a day. Here, that wasn't the case.

But what will happen if they start to realize that clients don't want to have sex with me because I'm getting fat?

What will—

THUNK! THUNK! THUNK!

The heavy knocks echoed through the house, nearly causing her to jump. Never before had anyone come to the door like this.

What do I do?

Another *THUNK* echoed, followed by the doorbell ringing.

She waited.

The bell rang again.

They know you're inside and…

Nothing followed.

She had no idea what to think and also didn't know what to do. People weren't supposed to come to the door, at least not people who knew anything about what they did. That was why they always met clients at the other houses.

No more knocks followed.

Heart racing, she moved to the window to peek outside. At first, no one was there, but after a second, she watched a man and a boy descend the driveway and step onto the sidewalk. After that, they stepped onto the neighbor's driveway and headed toward that door.

Selling something?

Is that allowed out here?

For some reason she'd been under the impression that cities like Wheaton, Naperville, and Glen Ellyn forbid such things, the rich homeowners not liking the bother of people pretty much begging for money, the typical plastic cup replaced with overpriced magazines, cleaning supplies, and other items that could be picked up for cheap at the local Walgreens.

At least it wasn't someone bad…

The relief of this was short-lived, her hunger pains reminding her of the growing weight issue. She also didn't feel very confident about the upcoming math test. Actually, the entire college thing seemed like a fruitless endeavor, given how much difficulty she was already having.

11

"So, how's your mom doing?" Stacy asked, nothing but crumbs remaining of what had once been a heaping basket of food.

Alan shrugged, debating his own last two bites of burger and the remaining fries. "She's good." He decided against the fries but reached for the burger. "Still working the travel agent job, putting groups together and going out to exotic locations with all these middle-aged women every couple of months."

Stacy grinned. "That still cracks me up, all those suburban housewives going out to see the world, taking the road less traveled. Your mom should totally have her own TV show with this group."

Alan finished chewing. "She really should. You know, she took a group to the Amazon and thought it would be cool to stay in this eco hotel thing that researchers often use. I guess the selling point for the group was that they would hear monkeys in the trees from their rooms. Nothing was said about the fact that the rooms only had three walls, and everyone had to sleep in hammocks with mosquito netting over them. The group was horrified when they finally arrived and took it out on my mom, who spent her entire first night crying."

"Oh, that's horrible." Then, after stealing one of Alan's fries, "Why did the rooms only have three walls?"

"So you could experience the jungle. Remember, it was typically a place for scientists and researchers to stay. Oh, and no AC…obviously."

"Ahhh, that makes sense." She took another fry. "I guess that's the one downside of trying to find the most untouristy ways of visiting a country."

"Yeah, but for the most part the groups always enjoy themselves. One of the best times they ever had was in India, of all places. Oh, and Egypt—before all the turmoil. Got tons of pictures of her seeing all the sights from the back of a camel."

"Shit, I totally need to sign up for one of these trips, as soon as I have enough money to throw at something like that. Where's her next one?"

"Antarctica."

"What?" She gave him a "are you bullshitting me?" look. "For real?"

"I swear. Actually, that isn't her *next* trip. I think the next one is to Cuba right after Thanksgiving, but the Antarctica one is coming up as well, toward the end of the summer months down there."

"Wow. Cuba and Antarctica. Your mom's awesome."

"She is."

The two went quiet, thoughts of his mother and how special she was dominating Alan's mind for a moment.

"So," Stacy said after nearly a minute, "now what?"

"All depends," Alan said. "I'm up for anything."

"Anything? Well, if that's the case, I heard about this game show where men have three holes to choose from. Behind one is nothing, behind another is a girl's mouth, and behind the next a Taser..."

"Yeah...so...I'm up for *almost* anything."

"Okay, well then, might I suggest we head back to my place and hang out there?"

"Sounds good to me. You still over in Lakeside?"

"Ha, I wish. Nope. Sadly I had to downgrade a bit and am now over a store in downtown Wheaton, one with no AC, very little hot water, and a fuse system that allows me to run one appliance at a time in the kitchen."

"Hey, better than having to live with your mother."

"I'd agree, if I thought you didn't have a choice in that."

"What do you mean?"

"Oh come on. Knowing you, I'm fairly certain you saved most of the money you earned while in the military and that you really had no expenses whatsoever beyond things that took your fancy." She paused to finish off the rest of her beer. "I also know that you were wounded twice and now, given what you said tonight, that you were medically discharged, which means you get something every month from the VA."

"Okay, you got me there. Still, it's really not as much as you think. Sure, I could move out, but without a job, my savings would disappear fairly quickly, especially while going to school, and I'd be back in my mother's basement before I knew it, this time without any savings." Plus, much of what he had saved was tied up in stocks, CDs, and mutual funds, some of which were earning quite a bit with interest and dividends, so he didn't want to put an end to that by pulling out the funds.

"I suppose that makes sense," she said. "So, what field of employment are you thinking of going into?"

"I have no idea." It was the truth. Nothing appealed to him.

"I was all set to be a career soldier and now..." He shrugged. "...everything has changed."

"Well, I'm sure something"—it was her turn to shrug— "actually, I have no idea either."

"Ha, that makes two of us." He liked her honesty and the fact that she hadn't said, "Everything happens for a reason." Nothing happened for a reason; people just applied what they thought the reason was in order to feel better about the events that unfolded.

12

Just like old times, Stacy said to herself as she got into her car, a fantastic feeling of comfort having descended upon her as the two talked. *But maybe this time it will last a bit longer...*

She didn't know why, but being with Alan felt right. The two of them clicked together perfectly, something she had noticed the very first time they met. It was weird too because she typically didn't click with anyone, her determination to succeed in her field and reluctance to pad the truth with anyone, even friends, always driving others away.

But not Alan.

Why this was, she didn't exactly know, but she thought it might have to do with the lack of bullshit between them. Five years ago, they had known what their relationship was all about and thus hadn't had to pretend with each other.

And the same will be true now.

No drama. We get along while together and, if it's like before, will enjoy having sex together, each of us always feeling satisfied afterward.

A lack of awkwardness about things helped. Back then, if something interesting had caught her attention, she'd had no qualms about calling him up to tell him about it, no thoughts of *Am I bugging him?* or *Is he getting annoyed with me?* entering her mind. And it seemed the same on his end. A day or two might pass where they each had their own things going on, and then suddenly he would call and be like, "Hey, you want to hang out tonight?" and they would. No "Why didn't you call me yesterday?" or anything. It was great.

And just think, you thought the interview was going to be a serious waste of time and talent.

Thinking about this brought a smile to her face, especially since she was now able to look back at that moment, and what followed, without a sense of loss. He was back, and they were once again going to enjoy each other's company, this time without another deployment looming.

Does he know how hard that was for me?

Was it hard for him?

A part of her wondered if she should bring it up, but then she decided against it, given that it could add an element of drama into what they had. Neither was at fault for what had happened. It was just life, thus best to simply enjoy the fact that the separation was over and they were together again.

And soon I will find out if he still has that ability to bring about pleasure within me that I once dared not dream of for fear of never getting to achieve such bliss. She turned down Main Street while thinking this, an eye to the rearview mirror making sure he was still back there, a warm tingle developing within her nether regions.

Hopefully, I can still work my magic as well.

It had been quite some time since she had been with anyone with whom the sex was more than a simple masturbation fuck. With Alan, and a few others, sex had been an experience; with everyone else it had been just...well...*meh.* And the *meh* wasn't because the men sucked or anything; they just hadn't clicked. The pleasure was still there, but it wasn't the PLEASURE! she craved, both in receiving and delivering.

Thoughts on how they would get started entered her mind

as she bounced across the train tracks dividing the downtown area, along with a moment of concern for her muffler and other items of rusting machinery that were barely clinging to the underside of her car.

I should probably do it, she decided a few seconds later, hand signaling a right turn that most drivers probably didn't understand. *After all, this was my idea.*

Looking back, she realized she had been the one to make the first move all those years ago, thoughts of the soldier she had interviewed dominating her mind to the point where she called him up and fibbed about needing to get together once again because the photographs she had taken to go with the article hadn't turned out. *"I also have some additional questions I want to ask,"* she'd lied.

Of course, having sex with him hadn't been the actual focus of getting together—she had just wanted to see him once more because he was interesting—but while together a moment had come when she made a move, and sex had followed. Really GOOD sex.

And it was fun!

Before that month, she had never really put much thought into experimenting with different things, but once they had gotten together, her mind seemed to go nuts with different ideas and activities she wanted to try. And she wasn't alone. Once she got the ball rolling, Alan had started thinking things up as well and often brought ideas to the table—*bedroom* (well, actually sometimes the table)—that he wanted to try. It was great. No boredom whatsoever with their sex life, or their time together when not having sex, their conversations always lasting a long time and naturally shifting from one topic to the next.

Is he thinking about all this? she wondered while reaching out to signal a left turn.

No answer followed as she guided them down the alleyway and pulled into her parking spot behind the storefront, an old wooden stairway with a sagging porch leading the way up to her place.

Alan pulled in next to her and, before he shut the car off, called out through his window, "This spot okay?"

"Yep," she called back. "No one else lives in any of these apartments right now, so it's all ours."

"Nice," he said and rolled his window back up, engine noises fading away as he twisted the key. Then, as he got out, "This place is pretty cool. I always love old storefronts with apartments above. Makes you think of the thirties and forties."

"Well, just remember there's a difference between vintage and dump, and my place leans more toward the latter, sadly."

"Still, it's unique, which I love. I'd never want to live in an apartment building where every unit is the same. That's boring. Places like this, and old houses that have been converted into apartments by floor, that's more my style."

"Really, well, once you decide to get your own place, there are quite a few like that around here, ones that are actually nice, which, as I've warned, isn't the case here."

"You know, with all this buildup about how awful your place is, I may be disappointed at how unawful it actually is."

"Yeah, that's the goal," she said with a laugh.

"Well, don't worry. Some of the places I've lived in weren't even suitable for roaches, and they can survive anywhere. So as long as it has four walls, a roof, and isn't mortared daily, it works for me."

"Well then, I think we'll be okay."

With that, the two started up the steps, the wooden structure actually shifting a bit as they climbed.

"You think that was freaky? You should have seen it when a friend helped carry up my futon." She pulled out her key. "He actually gasped as if it was going to crumble beneath him."

He? Alan wondered to himself and then said, "I probably would have done the same."

She smiled and opened the door.

Alan stepped in and stood to the side as Stacy followed, her hand reaching up in the darkness to grab a cord.

Click!

Nothing.

"Son of a—" she started and shook her head. "You know, I just changed this one a week ago too."

"Where are your bulbs? I can go grab one," Alan offered.

"No, I don't have any fresh ones, but I can take one from over the mirror in the bathroom. Hang on a second." She started down the hallway and turned toward the bathroom, hand reaching for the light switch.

Someone's here!

She sensed the presence seconds before the figure moved toward her from within the bathroom, his body slamming into her just as her hand caught the light switch.

A cry left her lips, followed by a grunt as her body slammed into the wall, the attacker crashing into it with her.

And then a fist slammed into her gut, toppling her as her stomach seemed to cave in on itself.

"Stay away from—" a heavy voice began, followed by a strange cry.

Something crashed.

Glass shattered.

A table flipped.

Several shouts echoed, none of them sounding like Alan, though she couldn't be absolutely sure.

She tried to stand.

Bad idea.

And then Alan was helping her to her feet.

"You okay?" he asked.

"Y-y-yeah," she said, voice strained. Then, "Uh-oh."

She almost made it to the toilet.

13

"What do you mean no?" Alan asked. "Someone didn't just break in; they waited around until you got home so they could attack you. That's not something you just brush aside."

Stacy sighed. "I know, and I agree, but I simply can't go to the police with this."

"Why not?"

She took a sip of the water Alan had gotten her. "I'm working a story right now. One that will make headlines all across the country once it breaks."

"And…" he asked, fairly certain where she was going with this, yet still wanting to hear it from her own lips.

"And I don't want anyone else to catch wind of it and beat me to the punch."

"Do you really think that will happen?"

"In this area, the news of a break-in followed by an attack on a young woman will spread really fast and attract a lot of attention." She took another sip. "Especially with Wheaton College right down the road."

"Okay, I'll admit, you're right about that." For the most part, Wheaton was a very upscale conservative area, one that actually had more churches per square mile than anywhere else in the world. It also didn't have very much crime, at least that was the perception many of its residents held. Thus if anything were to happen, it usually surprised the hell out of them. "Even so, do you really think that reporting upon it will cause this story you're working on to be picked up by someone else?"

"I don't know, but I don't want to risk it. No telling what a reporter will dig up should they decide to look a bit deeper into what occurred."

Alan thought about that and wondered if maybe she was projecting too much of her own style of reporting into the reporters that would report upon the attack. Then again, having seen how reporters were while overseas, maybe she had a point and was right to fear them catching a whiff of the story and scooping it right out from under her. Speaking of which, "So what exactly is this story you're working on?"

Stacy met his eyes for a moment and then looked away, a debate over whether or not to tell him obviously being waged within her.

He waited.

Nothing.

"I'm not going to scoop you," he said after a while, the frustration he felt toward her successfully masked.

"I know. It's not that."

Again, silence.

He continued to wait, debating whether or not he should push her toward telling him, or simply see if she did on her own.

Then, without any further pressing, she said, "I haven't told anyone anything about this story, so I guess I'm a bit apprehensive about saying anything, especially to someone whose opinion matters to me."

"Oh," he said, her statement unexpected. "What, are you worried I'm going to say it's ridiculous or something?"

"Yeah," she admitted and took another sip of water.

"Well, I won't. You know your field better than I do, so if you think it's a big story, who am I to claim differently?"

She considered this for a moment and said, "Okay, so, a little over a month ago I was asked to do a story on the local real estate market and assess whether or not it had actually improved or was still faltering. The editor at that particular paper is not a fan of President Obama at all, so I knew that if I discovered things had actually improved during the last couple of years, I'd better have a lot of sources and data to back it up, or else she wouldn't even consider running the story."

Fair and balanced, Alan said to himself with a mental shake of the head. No such thing as news these days, not when everything had a political slant to it.

"So, naturally, I went around and contacted every real estate company in the area while also looking up records online of home sales. Almost all of them were eager to talk with me, especially when I mentioned that having their name in the paper might help generate interest in their company. And if the story got picked up by other papers, specifically all those that would have web editions that would put a link up, their name would really get spread around."

"I bet they ate that up," Alan said. "Free advertising, especially in this market, is not something any company would want to pass up."

"Right? That's exactly what I thought. And it worked, except with one small company, which kind of surprised me, especially since the lady that ran it didn't just say no. She seemed downright hostile. It was like she was angry that a writer was calling her asking about her business. Very weird."

Alan smiled.

"What?" Stacy asked, seeing the smile.

"Oh nothing, I'm just picturing you hanging up the phone or leaving the office or whatever, the wheels of suspicion starting to turn." As soon as the words left his mouth, he wished he could take them back, because they sounded silly. At the same time, he knew they were accurate. Most people would have probably brushed off the moment, but not Stacy.

"Well, wouldn't you be suspicious too? I mean, here is a

place that should be welcoming inquiries into their business, one that interacts well with people, yet this one doesn't do either?"

"I would be," Alan said, though he wasn't really sure about this. Then again, he wasn't a reporter, and thus wasn't constantly trying to sniff out stories.

"Anyway, thinking something was off and wanting to know what, I started looking up stuff about this company and found out that it pretty much was a one-woman show up until this summer. After that, she suddenly had several agents working for her and several properties on display, only no one seemed interested in showing them to me when I called."

"Maybe because they knew you were just trying to write a story?" Alan suggested.

"Please, give me some credit. I used a different name and told them my family was moving in from out of state and that we were looking for a place in the Wheaton or Glen Ellyn area because of the good schools and all that bullshit."

"And they said no?"

"Yep. And every time I called them after that, with different names and people making the calls."

"Okay, that is bizarre."

"Tell me about it. You want to know what else is odd? Every one of their employees is female, and not just any female, but young and pretty, with a photo that has a very seductive feel to it. Here, let me show you."

Alan smiled again, this time at the enthusiasm she was displaying. Had he not been here for the attack, he would have been hard-pressed to believe such a thing had actually occurred. It was a good sign, unless she crashed later. He had seen that happen one time with a reporter just like her. The guy had always been eager for a story and didn't seem to care about the risks involved in getting it. An IED followed by a fierce firefight had changed that, though not until a few days had passed. He had seemed fine until it came time to go out on another convoy and he had a complete breakdown as they started to roll toward the gate. The following week, he was out of the country.

There's always a breaking point.

Wonder what mine would have been.

Stacy returned to the front room with her laptop and sat down next to him, her leg touching his and sending a pleasant tingle throughout his body.

In turn, he put his arm around her, both so it wouldn't become awkwardly crushed between them as she leaned in with the laptop and because he simply liked the comfort it provided. She seemed to enjoy it as well and snuggled in closer, an unexpected, "Thanks for grabbing the guy off me," leaving her lips while the laptop booted up.

"Aw, you're welcome," he said, his words seeming off somehow, given what it was she had thanked him for. Had it been thanks for a "Do you have twenty bucks I could borrow for gas?" moment, his reply would have seemed more appropriate. "Glad I was here," he added.

"Me too." She snuggled in closer. "I'm also kind of glad this happened, but only because it makes me think I'm really onto something, not because I get a thrill out of being assaulted or anything."

That one he didn't know how to reply to.

"And that probably sounded really weird," she admitted after a few seconds.

"Don't worry; I totally get what you're saying. Now let's just hope you don't have to experience such acts of reassurance again in the near future."

"I don't think that'll be a problem, especially not if you're around. That guy, whoever he was, isn't going to want to mess with you again."

"I hope you're right," Alan said, his own mind somewhat uncertain about this, which was why he still thought a call to the police would be wise. He wouldn't go against her wishes on that, however.

"Ah, here we go," she said. "Sorry it's so slow. I really need a new one, but I have to wait for some payments to come through."

"That's okay," Alan replied and then bit his tongue before an offer of giving her one of his old laptops slipped out. He didn't know why, but he had a tendency toward being really generous with things like that, and while he didn't think this was a bad thing at all, he did recognize the discomfort it sometimes caused with those on the receiving end. Thus he would wait a while before making such an offer. "Wow, nice site," he added while looking at the screen. "*Meet our girls,*" he read. It stood above a scrolling display of young smiling female faces.

Stacy clicked one.

On screen, a profile page appeared, one that displayed the girl in what could only be described as a seductive business type of situation. She wore a skirt with stockings and heels, a white blouse, and a jacket while carrying a folder, the blouse opened in a way that showed considerable cleavage, which was further exposed by the camera as it looked down upon her.

"This is one of the more conservative pages." She clicked something. "Now check her out. Have you ever seen a site like this that actually allowed the garters to show? And that pen at her lips and the glasses having slipped down her nose a bit…seems somewhat provocative, doesn't it?"

"Um…yeah," Alan agreed, though he thought it was a stretch. Considering what the site was supposed to be used for, however, he could see how one could say it was too sexual and looked more like a dating ad than an attempt at selling houses. "Have you tried emailing any of the girls?"

"I did. No reply."

"Hmm, kind of weird to show their ages. Not sure what the point of that would be, especially in a field where one would think youth might mean inexperience."

"I thought that too," she said. "And look at this one," she added while clicking another picture.

"Okay, yeah, that is…well, I don't know, but I'd never expect to see such a photo on a real estate site."

"I know, right?"

In the photo, the girl was pressed up against a For Sale sign outside a house, her conservative business attire looking completely unconservative, given her pose.

"I wouldn't be surprised if the sign needed a cigarette after this shot was taken," Stacy said.

"Tell me about it. I've never been to a strip club, but if I had, I'm sure I'd have seen moves like this on the pole."

"You've never been to a strip club?"

"Nope."

"Seriously?"

"Seriously. I view strip clubs like zoos. If you can't pet them, might as well just look at a picture."

"Huh, I never thought of it like that." And then, after a few seconds, "Remember that picture I sent you?"

"How could I forget?" he said with a huge grin, the memory of the picture adding to the tingle her body was creating as it continued to press up against him.

"Do you still have it?"

"The original, yes."

"What do you mean *the original*?"

"That picture was a gold mine. Copies of it went for twenty-five bucks each. Had I not gotten sick, I would have made a fortune and been able to retire once my tour was done."

The look on Stacy's face was priceless. "You didn't!"

He tried to keep a straight face but couldn't maintain it, not with the growing horror he was witnessing. "Okay, I didn't," he said. "But if you ever need some extra cash, I'm sure you *could* make a fortune in the sexy photo business."

"Actually, what I think I should do is make sure I get some photos of you in a compromising situation, so I can take you down with me should you ever decide to release said photo."

"Ah, the threat of mutual destruction to keep each other in check—how very Cold War of you."

"Better believe it."

Friday

October 25, 2013

1

Amanda felt the garage door opening before the sound registered, the struggle as the worn gears lifted the heavy piece causing the house to vibrate, which somehow filtered into the odd dream she was having. A second later, confusion plagued her as she opened her eyes, the surroundings momentarily unfamiliar, given that she had never before fallen asleep on the family room couch. Pain was present as well, the stiff decorative pillow a poor choice when sleeping was concerned. Not that she had chosen to sleep there, that just kind of happened, but for future reference, she knew the couch was a no-go unless she brought down her own pillows.

On screen, an infomercial about a microwavable egg-cooking device was playing. Earlier, before she drifted away, it had been a *That '70s Show* marathon. When younger, she had been forbidden to watch the show, given the immoral behavior of the teens, but now, within this house, she was able to watch whatever she wanted as long as the TV was free.

That's going to get harder and harder once more girls arrive, she noted to herself, wondering if they were really planning on filling all five bedrooms.

Of course they are, another part of her mind countered, astonishment at the idea that the boss would allow them the luxury of such a large house all to themselves echoing within her, especially considering the other house had four girls living in it.

But maybe they'll let me get my own TV?

Do I even have to ask?

She had no idea what the rules were for something like that and, given her exhaustion and the fact that Emily was finally walking back in, decided not to dwell on it. Instead, she headed into the kitchen and asked, "How was the *study date?*"

"Shit, you scared me," Emily snapped, a slight jump giving credibility to her statement. "What the fuck you still up for?"

"Why the fuck you so late?" Amanda countered.

"Why the fuck do you care?" Emily replied.

"*Why the fuck do I care?*" Amanda repeated. "Um, I don't know, maybe because you're always the one demanding to know where I was if I'm back ten to fifteen minutes later than expected."

"Um, hello, we both use the car, and when you come home late in the middle of the day, that means I might be late for my afternoon and evening appointments." She put her hands on her hips while saying this, hips that Amanda was sure someone else had put their hands on recently.

"Well, if you added all your extracurricular activities to the calendar, I might have a better idea of when the car is needed. Oh, but wait, you probably don't want things like tonight up on the calendar, in case the boss makes a surprise visit and asks about it."

"What're you talking about?" Emily said, not missing a beat. "They'd be happy I was going on study dates and putting effort into my education."

"I never heard of a study date ending at two in the morning."

"Haven't you ever heard of cramming?"

"Yeah, I'm just wondering what was being crammed and where?"

"Well, if you must know, it was a study date and party all rolled into one."

"A party?" Amanda asked.

"Yeah, couple guys invited me, and it was totally epic."

"And you didn't think that maybe I would want to go?" She crossed her arms.

"You weren't invited."

"You're telling me that these guys would turn away a second girl in a skirt and fishnets simply because she wasn't invited?" Despite the contempt she felt toward Emily, hurt was also present. No one ever invited her to parties.

"Sorry, you know how these rich suburb people are. They like to keep things all planned out and don't like party crashers." With that, she pushed past Amanda, elbow actually catching her in the shoulder, and started toward the stairs.

After a few seconds, even though she knew it would be pointless to try to sleep with all the emotions bouncing around in her head, Amanda followed.

Emily was coming out of her bedroom as Amanda entered the hallway, body now clad in a bathrobe.

Amanda glared at her as she headed into the bathroom and then, wanting to check something, waited until she heard the shower going before stepping into Emily's room.

Sure enough, her clothes from that evening were on the floor, carelessly tossed aside like so many other outfits were on a daily basis. Hopefully, however, this was the first time this evening that the clothes had been tossed onto the floor, thereby allowing the possibility that...

Ah ha! she silently cried, her eyes having found a small semen stain on the skirt.

Another one was on the sweater.

No money was found, however, which surprised her, the

pockets of Emily's leather jacket empty but for a receipt for the College of DuPage cafeteria.

Did she hide it somewhere?

If so, why leave the cum-stained clothes on the floor?

Was it because she feared me taking the money but didn't think I'd study the clothes?

Or maybe there really wasn't any money and she just gave someone a blowjob at the party.

Would she actually perform such an act without being paid?

Amanda thought about that for quite some time, her mind unable to fathom doing such a thing herself—unless, of course, it was requested by the boss, which was different because, in a way, it was like paying tribute to someone who worked hard on your behalf. But at a party with some other guy? Why go through such an act for free when there were so many men willing to pay for it? It didn't make sense.

2

Though exhausted, both from the gastrological disturbance the morning before and from the intense sexual debauchery the two had taken part in during the last couple of hours, Alan couldn't sleep. His mind was to blame. He couldn't shut it down, thoughts on the attack, Stacy's real estate investigation, and the sex they'd just had all filtering together into an odd mental collage. It was bizarre, yet also expected. And frustrating.

In his bedroom at his mom's place, he would have flipped on the TV in hopes of finding something mindless to watch, the focus on such shows usually helping to stop the wheels within from turning so that he could drift away. Now, here in Stacy's bed, with her head on his chest snoring, that wasn't an option, not unless he wanted to move out from under her and head into the other room.

No, just close your eyes and push all thoughts from your mind.

It didn't work.

With pain or discomfort, he was able to shift his focus and clear his mind to the point of almost forgetting about it—to the point where enduring it was actually possible. With thinking, however, he always failed. Even worse, it was like the thinking parts of his mind had a defense mechanism that piled on more thoughts when threatened, thus making it even harder to clear his mind when desired. And no one ever understood it. When he was talking to an army psychologist while in the discharge process, the psychologist had suggested it was the subject of the thoughts that was keeping him up, thoughts that needed to be resolved. Nothing Alan said could make the man understand that it wasn't the thoughts, but the fact that the thoughts were there. Sure, sometimes the thoughts were of horrific events that he couldn't clear from his head, but other times they were completely random things from his life, or from something he had read, or something that was said. Nothing traumatic about them, he just couldn't stop them from demanding his attention.

Stacy shifted a bit and then mumbled something in her sleep. Drool followed, the warm liquid feeling odd against his chest.

Don't tell her about it in the morning.

Though amusing, he knew such information would be embarrassing to her; therefore, he would keep it to himself. Hopefully, she would do the same for him should he ever expel any interesting odors while sleeping, something he knew occurred quite frequently, given that he could often smell them lingering within the room upon waking, almost as if they had permeated the bedsheets.

Stacy shifted again and this time her hands, which had been stretched across his body, shifted downward and came to rest upon his groin. Needless to say, the consequences of this, despite everything they had already done, were immediately evident and would make drifting off to sleep even more difficult.

Not that he minded. It didn't seem to matter the situation, having a female hand in that area was always welcome.

What about the catheter?

That hand wasn't welcome at all...

He thought about that for quite some time, not just the moment when the catheter had been removed, but the entire surgical experience. It had been one of the most painful moments of his life, far worse than when he had been shot for the first time, yet he also had been filled with relief, given that he had survived the operation.

Oddly enough, thinking had not been a problem when trying to sleep in the days following the surgery, thanks to the painkillers he was on, one of which went directly into his spine. One squeeze of the pain pump and he would be out within a minute, a nice soothing warmth cocooning him.

Could use that now.

Knowing how easy it could be to turn everything off when wanting to sleep was a big reason why he had decided to stop drinking. At no point during his life had he ever had a problem with alcohol—it was always simply a social thing with friends—but after he had come home and realized how difficult it was to get to sleep, he had decided the temptation to shut everything down before bed would be too great, especially if he did it once or twice and enjoyed the effect.

And so cliché, as Stacy would have said.

The thought brought a smile to his face.

Sadly, it didn't last, not when thoughts of the attack and his fears that she might have bitten off more than she could chew entered his mind once again. The question was what exactly had she bitten off? Also, why attack her if she didn't really know anything— something he had concluded, not her. Was it because whoever was protecting this thing from her thought she knew more than she did? If so, they had probably just shot themselves in the foot, because now she knew she was onto something. Then again, given her nature, she probably would have continued to seek out answers even if it seemed like no answers would arrive.

Moving slowly, so as not to jostle Stacy awake, Alan rubbed his right fist, knuckles still able to feel the moment of impact against the man's face as he had jumped in to rid Stacy of the attacker. No memory of the fight was actually present; instead he saw himself fighting the man in a type of mental reconstruction, all his actions known to him, yet seemingly not experienced in real time.

I could have killed him.

If he had, it wouldn't have been the first time, not unless one was tallying up kills within his own country. Such a decisive act hadn't seemed necessary, however; at least this was what his mind must have decided during the fight, because if it had, he surely would have killed the man. Instead, he had gotten him away from Stacy and then, once the area was secure, went to her, his concern that she had been stabbed or seriously injured in some other way guiding his actions.

How many people did you kill?

The thought came out of nowhere and didn't get an answer simply because he didn't know. When counting the times he had been face-to-face with people he had killed, he could answer that, but when it came to an overall total, the answer was a mystery.

"You okay?" Stacy asked, eyes closed, voice heavy.

"Yeah, sorry, didn't mean to wake you."

"S'okay," she mumbled. "Dreaming about you."

The words were so soft that he wondered if she had fallen asleep while saying them, his hand stroking her hair for a moment to help ease her back into such a state if she wasn't already there.

And then her hand, which had been pressed up against his penis already, gently took hold of it and gave it a slow stroke. "Dreaming of this too," she said, voice still soft.

Alan didn't know what to say.

She stroked him three more times before drifting away, the snores that started up once again evidence of this. Her hand didn't let go, however, which was something he had never experienced before.

What do I do now?

A part of him wanted to reach down and remove the hand, given the sensation it was causing, one that would most likely make sleeping impossible. The other part, however, liked it too much to put it to an end.

With this indecision came thoughts of Stacy and what exactly the results of this rekindled relationship would be.

Who cares? he eventually decided. *Just enjoy it.*

Not long after that he was actually asleep, his dreams, once they appeared, encompassing almost everything he had been thinking about during that hour of sleeplessness. It was surreal.

3

"Fuck, man, what happened?" Riley Woodman asked, shocked by the darkened area of flesh he saw peeking out beneath his brother's sunglasses.

"Sucker punched," Sam said. He lifted the glasses so Riley could see the full extent of the damage. "Fucker totally nailed me too."

"I'd say. What were you doing? You weren't in the city last night, were you?"

"No, guy nailed me as I was leaving the liquor store. Totally unexpected. Took my bottle too. Neighborhood is going bad fast." He shifted the sunglasses back in place. "I swear, if Kristi hadn't grown up in that house, and if we didn't own it free and clear, I'd let the bank take it and go elsewhere. Not even worth trying to sell."

"Shit, man, in this economy, nothing is worth trying to sell."

"Ha, yeah, don't I know it."

A waitress came through the cutout from the main dining room and asked, "Two?"

"Two," Riley confirmed.

She nodded, grabbed menus, and led the way through the cutout into the dining room, taking a zigzag path to a table on the far wall.

"This okay?" she asked with mild interest.

"Perfect," Riley said and took a seat.

Sam did the same, the booth just large enough to allow his body room to be comfortable.

"Coffee?" she asked.

"Yes," Riley said, turning a tiny cup over in the saucer.

Sam flipped one over himself, looked inside for a bit, and, after deciding it was gunk free, started opening tiny cups of creamer to pour into it before the waitress returned with the carafe.

"We always get the Wicked Witch," Riley said while looking up at the artwork above their table. "Ever notice that?"

"Yeah, but it's not the Wicked Witch."

"What do you mean?"

"Wicked Witch was *Wizard of Oz*. This is *Snow White*."

"Still pretty wicked though."

"Yeah, but that's a given since she's a witch."

"Okay, I guess you're right," Riley said, a smile threatening to appear.

The waitress returned with the coffee pot, poured, and asked if they were ready to order.

They were, their near-weekly visits these past two years having narrowed down their choices to a handful of entrée items, none of which required a study of the unchanging menu.

"So…" Riley started but wasn't really sure where to go with it.

Sam waited, his lips taking several tiny sips to test the temperature of the coffee before swallowing a mouthful of the brew.

Riley took his own sip and winced, his brother's coffee a poor indication of how hot his own was, given the volume of cream Sam always added.

"So…" Sam repeated after a bit.

"How's Vicky doing?" Riley asked.

"She's good."

"All the shit out of her system?"

"Completely. Has been for days."

"And the latest tests for Caroline? They come in today, right?"

"Yep. Kristi is taking her by the county this afternoon to pick them up."

"Okay, good. Let me know as soon as you hear something. Hopefully she's clean now. If not…shit, I don't know what we should do."

"Hey, most of these things clear up with antibiotics, which they put her on as a precaution before the first tests even came back, so chances are good it'll be gone now."

"I know that, I mean with the men and screening. Are we doing enough? I don't want situations like this to become regular, but at the same time I can't think of any way to prevent it."

"Yeah, I know what you mean, and Kristi thinks that tightening things up with the men would hurt more than help. As is, I'm worried we're not clearing enough to make it all worthwhile, not with your insistence on them going to college."

Riley shook his head. "You knew my terms from the start, so…" He held up his hands. "Plus, it's a good cover."

Sam looked ready to say something but held off as the waitress carried a tray of food to their table.

"Everything okay?" the waitress asked.

"Looks like it," Riley said.

Sam nodded and, after the waitress walked away, said, "Good cover or not, this entire thing isn't worth it if we don't start making more money."

"Well, if you think you can figure a way for making more money, I'm all ears."

"No you're not. Every idea I've suggested in the last two months you've shot down."

"None of them were practical. Suggest something that is viable and won't be like a calling card for the authorities to come investigate, and I'll go along with it."

"Okay, how about setting up cameras to videotape the scenes so we can sell them on some of those user-uploaded porn sites? Therefore we make money not just once on a scene but—see, you're already shaking your head."

"First, no guy is going to pay for sex if we're using the scenes for porn. Second, filming porn is technically illegal in Illinois. Third, to get quality stuff that will actually sell we'll need to spend a considerable amount on lighting and cameras, which we don't have and won't be able to keep a secret from the men during the scenes."

"Kristi and I were thinking about that. What if we offer the men a deal, either pay for the sex or get it for free if they agree to be filmed? That way we get the model statements and everything so it's legit, and we can have the cameras all positioned in plain sight."

"Okay, as great as that sounds, it's still illegal in Illinois."

"So is prostitution, but that hasn't seemed to stop us."

Riley winced at his brother's statement, both because of how loud it was and because he hated being reminded of the fact that what they were doing was illegal. He needed no reminder. It was constantly on his mind, as was the fear of being discovered, arrested, and thrown in jail. Hell, just last night he'd had a dream where he went to jail, his eyes opening upon the real world just as the bars slammed home.

"And besides," Sam continued, "there's got to be hundreds, if not thousands of people making homemade porn in Illinois and other states where it's technically illegal, so do you really think they're going to actually notice us?"

"Yes, I do, which is why all these sites have those model statements on file, and while I'm sure nothing ever happens to those producers even when it's discovered they're producing it in a state where it isn't exactly legal, with us, they would discover the prostitution side to everything and we'd totally be fucked."

"But how would they discover that if all they're doing is checking model stuff to make sure everyone is over eighteen and gave consent to be filmed?"

"I don't know. Maybe they wouldn't investigate, but why would you want to even set things up so the possibility existed?"

Sam didn't reply to this.

Riley ate a forkful of eggs and then took a bite of bacon. Both were good, but even so, he knew he would not be clearing his plate, not when his mind was racked with worry.

"Fine, if you don't like the porn idea, what about doubling up on the guys they see? One scene a day is crazy, especially considering how many some of them used to do each day."

"I'm open to that, just as long as the quality doesn't slack. These guys aren't going to pay all this money every month and go through all the hoops we require if the fuck is no better than what they could get on a street corner." He paused. "By the way, are more men inquiring about the girls?" Putting a limit on the amount of guys the girls took on each day hadn't been an original stipulation but one that had sort of become policy due to how few men were hiring the girls. Doubling up on a day seemed silly when they could be spaced out, thus allowing more rest between the scenes for the girls.

"Not really, but Kristi and I were thinking that we could beef up the advertising a little and make the girls more known in the area, then—"

Riley cut him off with another shake of the head and then said, "More advertising means more chances that the authorities will catch wind of it."

"*But you're the authorities*," Sam said, voice rising, "and if you catch wind of anything, we'll know to shut it down for a while."

"I know," Riley said, "but what if I don't catch wind of it? What if the FBI gets involved, or the ATF, or the DEA? Once they find out that law enforcement is involved, they're not going to let anyone in on what they're doing and—"

"But they'd have to investigate first to know you're involved!" Sam snapped. "And you'd know about that before they connected you!"

"Dude, chill out." Riley looked around to see how many heads had turned, but no one was looking their way.

"Sorry, it's just I get so frustrated sometimes. It's like you were cool with all this, but now you don't want any part of it and worse, don't want it to succeed."

"You know as well as I do that I was never cool with this thing and only gave in after you and Kristi bullied me into it."

"Dude, you know I had no part of that, and if you had just told me—" He stopped as the waitress returned to freshen their coffee.

"What good would that have done?" Riley asked before Sam could continue, his napkin dabbing at the side of his cup where the coffee had sloshed over the rim. "By the time we talked about it, you had already brought a girl home."

"That's because you gave me the green light!"

"Because she said she was going to rat me out for the drug money if I didn't!"

"I never even knew she said that."

"Why'd you tell her about it in the first place?" Riley asked. *Better yet, why did YOU tell Sam about it? Fuck, why did you even take the money?*

One moment of greed had turned into several months of terror. Talk about something not being worth it.

But it could have been, if you'd kept your mouth shut.

Taking the money had been dumb, but nowhere near as dumb as telling Sam about it. And the worst part, he had known it was dumb to tell him, his mind having told him over and over again not to say anything when he saw him, yet what did he do? Told him about it within two minutes of sitting down for breakfast during their Friday morning get-together.

While sitting beneath the witch that was wicked but not necessarily the Wicked one.

He let out a sigh.

"Man, I still feel bad about that, okay, but I was just standing up for you because she was going on and on about how you were too uptight to ever get involved in what we were talking about and how you'd probably rat us out if we suggested it—stuff like that." It was Sam's turn to sigh. "So I told her."

"And she used it against me. Thanks."

"I didn't know she'd do that."

"Dude, she has hated me from day one. She didn't even want me in the wedding. Doesn't that tell you something?"

"Yeah, well, it's not like you hold her in high regard either. I don't understand why you two can't get along."

"I was nothing but nice to her when you two first started dating, and I kept my opinion to myself for quite some time."

"Yeah, but she could always sense you didn't like her, and that's not an easy thing to deal with."

More like she got pissed when I refused to have sex with her while showing me the house and has hated me ever since.

Regret for having never told Sam about that moment filled his head. If he had...well, he really had no idea what would have happened. At the time, however, he hadn't wanted to ruin the happiness he saw in his brother's eyes, happiness that he had never before seen and hoped would last.

Totally should have fucked her brains out.

No...

Memories of that moment kept entering his mind, ones that wanted to play out into a fantasy he didn't want to indulge. Unfortunately, telling her no had been easier than telling his mind no, its rebellious nature doing the opposite.

"Anyway, I'm sorry you got roped into being a part of this, and I would fix that if I could, but I can't." Sam shook his head. "All we can really do is make the best of it, which means making sure we profit enough from it to nullify the risk."

Riley hated to agree with the statement but knew his brother was right. Even so, he felt compelled to say, "I'm not budging on the school thing, especially since it's my money and my job that's at stake."

Sam held up his hands. "I wasn't going to suggest that, but I do think you should relax a bit and let us get this thing really going."

Riley didn't reply.

"And stop worrying about things so much. The FBI, ATF, DEA...this doesn't fall into the parameters of what they investigate."

"Dude, come on, you know as well as I do that the lines are very blurred when it comes to those agencies. Now, I'll admit, I'd probably hear about it if they came into the area to investigate, but please don't be so naïve as to think they won't get involved in something like this."

Sam took several bites of his food before replying, and when he did it was a simple, "Okay."

Riley looked down at his own food but still couldn't get his hunger to return. Later, it would hit full force, of this he was certain, but right now, just the thought of adding any more food to his system was enough to turn his stomach.

A buzz echoed.

Sam looked down at his phone for a second and then said, "Kristi just dropped off Vicky with Amanda and Emily."

"Okay, good."

"And her photos should go up on the site soon."

"Tasteful ones, I hope," Riley said.

"Of course."

"Sam, I'm serious."

"Fuck, man, stop getting so worried."

Riley didn't reply.

4

Though exhausted from her sleepless night and not really in the mood to play the role of a schoolgirl attempting to earn extra credit with her teacher, Amanda gave a good performance that morning, one that earned considerable praise from Mr. McGregor.

"Of course, if you really were one of my students, I'd have to fail you," he said.

"Oh," she replied, finger rubbing away a drying spot of semen from the skin of her right boob. "And why is that?"

"So I wouldn't lose you to another teacher, one who wouldn't appreciate your skills quite the way I do."

"But if you did that, I'd realize all the extra credit I earned was for nothing and might not ever allow that lovely bit of manhood between my lips again."

"Ah, well then, maybe I'd pass you but then have you back once a week for tutoring." He pulled up his pants. "After all, those upper-level classes can be difficult."

"See, I like that better." Semen flakes removed, she buttoned her blouse and then ran a hand through her hair to pull strands of it free from where it had been trapped beneath the collar.

Is he really a teacher?

If so, wouldn't he be at school right now?

The questions, though intriguing, went unasked, mostly because she didn't want to get in trouble. Delving into the personal lives of clients was forbidden, and even though he had brought it up himself, she wasn't going to overstep by asking questions based on the offhanded statement.

He grinned and then, sounding a bit unsure, said, "By the way, I've been wondering, is it possible to have you and Emily at the same time?"

"Oh…um…yeah, I don't see why not." No one had ever suggested such a scene like that with her before, though, given men's fantasies, she was sure it would become more and more common as more men employed their services. "Just mention it next time you set something up and they'll give you all the details."

"Great. That'll be fun. Got some interesting ideas I want to try."

"Oooh, I can't wait." She gave him a hug and pecked him on the cheek. "Until next time."

"Yep," he said and then headed toward the front door, a quick turn to wave and smile before he stepped out.

Amanda went to the window and watched as he pulled out. Once gone, she headed into the back bedroom of the small ranch house and switched her plaid schoolgirl skirt for a pair of pants, the skirt going into her tiny bag. After that, she collected her tiny bottles of pepper spray, ones that she always placed around whichever house she was working in, and headed to the garage to where the car was waiting.

Fifteen minutes later, she pulled up to the house, startled to see Mrs. Woodman's car sitting in the driveway. A bit of panic followed, not because she had done anything wrong, but because one always grew a little apprehensive when coming face-to-face with one of the bosses.

New girl, her mind reminded her, the name Emily had said the day before momentarily forgotten.

But wasn't that supposed to be in the afternoon?

Things change.

Unable to pull into the driveway, Amanda parked on the street and left the car to head into the house.

"Ah, Amanda," Mrs. Woodman said from the family room where she sat with Emily and the new girl. "We've been waiting for you."

"Oh, sorry, I had a—" she started.

"You were with a client, I know." She smiled. "I set it up, remember?"

"Of course," Amanda said, a hesitant smile appearing. "Um..." She glanced at the new girl and then back at Mrs. Woodman.

"As I'm sure Emily told you, we have a new girl in our company." She motioned toward the new girl, who looked incredibly young yet far from innocent. "Vicky, I'd like you to meet Amanda. Amanda, Vicky."

Vicky stood up, hands smoothing out the dress she wore, and said, "Hi."

"Nice to meet you," Amanda said and gave the girl a hug, one that was returned without any warmth whatsoever and obviously done as a mere courtesy.

"As you can see, Vicky has quite the youthful appearance, one that we're hoping will bring in clients that have a taste for younger girls, *but* not in such a way that they would dare dip below the eighteen-year-old age restriction we're all familiar with and re-spect."

You making a press release or something? Amanda said to her-self, eyes noting the practiced smile that distorted Mrs. Woodman's face.

"And I know," Mrs. Woodman continued, "that you two will make her feel right at home here."

"Of course," Emily said.

Amanda nodded.

"Very good." Mrs. Woodman stood. "Now, as much as I'd like to stay and chat, I have an appointment that I can*not* be late for. You girls have a good day."

"Okay, we will," Emily said, standing.

Mrs. Woodman smiled at them and then headed toward the front door, heels clicking across the entryway tiles in such a way that Amanda felt it in her spine.

Once she was gone, silence settled within the room.

Amanda looked at Emily, who looked back at her, a sense of awkwardness dominating her face. She then turned toward Vicky, who was picking at something on her knee. "So...um...Vicky..." Amanda started.

Vicky looked up.

"Tell us about yourself."

5

I MISS YOU ALREADY, Stacy typed shortly after Alan had left, a midday criminal justice class demanding his time.

Hesitation about sending the text message followed, along with several mental statements about not coming on too strong or being too girly about this thing.

You don't want to make him uncomfortable.
Give him space.

Too much of a good thing…

Her phone buzzed.

Thinking—*hoping*—it was Alan sending her his own message, she deleted the one she had typed and opened what had arrived. Sure enough, it was a message from Alan, but one that differed considerably from what she had expected.

HEY, WHAT WAS THE NAME OF THE REAL ESTATE COMPANY? AND THE LADY IN CHARGE?

Disappointed, Stacy typed, KRISTI HOMES / KRISTI WOODMAN, and hit send.

OK, THANKS, Alan replied.

Stacy stared at her phone, a desire to ask why exactly he wanted to know this information dominating her mind.

Are you going to contact her?

Are you going to try helping me with this investigation?

Are you going to uncover something that I missed and make me feel foolish?

Naturally, it was the last thought that stuck in her mind, one that produced more fear within her than the idea of being attacked again.

Was the attack even related?

What if it has nothing to do with the real estate company but some other story I'm working?

What else could it be though?

Nothing followed this thought, the various stories she was working on for the various editors that had contacted her having nothing within them that could enrage a person to the point of attacking her.

That you know of…

No, it's this one.

She knew it in her gut. Something wasn't right with that real estate company and as she had told Alan, being attacked pretty much confirmed this.

And you lied to him, which is why he wasn't fully convinced the two are connected.

Well, maybe *lie* was too strong a word. She simply hadn't given him all the details, the most significant being that one of the girls had been in the papers a year earlier in a prostitution scandal involving a school principal, who, naturally, was forced to resign due to the outcry from local parents. Things got even worse for him when it was reported that the girl he had picked up was only sixteen, sparking fears that naturally led to several female students claiming they had been sexually molested by the principal. No evidence of molestation was ever uncovered, and no charges filed, but just the accusations alone were enough to completely destroy the man, who committed suicide a month later. The prostitute in question had been a girl named Caroline Garner, who seemed to have turned her life around fairly quickly. She also must have jumped up in age by five years, given that a person had to be twenty-one to obtain a real estate license in Illinois.

Leaving a message about the age question might have done it, Stacy told herself, though why they would have waited over a week to do something was a mystery. Add in the fact that she hadn't mentioned the prostitution angle at all, and she really couldn't understand why they would go so far as to attack her.

Because you spooked them, which means there really is more going on here than meets the eye.

And you have a pretty good idea what that "more" is...

Sadly, she had no proof, and without it there was no point in writing the story, not if she wanted it to go big time. Sure, reporting on a real estate agency that was employing unlicensed, underage girls would get some attention, but nowhere near as much as a story detailing how all those girls were really prostitutes. Add in the fact that they were working in one of the most conservative and religious counties in the state, and it wouldn't be long before her name was known all across the country.

After that... She looked around her shitty little apartment, knowing that her time in such dismal dwellings was coming to an end.

But only if YOU break the story.

If someone else caught wind of it, she would be fucked. They wouldn't even have to uncover very much. A simple story on how the girls were too young to be real estate agents would be enough because it would bring in unwanted attention that would probably shut everything down. Hell, she had almost decided against calling Kristi Woodman with the question about Caroline's age simply because she worried about spooking them into closing shop. After some thought, however, she had realized that if something big was going on, one phone call wouldn't be enough to shut things down.

But it may have been enough to have someone come here to try to scare me away.

Over and over again, her mind kept returning to this, an odd sense of triumph overpowering the anxiety and terror she should have felt. Anger was present as well, both at the fact that someone had actually violated her in such a way and at their idea that doing so would be enough to scare her away. Did they think she was a timid little female reporter that would run and hide? Not a chance. And just the unspoken implication of such a thing was enough to make her want to eviscerate everyone involved in that company, the Kristi Woodman bitch most of all.

6

Though he could probably have spent the entire class period on his phone looking up stuff about Kristi Woodman, Alan didn't want to be disrespectful to the professor. Therefore, he kept his phone in his pocket and only attempted to look up information on the real estate lady during a fifteen-minute break. Sadly, he didn't get as far into his research as he would have liked, his inexperience with browsing the web from the device making it difficult to get into any type of groove. He wanted his laptop.

And you need more to go on than just a name.

This thought led to a question about what exactly he hoped to find, the idea that he would learn something through Google that Stacy hadn't already uncovered seeming somewhat silly to him now.

And it probably insulted her a bit, which is why she never texted anything else. That was something he remembered fairly well about Stacy: she personalized things to the extreme, her mind often assuming things were directed her way for a specific reason. With his question on the company name, she had probably read it as, *you don't think I'm good enough to research this stuff on my own and need to do it for me.* Obviously, this had not been his intention, but nothing he could say would bring her around to realizing that. At the same time, he knew there was nothing she could say that would make him feel apologetic for his text and any misunderstanding it caused. Hurting her feelings, if he had actually done so, had not been his intention; thus he would not take responsibility for doing so—at least not in this situation. With other situations, he might, but only if he legitimately felt guilt from it. Overthinking something to the point where it caused hurt was not grounds for this. She might disagree with him, but that was okay. Plus, it wouldn't ruin what they had; at least he didn't think it would. Drama free had always been the rule and, honestly, if things were going to go down a drama-filled path this time around, he didn't really want a part of it. Hopefully, she would realize this. If not, and things did start to seem overly dramatic, he would say something. After all, she had come to him, which meant he pretty much had control. Now, he wouldn't be a dick about it because he did like what they had, but he also wasn't going to allow any games to be played.

7

"So what happens if we get caught smoking?" Vicky asked while taking a look around her new bedroom.

"Um..." Emily looked at Amanda then back at Vicky. "What do you mean?"

"You know, the guy in charge of all this and his bitch that brought me here, what do they do if they catch us breaking the rules? Coat hanger?"

"No," Emily said. "Nothing like that. Actually, I don't think I've even heard of anyone being punished." She looked at Amanda again, who shook her head. "Yeah, no punishments that I know of, but..."

"But what?" Vicky asked.

"I don't know. We have rules, so there must be punishments, but, well, neither of us has ever really been caught breaking them, so..." She shrugged. "I really don't know."

"Great," Vicky said with a sigh. "Figured this place would be lame, just didn't realize how lame."

"Wait a sec," Amanda cut in, "have you ever actually been hit with a coat hanger?"

"Like, duh," Vicky said, voice carrying a "what are you, stupid?" ring. She lifted her skirt so they could see the crisscross of welts that had yet to fade, ones that sat on top of scars that would probably never go away.

"And what, you want them doing that to us here?" Amanda demanded. "Is that what you're saying?"

"Well, at least I'd know they were serious about making money."

Amanda didn't know how to reply to that, nor did Emily,

who simply stood in the doorway, shocked.

"Is it true that I have to go to school?"

"Um…well…yeah."

"And that I'll only get to fuck one or two guys a day?"

Amanda nodded.

"Swell."

"*Swell?*" Amanda said, anger rising.

"Hey," Emily said before things could get heated, an odd cheerful ring present. "I know it all sounds bizarre, but trust me, you'll like it here better than any other place you've been. Just give it a chance, okay?"

"Whatever," Vicky muttered.

Emily turned to Amanda and asked, "Do we have any grocery money left for the week?"

"A bit."

"Okay." She turned back to Vicky. "I've got a scene this evening, but maybe before it we can all go shopping and see if there's anything special you'd like to eat."

Vicky stared at her.

"What's something you really, REALLY like?" Emily pressed.

"Do you have any Lucky Charms?" Vicky asked.

"We can get some," Emily said.

Amanda caught a glimmer in the girl's eyes, one that didn't last long as she quickly tried to mask it behind her tough-girl act—if that was what she was really doing. One thing she was certain of, the girl had seen some shit. The marks on her butt and legs were proof of this. And the way she kept scratching at her inner arm beneath her sweater sleeve…seeing it, Amanda couldn't help but want to scratch at her own long-gone needle marks. It was weird.

"You ever get hit with a coat hanger?" Amanda asked once she and Emily were alone, her voice soft so Vicky wouldn't hear them talking while up in her new room.

"Yeah, coat hangers, belts, anything handy really," Emily said. "You?"

"Yeah."

Nothing else was said after that, words unnecessary since they both understood the pain involved in creating the marks they had seen on Vicky's legs. Just the threat of a single swat from Matt, her ex-boyfriend-turned-pimp, had been enough to keep Amanda in line, so to go through what Vicky had…well…she doubted anyone could stay conscious through something like that, let alone stay sane if it occurred on a frequent basis.

And yet she seems almost proud of her marks…

Amanda had no idea what kind of mind-fuckery she must have gone through in order to feel this way about such a thing, but she knew it had to have been bad. She also wondered if the girl was ready to be a part of their company. Was she stable enough? Could she be trusted?

They wouldn't have brought her here if she wasn't ready, Amanda said to herself, memories of her own path to employment filling her head. For days, she had been locked in a room, body going through withdrawal, the stench of piss, shit, and vomit so strong that toward the end, when lucid enough to understand things, she had wanted to scrape away her own skin in an effort to get clean. It had been a nightmare, the agony so intense that now, three months later, she actually had difficulty comprehending just how extreme it had been, despite having experienced it.

What if she isn't ready?

What if they rushed things?

What if they needed the room for another girl, or two girls, and had to scoot her out, their thinking being she was clean enough.

They would have said something.

The last thought was more of a hope than a certainty, her fears that something bad could bring ruin to her current situation and force her back onto the streets fairly significant. In fact, her fears were so great that she wouldn't be all that upset if the boss decided upon certain physical punishments should rules be broken, though only if they were fair and not used beyond the extent that was necessary for curbing behaviors that put the company in jeopardy.

Even coat hangers?

Memories of being held down by one arm while the other whacked away at her butt returned, along with the terror of facing it again simply because she hadn't earned enough money one evening.

Here it would be rule-based since we don't have to bring in the men, the punishments delivered due to the willful breaking of a rule.

But what if all that starts to change?

What if they start putting us out on the street corners like Matt used to do...

No, that wouldn't happen.

The Woodmans had put too much effort into the setup they currently worked and wouldn't want to jeopardize things by turning them into common street-corner whores.

And they probably also wouldn't want to inflict punishments upon any of us that would cause damage and unappealing marks.

But would someone like Vicky understand any other type of punishment?

This thought chilled her to the core.

Nothing you can do about it.

Though true, the thought did little to ease her concern. All she could do was hope that the Woodmans knew what they were doing. If not...

HEY, YOU GOING TO BE HOME FOR DINNER?

The text came as Alan was pulling out of the College of DuPage parking lot, his car failing to catch the green on the only light that sat between the school and his house.

YEP, he replied back, eyes keeping a check on the light and for college cops since he wasn't completely sure if texting and driving was still legal in this area. WHAT'RE WE HAVING?

PORK CHOPS OK?

YEP.

AND MASHED POTATOES AND BISCUITS.

SOUNDS GOOD.

Behind him, cars began to stack up, though the line didn't get as long as it would have had the class ended at noon. On days when that happened, he simply walked to class, his experience in late August and early September having shown him that it actually took less time to get home than waiting through the three or four cycles it would take for him to catch the arrow.

Really should just walk every day, he said to himself, foot easing off the brake as the light changed. *It's so close and would be good for your body.*

His body, however, was the reason he didn't do this, his fear of being hit with diarrhea at some point during the journey difficult to shake away.

Twice a week he could risk it, but five times…nope. The moments of gastrological distress were just too frequent. In fact, thinking about it, the longest period of time he had gone without having diarrhea was the week following his surgery, mostly because his body had been pumped full of painkillers. After that, well, he was lucky if he went three days without having to make some mad dash to a toilet, that horrible bubbling sensation in his gut always arriving without warning and letting him know he had five to ten minutes to find a secure location.

It will get better, a surgeon in Germany had told him during his second week of recovery, a period which saw him having so much diarrhea that it was almost like someone had left a hose running within his bowels. *You just need to give your body time to adjust to the shortened digestive track.*

Yeah, it's SO much better, Alan mumbled to himself within his head, car pulling into the driveway. Sure, the diarrhea wasn't as frequent as it had been during that second week of recovery, but it still wasn't as infrequent as he had pictured it would be when visualizing what the doctor meant by the word "better." Making things worse, during his last visit to the VA, he had asked about his bowel troubles and what could be done and had gotten a "nothing, you have Crohn's disease" response from the doctor.

"But that's the VA," his mom had scolded. *"You should go to Loyola and have them check you out."*

Loyola was a teaching hospital right next to the VA, one that supposedly had a good gastroenterology department. Alan, however, had a feeling the VA doctor, who also worked at Loyola, was right about what he could expect, his research on the web having said similar things.

Accepting reality doesn't mean you have to like it, an officer had once said to him.

Like it he did not, that was for sure.

Well, the diarrhea and living with an incurable disease aspect. Being back home, spending time with his mom, watching horror movies, going to classes, and now getting to hang with Stacy was enjoyable and made him feel good. Even so, if he'd had his choice, he would be back with his team in Afghanistan.

All that time and training…

Not your fault.

Despite the thought, he couldn't dismiss an unrelenting sense of guilt. He knew it was ridiculous to feel this way, not to mention overly cliché, but that didn't make it any less real. It was weird, especially given how rational he typically was about such things. In fact, if someone else on the team had gone through what he had and said he felt guilty, he would have smacked him upside the head and told him to snap out of it. *Nothing you can do. Fate dealt you a crappy hand. Just have to deal with it and move on.*

He shook his head and walked into the kitchen to make a pot of tea, all while checking his phone to see what the latest horror movie on AMC Fear Fest was. *Omen III: The Final Conflict.* Though he loved Sam Neill, he wasn't really a fan of this one—or any beyond the first one—and decided to pass.

Need to get that memoir moving again.

Or some thought-provoking blog posts.

His phone buzzed.

HEY, WHAT'RE YOU DOING TONIGHT? Stacy asked.

Alan stared at the message for a while, unsure what to say. The answer was nothing, but saying that would probably result in her wanting him to come over and, at the moment, he wasn't fully sure if he wanted to do that. It wasn't a matter of not wanting sex, because a repeat of last night would be great, just that he wasn't sure if he wanted this to become an everyday sort of thing. Last time, they had gone down that path, given the limited time they had, which was fine, because that limited amount of time made it so they never got bored. This time around, such a thing could easily happen and ruin the fun.

JUST WRITING AND WATCHING HORROR MOVIES, he typed after a few minutes. YOU?

Once sent, he got his tea leaves ready, his choice this time around being a first-flush Darjeeling from the Puttabong Tea Estate.

TRYING TO FIGURE UP A NEW ANGLE TO TAKE ON THIS REAL ESTATE THING, Stacy replied. Then, before he could get a response in, she also sent, DID YOU LEARN ANYTHING

ABOUT THE COMPANY TODAY?

NO, NOT REALLY.

The teakettle whistled.

His phone buzzed.

Ignoring that for a moment, he dropped a cube of ice into the spout of the teapot to cool the water down a bit and then poured it over the tea leaves into the glass pot. Once that was finished, he set his timer for two and a half minutes and then looked at his phone.

WAS WONDERING, HOW'D YOU FEEL ABOUT HELPING ME WITH SOMETHING?

WITH WHAT? he asked.

SETTING UP AN APPOINTMENT WITH ONE OF THOSE GIRLS ON THE SITE, SEE WHAT'S GOING ON.

He thought about that for a moment and then, with thirty seconds left to go before he had to pull the tea leaves, typed, YOU REALLY THINK IT'LL WORK?

MAYBE. DOUBT THEY'LL BE ABLE TO CONNECT THE TWO OF US.

He pulled the strainer from the pot and, using a spoon, pressed out the remaining liquid from the leaves. After that, he typed, OK, GUESS WE CAN TRY THAT.

GREAT!

WHAT DO I DO?

IF YOU WANT TO SWING BY TONIGHT, WE CAN TYPE UP AN EMAIL FOR YOU TO SEND THEM.

ABOUT LOOKING FOR A HOUSE? Alan asked.

SOMETHING LIKE THAT, she said.

Something like that? he said to himself, a desire to ask what exactly her suspicions were unfolding. Instead, he typed OK and hit send, a decision to wait and hear what she had to say later on guiding him.

And she better tell me.

He wasn't going to help her if she didn't, not when it was obvious that the people behind it were willing to become violent in order to prevent others from seeking information about them.

10

After breakfast with Sam, Riley wasn't sure what to do with the rest of his day off and spent several hours cruising the quiet streets, car occasionally stopping at random locations so he could get out and walk around. One such location was Northside Park in the old part of Wheaton, a place where he and Sam used to play as kids, their adventures on the old splintery wooden structures having been catalogued on several VHS home movie cassettes that he had sitting in a box at home collecting dust. Nearly twenty years had passed since the last time Riley had raced across the playground, imagining himself a part of some fantastic fantasy, a toy sword in one hand, plastic shield in another. Sam had been with him but wasn't playing within the same fantasy, Riley having reached the age when the presence of a younger brother would always ruin the fun, no matter the game.

A sense of loss filled his head, though he wasn't sure why. Was it because he wanted to go back and relive his childhood, one that had been pretty much drama free and thus carefree? Or was it the plastic structures that now stood where the old wooden ones had been, structures that while bright and cheery, didn't look nearly as fun as the ones he had played on?

Probably a bit of both, he told himself.

A young mother with a bundled-up toddler eyed him as he walked around. She was the only parent present at the moment, which was probably a bit disconcerting for her now that he, a lone unshaven adult male, was near. Fortunately for her, he didn't plan on staying long, his body not dressed for the cold that had descended upon the area, one that had actually brought morning frosts every day that week.

I'm also a state police detective, he noted to himself but wondered if that would really settle any fears the young mother held. Had he been in a standard police uniform with a patrol car the answer would probably be yes, but simply walking around with nothing more than a firearm and badge…that might not cut it.

Image is everything.

It didn't matter the situation, what one perceived to be reality was often more significant than reality itself. Security cameras were a perfect example of this. Many times small retail businesses installed cameras that didn't even function, the sight of them more important for deterring theft than the ability to actually review what had gone on in the store after the fact. Gun violence was another. Recently, thanks to the media, many people thought violent crime in the US was on the rise and had reached a point of such high levels that something had to be done about it, especially where schools were concerned. In reality, gun violence had been on a steady decline for years, ever since the crack cocaine epidemic of the '80s had subsided.

Image, image, image.

He shook his head, recalling the threats to his own image that Kristi had used against him, ones that would have painted him as a dirty cop, despite the near-perfect record he held.

All because you took the money…

Why exactly he had grabbed it was a mystery, one that he hated to think about, given the sick sense of despair it always brought. The only comparable feeling was the overwhelming moments of heartache he had felt after his wife had left him, heartache that still had the power to plaque him from time to time, though not in the way it had during that first year of separation.

Both were moments he wished he could simply erase from his mind, the latter more so than the former.

Would you have taken the money if not for the separation and divorce?

Though he liked to think the answer would be no, he knew he couldn't blame his actions on the divorce, not when the decision to take the money had been his and his alone. No getting around it. He had been first on the scene thanks to it being his turn in the surveillance schedule, seen the taped-up bundles of money in the black Hefty bag near the couch, realized no one would know about it, and swiped it before anyone else could arrive. Nothing to it really, unless one counted the hours of anguish and guilt he felt. And it wasn't simply Kristi threatening to spill his secret that made him feel this way. No. Guilt had arrived within minutes of him taking the money, a desire to put it back heavy on his mind but undoable, given the patrol officer who arrived moments after he had dumped the bag in his car.

Nothing you can do about it now.

And honestly, the threat of being painted a dirty cop was nothing compared to the horror of having the prostitution gig uncovered. One would result in the loss of his job, the other, jail time.

And no one will really care how well treated the girls are, or that you're helping them build a foundation for the rest of their lives.

Again, image would be to blame. People would hear the word "pimp" and picture him with a dozen girls, driving them to motel rooms and alleyways, bodies used over and over again at twenty bucks a pop. The inaccuracy of the imagery and the fact that he had actually helped rescue the girls from such setups would never be mentioned or really considered. Even worse, Kristi would probably paint herself as a victim, forced by them to turn her failed real estate business into a front for a suburban prostitution gig. Their connections to the world of law enforcement would only serve to vilify them even more, a sense of "they betrayed our trust" and "abuse via authority" being voiced from those who always jumped on any story involving police officers who fucked up.

And again, no one to blame but yourself.

Sure, Kristi had bullied him into it, but if he hadn't taken the money, then she would have had no leverage. And honestly, what could she have done with so little evidence? Being painted as a dirty cop would be bad, but would it have really ruined everything like he had feared at the time? Would an investigation, if instigated, have revealed anything?

You shouldn't have freaked out.

It would have been your word against hers.

He sighed.

Nothing you can do about it now.

What's done is done.

This thought stuck with him as he walked up the hill that sat next to the park, having made a sudden decision to brave the cold a bit longer just so he could take a moment to view things from the top.

Once there, he looked to the left toward Cosley Zoo and then panned over to the right where the Northside pool sat, childhood memories of each flowing through his mind. As always, his brother was present in the memories, his mother's insistence that he take Sam along and look out for him something he never dared to argue against.

Nothing has changed.

You're still looking out for him.

Unfortunately, he had failed to protect Sam from the biggest threat of all, that being Kristi. So many times during their relationship, he had known the girl was trouble but never wanted to say anything, given how happy Sam seemed.

Would it have really made a difference?

Would he have been able to see beyond his happiness?

No answers arrived. Instead, he wondered if his brother was

happy now, happy in the way that while sometimes down—as he had been today, given how little money they were currently making—he overall had an enjoyable existence.

As before, no solid answer arrived, though he was leaning toward a NO. His brother wasn't happy. Probably hadn't been since the end of his career, which was why it had been so easy for Kristi to get him involved in the prostitution stuff.

Get us both involved.

A bitter gust of wind arrived, one that seemed to pass through his coat and skin with little effort and chill his bones.

Time to go, he decided, noting that the mother with the toddler had called it quits at some point, the playground now completely empty.

Is Sam right? he asked himself while heading toward the car, steps careful on the downslope of the hill so he didn't stumble. *Am I holding the girls back and making it impossible to earn a profit?*

The question stuck with him for most of the day, though it wasn't the lack of an answer that kept it present. Instead, it was his unease with the answer, one that Riley tried to dismiss over and over again without success.

Sam's right.

I'm holding things back.

11

Try as she might, Stacy couldn't get into the piece she was supposed to be writing about the new Mariano's store opening on Main Street and Roosevelt Road, the purpose of the story being to ease the traffic congestion concerns that had been voiced by local residents. Trouble was, Stacy knew the concerns were valid and that the store might very well cause traffic problems, especially during the rush-hour periods. To claim otherwise was just foolish. Making it worse, the editor didn't simply want a bunch of quotes; he wanted her, as the voice of the story, to validate those quotes by expressing confidence that they were solid enough to erase any doubts within her mind. Writing such a thing would be a lie. It also went against her principles as a journalist, principles that said a written news article should cause an emotional response, not be comprised of one. Such was not the style of reporting these days. People didn't want to have to work toward their own conclusions; they wanted those conclusions to be given to them. Not that anyone would ever consciously admit this. In fact, most probably didn't even realize it was true, their brains having been slowly but surely indoctrinated into the thoughtless media cycle of being told what to think.

I should write a story on that, she said to herself, even though she knew none of the editors she worked with would allow such a piece, not when it would be viewed as belittling their readers.

Unable to get anywhere with the Mariano's article, she turned her attention to her email to see if anything interesting had come in. Several comment notifications were present, ones that meant a story she had submitted a few days earlier about the "sugar makes kids hyper" myth had gone live. Requests to write such pieces were common around Halloween, the topic, while rarely showing anything new in terms of studies, always gaining quite a bit of traffic, mostly because it was a comment magnet. Sadly, most of the comments seemed to ignore the science presented by the studies quoted in the piece, people always seeming to think the hyperactivity they saw in their own kids after eating sugary treats proved the myth to be true. How anyone could continue with such ignorance when presented with countless research studies was beyond her understanding, but they did. Flu shots and pieces about vaccines were traffic snares as well, thanks to the comments they generated, comments that, in Stacy's opinion, carried an element of terror due to the realization that the anti-vaccine proponents not only preached their stupidity but lived it as well. One of the greatest medical advancements humanity had ever achieved, and people actually rallied against it, and did so in such numbers that viruses that should have been nearly unheard of in this day and age were making comebacks. It was mindboggling. Equally mindboggling was how often readers would email her after such articles were published. Their anger toward her for pushing a "pharmaceutical agenda" created rants that not only showed how ignorant many were toward scientific fact, but also how seriously lacking many were when it came to being able to communicate with the written word.

Perhaps the most appalling of all, however, was the response she got from an editor after suggesting to him that she write a piece on how illiterate many of the people who emailed her seemed to be.

"I could use it as a jumping-off point to bring attention to how often people graduate from high school without being able to read and write, and how colleges are now having to test new applicants just to see if they are ready for the entry-level classes they want to take," she had said.

"No," he had replied. *"We don't want to give the impression that we feel superior to our readers simply because we understand where a period goes."*

"Okay, what if I leave out the stuff about the emails I receive and simply write about the fact that many people are graduating from high school without the ability to read and write?"

"No, it's never a good idea to call attention to the flaws of our readers, not when we depend upon them to make a living."

Sensation and reinforcing the reader's self-reassurance…that pretty much summed up modern-day reporting.

And there is nothing you can do about it, so why get all upset over it? she asked herself with a sigh.

A moment later, she pushed away from the laptop, her mind needing some time to calm itself down now that she had needlessly worked it up. While doing that, she checked her phone to see if Alan had sent her anything else about that evening, but nothing had arrived.

Questions about how he would react once she filled him in on what they were doing entered her mind, as did possible outcomes of what could follow once the email was sent.

Would they bite?

Earlier, when she sent messages requesting time with the girls, nothing had happened. Those had been sent from fake email accounts set up to look like men, a fact that must have somehow been discovered by whoever received the emails. With Alan, everything would be legit—everything but his actual desire to pay the girls for sex. Hopefully, that would be the key, and once a connection was made, Alan would learn how things worked, thus allowing them to gather even more information that would help her break the entire thing wide open.

What if he doesn't want to actually have sex with the girl we solicit?

This was one of her biggest concerns at the moment, thinking the best way to establish trust would be for Alan to go all the way. He might not agree, however, and could easily ruin everything if he went in and simply tried to talk to the girl once an appointment was scheduled.

And if that happens…

She didn't even want to think about the consequences, not when her future was riding on it.

Just make sure he knows how important this is, not just for your career but also in putting a stop to this setup.

Putting a stop to it?

Do I really care about that?

The answer was NO, she didn't really care, but if asked, she would say YES. People didn't like it when the sole purpose of acting upon something was to better oneself economically, even if that truly was the justification for the majority of the actions people undertook. She also couldn't help but feel a sense of pride in the fact that she could admit this about herself, pride that others would probably condemn without realizing they would feel the same way. That was the thing about most people: they often tricked themselves into believing things about themselves that weren't true. Everyone worked in his or her own self-interest. Anyone who claimed different was either lying or oblivious.

And this is why you don't have any friends or family members that want to speak with you on a regular basis.

Except Alan.

Is he a friend?

No answer arrived, mostly because she couldn't really define what it was they shared.

Does it really need defining?

No.

Then just let it be.

Though the advice was solid, she knew it was something she would not follow. Questioning what it was the two of them shared would not stop, nor would the desire to bring it up with Alan when together.

Which will spook him.

Yet asking him to sleep with a prostitute won't?

Oddly enough, she had a feeling it wouldn't, at least not in the same sense that talking about themselves would. This wasn't to say he would agree to it, just that it wouldn't spook him to the point of stepping back from her and, slowly but surely, distancing himself until they occasionally shared "hey, what's up?" texts every couple of weeks, if that.

12

Though the desire to do so was strong, Amanda couldn't get into the novel she was reading, one she had picked up from a Half Priced Books the other day after servicing a client she had met at the house up by the Park Place Mall. Curiosity had been her main reason for stopping, the client having said something about finding a bunch of Fear Street books for his daughter at the bookstore while killing time before their scene. The comment had been totally off the cuff, something he probably said due to how nervous he was, yet it stuck with her, memories of reading those books herself in grade school filling her mind. Triggered by those memories was a desire to recreate the joy she had often experienced while tucked away in a bedroom chair with a good book, lower half cocooned by a blanket, mug of hot chocolate at her side, and her cat Misty purring in her lap—joy that she had not experienced since leaving home all those years ago. Unfortunately, setting up a reading nook similar to the one she had when younger didn't automatically mean she would be able to get the same sense of joy she had as a kid, especially when her mind kept getting overly nostalgic about the past and how simple her life had been. Such thoughts brought about an unobtainable yearning to go back and change a couple of decisions she had made following high school, most particularly the one where she had fallen for Matt.

But you can't, so why—

Downstairs she heard the front door rattling in its frame as it was yanked open, followed by a slam as it was pulled shut. With that came the realization that the TV was no longer going, the theme from *Full House*, which she had heard just seconds earlier, having ceased.

Startled and somewhat panicked, Amanda jumped up from her chair and hurried from the room, her feet just barely escaping what could have been a devastating tangle as the blanket pooled on the floor.

And then she was at the front door, a shout to Vicky, who was already two houses down, echoing.

"What?" Vicky called back, hands on her hips.

"Where are you going?"

"7-Eleven!"

"What for?"

"Cigarettes."

"But you're not allowed to smoke!" They'd been over this twice already, the second time while in the grocery store, Vicky looking ready to throw a temper tantrum as if she were a kid that couldn't get a candy bar. Amanda hadn't really wanted to go on that errand, but Emily had insisted, a statement on "we need to make her feel like we're a family" leaving her lips. Why they needed to feel this was beyond Amanda's understanding, but in the end, she figured going along with it was less taxing than arguing.

"What're you gonna do? Fucking tattle on me?"

"No, but—" She stopped, realizing that shouting across two yards toward a girl who barely looked like a freshman in high school was probably not the best way to keep a low profile in this neighborhood.

Vicky waited, foot tapping on the sidewalk.

"Fine, go ahead!" Amanda shouted and started to pull the door closed.

"Wait!" Vicky called.

"What?" Amanda asked.

"Am I going the right way?"

"Guess you'll find out!" With that, Amanda closed the door and waited, half expecting Vicky to come back and demand to know the location.

Nothing.

Amanda peeked out the window.

Vicky was several houses down, hands in her coat pockets, steps hurried due to the cold.

If she gets lost, everyone will be pissed at me.

But I told her not to go.

Won't matter.

"Fuck!" she shouted and then opened the door. "Vicky, wait!"

Vicky stopped and turned.

"I'll show you the way," Amanda called, a sense that dozens of neighbors were now peering out their windows causing her to shudder. *She is going to ruin us. I know it.* "Let me get my coat!"

Vicky didn't reply, but she also didn't start walking again, which hopefully meant she would wait for Amanda to catch up.

Two minutes later, breath heaving in and out from sprinting down the sidewalk, Amanda was at Vicky's side, her mind doing everything it could to keep a lid on the volatile mix of anger and frustration brewing within

"This way," Amanda said, turning to the right and starting across the street.

Vicky followed.

Nothing else was said for half a mile, and then, "You have an ID, right? Because they're totally going to card you."

"Seriously?" Vicky asked.

"Um…yeah," Amanda said, halting.

"Fucking lame!"

"You don't have it?"

"They haven't given me one yet."

"Jesus Christ, how were you going to buy cigarettes then?"

"Didn't think they'd ask." She shrugged, body starting to bob a bit to stay warm.

"You didn't think they'd ask?" Beyond that, Amanda didn't know what to say, her mind completely at a loss for words.

"I didn't know," she snapped and kicked at a stick near the edge of the sidewalk. "No one ever asked me for ID before!"

"Really?"

"Really!"

Amanda thought about this for a second, a question about where exactly Vicky had been recruited from entering her mind. Had it been a small-time pimp like Matt, or someone bigger, someone connected?

Someone who local shop owners wouldn't want to piss off by denying one of their girls a pack of cigarettes?

Seems so Hollywood.

But maybe Hollywood actually got it right when it came to things like that?

Emily would know.

She had been deeper into the underworld of the city than Amanda had.

"So?" Vicky asked. It was almost a demand.

"What?" Amanda replied, her own body bobbing against the cold.

"Are you gonna buy them for me or what? I'll pay you back."

"My license is back at the house," Amanda said.

"Why didn't you grab it?"

"I thought you had one!"

"But I don't!"

"Yeah, I know that now!"

"Well, thanks for nothing," Vicky snapped and twisted back toward the house.

Let it go, Amanda said to herself, a desire to reach out and grab the brat by the ponytail difficult to resist. *Just let it go.*

13

"Wait, you want me to have sex with one of them?" Alan said, completely shocked.

"Well, it's the only way to really learn what's going on,"

Stacy said.

"What do you mean it's the only way?" Alan asked. "I can think of a dozen other ways to find out what's going on."

"Really?" Stacy crossed her arms. "Well then, I'm all ears."

Alan sighed and put a hand up. "Okay, maybe not a dozen, but seriously, what about just setting up a date with one of them and getting confirmation it's for sex? Isn't that—"

"No!" she snapped. "It's not enough."

"Why not?" Though he wanted to, he resisted the urge to cross his own arms, knowing such a pose could prove destructive, given its defensive nature. This wasn't to say he didn't feel a bit defensive right now, just that he didn't want Stacy to note that, even if only on a subconscious level. Instead, he wanted to appear open to discussion and help work up a plan that would be beneficial to her while not compromising his own feelings toward the act of exchanging money for sex.

"*Because!*" She threw her arms up. "*Anyone could write about these girls being prostitutes and leave it at that, story broken but not really detailed!*" She took a deep breath and calmly added, "I want a story that explains how they got there and what the inner workings are. A story that really lets people know who the clients are for this sort of thing, and how our society's closeted views on sex are responsible for setups like this."

Alan nodded.

"And I want to know what these girls think and how they feel about their situation."

Alan nodded again and then simply said, "I see."

Stacy looked at him for a second and then let herself fall back onto the couch, body looking as if all her strength had suddenly disappeared.

"So…" she started.

Alan knew where this was going and said, "I'm sorry, I

really don't know." He shook his head. "Setting up an appointment to help you confirm that this is a prostitution gig is one thing, but actually employing their services over and over again…that's pretty extreme." *And illegal,* his mind added.

"Sometimes extreme acts are necessary," Stacy muttered.

"Necessary for what?" he asked. "If it were just a matter of putting a stop to this, you could go to the police with your suspicions and let them handle it."

"But no one would take notice of it."

"What do you mean? Last night you said this story would make headlines across the country and were worried that someone might scoop it. Has that changed?"

"No," she said. "But if it just becomes a police headline, people are going to view it as another prostitution sting that they can easily distance themselves from."

"And that won't happen if you report it?"

"Not if I can put a human face to it, make people realize they are connected to these girls." Her voice seemed strained, his questioning having taken a toll.

He waited, his ears wanting to hear her admit the real motivation for breaking the story. Appearing altruistic and presenting a desire to help the girls was fine when talking to the masses, but with him, given what she was asking and how intimate they had been, he wanted the truth.

But does it really matter?

You know she wants to make a name for herself, and she knows that you know this, so does she really have to say it?

To me, yes.

But will she without prompting?

Alan didn't think she would and didn't really want to force it from her, because then it wouldn't really mean all that much. Plus, he knew she would say and do whatever needed to be done to get a story and advance herself, so, if he pushed, she would probably tell him what he wanted to hear.

Would that even work? he asked himself. *Would you pay one of these girls to have sex to help Stacy get a story if she admitted her true motivation?*

No answer.

In principle, Alan didn't take issue with the idea of prostitution and felt that if such a career was desired, then it should be allowed as long as it was handled in a safe manner. That said, even if legal, he would probably never utilize such services himself since half of what made his sexual experiences enjoyable was knowing the woman he was with enjoyed it as well. Her pleasure increased his pleasure. If paying for it, he would never really know if she enjoyed it, which in turn would cause him to overthink things to the point of not enjoying it himself.

With this, however, he wouldn't really be paying for the sex. That was just a cover. Instead, he would be paying to get information for Stacy's story.

They might say no.

But if they say yes, you have to go through with it.

Telling Stacy yes on the gamble of the girls saying no so he wouldn't damage their friendship would be wrong. On the flip side, just the fact that he knew he could possibly damage the friendship if he said no was pretty bad as well and said a lot about Stacy's character. What really sucked was that he knew she wouldn't consciously go this route. It would be her subconscious that did it, constantly implying that the failure of her story, if it failed, was because of him. Over time, this would destroy whatever bonds they shared.

But do you want to say yes simply based on the fear of that? Or do you want to say yes because you truly want to help her?

He leaned toward the latter but couldn't dismiss the former, which irritated him, given that it meant he didn't have control of the situation.

"Well…" Stacy urged. "Are you going to help me or what?"

You should say NO.

Nothing good is going to come of this.

"Okay, I'll do it, but on one condition."

"What?" she asked with a sigh.

"If, for some reason, I get a bad vibe once I meet up with the girl, you understand that it is my call on whether or not I go through with it."

She stared at him.

He waited.

"I suppose that's fair. I just hope you're not saying yes now knowing you will say no when the time comes."

"If I say yes, it's because I mean to go through with it," he said, slightly irritated, though he wasn't sure if it was due to her suspecting him capable of such a thing or because he had actually thought along such lines.

"Okay," she said, a skeptical tone present.

"So now what?" he asked.

"We need to pick you out a girl and then write the email, only I don't think sending it from here is a good idea. Chances are they don't have the ability to figure out what computer sent it, but even so, why risk it when it's so easy to eliminate the threat altogether?"

"Ah, good point."

14

"Hey, you got a second?" Amanda asked as Emily came down the hallway toward her own room, presumably to change out of her scene clothes before relaxing for the rest of the evening.

"Yeah, what's up?" Emily asked, voice heavy with exhaustion.

Amanda listened for a bit to make sure Vicky was still downstairs and then quietly said, "Did Kristi or Sam tell you anything about Vicky's background?"

"Um, not much really, just that she was in a pretty bad setup on the south side and wanted out, so..." She held up her hands.

"Huh."

"Why do you ask?"

"I don't know. Something just isn't adding up. For one, it doesn't seem like being here is her idea, not with all the 'I knew this place would be lame' and 'fuck the rules' stuff."

"I was actually thinking about that today," Emily said.

"And?" Amanda asked.

Emily shrugged. "I think she's probably just trying to sound tough or something."

"Hmm."

Emily waited a second and then said, "What're you thinking?"

"Honestly, I think she's trouble."

"Why's that?"

"For one, I had to chase after her tonight because she decided to go buy a pack of cigarettes. Caused a big scene right outside."

"Really?"

"Yeah, and to make it worse, she doesn't even have an ID, so in the end I had to buy them for her." *After coming all the way back for my own ID.* That still pissed her off.

"You shouldn't have done that."

"I didn't have a choice. She was throwing a temper tantrum where everyone could hear, and someone would have probably called the police if it carried on for very long."

"Oh come on. I don't think —"

"Wait, there's more. She said something about not having to show ID to buy cigarettes and booze in the past, yet she looks like she's fifteen."

"And…" Emily pressed.

"Don't you find that weird?"

"Not really. The area she was living in…shit, city officials wouldn't venture into it to check that places are checking IDs even if they got pummeled with reports, not unless a news crew was with them." She shrugged. "Happens all the time."

Amanda thought about that, and while it made sense, it didn't nullify her suspicions that something more was going on with Vicky than met the eye.

"Anything else happen? Because I really need to shower and get some sleep."

"No, go ahead," Amanda said with a wave of her arm. "I think I'll call it a night too."

"Okay. See you in the morning."

"Yep."

Amanda watched as Emily stepped into her room, and then turned and headed back into her own. A few minutes later, the sound of the shower filled the upstairs, along with music from Emily's phone.

Though she really was tired, Amanda knew sleep would not come, so rather than getting into bed to stare at the ceiling or read more of her book, she pulled out her sketchpad and sat on the floor in the corner beneath an eave. From there she eyed the chair that sat by the desk, the schoolgirl outfit from that morning still draped over the back. Why she chose to sketch that scene was beyond her under-standing, yet that was what she did until her eyes could no longer focus on the chair or her pad, and she crawled into bed.

Saturday

October 27, 2013

1

He heard the buzz in his sleep but didn't register it until Stacy nudged him awake. "Your phone," she said, voice barely audible. "Someone's calling."

Who would be calling? he asked himself while twisting to the side of the bed, uncertainty about the location of the phone plaguing him until he saw his pants. They were crumpled up in the corner of the room, Stacy having tossed them there after pulling them free so she could wrap her mouth around him, a resurgence of energy and happiness appearing within her after the two had typed up the email to send to the girl he had chosen.

And then it clicked.

Saturday. Mom.

"Shit," he said and slipped out from beneath the covers, a cold draft that had seeped through the thin walls instantly causing gooseflesh to bubble up on his skin.

"What?" Stacy asked, eyes finally opening.

"I forgot about breakfast with my mom. We do it every Saturday." He fished into the pocket of his pants for his phone, which had stopped buzzing but now was indicating a missed call. Sure enough, it had been from his mother.

He waited a second, phone in hand, and it buzzed again, this time with a text that read: ARE WE STILL DOING BREAK-

FAST?

"Call and a text," Stacy muttered. "She must be really hungry."

"Ha ha, that's standard operating procedure for her. Rather than leaving a voicemail, she'll just send a text afterward. Doesn't matter the situation. If she calls to tell me she's on the way home from work, she'll send a text too if I don't pick up. Never fails."

"She calls when she's on her way home," Stacy said. "Good to know should we ever decide to have some fun at your place."

"Honestly, I think that's why she does it."

"Really? Did she ever come home while you had a girl there?"

"Only that one time with you."

"Oh wow, I forgot about that."

"I don't think she did," Alan said with a grin. "Hey, I hate to wake up and run like this, but…"

"No, it's cool."

"Unless you want to come with?"

"Um…you know, as much as I'd love to, I think I will pass for today. I'd like to be a bit more presentable upon meeting your mom again after all these years."

"You sure?" he asked. "Because she probably won't be all that presentable herself."

"I'm sure. Have a good time and let me know when you send the email."

"Okay, will do." He hobbled around with his pants for a moment, right leg meeting up with a tangle that didn't want to break. Once through, he got his other leg in, buttoned them, and then went in search of his shirt. After that, he walked over to Stacy and gave her a hug, the cool air causing her bared nipples to poke him through the thin fabric of his shirt.

Sensing the effect this had on him, she cupped his testicles before he could break away and said, "If I had known you had to leave so soon, I would have woken up earlier so I could send you off a happy man."

"You already are," he said with a smile.

"Happier then." With that she leaned down and pressed her lips against his firmness and then, once the kiss was done, said, "Now get out of here so I can get another couple hours of sleep."

"Ha, okay," Alan said, right hand adjusting himself, mind wondering how the hell he was supposed to sit through breakfast with his mother after being teased like that.

2

"Two nights in a row," his mom said once they had a table at the Egg'lectic Café in Danada Town Square. "Certainly seems like you and Stacy have hit it off again."

Alan felt blood rushing to his cheeks as he nodded, the openness the two had with each other not enough for him to welcome this topic into their breakfast conversation. Or any conversation really.

"I'm glad," she continued. "She seemed like such a nice girl and was pretty devastated by you having to leave all those years ago. She used to message me all the time to find out if I'd heard anything."

"Really? I didn't know that."

"Yep, and for nearly a year her profile picture was of you two at the pool, the one I took right before you did that amazing twisting front-flip face-plant into the water."

"Oh god, the one where a ten-year-old followed me up with a perfect front flip into a dive. Glad you didn't video that too."

"That's the one," she said, head twisting a bit as Jody, their favorite waitress, approached with a coffee carafe.

Alan quickly turned his mug over and smiled at Jody while

his mother greeted her with a "good morning" and questions about how she was doing and if she was getting excited about Halloween.

"Speaking of Halloween," his mother said once Jody had left with their order. "When are you going to set up your display?"

"Probably on Monday, maybe Tuesday. I was going to do it today, but the weather people said we're supposed to get high winds all weekend, so I figured it was better to wait. Don't want the tombstones blowing away again like they did last time."

"What year was that?" she asked.

"My senior year, so 2001." He sipped his coffee. "Hard to believe, isn't it?"

"Wow."

The two went silent for a moment, both contemplating the passage of time. During this period, Jody returned with the coffee carafe and checked to see if they were ready for more. Both were.

"So…what are your plans for today?" his mother asked.

"Nothing much." He took another sip of coffee. "Just going to study a bit for that history test and hopefully get some more writing done on my memoir."

"How's that going?"

"Eh…" He shrugged. "I've gotten bogged down."

"How so?"

"Trying to convey what it was like to be home between tours."

"Okay, and what's making that difficult?"

Alan shook his head. "It's hard to explain."

"Well, try. Talking might help you work though the problem."

"No, it really isn't that kind of problem. More like…I don't know, but it isn't really something I can think through. I just have to work through it."

"What do you mean?"

"See, I know exactly what I want to say, but when I sit down to write it I just can't get it out." He shook his head. "I just stare at the screen, typing a few words here and there, but can never get a flow going."

"Writer's block," she said.

"Maybe, though it isn't that I'm struggling for ideas, just how to present them. I know exactly what I want to say, just can't."

"And what is it you want to say?" she asked.

He thought about that for a second and then looked toward the kitchen to see if Jody was near with the coffee carafe, his mind and body really needing another dose.

Catching his glance, she started heading their way.

Alan waited until she had filled both their mugs and then said, "Remember that time when we were in the car and I was startled by the guy with a cell phone?"

"No, not really."

He sighed. The incident stuck in his mind in such a way that he could recall almost every detail, yet it had barely made an impression upon her, which, ironically, was something else he wanted to convey in his memoir but was unsure how to go about it.

"Okay, you know that in Iraq insurgents often used cell phones to set off IEDs. Well, back when I was stateside for the first time, I would get apprehensive anytime I saw someone on a cell phone, my ears ready to hear a blast of some kind somewhere near."

She nodded. "I remember you talking about things like that."

"Yeah, well, what I want to do is try to convey that feeling, make readers understand what it is like to come back to a society where the actions you fear are everyday occurrences, and how difficult it can be to adjust to such a thing."

"I think that would be good."

"Me too, only I can't seem to write it."

"Why not write what you just told me?"

He shook his head. "Doing that isn't the problem. I can write about the events that unfolded in my life all day long. It's writing it in such a way that I get people into the mindset that I'm having trouble with. And it isn't just with the cell phone thing. Just leaving the house to run to the store was difficult because I didn't have my rifle with me. Believe it or not, that made it so I felt like I was forgetting something every time I went somewhere, and even though I knew what it was, I couldn't shake the horrible feeling."

"Do you still feel that?" she asked, concern present.

"Not really…well…sometimes, but hardly ever."

"How come?"

"Well, I haven't really been in deployment to a combat zone for an extended period of time. Not since early 2008. After that tour, I spent most of my time training, and when I was deployed again I got sick, so I wasn't out in the field as much." Plus, going out into the field in Afghanistan had been different than going on patrols during his tours in Iraq, though it was hard to describe why. The setting was one thing, the terrain of the two countries and the way populated areas were set up completely different from one another. Afghanistan had also felt more open and more displaced from the rest of the world. It was weird. "In fact," he continued, "being sick probably helped a bit since it gave my mind something to focus on."

"Huh, I never thought about that. For me, there were only two periods, time when you were home and time when you weren't, and the time that you weren't, all I could really picture was you in Iraq."

Alan wasn't sure how to reply to that.

"I think that's a perspective not many people can understand," she added.

"I think you're right. We should each write a memoir and then can sell them side by side, a mother-son perspective on what the war on terror has been like."

"You know, that's not a bad idea."

Uh-oh, he thought. *What have I done?*

In all honesty, it really wasn't a bad idea. He just feared the potential for it turning into a joint project, which he knew would be a maddening experience.

"I think you should write about your travels," Alan said. While saying this he saw Jody coming out of the kitchen with a tray that looked to be their food.

"I keep thinking about that too, but I just don't know where to begin."

"That's always the hardest part."

Jody appeared as he said this and presented them with their orders, the freshness of the food evidenced by the steam still rising from the plates.

"More coffee?" she asked.

"Yes, please," Alan said.

With that, the two started eating, all talk about writing projects pushed aside while they enjoyed their food.

3

OKAY, JUST SENT THE EMAIL. FINGERS CROSSED.

The text message had arrived while Stacy was in the shower, one that had been desperately needed after everything she and Alan had done the night before.

In reply, she typed: EXCELLENT. LET ME KNOW WHAT THEY SAY.

If they reply, her mind added.

They will.

Unfortunately, the inner statement was not enough to curb her doubt. With the doubt came fear that Alan would back out if they said yes.

Or fall for the girl.

Could that actually happen?

Would Alan fall victim to a "rescue me because I'm a damsel in distress" type of situation?

Stacy tried shaking the thought away but couldn't. Even worse, she knew that if such a thing happened, she would have no one to blame but herself.

But it is necessary.

The story depends upon it.

Afterward, if need be, she would do her best to fix any problems that arose from having been so focused on the story. Until then...well...

She looked around the dump she called home, frustration at how little she had achieved since college hitting hard.

4

The last thing Riley wanted to do after leaving work that afternoon was talk to Sam about adding more girls to the setup, but Sam insisted, and while Riley could have put his foot down, he relented and headed out to meet up with him.

"I have a bead on a guy that's been peddling a couple teens from the back of a van at a motel on the south side," Sam said. "I'm thinking we might be able to swing in tonight and take a look and if you think they're okay, grab them. I got room now that Vicky is gone if we need to detox."

"How'd you find out about him?" Riley asked.

"He's been picked up several times in the past during UC operations in that area, and last night I swung by and took a look, and sure enough he's back, new van, new girls, same motel."

"Anything going on in that area?"

"No, not that I've heard."

"You sure?"

"Dude, I wouldn't suggest it if there was."

"And the ages he usually works with?"

"Upper teens. Runaways mostly."

Riley thought about it for a few minutes and said, "Okay, we'll take a look, but I'm telling you, if I get the impression that they're underage, I'm putting my foot down."

"I know," Sam said, palms up. "You made that very clear last week." He paused for a second and then added, "But you do have to admit, Vicky is much better off with us than she was."

Riley sighed. "I agree. I just don't want to make a habit of stocking our rooms with girls her age."

Sam nodded. "Me either, actually, but...well...it won't happen again."

You're damn right it won't, Riley said to himself, frustration over the Vicky situation bubbling up to the surface once more. *And if it does...*

Sadly, Riley wasn't sure what he would or even could do if his brother defied him. Sam and Kristi held all the cards in this thing. They also didn't really need him all that much, not anymore. He, however, couldn't walk away, not when he knew that doing so would allow Kristi to get reckless with things, eventually landing all of them in jail. It wouldn't matter that he had walked away; she would make sure his early participation was known and that he was punished right alongside them. He was stuck.

"What time you want to head out?" Riley asked.

"Seven, seven thirty," Sam said.

"Okay."

"Also, if this falls through, I know of a small dope house not far from the area that probably has quite a bit of money stashed in—"

"No," Riley said.

"But there might be—"

"NO!"

Sam held up his hands again. "Okay, okay, was just a thought. Figured your stash is running low and it would probably be a nice score. My buddy did a raid on another place not too long ago that netted nearly thirty grand, all of which is now just sitting in an evidence locker collecting dust."

"Yeah, and that raid was meticulously planned out and probably had a dozen well-trained tactical officers in full body armor carrying MP5s on the chance that things could get messy. If the two of us went in on our own"—he shook his head—"no, I can't even consider doing it."

"Okay, just wanted you to know the possibility exists, that's all."

"Possibility noted," Riley said. Though he didn't show it, he was now very uneasy about things, his fear being that Sam would hit the house on his own one day and get hurt.

Not your fault if he does.

But...

No, don't even consider it.

Once they opened such a door, they would not stop. Two, three times, they would probably be okay, but then their luck would eventually run out and something horrible would happen.

And even if they did manage to make several successful scores and then stopped, word would spread of the robberies, which would beef up security at other houses, making it more dangerous for everyone. It could also spark conflict between rival areas, which would claim innocent lives and increase the police presence, which could then lead to their own activities becoming known.

Not worth it at all.

None of this is.

"Hey, you okay?" Sam asked.

"Huh?"

"You seemed out of it for a moment," Sam said. "Worried about the girls? Tonight?"

"Fuck, man, the entire thing has me worried, but...well, nothing I can do about it now."

"Yeah," Sam muttered. Then, "So you'll be at my place around seven? We can take my car."

"Fine."

"And don't worry, nothing's going to happen."

Riley just looked at him, his doubts about that impossible to mask, and then turned to leave.

5

ANYTHING YET? Stacy texted Alan as the afternoon slowly progressed into evening.

NO, NOTHING, he texted back a few minutes later, followed by, IS THAT BAD?

DON'T KNOW, she replied. NOT SURE ON THE TURN-AROUND TIME.

AH, OKAY.

Feeling foolish because she knew he would have messaged her if he had received a reply, yet she had asked anyway just to get his attention, Stacy set the phone down and went to the fridge. Nothing within looked appealing, however, and though she really couldn't afford it, she decided to head out and get something for dinner, a quick check on her credit card balance showing she had six dollars worth of credit available.

6

Though he still wasn't fully comfortable with the idea of getting together with one of the girls from the real estate company, Alan had to admit a sense of sexual excitement when looking at the picture of the one he had selected. He also couldn't help but feel anxious about getting a reply, hope of receiving one that said *yes* growing within him and causing him to check his email inbox every half hour or so. Of course, an answer of *no* wouldn't be devastating either, though it would be disappointing simply because he really did want to help Stacy. And the sex with the girl, well, he wasn't really sure what to think when it came to that, though he was fairly certain it would not even come close to delivering the pleasure he experienced when with Stacy.

Footsteps echoed on the stairs beyond his basement room, and even though he wasn't looking at anything questionable, Alan minimized the real estate company website. A second later, his mother poked her head into his partially open bedroom door and asked, "You have any clothes you want me to wash?"

"Not really," Alan said and motioned toward the near-empty basket by the bed. "Did it the other day."

"I could still toss what's in there with my stuff if you want."

"No, I'll do it when it's full."

"It's really no trouble. I can throw it—"

"Mom!" he snapped. Then, voice calmer, "Please, I said no."

"Ohhh-kay," she said, trying to mask her hurt.

Guilt flowed through him, but he held back an urge to apologize, the fact being that he had asked her over and over again to simply leave it at that if he said *no* to something.

Nothing else was said and soon she was heading back upstairs, the washing machine rumbling in the room next door.

Alan shook his head and then noticed he had a new email message waiting, the tab at the top of the screen showing a (1). Hoping it was a reply, he clicked the tab and watched as his inbox filled the screen.

No reply.

Instead, it was a message telling him he had a new comment on his blog, one that had a link for a Viagra-like product.

He sighed and then went back to looking at the real estate webpage, clicking on each one of the girls even though he already had one selected.

Kristi Homes, he noted to himself while looking at one picture, the sign and logo of the company clearly visible next to the girl. *Is it a prop or a real sign at a real house that really is for sale, and, if so, how do they differentiate between those who want to buy a house and those who want to buy a girl? Is there some sort of code for those who want a girl, one that we didn't use and therefore we won't be approved?*

The more he considered this, the more likely it seemed. After all, the site wasn't exactly set up in a way to lure in men seeking sex. Sure, some of the pictures were erotic, but many might feel that was just an attempt to sell houses, the fact being that sex did sell. Only those who went to the site already knowing the girls were available for more than a house showing would understand what the photos were really advertising.

If that is what's really going on.

Though slim, he still had doubts, simply because the idea seemed too fantastic. He also didn't understand how they could be making money, though he did know a simple lack of information could be to blame for this, and once he did have all the information on how the setup worked, it might make sense.

Alan clicked on a picture of a girl named Amanda. Unlike some of the photos, her image wasn't provocative at all. Instead, she simply stood by the sign, smiling, body clad in a white shirt and dark skirt, hair falling to her shoulders and ending at the top of her breasts. Nothing about the picture screamed sex, yet somehow it was one of the more erotic ones, probably because it had a very innocent, girl-next-door feel to it.

Something else...

He couldn't put his finger on it, but something about the girl was bugging him—had been since first considering her last night.

Whatever it was, however, his mind wasn't going to release it just yet; thus he would just have to wait.

Another new email appeared.

He clicked that tab, but once again, it wasn't a reply from Isabella or the company.

Growing weary, he went to exit out of the Internet altogether, but then stopped and went back, a new thought occurring.

A moment later, he had the first picture of a girl on the real estate site open, trying to see if he could make out the address on the house that stood behind her.

Nothing was visible in that one, so he moved on, and then on again, and again, until he came to a picture of a girl named Caroline. In it, he could make out the first two numbers of an address, but none beyond that due to an ill-timed shadow. In another picture, this one of a girl named Sophia, the same house was visible, and he could make out the final two numbers.

A couple other pictures provided him with more address numbers, a full one visible in Amanda's and another in one displaying Isabella. The rest were all partials or didn't show any numbers at all.

Now what?

Without street names, the numbers didn't really mean much.

And even if he had street names, he wasn't really sure what could have been gained from visiting the addresses of the photos. In fact, all he really wanted to know was whether or not the For Sale signs were real and if the houses themselves were being offered by the Kristi Homes Real Estate company. Why exactly he wanted to know this was a mystery, but he figured every detail helped. Plus, such information could prove useful at some point.

But without the street names...

Was that really an obstacle?

More had been done with less in other situations, a documentary he had watched on how they had uncovered that it was Bin Laden living in the house in Islamabad coming to mind. Then again, the intelligence agencies involved had had a few more tools at their disposal than he did, tools that were used by experts working around the clock for years. All he had was himself, Stacy, and, if he could find one, a list of addresses in the Chicago area, one that he would have to go through entry by entry in an attempt to match up the numbers he had just found. After that, he would drive out to the addresses he had highlighted and find out if they were the same houses in the pictures.

All this so Stacy can get a story and win a Pulitzer.

Actually, he had never heard her mention the award, but he had no doubt it was on her mind when writing. How could it not be when she always aspired to be the best in her field?

Maybe she'll share it with you, he silently said with a chuckle. *On the weekends, you could put it in a drawer next to the Bronze Star and Purple Hearts.*

While contemplating that he typed "DuPage County Address List" into Google to see what would happen. Nearly one million search results came up, the first of which looked promising until he realized it was just a list of county offices. From there he added the word "residential" to the search, but it didn't really help.

There has to be some sort of list, he silently said, frustration present. After all, if one could search out an address on Google Maps and MapQuest, then there had to be something public that was providing the data.

He wondered if his mom would know. She was pretty savvy when it came to things like this. Unfortunately, asking her would probably result in her asking him quite a few questions, ones he didn't really want to answer.

You might have to...

An image of his mother helping uncover the prostitution scheme entered his head, all her years of watching *Murder, She Wrote* and *Magnum P.I.* giving her a false sense of expertise in how to investigate such things. Not that he was any better, all his investigative skills having come from private-eye novels and *Columbo* shows. However, he did feel he was better equipped to deal with trouble, should it come along.

Would she stop if asked?

Or would her excitement get the better of her?

Not wanting to find out an answer, he continued plugging search strings into Google in hopes of finding an address database. Nothing useful ever popped up, however, and in the end, he decided to go upstairs and ask his mother.

"Wait, what?" she asked after hearing his question, his wording so careful that it hadn't really made sense even to him.

He tried again, this time with more detail.

"Oh, just start typing the numbers into the Google Maps search thingy," she said.

"But I don't have the street address," he repeated.

"I know. It will give you suggestions local to this area. I'm not sure how it works, but I do it all the time."

"Really?"

"Yeah."

Somewhat startled, he went back down to his room, opened up the Google Maps webpage, and started typing in the numbers of the first address. Sure enough, several options appeared in a drop-down menu, all of them local to the Chicago area.

7

Amanda was not having a good afternoon. First, she nicked herself while shaving her legs and couldn't get the bleeding to stop, which forced her to use a Band-Aid that was visible through her stockings.

Second, she couldn't get the back left garter on her new corset-like top to stay in place, the clasp slipping free from the stocking every time she bent over. Third, the skirt she had been requested to wear, one that the client had actually bought her, was nowhere to be found.

Frustrated, she walked down the hallway toward Emily's room and tried the knob, the door opening without any trouble. Emily was sitting on her bed with her laptop, earbuds connecting her to the device.

"Hey, Emily," she called.

Emily looked up and pulled one of the earbuds from her ear, a faint cackle of what sounded like sex escaping before she clicked something with her mouse, silencing it. "Yeah?" she asked.

"Did you take any of my outfits?"

"No."

"You sure, because the leather skirt I'm supposed to wear today is missing."

"I didn't take it," she said.

"Really?"

"Really!"

Amanda considered things for a moment and then, while turning, said, "That little bitch!"

Emily, probably realizing what had happened as well, jumped up from her bed and followed Amanda, a statement of, "Don't freak out," leaving her lips.

Amanda ignored it and threw open the door to Vicky's room, the anger displayed by the act pointless since the girl was downstairs, and stepped toward the closet.

Inside, several dresses were present. They looked like outfits that a little girl would wear on her first day of school. Also present were several schoolgirl jumpers, skirts and blouses with overly rounded collars.

"When did she get these?" Amanda asked, somewhat startled.

"Kristi brought them with her when she dropped her off. You weren't back yet."

"Oh." Though disturbed by the idea of men wanting to have sex with Vicky as if she were a young innocent child, Amanda didn't have time to dwell upon or discuss the issue and went from the closet to the dresser, her hands grabbing and throwing the items onto the floor, eyes on the lookout for leather.

"Amanda, easy," Emily said and then, when Amanda moved on to the next drawer, left the room, her voice filling the house as she called for Vicky to get up there.

The skirt was not in the second drawer either.

Panic growing, Amanda opened the third drawer and momentarily thought she had found it when her eye caught sight of something black. To her surprise, it was a different skirt, one she hadn't realized was missing from her room. Seeing this, she turned back toward the pile of clothes she had tossed on the floor and wondered how many other items of hers were within, and then turned back to finish with the drawer, her skirt finally appearing after she had pulled out a chunk of clothes.

"What the fuck?" Vicky cried.

Amanda spun around and shouted, "Don't you ever go into my room and take my stuff!" She waved the skirt.

"I didn't," Vicky protested.

"My stuff was in your drawer!" Amanda snapped.

"I didn't do it." Vicky looked at the floor while saying this.

"Vicky, come on," Emily said. "It's kind of obvious that you did."

"Why would I take her stuff? She's so *fat* that none of it fits me."

The comment tore into Amanda like no other, and before

she knew it, she was across the room, hands ready to grab and throw the little bitch to the floor. Emily moved as well, blocking her.

"Amanda," she said. "You have a scene you need to get ready for. I'll deal with this."

Breathing heavily, Amanda nodded and left the room. While doing this she heard Vicky starting to say something, only to be cut off by a swift, "Shut up!" from Emily.

Back in her own room, Amanda went to step into the skirt, when she realized one of her stockings had slid down to her knee, both garter straps having come undone.

Overwhelmed, Amanda threw herself onto her bed and let the tears start to flow.

"Amanda, you okay?" Emily asked.

Amanda didn't reply.

"Come on, don't let her get to you like that. She's just a brat." Then a few seconds later, "And you have a scene you need to get to, so get up and finish getting ready."

Amanda knew Emily was right and did as instructed, her fingers once again beginning the struggle with the garters, which, thankfully, Emily stepped in and helped with.

After that, she put the skirt on, grabbed a sweater to wear over the corset, took hold of her purse and makeup bag, and said, "Okay, I'm off. Can you make sure all my stuff is put back? I saw other outfit items in there."

"I will, and I'll try to make her understand that she can't do stuff like that."

"Good luck," Amanda muttered and started out of the room.

"Oh, and Amanda?"

"What?" she asked with a sigh.

"You know what she said isn't true. Calling you fat, that was just an immature schoolgirl jab to get a rise out of you."

Amanda didn't reply to that and instead said, "I gotta go."

"Okay," Emily said and followed her out, quickly stepping to the right so as to be between Amanda and Vicky if Vicky decided to step out of her room and say anything.

Downstairs, Amanda donned her coat and grabbed the keys from the shelf above the rack, mind desperately trying to push everything that had just happened out of reach so she could focus on the scene.

While doing this she heard the floorboards above creaking in such a way that she was certain Emily had gone back into Vicky's room. Voices could not be heard, however, and, sadly, she didn't have time to sneak back up and listen in on what was discussed.

Probably for the better.

Might not like what you hear.

In fact, the only thing she would really want to hear would be the smack of something across the girl's ass, followed by pleas from her to stop and promises of never doing anything like that again.

Such would not happen, not unless the Woodmans approved, which she doubted they would do. It just wasn't the type of setup they had in mind. At the same time, girls behaving the way Vicky was behaving probably didn't fall in line with their setup plans either, and because of that, maybe changes would be made.

Okay, enough, she told herself, fingers turning the ignition key. *Time to focus on Brian and how you're going to get him off.*

After all, the last thing she wanted was changes to be made due to her not living up to the expectations that came with the cost of her services, especially if the change was her being fired.

Would they do that?

If she were running things, she would be worried that firing a girl would result in the girl telling the authorities what was going on, which would be really bad. So what did one do with a girl if her services were no longer required or desired?

The answers that followed were disconcerting.

8

"Are you still planning on staying in tonight, or has that changed?" his mother asked as he got his coat.

"Oh, I'll be staying in," Alan said. "Probably won't even be gone all that long. Just need to check out these addresses for Stacy."

"Ah...I see."

He could tell she wanted to come with him and was waiting for an invite, which was why he shouldn't have been so forthcoming about the "checking out addresses" part. Hoping to redirect her, he said, "Hey, I was thinking when I get back we could watch some old horror movies. Maybe *The Haunting* or *House on Haunted Hill*? I got tons of DVDs and lots of stuff on my hard drive that we can stream onto the TV."

"Hmm, that's an idea, or is there anything new we could get? I heard those *Paranormal Activity* movies were pretty creepy. Bet the Redbox at Jewel has them."

"We could do that." Alan wasn't a fan of point-of-view films but figured he could go along with it if that was what she wanted. "Want me to grab them on my way back?"

"Um, I can do it. Have to go to the store anyway, and I'll get some goodies for us to eat while we watch them."

"Okay." He grabbed his keys.

"Are there any other new ones that sound good, just in case they don't have it?"

"Um...I can't think of anything off the top of my head. Let me think about it a bit and I'll text you."

"Okay. Be careful."

"I will." He reached for the front door.

"Oh, wait, what kind of candy do you want?"

"Anything," he said with a sigh. Then, "Well...no, something fruity and chewy, like Dots or Jujyfruits."

"That it?"

"And some Junior Mints."

"So, Dots, Jujyfruits, and Junior Mints? Anything else?"

"Nope, that should be enough."

"Okay."

A few seconds later, he was in his car, finger programming the first address into the GPS on his phone. Ironically, he had actually protested his mom getting him the phone upon his return to the States, his thinking being it was too expensive and had too many pointless functions.

"I don't even like texting," he had told her.

"Give it a try. If it doesn't grow on you, we can sell it on Ebay," she had replied.

Grow on him it had, as she had probably known it would, and now he couldn't imagine his life without such a device. It was so surreal. Leaving the house without a cell phone...how did anyone ever manage such a thing all those years ago? It was unthinkable. The same was true with things like Google and Facebook. Some of his fellow students couldn't believe he had made it through high school without them and, honestly, given how important the two were to him now, he couldn't believe it either.

"Turn left onto Brentwood," the mechanical female voice instructed as he backed out of the driveway and into the cul-de-sac.

"Nope," Alan replied. Going left would require him to make another left turn onto Butterfield without a light, which was just stupid when he could make the same turn a couple blocks down at an actual light.

Actually, looking at where the first address was, he was surprised the GPS actually wanted him on Butterfield at all. He knew a better way.

Now let's just see if the address is actually one of the houses…

Given that only three options had been given on the drop-down suggestions when typing in the numbers of the first address, he felt chances were good that it was. However, if it wasn't, the other two suggestions weren't that far either, so no matter what, it wouldn't take long to find the house.

If one of them is it.

Nothing short of finding the actual house would shake the tiny bit of doubt that was still floating around inside his head, doubt that wasn't shared by most of his mind yet still had to be acknowledged.

This doubt was given a boost when the first house he drove to didn't have a For Sale sign in the yard. It also didn't have any resemblance to any of the houses from the images on the website, which he double-checked on his phone just to make sure.

The next one was about five minutes away.

It too didn't have a sign or any resemblance to the house in the photo.

Growing worried, he started the ten-minute trip to the next house, which was in Lombard just off Main Street, not too far from Enchanted Castle. Fond memories of his visits there with his mom entered his mind as he passed it, all of which were quickly displaced the moment he saw a For Sale sign sitting in a yard up ahead.

Is it…

"Your destination is on the left," the GPS announced as he slowly passed the house, eyes catching the familiar Kristi Homes logo.

The house itself was familiar as well, so familiar that he didn't even have to match it up with the image on his phone.

Now what? he asked himself.

No answer followed.

Finding the house had been his goal, so he hadn't really

thought much beyond that.

Take a *picture!*

That was really a no-brainer.

He snapped two of them with his phone and quickly emailed them to himself without even thinking about it, the extensive training he had received on how to conduct surveillance operations prior to his first deployment to Afghanistan guiding his hand.

Once that was done, he looked at his list for the next house and what the possible locations were. Three addresses were up north, and two were south. He decided upon the ones to the north, simply given that the odds were better.

His phone buzzed.

GOT THE FIRST TWO *PARANORMAL ACTIVITY* MOVIES. ANYTHING ELSE I SHOULD GRAB? THEY GOT SOMETHING CALLED *THE COLLECTOR*, WHICH SOUNDS PRETTY INTERESTING.

Alan thought about that, memories of past moments when his mother had selected "horror" movies for them to watch surfacing. *Hostel* came to mind, the brutality so extreme they had shut it off, their disgust at what they had seen—and that it had carried the label of horror with it—overwhelming.

NO, LET'S JUST STICK WITH THOSE TWO SINCE THEY'RE LIKE A DOLLAR A DAY.

AH, GOOD POINT. OKAY.

He waited to see if anything else would be sent and when nothing was, started typing the next address into his GPS. While doing this he caught sight of a car approaching in his mirror, one that slowed considerably as it neared the house.

Could it be?

The car turned into the driveway, his eye catching sight of a female driver. He then watched as she exited the vehicle and hurried to the garage, where a keypad was waiting for a code.

Appearance-wise, she didn't look like a prostitute, just a realtor, but he knew that was probably standard when going to and from a house. Once inside, there was no telling what type of outfit she might be wearing, if anything.

Is she meeting someone?

Why else would she be here?

Without really needing to think much beyond that, Alan shifted the car into drive and headed down the quiet street until he came to a four-way stop. Once there, he took a right and then used the first driveway he came upon to turn around and pulled himself to park in a position that allowed him to look down the street to the house in question.

Though he had never done any actual surveillance from a vehicle, he felt confident that his location would go unnoticed, especially to the untrained eye. He also doubted anyone would see him as he pulled up to snap a picture of whatever vehicle arrived, the client and the girl being too busy to notice anything happening beyond the windows.

Then what? he asked himself.

Follow the guy home to see where he lives so we can ask him questions, or follow the girl so we know what the main address is?

Or can we find out that information with the license plate number?

In the movies, reporters always seemed to have contacts they could milk for such information; in reality, it probably wasn't that common. However, if anyone did have such contacts, it would be Stacy, her determination and unapologetic drive to achieve glory in her field having probably snared a few useful sources.

9

Though somewhat calmer than she had been upon leaving the house, Amanda was nowhere near as calm as she wanted to be for her scene, the fifteen-minute drive from the house in Glen Ellyn to the one in Lombard simply not a long enough period of time to allow for such an outcome. The fact that nothing good was on the radio had added to the difficulty, the frustration of not being able to find a song she wanted to listen to mixing with the aggravation she felt.

Thankfully, her scene wasn't scheduled to start for another forty minutes, so once she did her makeup, she would have a good chunk of time to try to decompress. Before she did that, however, she went to a second-floor bedroom to check the road in front of the house, the red Saturn she had seen with a driver sitting inside somewhat disconcerting.

Gone, her mind said needlessly as her eyes carefully peeked through the blinds.

No relief followed, an idea that maybe she had scared him away entering her mind.

But why would he be right out front to begin with? she asked herself.

Such a position would be downright stupid if surveillance of the house was the goal.

Unless he knew the scene wasn't supposed to start for a while yet and was just getting a look at the place, a voice within suggested.

But how would he have even known about the scene?

No answer arrived.

No relief either.

And then her eyes settled on the For Sale sign, a cry of *DUH* echoing through her head. He had probably just been a prospective house buyer jotting down the phone number. After all, the house was for sale, had been for some time, and was sure to catch attention from people in the market for a new home. In fact, now that she thought about it, she was surprised she had never noticed anyone checking out the signs before while at houses, but then she wondered if maybe she simply hadn't been paying attention to such things. Hell, the only reason she had noticed it this time was because she had pulled up while he had been sitting there. Had he arrived two minutes later, once she was inside, she might never have seen him.

Glad he didn't come up to try to talk to me about the house.

Has that happened with anyone else?

The signs in the yards all clearly said By Appointment Only, but she knew many people often decided such rules were clearly meant for other people.

Apparently, this guy actually follows rules.

Probably calling the number right now to see if he can get a showing...

She wondered what the answer to such a question would be, but then pushed it from her mind while applying her makeup. Once that was finished, she went around placing her defensive sprays around the house, knowing that just because she had done scenes with Brian several times, she didn't really know the guy. The day she decided to skip the safety measure would be the day one of her trusted clients would attack her, her body found strung up and eviscerated in the basement a few days later.

Or he will take you somewhere and rape you over and over again for several weeks, maybe even years, before growing tired of your body...

Such things happened more often than people wanted to believe, especially to people like her, people that society didn't really want to know about unless it was while viewing law-enforcement sting operations on TV or *Dateline* documentaries about human trafficking.

But such was life.

And the danger wasn't just limited to girls in her field. Standing at a bus stop could be just as dangerous, or waiting tables, or being a teacher. It all depended on who was lurking in the area.

She sighed and then, with nothing else to do until the scene began, went back to the window for a moment to look at the street. After that, she headed downstairs to wait on one of the couches in the family room. A few minutes later, she went to get a drink from the fridge, which was always stocked with water and soda. Other items could be requested by the men in advance if they desired particular beverages or food items for before, after, or even during the scenes. None of her clients ever asked for anything, but she knew that Emily had a guy who really liked drinking liquids from her pussy and, on occasion, her ass.

Just thinking about that latter act made her want to vomit. Emily, however, thought it was great, though she did admit that it felt really funky when the liquid was in, especially if it was something thick like milk.

"You feel like you have to take an explosive shit," she had said. *"All you want to do is run to the bathroom, but you can't, and then when his tongue starts to poke at you—"*

Amanda had stopped her right there, a hand raised and a cry of *"you're going to make me sick"* leaving her lips.

Emily had laughed but also complied with her request and never said another word about it. Sadly, removing the image that had been created within her mind was not an easy task. In fact, the more she tried to destroy it, the more detailed it seemed to get. Fuck, even now, the imaginative gears were turning to create a video-like display of what the scene could have looked like, one that was so disgusting she actually tried to shake it away.

A few minutes later, the doorbell rang, jolting her.

It was Brian; a peek through the peephole confirmed this.

She opened the door, a practiced smile upon her face. A greeting of welcome followed, punctuated by a motion for him to step inside, one that would look like nothing more than a standard "come on in so I can show you the house" display to anyone who might be watching.

10

And…no, Alan's mind said as a car drove by the house, his impatience growing as he waited for someone to show up. Had he been in the military still, watching a known Taliban convoy route through the mountains, ambush ready to be unleashed, he would have been fine, his training and confidence in his team members keeping him at ease. Now, things were different, mostly because he had no official capacity here. He also wasn't entirely sure that someone would actually show up, and while such outcomes were always a possibility while taking part in military operations, this felt unique.

Another car appeared and slowed, but only so it could turn into a driveway two houses down, kids exploding from within to run inside while a woman took her time.

Alan sighed.

What if she doesn't have a guy coming?

What if she simply decided to stay at the house for a while?

Questions like this didn't help his anxiety, mostly because he really had no idea how this gig worked. Logically, it made sense that the houses would be used to service the men, but that didn't mean it was the reality. Every day things happened that went against logic, mostly because people often acted in haste rather than after careful consideration. That said, he had a feeling quite a bit of consideration had gone into this setup, but even so, that didn't necessarily mean logic had guided it.

Or that logic is guiding it now.

Best-laid plans…

Behind him a car appeared.

Though he doubted anyone would really be paying attention, Alan put his phone to his ear as if he were talking, which hopefully would make it seem as if he had pulled over to ask directions or something.

And if someone comes out of a house to ask what you're doing?

Technically, given that the street was public property, he wouldn't have to say anything, nor did he have to fear getting in trouble for sitting here. Refusing to answer, however, could draw unwanted attention; thus, if asked, he would tell people he was waiting for his girlfriend to show up to check out the house that was for sale.

And why are you waiting way over here?

Because she is easily lost and I figured this way, she would see me right away when turning from Main Street.

It seemed legit, but even so, he hoped he wouldn't have to say anything.

Holy shit, is that him?

Seeing the car turn down the road the house was on hadn't really made an impact upon him, but seeing it slow as it neared the house did.

And then it pulled to a stop alongside the curb.

Alan waited.

So did the driver.

What if they're just checking out the sign, writing down the number?

While he was thinking this, the driver got out and headed to the front door, steps seemingly purposeful.

Though the house was slightly blocked from view due to the position of a van in another driveway, he could sort of make out the front door and the girl standing in it.

And in he goes, his mind noted.

He looked at the clock and decided he would give it five minutes before he drove up to snap the picture of the license plate.

Maybe ten would be better…

By then they would surely be engaged in whatever had been

planned on for this visit, the likelihood of him being seen from within slim.

Two minutes came and went, and then three, his eyes constantly checking the clock.

Waiting to act was always the hardest part, especially once the target was visible, the risk of acting too soon or too late weighing heavy on the mind, especially if lives were at stake.

Even now, without the threat to life and limb, it was difficult.

Six minutes.

Up ahead a man with a dog appeared.

Seven minutes.

A car drove by.

Eight minutes.

The man with the dog stopped at the intersection, the dog sitting down and waiting even though no cars were present. Alan remembered teaching his dog to do the same as a teen and then, without warning, felt emotions building about the fact that he hadn't been there when his dog had been put to sleep, his body riddled with cancer.

Nine minutes.

Alan shook the emotions away and checked his phone, fingers switching it into photo mode so he wouldn't have to do it while behind the car, his actions visible to anyone in the house.

Ten minutes.

Alan twisted the key, the man and dog, who were crossing the intersection, both looking his way as the engine came to life.

He nodded toward them before shifting to drive, his training having taught him that acknowledging people when observed was less suspicious than making as if you didn't know they were there. Not that he actually thought about this while doing it; the act was purely a reflex, given how deeply it had been ingrained into him.

Moving slowly, but not too slowly, he maneuvered his car down the street until it was behind the car in question and quickly, but carefully, took a picture.

He then looked at it to make sure everything was visible before driving away.

It was.

Two minutes later, he was back on Main Street, a sense of accomplishment causing endorphins to rocket through his body.

What about the other houses? he reminded himself while nearing Roosevelt Road, realizing he was going the wrong direction.

Probably best to wait.

The last thing he wanted was to be noticed at another house, though he doubted he would be, especially if he simply drove by the others, confirming the address. Still, why chance it now? He had done well at this location. So well that confirming the addresses of the other houses didn't seem necessary now. Later, he would probably feel differently, and he knew without a doubt that Stacy would want the information for her story, but now he just wanted to go back home and call it a day.

11

Stacy heard her phone buzz in the other room and hurried to retrieve it from the table, hoping the message was from Alan. It was, though once again, it didn't contain the message she was anticipating. Instead, it simply said, CHECK YOUR EMAIL.

She did, curiosity growing once she saw that pictures were attached to whatever it was he had sent her. And then, once the email actually loaded and she read the descriptions he had typed up, *Holy fuck!*

12

"You see the pictures?" Alan asked once the phone was to his ear.

"I did. When did you—"

"About an hour ago," he said before she could finish her question. "Figured maybe you could find out who the guy is with the license plate and then lean on him for information, you know, if they don't approve me to see one of the girls."

"Fuck that. Even if they do approve, I'll still totally use him."

"Okay, anyway, I have to run. Promised my mom I'd watch a movie with her, but I figured you'd want to see those before I did anything."

"Figured right. I still…why didn't you tell me you were doing this?"

"It was kind of last-minute and a total whim, so I didn't want to waste your time just in case it didn't pan out."

"Last-minute? Figuring out where one of these houses was and being there when one of the girls was fucking a client was last-minute?"

"Honest to god, I just wanted to see if the house was real after realizing an address was visible in one of the photos. I didn't expect anyone to show up while I was doing it. Anyway, my mom is waiting for me, so I should head up there."

"Okay, yeah. Let me know if you learn anything else."

"Will do."

Alan disconnected the call and headed upstairs.

"Ready?" his mom asked.

"Yep," he replied. "Let me get the lights."

13

"So…where is this guy?" Riley asked, eyes growing weary from staring at the motel parking lot, which constantly went from being somewhat lit to dark, due to a overhead light that seemed to lose power every couple of minutes.

"Not sure," Sam said. "From everything I heard, this fucker typically sets up shop around four and keeps at it until the early morning hours."

"And he was here last night, you said." It wasn't a question, more of a confirmation.

"Yep, watched him for hours." Sam looked around and then lifted the binoculars to his eyes so he could scan the lot. "Fucking light is giving me a headache."

"Yeah, me too." It actually wasn't, but maybe he could end their evening early if Sam thought they were both suffering.

Silence settled upon the car.

Riley rubbed his hands together and then crossed his arms.

"Cold?" Sam asked.

"Yeah," he admitted. "Forgot what it's like to be on a stakeout as winter nears. Once that sun goes down...shit."

"You know, as bad as it can be, I always preferred it over the hot summer days—especially when wearing a vest."

"True that."

"Fuck, there were times when I probably lost ten pounds while watching crack houses from the backseat."

Riley nodded.

"But it was all worth it for the takedown moment," Sam said, a longing in his eyes. "Man, nothing could top that."

Riley didn't reply.

"You don't agree?" Sam asked.

"It's not that I don't agree or disagree, I just wonder what the point is sometimes. Drugs, prostitution, gambling...everything we do and yet we barely put a dent into it. And don't get me started on why a lot of this stuff is even illegal in the first place. I mean, the other day I heard someone saying on the news that legalizing dope is bad because it's addictive. Are people really that dumb?"

"Yeah, they are," Sam said, binoculars to his eyes once again. "It's sad."

Riley smiled. Conversations like this were something he really missed. Before Kristi, the two of them would spend hours shooting the shit about topics that were so random they often had trouble remembering everything they had touched upon. One thing just led to the next, the starting and ending points so different from one another that it was hard to believe a path even connected the two.

"Fuck it, I don't think he's going to show up tonight," Sam said, hand returning the binoculars to the console between them.

"You think maybe he switches things up now between different locations?" Riley suggested. "I mean, I can't imagine a guy like that not bringing his girls out on a Saturday night."

"Me either."

"Or maybe he was nabbed." Just because no one had him in their sights didn't mean he hadn't been picked up on something else, say a rolling stop or speeding—something that had resulted in his being arrested, because people like that always seemed to have something in the car that would land them behind bars.

"Yeah, maybe." Sam paused, eyes once again focusing on the motel. "So, want to cruise a bit and see if we find anyone promising?"

"No," Riley said.

"You sure? Might be able to convince a street-corner girl to come back with us."

"No, it's too risky."

"Yeah, you're probably right." Sam sighed. "Fuck, I told Kristi we'd at least be bringing one new girl back tonight. She's gonna be pissed."

"Dude, she has to know this isn't an exact science."

"Yeah, well, she expects results, and so far we haven't really been delivering on what she expected."

Riley wasn't sure how to reply. He had things he wanted to say but knew doing so would put his brother on the defensive.

"Fuck, fuck, fuck," Sam said, hand slamming the dash several times.

Riley was a bit startled by the outburst and by the knowledge that it was due to Sam's desire not to disappoint Kristi. Had she not been a factor, he would have simply brushed this off as a "shit happens" moment, something that anyone who had worked their field learned to deal with fairly quickly. With her on his mind, Sam could no longer do that, which was troubling. Even worse, Riley had a feeling that Kristi knew she wielded such power and got a kick out of it. Their relationship was abusive, but not in a stereotypical, husband dominating the wife type of way. In fact, it wasn't even physical abuse but mental, which unfortunately was difficult to put a stop to because the one being abused often helped put himself into the situation.

And there is nothing you can do about it, Riley told himself, not without Kristi twisting it around to make it look like he was trying to ruin their relationship. That was the biggest problem with such situations. Those who tried to help were often painted as the enemy. All he could do was wait for Sam to realize what was going on and pull himself free.

Sadly, the best way to do this would be for him to disconnect himself from Sam and force him to live in the "Kristi is all that matters" world for a while, which hopefully would open his eyes to the true nature of his relationship. His ties to the prostitution setup would not allow for this, however, because doing so would put his own future in jeopardy. Tonight was a perfect example. If not for his presence in the car, chances were good Sam would drive around trying to find other girls and would run into trouble, either from the Chicago Police Department or because he stumbled upon something he wasn't prepared for. Once something like that happened, they were all in trouble.

As if to emphasize how easy it would be for law enforcement to come across them while in the act of soliciting a girl, a patrol car came down the road, the two officers inside eyeing Riley and Sam as they passed.

"And they're checking out the motel," Riley said as the patrol vehicle turned into the motel parking lot. "Guess it's a good thing the guy didn't show."

"Yeah," Sam said, voice carrying a startled ring to it. "Not a single patrol last night and now…shit."

"You never know."

Chances were, the two officers, knowing the area was frequented by pimps and dealers, had decided to do a simple drive-by to make their presence known. Such a pass could have a huge impact on an area.

"You know, these fuckers are probably the reason no one's here tonight. They probably did a pass earlier and scared everyone away and are now swinging by again just to make sure no one came back."

"Well…kind of what they're here for," Riley said.

"Yeah, I know," Sam muttered. He waited for the patrol car to disappear down the block before starting the engine and pulling away from the curb.

Nothing else was said as they headed back to the expressway, Sam maneuvering the car in such a way that Riley knew he was keeping an eye out for girls who might want to join them.

None caught his eye, however, and soon they were cruising back toward Sam's place, one of them relieved, the other feeling like the night was a complete bust.

Stacy was in bed staring at the ceiling, contemplating how empty her apartment felt without Alan there, when the buzz from her phone suddenly echoed through the dark room.

WHAT'S THIS? the message from Alan asked.

THE HOUSE WHERE THE GIRL FROM THE HOUSE YOU FOUND LIVES, Stacy replied, wondering why it had taken him so long to reply.

REALLY!? HOW'D YOU FIND IT?

FOLLOWED HER AFTER SHE LEFT THE HOUSE YOU WERE AT. Then, before he could reply, she typed another message that read: YOU'RE NOT THE ONLY ONE WITH AMAZING IN-VESTIGATION SKILLS!!

APPARENTLY NOT, he replied a few minutes later. NICELY DONE.

"Thanks," she muttered to the empty room, the praise an-noying her because it felt as if he were somehow elevating himself over her in a field where she was supposed to be the professional. The fact that she was still embarrassed by not having uncovered the address herself added fuel to her resentment, a sense that maybe she was kidding herself about ever becoming a world-renowned jour-nalist overwhelming her.

The phone buzzed.

She looked at the screen.

SO, WHAT DO YOU DO FROM HERE? he asked.

I don't know, her mind answered, despair growing. *I just don't know.*

STILL NO WORD FROM THEM ON YOUR END? she asked a few minutes later.

NO, NOTHING, he replied back. AND I'M STARTING TO WONDER IF MAYBE WE NEED SOME KIND OF CODE OR SOMETHING.

CODE? she asked.

YEAH, SO THEY KNOW WE'RE FOR REAL. LIKE A RE-FERRAL THING OR SOMETHING.

I DON'T KNOW, she typed. THAT SEEMS KIND OF RE-STRICTIVE. HOW WOULD THEY MAKE MONEY?

BEATS ME.

A few minutes passed.

MAYBE WE CAN ASK THE GUY IF WE DON'T HEAR FROM THEM SOON. MAKE HIM THINK WE'LL TELL EVERY-ONE WHAT HE'S DOING IF HE DOESN'T GIVE US DETAILS.

Stacy stared at the message for a bit before typing, BLACK-MAIL? DIDN'T THINK YOU'D CONDONE SUCH A THING, LOL.

I'M OK WITH US BLUFFING IT TO GET INFO.

AH, WELL, I'LL SEE WHAT I CAN DO ON THAT END, she typed.

HOW LONG DO YOU THINK IT'LL TAKE TO FIGURE OUT WHERE HE LIVES?

Stacy considered the question and, figuring it sounded right, typed: DEPENDING ON HOW WILLING MY SOURCES ARE, A FEW DAYS. Guilt at the lie followed. She had no sources and had no idea how one went about obtaining information using nothing but a license plate. This wasn't to say she didn't think learning such in-formation was impossible; she just wasn't going to be able to do it the way he suggested. Instead, she would simply wait until another man showed up at the house and follow him home.

THAT'S SO COOL THAT YOU CAN DO THAT, he replied. SEEMS SO HOLLYWOOD. DIDN'T REALIZE IT WAS ACTUALLY POSSIBLE.

WELL, IT'S JUST A MATTER OF MAKING THE RIGHT CONTACTS AND MAKING SURE THEY OWE YOU A FAVOR OR TWO. Hesitation hit before she pressed send, the guilt about not only lying but also adding details to it getting the better of her. After a few seconds, however, she realized she wasn't really saying she had done this, only that it was how things like this worked, which, in all actuality, was true.

Message sent.

She sighed and then, hoping to change the subject a bit, asked, HOW WAS YOUR MOVIE?

OMG! HAVE YOU EVER SEEN THE PARANORMAL AC-TIVITY MOVIES?

NO, HORROR'S NOT REALLY MY THING.

WELL, LET ME TELL YOU, THEY ARE CREEPY LITTLE BUGGERS. IT'S WEIRD TOO BECAUSE THERE ARE LONG MO-MENTS WHERE NOTHING HAPPENS THAT JUST MAKE IT MORE TERRIFYING WHEN SOMETHING DOES.

NEAT!

YEAH, MY MOM AND I BOTH ARE TOTALLY SLEEPING WITH THE LIGHTS ON, LOL.

Stacy almost typed up a reply suggesting he come over so she could protect him from all the scary ghosts, but then she decided against it.

OKAY, WELL, LET ME KNOW IF YOU HEAR ANYTHING BACK.

YEP, WILL DO.

With that, the two went quiet, Stacy's mind once again drift-ing into a pool of self-doubt. Disappointment followed.

Tomorrow will be better, she told herself. *Tomorrow you'll locate more houses and follow a guy home.*

If any of the girls actually see a guy tomorrow, and if you manage to be at one of the houses when they do…

Might have to get Alan to help.

With both of them watching different houses, the chances were better that they would be in the right place at the right time.

And who knows, maybe we'll catch a break and each get a guy to follow. If that happened and if each one presented an opportunity for their blackmail bluff, the information uncovered could be incredible—maybe even enough for her to finally break the story.

She pushed the thought away, fear that just thinking about it might put her success in jeopardy flowing through her mind.

Sunday

October 27, 2013

1

Jesus Christ! Alan's mind cried as he lay curled beneath the sheets in his room, hands clutching his knees, his insides feeling as if they were being twisted in a vice.

And then it faded.

He took several deep breaths and awaited the next cramp, which arrived within thirty seconds, a small ripple actually flowing through his body as all the muscles in his abdomen squeezed together.

What was I thinking? he demanded of himself. *All that candy, popcorn, and—*

The thought was cut off by a sudden rising in the back of his throat, one that forced him to a sitting position despite the pain.

Thankfully, whatever had been rising went back down, the sensation that he was going to vomit fading. Unfortunately, the same could not be said of the fear the moment had brought, the reading he had done about his disease making him aware that throwing up while in such pain could mean that a blockage in his bowel was present, caused by the buildup of scar tissue.

Another cramp hit.

With it came a gurgling sound that echoed throughout the room.

Taking another deep breath, he stood and slowly walked to

the bathroom, a hand pressed into his stomach in hopes of keeping the pain at bay.

It worked…until he sat down, a cramp nearly knocking him from the toilet.

Tears welled up.

Learning forward, he rested his forehead on the edge of the sink and silently chanted the word *please* over and over again. While doing this he also pressed a fist into the lower right side of his abdomen, knuckles trying to knead away whatever it was that had clogged up his intestinal track.

The next cramp, while horrific, wasn't as severe as the previous one had been, and the one that followed that one even less so. Both were still crippling, however, and would have toppled him if he had been on his feet.

Not long after that, using the sink for support, he stood up, past experiences having made him aware that sometimes the up-down movements would help move things along.

A nasty cramp hit during his first moment of standing, his face lowering itself into the sink as he bent forward, elbows painfully pressed into the porcelain edge.

Once it passed, he took another deep breath and pressed his fingers into the area of concern, the tips actually registering what felt like a clump, one that he pictured being broken free like a chunk of flavored ice in a freeze pop.

Three more cramps hit before anything came out, after which it felt like his colon had been turned into a fire hose. The force was so powerful that he actually had to take a shower afterward, the splashes as everything hit the surface of the water having risen halfway up the underside of the seat and his backside. It was disgusting.

Exhaustion followed the shower, his body feeling as if it had been up for days, the muscles and joints completely used up and unable to do anything beyond pulling the bedsheets to his chin once he made it back to the soft mattress. Even reaching for the TV clicker, which sat on the nightstand, seemed too strenuous.

Not long after that, he was in a dream, his face pressed against the glass of a house as he watched one of the girls from the Kristi Homes company moving about within. Eventually, having known he was there the entire time, she motioned for him to come inside and join her. He complied. Sex was not on the agenda, however. Instead, they started working on a project together for school. It was surreal. Even more bizarre, Stacy was there and didn't seem too pleased about the two of them working together.

2

Someone was here!

The realization arrived as Riley was reaching for the coffee container in the cupboard, one that had a handle built into the plastic. Normally the container would have the handle facing outward, given that there was no point in twisting it around once he had returned it to the cupboard, but this morning, it was reversed.

But why would someone do that?

Nothing else seemed amiss, and the idea that someone would break in to simply twist the container around so that he had to twist it back when reaching in was ridiculous.

Once he started investigating his place, however, he realized there were other things that seemed off, the most noticeable being the couch cushions. Many years ago, back when he had been a smoker, he had accidently burned a tiny hole in the cushion on the left side, which he now put on the right side of the couch because he hated feeling the hardened edges of the hole when lying down to watch TV. Today that hole was back on the left where his left side would snag it.

Someone was looking for something.

Someone who didn't want to simply tear the place apart.

But what were they looking for?

It wasn't like he had anything of value that—

Oh fuck!

He hurried into his office and opened the closet. Inside, among files and empty product boxes, was his old computer, one that he had never been able to throw away despite the fact that it was completely obsolete now. It also had a serious virus problem, which might have been fixable if he could get up the motivation to bring it into a computer repair center, something that seemed overly trying given how bulky the old tower was. Plus, given the computing power of his laptop, getting the old computer fixed seemed pointless, especially considering the space it would eat up if he put it back on the desk. That wasn't to say it was worthless. A couple months ago, he had discovered an interesting use for such things after coming upon a stack of computer towers in the back of a truck, towers that had seemed so out of place in the known drug-trafficker vehicle that Riley's team couldn't help but take them apart to see what was inside. Sure enough, the electronics within had been removed to make space for bags of dope, space that would have probably been used for money on the return trip.

Money was what he used his for now, money that hopefully would still be there when he opened it up. If it wasn't…

Actually, Kristi and he were going to be having a talk no matter what, one that would be really unpleasant if the money was not returned to him when asked.

The money was still inside.

Relieved, but also angered by the intrusion, he went into the kitchen, grabbed his phone from the counter where it had been sitting since the coffee container discovery, and called Sam.

"Hello?" a sleepy voice answered.

"We need to talk," Riley said. "And by we, I mean you, me,

and Kristi."

That got his attention.

"Fuck, man, something happen?"

Riley waited a second before answering, trying to figure out if Sam knew why he was calling, or if he was in the dark and now really thought something bad had happened.

"You there?" Sam asked.

"Yeah, I'm here." Then after a deep breath, "What was Kristi doing last night while you and I were out?"

"Huh, what do you mean?" Sam asked, question sounding sincere.

Regret that he hadn't waited to ask in person appeared, though then he wondered if he would really have been able to see through any deception that his brother might use. The guy, after all, had done quite a bit of undercover work a few years back, undercover work that had been so successful that once his identity was revealed following a huge takedown, a website had actually gone up warning the underworld about him.

"Is she there with you right now?" Riley asked.

"In bed, no. You want me to go get her?"

"No..." He hesitated, mind shouting at him to wait. "But when you see her next, let her know that if she *ever* breaks into my place again, there will be hell to pay." With that, he ended the call and ignored the phone when the anticipated return call vibration caused it to dance upon the counter.

And you totally fucked that up, he told himself as the vibrations stopped, the mental image he had held of going there and making her sorry quickly fading.

He really should have waited.

Oh well.

He began preparing a pot of coffee.

His phone buzzed again, this time with a message.

WHAT DID SHE DO? Sam asked.

Riley considered the question, debating whether or not last night's failed attempt to get some girls had been a simple ploy to get him out of the house.

Would they really have needed to set something like that up?

She could have just waited for me to go to work.

In fact, if Sam had been in on it, he probably would have suggested that, so maybe Kristi had acted alone.

But would she?

God, what a mess!

The first drops of coffee hit the bottom of the carafe, the hard glass surface causing them to splash outward, the fragmented drops slowly coming back together to form a liquid surface. Soon, a layer of coffee was in place, the drops now causing bubbles to form upon impact. He recalled a period of time when he had actually been convinced that the churning one saw at this stage added flavor to the brew.

His phone buzzed.

DUDE, TALK TO ME!

Riley sighed. SOMEONE BROKE INTO MY PLACE LAST NIGHT, he typed and then before sending it changed SOMEONE to KRISTI so that it didn't appear as if there was any question as to who it had been.

WHY WOULD SHE DO THAT? Sam asked.

SERIOUSLY!? WHY DO YOU THINK?

Nothing followed for nearly five minutes, Riley having managed to pour and sip at his coffee before the familiar buzz echoed once again.

I DON'T THINK IT WAS HER.

Of course you don't, he muttered silently while taking another sip of coffee. *I could have video of her going through my things, and you'd still figure out a way of being in denial about it.*

OH, SO THEN, WHO DO YOU THINK IT WAS? Riley asked.

THAT REPORTER.

Riley thought about it for a second but then shook his head and typed, HOW WOULD SHE KNOW ABOUT ME AND WHY WOULD SHE SEARCH MY PLACE?

LOOKING FOR INFO.

UNDER MY COUCH CUSHIONS AND IN MY CUPBOARDS!?

YEAH. THAT'S WHAT THEY DO.

Riley shook his head again even though Sam couldn't see him, his mind unable to get on board with the idea that the reporter had broken into his place. It just didn't jive with him. Looking into things, asking questions, and following Kristi around was one thing, but going so far as to break into the place of a state police detective who had no connections to what she was investigating beyond family ties...not likely.

I DON'T THINK SO, Riley typed.

WHY NOT?

SHE WAS NOSY, BUT THERE IS NO WAY SHE LEARNED ENOUGH FROM JUST BUGGING KRISTI TO FIGURE OUT WHAT IS GOING ON AND BREAK IN HERE.

A few seconds passed, during which Riley added, YOUR PLACE, MAYBE, BUT NOT MY PLACE.

He took another sip of his coffee, the temperature having finally reached the level where he could gulp it.

I THINK YOU UNDERESTIMATE HER, Sam said. YOU KNOW SHE KNOWS SOMETHING IS GOING ON AND SUSPECTS PROSTITUTION.

NO, WE DON'T KNOW THAT, Riley replied.

SHE PRETTY MUCH SPELLED IT OUT THAT ONE TIME.

ONLY IF YOU'RE LOOKING FOR WHAT SHE HINTED

AT. Sam and Kristi were like those 2012 end of the world nuts. Once they had the date set within their minds, they were able to manipulate other vague prophecies and statements to point toward it. Kristi, naturally, was the worst of the two. From the very beginning, she had suspected something of the reporter, even though there really was nothing to worry about. In fact, if anything, appearing worried and standoffish had only helped to fuel the reporter's suspicions, which was why Riley had constantly told Sam to calm her down.

SHE ASKED KRISTI ABOUT THEIR AGES AND WHY SHE WAS EMPLOYING A PROSTITUTE! Sam said.

AND I TOLD YOU TO TELL HER THAT SHE WAS SIMPLY A GIRL WHOSE LIFE YOU WERE TRYING TO HELP STRAIGHTEN OUT. Places did things like that from time to time, and just because she wasn't old enough to have a real estate license didn't mean she couldn't help show houses. She simply couldn't sell them.

SHE DIDN'T BELIEVE US.

Because you two probably didn't word it properly and seemed confrontational about it, he said to himself, an audible sigh following. If there was one thing both Kristi and Sam were good at, it was provoking conflict in a situation where conflict was avoidable, all because of the vibe they gave off when engaged in such discussions. For Sam, the trait had actually helped him in being accepted into crime organizations when undercover because being hot tempered was fairly common in such circles. Oddly enough, given the danger of such undercover work, Sam had been calculating and cautious with his temper and made sure it didn't get the better of him. Once back in the real world, however, that control seemed to disappear.

HAS SHE DONE MORE THAN ASK QUESTIONS? Riley asked, feeling a sudden concern that maybe Sam hadn't been forthcoming about something involving her.

NOT THAT I KNOW OF, BUT GIVEN ALL THE QUES-

TIONS SHE DID ASK, AND THE TYPES, I'M CERTAIN SHE HASN'T SIMPLY LEFT THINGS ALONE.

The phone buzzed again.

YOU KNOW HOW THESE REPORTERS ARE. THEY KEEP PICKING AND PICKING UNTIL SOMETHING IS UNCOVERED.

YEAH, Riley replied. WHICH IS WHY WE DON'T WANT TO GIVE HER MUCH TO PICK AT.

Eventually, if nothing broke, she would move on to something else. Reporting was just like detective work. The flow of cases coming in did not slow simply because one was already working something, and newer items often took precedent over older ones that didn't seem to be going anywhere.

AND IF SHE DOESN'T STOP PICKING? Sam asked.

Riley thought about that for a while and, even though he knew it was extremely unlikely, did allow into consideration the possibility that she would uncover something. IF SHE KEEPS PICK-ING AND IF SHE UNCOVERS SOMETHING THAT COULD HARM US, THEN WE WILL HAVE NO CHOICE BUT TO PUT A STOP TO IT.

HOW?

I DON'T KNOW, he admitted, though only because he didn't want to consider violence toward her as an option. Breaking the kneecap of a pimp who was abusing teenage girls was one thing, but taking a pipe to a twenty year old girl simply because she had stumbled upon a news story she wanted to share…that was a line he didn't want to cross.

Yet it is a line you may have to cross in order to ensure your survival…

The thought, and the fact that he knew it was right, caused him to shiver. He also couldn't help but feel a sense of anger and resentment toward Sam for getting him into this, but at the same time he knew that passing on the blame was childish since he could have and should have said no.

But you didn't and now this is your reality.

What's done is done!

He needed to stop dwelling upon what could have been and focus on the here and now—focus on what was best for him and the girls.

An image of a man beating a skinny undernourished teenage girl entered his mind's eye, along with an inner statement of how he was in danger of becoming the very thing he wanted to put an end to.

Only you did end such things for several of these girls and now simply want to make sure they are not forced back into such a lifestyle.

Plus, you don't know if the reporter will actually uncover anything...

But if she does...

His mind was stuck in a loop, one that he wouldn't be able to free himself from anytime soon, not without an outside source entering in and shifting his focus.

Maybe go into the office, one part of his mind suggested.

Maybe change the locks on your door, another said.

He decided upon the latter, the idea of going into the office unappealing, given that he knew that as soon as his team caught a break in the case they were working, he would be pretty much living with the case twenty-four seven.

3

SORRY, SLEPT WAY LATE TODAY, the message from Alan read, one that was in reply to a message she had sent two hours earlier asking if he wanted to join her in staking out the house where the girl from last night seemed to live, Stacy's hope being to follow her—or anyone else that lived there—as they went out to service clients.

WOW, THAT'S NOT LIKE YOU, Stacy replied. EVERY-THING OK?

Once sent, she set the phone back into the cupholder and re-turned her eyes to the house, which was lifeless.

What'd you expect, coming here at ten in the morning? she scolded herself. *Girls like this, probably not the morning types.*

It was all Alan's fault. His lack of a reply to her first message of the day had made her restless, a mixture of concern for him and concern for their relationship getting the better of her. Staying in her apartment in such a state had been out of the question. She needed a distraction, something to take her mind off the silent phone.

At first, she'd decided to locate the rest of the houses where the real estate whores would fuck the men, but then realized she had no idea how Alan had actually uncovered the full addresses with nothing but the numbers. Frustrated, she'd searched Google for other sites that might reference the Kristi Homes Real Estate com-pany, in hopes of finding a list of locations available for viewing, but nothing was posted anywhere.

And why would they, when the houses probably aren't really for sale? she had voiced to herself, a decision to simply go out and watch what she now considered the "main house" arriving.

Her phone rattled the change in the cupholder.

She looked at it and the message.

DOING OK. GOT SICK LAST NIGHT, SO ONCE THAT PASSED, I ENDED UP SLEEPING A LOT LONGER THAN NOR-MAL.

The phone buzzed again while she was typing up a reply.

WHAT TIME DID YOU WANT TO WATCH THE HOUSES? he asked.

HA HA, I'M WATCHING THE MAIN ONE RIGHT NOW.

REALLY? WOW. ANYTHING HAPPENING?

SADLY, NO. I'M TOO EARLY, IT SEEMS. HEY, DID YOU

FIND THE ADDRESSES OF ANY OTHER HOUSES OR JUST THAT ONE?

She held the phone, expecting a quick reply now that they had gotten into a texting rhythm, but then a minute turned to two minutes.

In the end, six minutes passed, her hand having once again returned the phone to the cupholder before the next text arrived.

JUST THAT ONE. I HAVE OTHER POTENTIALS THAT I STILL NEED TO NARROW DOWN.

AH, I SEE. She didn't want to ask how he had narrowed it down since she hadn't been able to figure it out herself, so instead she asked, DO YOU THINK YOU'D BE ABLE TO CHECK THOSE OUT WHILE I STAY AND WATCH THIS ONE? I DON'T WANT TO MISS ANYTHING.

Again, several minutes came and went before he answered with a SURE, NO PROBLEM.

EXCELLENT, she replied.

Nothing else followed and she went back to watching the house, her stomach starting to regret the decision to hold off on eating anything that morning.

Less than ten minutes later, house still lifeless, she started counting the change in her cupholder to see if she had enough for something at a local drive-through.

The answer was no, though not because she didn't have enough money, but because when it came to quarters, she only had four dollars, and she really didn't want to have to deal with handing out two to three more dollars worth of dimes and nickels. Too embarrassing.

Maybe Alan will bring you something?

Chances were he would have to drive this way in order to get to another house anyway, her guess being that this one was in the center of things for the girls.

The question was, what did she want? Though hungry, nothing seemed appealing, especially in the fast-food department, and while she knew he probably would shrug it off, she wanted to be able to at least offer him money to cover what he brought her.

Maybe a sandwich?

She opened her phone to look at some menus for some sandwich places, only to notice that many of the chain places didn't list any prices next to the items. In fact, no price was shown at all until one got to the online ordering platform, and even then, it wasn't until after she had punched in her location.

Do the prices change from location to location?

The possibility had never occurred to her before, though now that she thought about it, she had noticed price changes depending on location for places like Dunkin' Donuts and McDonald's throughout various suburb locations.

Why? she asked herself, the journalistic part of her mind taking control. *Taxes? Food costs? Gas prices? Greedy franchise owners? All of the above?*

A car drove by while she was contemplating this, thinking she might be able to get an editor at one of the online sites to let her do a simple story on this, one that would then ask people to report the prices at such places in their areas. If nothing else, the site would enjoy an increase of page views as people checked out the prices other people were submitting to compare with their own locations, views that would help in earning money from advertisers.

The car that passed by turned into the driveway of the house in question, a young lady getting out and walking up to the front door. Stacy watched this for several seconds without really processing it, her mind still tangled up in the possibilities of a fast-food story. And then it clicked, a *holy fuck* echoing within her mind as she watched the lady leave the house with a young girl, who quickly headed around to the passenger door.

Shit! Shit! Shit! her mind chanted as indecision plagued her, the question of whether or not to follow the two bouncing around within her head.

Five seconds later, she was twisting the key in her ignition, engine protesting the end of its break. The protests continued as she pulled away from the curb, the groans so loud this time around that Stacy actually feared it would call it quits at some point during this trek, fate once again deciding against her achieving success.

No breakdown occurred, and soon the angry protests downgraded themselves to the standard rumbles that had been echoing ever since the Check Engine light had flickered on a few weeks ago, which she could no longer brush away as a simple gas-cap issue.

Repairs will probably be more than the car is even worth, she mumbled to herself while following the new, freshly washed Lincoln Town Car, a small bit of jealousy building within.

Cry about it, why don't you? another part of her brain said as the two in the Lincoln made a left turn onto Lambert Road, which was thankfully free of traffic, thereby allowing her to make her own left turn without having to wait for an opening.

4

"Mom, do we have any of the pink stuff?" Alan called out while searching the bathroom medicine cabinet.

"Um...we should," she called back from the kitchen. "You having diarrhea again?"

"No, but I may later and want to be prepared." He scanned each shelf again, yet still didn't see any. "Going to be helping Stacy, so..." He left it at that, not really feeling the need to get into any details about what could happen while sitting in a car during a stake-out-like situation.

"Wow, you two are spending a lot of time together on this

thing. I really hope she gives you credit for it when it comes out."

"I'm sure she will," he mumbled back, voice probably failing to reach her as his eyes did a third sweep of the cabinet. Peroxide, Band-Aids, Advil, Tylenol, Nyquil—everything one would expect in a medicine cabinet except for Pepto-Bismol.

"Did you find it?" she called.

"No. You sure it's in here?"

"Yeah," she said, footsteps now coming down the hallway.

"Then I must be going blind," he said while backing up so she could take control of the medicine cabinet.

"Let's see," she said, starting her own scan. Nothing followed for several seconds, her eyes obviously going back and doing a second and then a third scan. "Where in the world did it go?"

"See, I told ya," Alan said.

"Did you move it?"

"No."

"You sure. Maybe on a day you had diarrhea before class?"

"No, I haven't touched it."

"Really?" Her tone was skeptical.

"Really!" he insisted. "Last time I took any was at Bragg, and it made me so constipated I was on the ground with tears in my eyes." That had been about a week before his medical discharge went through and had been the first time he had recognized how correct the military was in their assessment of him and whether or not he could return to active duty. Gastrological attacks like that, while on patrol or during a firefight, would put his team in danger and was not something he, or they, wanted to risk.

"Well then, I have no idea what happened to it," she said, arms going up into the air. "I know it was here."

"Ah, it's okay. I'll just pick some up on my way. Chances are I won't even really need it, but I'd rather have it and not need it than need it and—" His phone buzzed.

"Stacy?" his mom asked.

"Yep." He opened the phone, read the message, and let a "Huh" escape his lips.

"What?"

"Oh, um…she was following a lady that she's doing a story on and says that for some reason the lady pulled into the COD parking lot and went inside."

"COD? You mean right down the street?"

"Yep."

"Wow, that's weird. Do they have classes on Sundays?"

"Actually, I don't know. Maybe?"

His phone buzzed again.

"What'd she say?" his mom asked.

"She wants to know if I can go over and watch her, see what she's doing. She says she would, but she's fearful that the lady would recognize her, given how empty the place is and the fact that the lady might know who she is."

"Are you?"

"Um…I don't know." Following a lady around the campus hallways sounded a bit risky, the idea that he could do it without being noticed unlikely. Then again, he was a student there, and if he made it look as if he were there to study or do some sort of paperwork at one of the offices, then maybe his presence could be justifiable in the eyes of anyone who noticed him. "I think I'll go talk to Stacy a bit and figure out what exactly is going on."

His phone buzzed again.

"Now what?"

"Oh, she just says that the lady is in the library," Alan said. He wisely left out the part about her meeting a man there while with a girl that Stacy described as "young looking." "Not sure what exactly is going on, but I better get moving so I don't miss her."

"Yep, okay. Let me know what's going on and if you'll be

home for dinner."

"Okay, I will."

"And be careful."

"Don't worry," he said and gave her a hug. "I always am. See you later."

5

The College of DuPage had gone through quite a few changes over the years, the biggest being a coffee shop smack-dab in the middle of the old hallway across from the main offices. Originally, that hallway led down a long narrow building that had classrooms on either side, labs in the middle, break rooms with vending machines, and three or four open-air courtyards that no one ever used. That was the biggest change in the area Stacy was roaming. The recently built Homeland Security building on the other side of Lambert, the new Technology Center, and the long wing that jutted out into what had once been a prairie restoration project were all grander and probably considered more significant than the coffee shop.

The library itself, however, seemed unchanged, though she couldn't tell for sure, given how little time she had actually spent in it when going to school. This wasn't to say she had been a slacker during her college days. In fact, she had graduated with a 3.8 grade point average. She simply never really needed the library as a resource for any of her classes, not when her textbooks and web searches provided all the information she ever required. High school had been the same way, though without the use of the Internet since that had been frowned upon as a research tool when doing papers in those days.

Still is to some, she said to herself, recalling many times when people were like, "In my day we actually had to open books..." Such individuals never seemed to realize that information was information, and it didn't really matter where one gathered it as long as it was accurate. Plus, in those days, those people would have used the Internet as well if it had been available.

Her phone buzzed.

She looked at the screen and saw that Alan had arrived at the college and wanted to know where she was.

Not wanting to actually text while in the library, given all the signs that discouraged cell phone use, Stacy headed back into the main hallway area and sent him a reply. A few minutes later, he entered through the doors below, a backpack slung over his shoulder.

She waited, momentarily thinking he would come up the steps to her level, but then realized he was staying down there, waiting for her, out of view from the library windows that overlooked the hallway.

"Thought you were going to hang back?" Alan said once she was face-to-face with him.

"I was but…well…I got curious and wanted to see what exactly they were up too." Though she was certain she hadn't been noticed, she still felt foolish for taking the risk, given the dismay he displayed.

"So how should we play this?" he asked.

"I was thinking you could watch them and see what happens and, depending on what does, maybe follow the man while I go back to the house to watch the other girls."

"Do you know where his car is?"

"Um…no."

Alan thought about that for a second. "Okay, chances are, if he came here knowing he would go to the library, he would have parked out there somewhere." He motioned toward the entrance he had come through. "If not though, I'd totally lose him once he leaves, because by the time I followed him to his car and then got back to mine, he'd be long gone."

Stacy hadn't considered that.

"So instead of heading back to the house, maybe it would be best if you waited in your own car on the other side of the parking lot and then, if he goes that way, I will call you so you can follow him."

"And if he doesn't, you will just follow him yourself," she confirmed.

"Yep. And then you can head back to the house and see what happens there."

"Okay." It seemed like a good plan. "Will you be able to find them?" She nodded toward the library while asking this.

"You said they were to the right of the entrance in those chairs along the glass wall that wraps around the hall."

"Yeah," she confirmed.

He nodded. "Shouldn't be a problem. I'll let you know if there's an issue. In the meantime, why don't you go position your-self by the other exit somewhere and I'll go keep an eye on things."

"Okay."

6

"What's wrong?" Emily asked as Amanda set the phone down.

"What? Oh, nothing actually, they've just never done that before."

"Done what?"

"Put two clients back-to-back at the same house."

"Oh, huh, yeah, I've never had that happen, especially last-minute like that." She shook her head. "Wonder if this will become a trend as they bring in more clients?"

"Yeah, same here."

"Is it a regular?" she asked. "The add-on guy?"

"No, that's the thing, it's someone new."

"Really? Okay, that's a bit odd."

"Yeah."

Given the cost of their services and the expectations, adding a new guy right after a scene seemed risky simply because she would be tired and unable to give her best. If it had been a simple twenty-dollar fuck, it wouldn't have been a problem; she could simply lie back and let him use her until he popped his cork. That was not what he had paid for, however; thus he would expect more. Add in the "post-orgasm depression" many guys felt, and it became very possible that they would lose the client if she didn't do a good job, something the company would not like.

"What time is the second guy?" Emily asked.

"Five," Amanda said.

"And the first one at two thirty?"

"Yeah."

"Hmm, that's not much time in between."

"I know. And what if the first guy wants to chill for a while? I don't want him to feel rushed."

"Is he one that likes to stay afterward?"

"Actually, no," Amanda admitted. "He typically cuts out within twenty minutes. It's the principle of the thing though, you know. What if they keep scheduling back-to-backs like this and I get a guy who wants to stay, one that needs to shower or something so his wife won't smell the sex. How am I supposed to get things ready for the next guy?"

"They are at least two bathrooms in all the houses," Emily said.

"Are you crazy? I'm not taking a shower while a guy is there!"

"Aw, come on, you know they screen these guys really well. Why would anyone go through the entire process, providing tons of details about himself and laying down a lot of money, just to kill you, when they could simply pull up to a dozen willing girls on a street corner and open the door?"

"Because they know I'm clean and not worn-out like those girls. And they probably also know that if something happens it's not like the boss will go to the police and report the guy."

"No, they'll go and kill the guy...slowly."

"Yeah, right," Amanda said with a sigh.

"Seriously, remember that guy that got a little rough with Sophia?"

Amanda nodded. Rumor had it that a week after nearly choking Sophia to death with a belt while fucking her in the ass to the point of tearing her rectum, the man had been jumped, sodomized, choked out, and woke up naked in a Gangster Disciple neighborhood with racial slurs written all over his body. Whether or not the story was true was up for debate, the only known fact being that the man was no longer a client. "Of course, that just proves they're good at reacting when something happens, which doesn't do me any good if I'm the one that gets raped and killed."

"Okay, good point," Emily said and then looked as if she was going to say more but stopped as a musical score began to echo from her pocket.

She pulled her phone free.

Amanda waited, having recognized the musical ringtone as the one that belonged to Mrs. Woodman.

"What, really? Wow, okay, um...yeah, that shouldn't be a problem." Emily listened for a bit. "Um, no, she's still here, and I'm sure she won't mind since she'll be up that way anyway." She listened some more. "Oh really, yeah, okay, that sounds great." She listened some more while backing up to lean against the fridge. "Tuesday afternoon? Okay." More listening. "Yep. I'll have everything ready."

She ended the call.

"What's going on?" Amanda asked.

"Well, seems I now have a scene as well, very last-minute with a new guy. It's not far from where you'll be, so if you can drop me off on the way to yours and then pick me up afterward, that would be great."

"Okay." She waited a bit. "What's happening Tuesday?"

"Oh, so get this, me, Caroline, and Isabella are all going to be in a porn film and, if all goes well, will have our own sites."

"What?"

"I know, totally unexpected. Mrs. Woodman thinks it will be a great way to generate more income for the company and for those of us who agree to do the videos."

"Wow," was all Amanda could say.

"Oh fuck," Emily said, looking at the time. "I gotta get ready! Do you need the bathroom for anything else?"

"No, I'm good." The house had three bathrooms total, yet they both kept all their favorite items in the one upstairs. Vicky was using it too, though she hadn't actually established her own set of products yet.

Vicky.

Amanda couldn't help but wonder what type of client she was with today. The fact that Mrs. Woodman had personally picked her up to drive her to him and specified a "little girl" dress made it difficult to focus elsewhere. It also brought concern into her mind, the idea that men with "little girl" fantasies would be helping to spread the word about their services disconcerting because there was no telling what type of sick and twisted minds might be brought into the mix. This wasn't to say the threat of sick and twisted individuals wasn't present already, just that having men who were already sick in the head spreading word about them made the chances of them being discovered by such individuals greater.

Nothing you can do about it, she said to herself with a silent sigh. *And it's so much better than before.*

Twenty-dollar fucks. No time to clean. Cum from one man still dripping down her leg as the next man climbed up onto her and began thrusting away. Mouth always sour from the blowjob guys. Lips swollen and stinging during the winter. Standing on the corner in seventeen-degree weather in a halter top, skirt and heels, stockings torn to the point of uselessness, cum actually freezing within the two-day-old stubble on her legs. Being arrested. Giving cops handjobs so she could be released and bring in the required money to prevent a beating. Trading sex for antibiotics from a clerk at a pharmacy so she could treat any STDs she had, the clerk seemingly unfazed by her choice of drugs and the wincing she couldn't hide when he thrust himself into her, a comment on how his amazing girth always made girls moan leaving his lips. Being strung out for days once heroin entered the picture and waking up to find herself not only dripping cum from all three holes, but being soiled in piss and shit. Someone had even spread it all over her face—the memory of waking up and realizing what it was that she tasted and felt when touching her right cheek one of the most horrific moments of her life.

Even now, the horror and disgust of that moment was impossible to shake, the small meal she'd had an hour earlier threatening to come back up.

All because you were in love.

She shook her head and scolded herself for being so young and stupid, and then added scorn toward the fact that she occasionally would miss those early moments of romance the two had shared.

Upstairs music blasted for a second before being drowned out by the spray from the shower and the sound of Emily singing along to the lyrics.

She had it even worse, Amanda said to herself. She didn't

know the details of Emily's time on the street but knew, just by the way she talked from time to time and the look that came over her, that there had been moments of horror that she herself could never even imagine.

Vicky too, though she wasn't yet ready to have any sympathy for the little bitch, not with the way she had been acting.

But that's probably a defense mechanism.

You should be the better person and...

...blah, blah, blah, another part of her mind interrupted. *Having it rough doesn't give one the right to be a bitch.*

Even as she thought this, she knew the bitch label was hovering dangerously close to her own skin, but she couldn't help it. Something about that girl...

She let out a silent roar, triggered by the Katy Perry song she could just make out from the bathroom upstairs, and then headed up there herself, a need to figure out her wardrobe options for the two scenes guiding her.

7

One walk-by of the three in the library was enough for Alan to imprint the man into his mind and position himself elsewhere to follow once the man left, his desire to go unnoticed keeping him from planting himself close enough to listen in on whatever it was they were talking about. While waiting, sitting on a bench beneath the library, eyes constantly looking up to see if the man was leaving, he thought about the girl with the two adults, concern over how old she was and what the plans were for her plaguing him.

Could she actually be eighteen?

It seemed so unlikely, yet, having browsed a few adult sites in his day, he knew there were plenty of young-looking female adults, and they were in high demand on the "barely eighteen" type of sites.

Is that what this is? A barely eighteen type of setup?

Or does the guy really want someone that is younger than eighteen?

This brought about a question of whether or not the girl was a trick, one who they claimed was under eighteen when really she wasn't, the illusion made greater by the clothes she was wearing.

Hope followed the question, hope that he had hit the nail on the head with the "trick" idea. If not, and she was just a minor and currently in the process of being sold, he didn't think he could just sit back and mentally record what happened. No. He needed to act.

But there is no way to know for sure, and if you do interfere…

He would never hear the end of it from Stacy.

Actually, he simply wouldn't hear from Stacy. She would cut him out of her life, her belief that he was responsible for ruining her chance at success unshakable. Any statements he made to the contrary would be ineffective. In fact, the only thing that might keep her from hating him should he interfere would be if he stepped in to save the girl's life, though even then she probably would still keep him at a distance anytime an important investigation for a story was taking place.

His phone buzzed.

It was his mother.

ARE YOU STILL WATCHING THEM? she asked.

YA, he typed quickly, eyes barely glancing at the phone, and hit send.

His phone buzzed again.

Jesus!

WHERE ARE THEY?

He shook his head and was about to type another quick reply reminding her that he was busy and would tell her about it all later, when he caught movement up above. It was the three, the swish of the girl's yellow dress as she impatiently toyed with the fabric while the two adults talked impossible to ignore. And then they split, the guy and girl going one way, the lady another, the former heading toward where Stacy was waiting rather than the library entrance.

Alan waited a second to make sure they didn't twist around and come back, opened his phone, selected Stacy's name, and typed, THEY'RE HEADING YOUR WAY.

OK.

A few seconds passed and then she asked, CAN YOU GO TO THE HOUSE AND SEE IF THE GIRLS GO ANYWHERE?

SURE, he typed as the lady who had brought the girl walked by him, eyes never even glancing his way. Even if they had, she most likely would have thought he was nothing more than a student killing time on his phone.

Not wanting to get up and look as if he were following her into the parking lot, he took a moment to plug the address of the house Stacy had sent him earlier into his GPS.

On screen, the route popped up, as did an estimated driving time: eight minutes. The house was literally right down the street. Seeing this, and knowing how close it was and how close all the houses the company used were, was still a bit mindboggling to him. A house of ill repute right in the middle of the suburbs, and the most conservative suburbs at that, seemed completely unthinkable. Stacy was right. Once the story was exposed, people were going to freak — especially if some of the girls truly were underage.

His phone buzzed.

I GOT THEM, Stacy said. LET ME KNOW IF ANYTHING HAPPENS ON YOUR END.

WILL DO, he replied.

Nothing else followed, and soon he was back in his car, engine running, maneuvering himself through the new parking lot areas toward the new stoplight that would allow him access to

Lambert Road. Ironically, the lady who'd brought the girl was next to him at the stoplight, turning left instead of right, talking on her cell phone, paying no attention to him whatsoever as he edged his way forward to see if he had an opening.

He turned.

Six minutes later, thanks to the lights that were all green, he was driving down the road the main house was on, eyes scanning the actual addresses since this one didn't have a For Sale sign in the yard.

Once located, he assessed the area, figured out the best place to park so as not to be too conspicuous, and planted himself.

Up ahead, a blue Volkswagen Beetle crossed the intersection, one that looked identical to his mother's car.

No, she wouldn't, his mind said, unease building.

He looked at the two messages she had sent, the first asking if he was still watching them, the second, where they were, a sudden understanding of her word choice now unfolding.

Up ahead the blue Volkswagen Beetle crossed the intersection again, this time going the opposite direction, and then came to a sudden halt.

I don't believe it! his mind cried as she backed down the road until she had room to turn and then headed toward him.

Actually, that wasn't true. He did believe it and was now surprised with himself for not anticipating it, especially given how close the college was to the house.

If you hadn't said anything…

Nothing he could do about it now.

His mother pulled up to his car, window down despite the chill in the air, and waited as he rolled down his own window.

"Mom! What are you doing?" It was all he could say, his frustration and dismay too much to allow anything else to come out.

"I thought you could use an extra set of eyes," she said. "On

TV they always have teams of people when on a stakeout."

"This isn't TV, and your car stands out from a mile away!"

"But it stands out so much that no one will think it could be a stakeout vehicle."

"Jesus Christ! Please go!"

"But—" she started.

"God dammit!" he shouted and switched his engine back on, frustration overflowing.

"Wait, you're leaving?" she asked.

"Yes!" he cried.

"Oh, come on, don't be like—"

He rolled up the window, cutting her off, and shifted to drive.

While he was doing this, a car pulled onto the street and honked at his mother's car, which was blocking the road. Alan started to pull away.

In the mirror he saw her pull to the right in order to give the other driver some room, and then into a driveway so she could turn around and follow him.

Though traffic was light that day, he still had to wait a bit to make a left turn, his frustration continuing to build as more and more cars came down the road, their spacing perfect so as to make it impossible for him to turn.

His phone buzzed.

He ignored it.

It buzzed a second time.

He still ignored it.

It then buzzed with the vibration of a call.

He sighed and answered it. "What?"

"I'm sorry. I just thought I could help. Please go back and watch whatever it was you were watching, and I'll go home."

Alan considered this, questions about the risk of going back unfolding. *Had the two been noticed? Had the girls seen his mother's car pulled alongside his and realized something was going on?* Even if they didn't realize something was going on but had seen the commotion, would they now have more awareness of his car?

No, he finally decided, and then into the phone, "Okay, I'll see you later."

"Okay," his mother said.

He put the phone down and changed his left-turn signal to a right one. A moment later, he turned, eyes staying glued to the rearview mirror as he drove down the road toward the next intersection, waiting to see his mom make the left.

She did, the blue Beetle pulling out and swinging into a tiny opening between two cars, horn echoing as brake lights appeared.

Alan shook his head and took the next right, maneuvering the car back into a position of observation. Up ahead at the house, everything looked as it had a few minutes earlier. In fact, the entire street looked unchanged.

Hopefully nothing was noticed, he said silently while sitting there. *And hopefully she learned her lesson.*

Yeah, right.

8

Following the man and the girl had been fairly simple in the beginning but then got complicated once they got onto I-355, Stacy's car not enjoying the speeds necessary for the traffic on such a road. Her lack of an I-pass also concerned her, memories of going through various booths in the past when lacking the correct change making her fairly certain that one more violation would result in a letter with an exorbitant fine attached for each toll she had missed. In the end, the decision was not hers but his, and one after another they each passed beneath the giant camera-heavy contraption of the open-road-tolling system, a computer probably clicking into gear as it processed her information and readied the letter.

Oh well, by the time I get it I'll be overwhelmed with writing assignments and the money they bring in, she said to herself, a scene of thoughtlessly writing a check for the fine as if it were nothing but a mere convenience fee playing in her mind.

And if you don't have the money…

Fuck 'em!

Up ahead, brake lights began to appear, the never-ending construction that plagued such roads finally making an appearance. Also looming was the I-55 exit, which could take a driver into Chicago or down toward St. Louis.

St. Louis seemed to the choice of the man with the girl, though hopefully they would be stopping a bit closer to home than the Gateway City. If not, well, her pursuit would be short-lived, given her gas-fund situation. Had credit cards still been an option, she could follow them across the country and back, but with the cards all maxed out and, in some cases, shut down, all she had was her debit card and cupholder change, neither of which amounted to much.

St. Louis was not the destination. Instead, it was Joliet, something that became clear as they got off at the Plainfield Road exit and cut across to Route 30.

"Easy does it," she voiced as they came to a stop at a light, her frustrated engine causing the entire car to vibrate. "Almost there."

The words were more for her than the engine, the soothing sound somehow helping ease her fear of a breakdown. The turn into an old run-down neighborhood of single-story homes helped with the fear as well, the likelihood of them stopping somewhere soon growing with every house they passed.

Up ahead the two took a right.

Stacy pressed the gas a bit so she could be sure to see the car if it turned again.

No Outlet.

Seeing the sign, she breathed a heavy sigh, the idea of arriving at a destination certain.

And then she saw what loomed ahead and felt the uneasiness returning.

The road, though providing no exit beyond the entrance, seemed to go on forever into the distance, both sides littered with poorly parked cars as the drivers had simply pulled into the front yards of the houses whose occupants they were visiting (doing deals with?). Even worse, there were actually turns from this road onto short dead-end ones, houses lining each as if it were a cul-de-sac, only without the well-crafted aesthetically pleasing circle part.

Thankfully, the two hadn't turned onto any of these dead-end roads just yet, the man driving slowly—probably due to the frequency of potholes and cracks that littered the road.

Stacy drove slow as well, both because of the danger the potholes presented to her thin, bald tires and rusted underbody and the continued fear that she would be spotted if she got too close.

What if he's already spotted you and all this is just a waste of time as they randomly drive around?

No answer followed, and soon she watched as they turned onto one of the short dead-end roads, one that she passed without turning onto so as to not draw attention to herself, eyes peering down to see where they had stopped.

Seven houses were crammed together on the tiny road, the man having pulled up into the angled yard between two of them, one that had three giant pine trees in it, all of which could easily destroy either of the two houses should they fall over in a storm.

Not wanting to linger, Stacy continued forward, found an area to turn around in, and then parked along the main road, a question of whether or not to get out and walk by the house so she could get a better feel for it entering her mind.

In the end, she decided against doing this, her thinking being that, given the nature of what was probably going on within the house, those inside would be overly cautious and think it odd for someone to walk by. Had the house been on the main road this wouldn't have been the case since people probably walked back and forth all the time on their way to and from work at the various fast-food and retail joints out near the entrance of the main road, but being at the back of the dead-end made it unlikely that people walked by on a daily basis.

If I had a dog…

That would probably work. Unfortunately, it was not an option. Taking a photo of the street sign was, however, and if she repositioned herself a bit, she was sure she could zoom in and get a decent picture of the car and its license plate.

While she was doing this, another car started down the road coming toward her and slowed as it neared the dead-end turnoff. Two men were within, the passenger keeping his eyes to the right as if looking for something, the driver keeping focus on the road.

And then they turned, the passenger having most likely been looking out for the tiny road sign that she had just snapped a picture of.

The two parked by the first car, both getting out and walking between two of the pine trees.

Seeing this, she suddenly realized there might actually be another house back there, one that was pretty well hidden due to the pine trees and overgrowth beyond. The lack of a driveway only added another layer to its concealment, something that might not be uncommon in neighborhoods like this, given how old some of the structures were.

You could probably walk up to that, she said to herself. *No one will see you if you keep a house between you and the one they walked back to.*

Doing so would give her a better look at the cars, as well as a chance to see the actual house rather than just the mental impression she had of what it probably looked like.

And if you can get close enough—

Don't be stupid!

Getting details on the cars and having the address of the house was all she really needed. A picture of the house would be nice too but wasn't absolutely necessary, especially if she had shots of all the other houses.

Though if this one is really run-down and decrepit looking...

Such a photo would work well in inciting anger toward what was going on, especially when it was noted that this particular house was one where a young-looking, possibly underage, teen girl was taken. Such anger would help in getting her name spread as the story was talked about and shared all across the web.

And if I can get one of them coming out with the girl in tow...

Is it worth the risk?

Fear that she would be seen while taking it was present. At the same time, a photo like that added to the details she had already gathered and the speculation about what was going on might be enough.

Might be...

Still no proof.

What she really needed was confirmation. She needed them to say yes to Alan, and for him to be able to say that he did, in fact, hand over money so he could have sex with one of the girls. Once she had that, the story would be solid. All she would have to do was write it.

Her phone buzzed.

Speaking of Alan.

EVERYTHING OKAY?

Seeing this, she realized she hadn't said anything about where they had gone, and she now quickly typed: YEP. IN JOLIET. LET YOU KNOW MORE SOON.

Once sent, she left the car, walked down the main road a bit, and then crossed, feet taking her toward the two cars, body shielded from view by the house next door.

Within seconds, she had a picture of each car, the license plates clearly visible in both photos. A third was then taken of the right-side windows of the second car, her thinking being that the playful cartoon stickers that decorated the back right window would be an interesting addition to the story, given how creepy it would be for people to realize that such stickers could possibly be a lure to attract children to the car.

Or maybe the owner of the car has kids?

For some reason this seemed more disturbing than the idea of luring in children simply because it showed the human side of such monsters.

Fucking a kid during the day before going home to play father to another…

She shook her head.

But you don't know that anyone is fucking anyone in there, or if the girl is still just a kid.

Need more information.

She looked over at the house while thinking this, body still somewhat shielded, and contemplated sneaking across the grassless yard and peeking through the windows. Given the single-story structure, one of the windows would have to give a view of what-ever was going on inside, unless, of course, it was somehow blocked from within.

Or the place has a basement.

Given the overgrowth surrounding the house, she could not see any basement windows; thus she had no idea if the place did actually have one, or if it had been built upon a slab. She could, however, see basement windows on the houses to either side of it, which meant, if built upon the same design, it probably had one as well.

Only one way to find out, she told herself, the inner statement overwhelming the one that suggested she hold back and not approach the house in broad daylight.

She crossed the yard.

No alarm sounded.

No shouts from within echoed.

Heart racing, she tried pushing herself through the tangle of brush that grew up against the side of the house, her goal being to press herself as close to the house as possible so that if anyone did happen to glance out a window while passing, they wouldn't see her. Something stuck her, body instinctively jerking away only to be stabbed from the other side.

Gritting her teeth, she peered down at the vegetation while pulling her leg free, eyes noting that within the relatively harmless overgrowth she had first spotted were several vine-like growths covered in thorns that had tangled themselves within the tiny branches. Beyond that were dozens of tall thistle weeds that had thousands of tiny needle-like spears, which would make pressing up against the house incredibly painful.

"No, no, I got it," a voice said, followed by the slamming of a screen door as it swung shut.

Stacy froze as one of the men hurried toward the cars, his hand pulling free a key and hitting the trunk release, and then, without really thinking, she ducked down into the brush and scooted backward, thorns and needles piercing through her jeans and sweatshirt without mercy.

Please! Please! Please!

A duffel bag in one hand and a large tripod in another, the

man used his elbow to close the trunk and then started back toward the front door, which he struggled to open.

Stacy sighed and then winced as she started to pull free, only to freeze as the door opened again.

This time the man only walked halfway across the yard, his finger hitting the lock button twice, the double beep of the alarm system echoing.

Stacy held her breath, praying that her momentary attempt at freedom from the thorns hadn't shifted things to the point of ruining her concealment.

The man returned to the house, focus never shifting her way.

Stacy let out a second sigh and then finished pulling free from the thorns. After that, she twisted a bit to see if she could see any basement windows.

Sure enough, one was there.

Even better, if she stayed low, it looked as if she might be able to slither her way to it beneath the vines and then, if she were really careful, snake her hand between two of the thistle weeds with her camera. Whether or not the picture would actually capture anything within was a mystery, but it was worth a try.

And…nothing, her mind noted once she looked at the screen capture from the picture, her forearm burning where the thistle thorns had gotten her.

Whoever was inside had blackened the basement window with a curtain. The same was true with the next one, which she slithered her way to, the flesh of her forearm being pierced repeatedly as she pressed her camera against the glass.

After that, she decided against trying to get a look inside any of the other windows, her thinking being she had pushed her luck far enough.

And then the door opened again, the man who had driven

the girl to this location stepping out on the front steps to smoke a cigarette.

One look down and he would see her, the vegetation between the two not enough to conceal her presence.

Don't breathe.

Don't move.

Don't think.

9

About forty minutes into watching the house, Alan began to feel a grumble of discontent from his bowels. Pain wasn't present with the grumble, just a slight feeling of liquid discomfort, one that he knew would want to come out of him within the next half hour.

Should have eaten a banana, he told himself, past experience helping him recognize that this was nothing more than bowel juices that could have been soaked up if he had put something small inside.

Such action would have been a gamble, however, other past experiences having taught him that after an attack like the one he had suffered, the inflammation within could make it so everything he ate, even if it was something that typically prevented diarrhea, would go through him at the speed of light.

Taking a deep breath, he willed the grumble to go away and his mind to think about something else.

Anything else!

Movies, Mom, Iraq…anything but pooping!

At the house, the garage door opened, allowing a car to back up.

Alan switched on the ignition and waited to see which way it would go. If toward him, he would go the opposite way and then catch up with them on the main road. If away, he would simply follow.

The car came toward him, two girls within, neither looking his way as he pretended to stare at his phone.

Once they passed, he drove forward and took a right and then another right, the road momentarily clear. After that, it wasn't long before he had the two girls in sight, his theory that they would be heading north on this part of Lambert, given their initial direction, correct.

Now he just wished a car would come between them so that if they did look back they wouldn't automatically note his presence.

A stop sign a minute into the drive granted him his wish. Unfortunately, the car didn't stay between them for long, the girls taking a right a few blocks ahead while the car between them continued northward.

Alan followed.

The girls continued east through two intersections, each one requiring a stop but not providing a new car for cover, before making a left onto Main Street. Here, thankfully, a car got between them once again and stayed between them through the complicated downtown Glen Ellyn area.

Once beyond that, the car between turned off on St. Charles Road while the girls continued forward, Alan having to race a yellow to stay with them, only to come to a halt at the next light.

While waiting, he played over the list of addresses he had created, his mind trying to remember the various city and town names that had been on it and what the possible location for them would be, given how far north they seemed to be going.

Bloomingdale was one, and if they continued north on this road they would hit it soon. He didn't yet have the exact address of the house up there, but he did have a few possible ones for the area.

Should I back off and just go to the addresses?

But what if they're going to one that isn't on the list?

At the next light, he decided to turn off and risk taking a different route toward the first of the Bloomingdale-area houses, the chance of being seen after all this time too much. Had the outcome been unlocking all the mysteries of this real estate prostitution setup, he might have decided differently, but it was most likely to see a client or two, so really, losing them wouldn't be too big a deal.

Probably shouldn't have even followed them.

Not if the only reward was the chance of locating another house that wasn't in the website pictures.

10

"Okay, he turned," Emily said as they crossed North Avenue, an unmistakable layer of relief present within her voice.

"Thank god," Amanda replied, eyes glancing up into the rearview mirror even though she trusted Emily's observation.

Neither said anything after that, the anxiety that had been growing after Emily had noticed the guy making the same turn they made not just once but twice leaving a sense of exhaustion as it faded.

Up ahead, Army Trail Road appeared.

Amanda signaled a right and then, before taking it, nodded toward the gas station and asked, "You need anything before we get there?"

"No, I brought a ton of crap there last time, and I doubt anyone would have used it all between then and now."

"Okay."

Amanda turned and then quickly got all the way over so she could make a left onto Swift Road, the house half a mile down on the left.

"Jesus, I don't know how you can relax in this place," Amanda muttered as she pulled the car into the driveway.

"What do you mean?" Emily asked, hand reaching back to grab her purse.

"It's just seems so out of the way and rural, like you're in the middle of nowhere." She shuddered.

"But it isn't," Emily said, purse now in her lap.

"I know, but it feels that way, what with all the trees and the overgrown field behind it. Eerie."

"Thanks. I hadn't really thought about that before, but now that you mention it, it is a bit spooky." She smiled to show she was only half serious and then opened the car door. "Shoot me a text when you're on your way back?"

"Sure."

"Okay. Good luck with the new guy."

"Yeah, you too."

Emily gave her another smile and stepped out of the car.

Amanda waited a moment to make sure Emily got inside, this location being one that had a key tucked away rather than a garage door keypad, which was another reason why she wouldn't want to scene here. Way too easy for someone to find the key and let himself in.

Door open, Emily turned, gave Amanda an "all's good" wave, and stepped inside.

Door closed, Amanda headed back toward Army Trail Road, finger toying with the radio now that Emily's music selection was gone, her hope being that she could find something that would give her a little uplift during the ten-minute drive. She didn't, all the stations conspiring to give her commercials, a vow to start downloading her favorite songs onto her phone as Emily had done once again being voiced by her mind.

11

Alan located the address of the house in Bloomingdale without too much trouble, it having been the first address on the list of possible addresses he had made for this particular location. Unfortunately, no one was there upon his confirmation of the location and, given its position in the back of a cul-de-sac, there really was no way to watch the place without being noticed.

But you could watch the cul-de-sac to see if anyone pulls into it and then check to see which driveway they park in.

Of course, driving back and forth every time someone pulled in could draw unwanted attention as well, as would driving up to gather information on any client car that pulled in.

So, do I stay here or go and track down the other addresses on the list?

In the end, he did pull away from the house, though not because any decision had been reached. Instead, he had to use the bathroom, the earlier grumbles from his bowels having returned and shifted so far south that he knew it was only a matter of minutes before the liquid-like substance within would demand to be let out.

A gas station was his destination, one that seemed to have an overstock of soda since they had stacked several crates of two-liter bottles in the corner of the men's room. Thoughts on whether or not this was in violation of any health codes played across his mind, as did questions about what Stacy was uncovering all the way down in Joliet.

12

The cigarette butt landed a few inches from her face, a tiny bit of smoke drifting up from the poorly crushed tip. Fortunately, nothing but dirt was present in this area, the large pine trees apparently a nice buffer for the yard when it came to falling leaves from the other neighborhood trees.

The front door opened as the man stepped back in, the sounds of a girl moaning sexually echoing.

They're somewhere on the first floor, she realized.

But the windows are blocked.

Or are they?

Despite having almost been discovered, she actually began contemplating an attempt to see if she could capture any pictures through the windows that she hadn't yet tried peeking through. First things first, however, she had to get away from the front door just in case—

In case of what?

He isn't going to want to have another cigarette this quickly after his first, and the others seem to be in the middle of having sex, so...

A new thought appeared as that one faded, one that wondered how far from the front door they were and whether the layout of the house within would allow for her to enter and get herself hidden somewhere.

No, that would be too risky.

But if I could get a camera inside for next time...

One of those nanny camera things that's triggered on by motion...

Shit, not only would she have pictures of the houses and a written story, but also video that could easily go viral, her name being spread to those that never read news stories and weren't patient enough to click through pictures.

Could I get inside?

Given how old and run-down the house was, she bet there was enough of a gap to slip a credit card through to unlatch the lock.

Not if it's deadbolted too.

You'll just have to wait and see.

Slithering backward, she pulled herself free of the overgrowth, body narrowly missing an unseen vine with thorns, and retreated back to her car to wait, her hope being they would finish up with the girl soon so she could check the door.

While waiting, she sent a text to Alan asking if he knew anything about nanny cams and what they might cost, hope brewing that talking about them would help lead into her approaching him with the possibility of fronting the money for a few that she could put inside.

If you can even get in.

If not here, maybe one of the other locations would be accessible.

13

Nanny cams? Alan wondered as he left the bathroom and returned to his car, the irritation that had plagued his backside having returned with the fresh squirts that had shot out of him. Later, a warm bath would help soothe things, if he got a chance at one. No telling what might unfold in the hours to come and whether or not he would have the time to fill the tub and soak once he got home.

AH, GOOD IDEA, he replied a few minutes later after an explanation for the nanny cam text arrived. Then, IF WE CAN AC-TUALLY GET INTO ANY OF THE HOUSES.

I THINK WE'LL BE ABLE TO DOWN HERE. IT'S REALLY OLD.

Old didn't mean anything if new locks had been installed, but Alan decided not to press such an issue and instead would wait and see if she could get in.

I'LL LET YOU KNOW, she added.

OKAY. BE CAREFUL.

I WILL.

Nothing else arrived as he drove back to the house, a decision to see if the two girls or anyone else had arrived while he was away guiding his actions. If not, he would check out the other locations. If so, he would watch the cul-de-sac to see if a man arrived, if one wasn't there already, and gather some basic information about the car for Stacy.

After that...well, he didn't know and would play it all by ear.

The car he had followed was sitting in the driveway when

he drove by. No one else was present, so he headed down the street to see if he could find an area of observation. Nothing really worked; the one spot he really wanted that gave the best view unappealing now because the homeowner had decided to start raking his front yard. In fact, parking anywhere near that area would make him uneasy, the man with the rake sure to notice him and grow suspicious. And going to the opposite side of the cul-de-sac seemed risky, the possibility of being noticed by whoever showed up to be serviced at the house, due to how wary someone in that state might be, too much for him to chance.

So...now what?

Not wanting to lose the opportunity of gathering information on another client, even if the information would be minuscule, Alan decided to leave the area for a bit to see if he could locate the next closest house, and then come back and see if a new car was at the house. After all, the fact that the car the girls had driven was in the driveway rather than the garage meant that he could easily verify if they were still there when he came back, and it stood to reason that if another car was parked next to them, it would belong to a client.

Now he just had to figure out how to get back to Army Trail Road. Pulling into a driveway to turn around wasn't something he enjoyed doing, especially on days when people were typically home, so he tried to find a cross street he could use to loop around. No cross streets seemed to exist though, this street simply going on and on at an angle, almost as if it was going to wrap around itself.

Another cul-de-sac appeared, one that he used to turn around.

Two minutes later, he was nearing the cul-de-sac he had wanted to watch once again, eyes peering into it as he drove by.

A new car was parked within, only they had pulled up alongside the curved curb rather than into the driveway.

Is it a client? he asked himself.

When it came to cul-de-sacs, parking was kind of wacky, the angled yards and narrow strips of curb between some of the drive-ways making it so people could park in front of one house while actually visiting another simply because there was no space in front of the house they were actually going to. Because of this and his failure to actually watch a man get out and walk up to the front door of the house the girls were in, he couldn't say for sure if the owner of the car truly was a client and thus was hesitant to gather information on it. After all, the last thing he wanted was for Stacy to ruthlessly pursue some guy for information on the prostitution setup when he didn't actually have any information, especially if he was in another relationship that could be damaged by such inquiries.

So…now what?

He couldn't simply stand on the corner staring at the car until someone left the house and got in. That would be more conspicuous than parking near the entrance to the cul-de-sac and watching it.

And driving by repeatedly in hopes of timing things perfectly so that he was passing by just as the man left the house and headed to the car was unrealistic.

Just go and locate the other houses.

Nothing more you can do here.

A sense of failure arrived with this decision, even though the terms *success* and *failure* didn't really seem correct when considering any outcome of this little investigative quest. Plus, he had uncovered another location, which was good.

And will find more.

His phone buzzed with a call, the number blocked.

Normally he would not answer such things, but this time, hoping that it might be the real estate people responding to his inquiry about being serviced, he did.

"Hello?" he asked.

"Alan Miller, please," a man asked.

"Yes, this is he."

The call ended.

Alan looked at the phone for a moment, questions and theories entering his mind.

Could it really have been them checking the number?

If so, why not just hang up when I answered?

Was it because they wanted confirmation of my name?

Nothing else seemed likely, yet even so, he felt like such a step was odd. But maybe such things worked for them, and even if it was truly pointless, maybe they got a sense of security out of it.

14

Changing the locks on the front and back door was, in theory, a fairly simple task. Sadly, Riley was not wired for such things, something he should have learned once and for all back when he had attempted to change his spark plugs with the aid of a webpage. He hadn't, however, and naturally, screwed everything up to the point where he just put the old knobs back in and called a professional. Wednesday was the next available time, much to his dismay. Equally dismaying was the amount of money he had spent on the new knobs and deadbolts, though he eased the mental pain of that by thinking that maybe the guy who came could use them instead of getting his own and subtract the difference from the total bill.

What are the chances that she'll try again before then? he asked himself after all was said and done, his body in his main chair, TV clicker in hand while he sipped a glass of water.

Knowing Kristi and how determined she could get about certain things, she would probably try again while he was at work the next day, and then again and again until she either found what she was looking for or was found out and forced to stop.

Even if she does get in again, she won't find it.

His confidence on this was solid, though he did wonder if maybe he should put the computer somewhere else to make it even more unlikely of a discovery.

Then again, she might think it odd that the computer was tucked away in a different spot and move in for a closer look. Such things happened all the time, the brain actually absorbing everything one saw but not always realizing it until something else triggered the memory. Because of this, he decided against moving it and then, since nothing was on TV, went into his office to see what was going on in the world of Facebook and OkCupid, a tiny hope of having made some worthwhile connections on the latter entering his mind.

"If you want sex, you could always get it from one of the girls," Sam had said a few weeks earlier when Riley had voiced dismay at being unable to find a girlfriend.

"I want more than just sex," he had replied back, though, admittedly, the idea of being able to get off with someone who was good at such things was appealing.

The current lack of connections or communications once he was signed onto the dating site brought the consideration of getting together with one of the girls back into his mind, along with thoughts on which one he would choose should he wish to go that route.

Silly question.

Isabella, as always, was the one he settled upon. He wasn't sure what it was about her, but ever since they'd been introduced to each other two months earlier, he had trouble pushing her from his mind. It wasn't just her body that had snagged him, though he wouldn't deny that it played a part. Something about her personality and the vibe she gave off just seemed to work magic upon him and turn him into a stuttering schoolboy who wanted nothing more than to please her.

You can't have sex with her, get a blowjob, handjob, or even exchange dirty messages while you jack off, so just forget about her!

Doing so would be too similar to the sexual advantage that everyday pimps took of their own girls, which in turn would once again add another element of difficulty in separating what went on in the cheap motels and abandoned alleyways of the city from what he and Sam were trying to do.

It isn't the same, though, another part of his mind attempted. *We're not like them.*

The thought wasn't enough.

Despite the appeal, he would not go down such a path.

Others in his position might, but not him.

Has Sam?

Shit, thinking about Sam in a normal sexual situation was disturbing, but then picturing him with one of the girls...he didn't know why, but it was even worse.

Kristi would never let him do that.

But if she didn't know?

Would Sam risk going behind her back for something like that?

If so, having such information could prove useful at some point.

The hard part would be looking into it without tipping them off, especially considering Sam and Kristi had way more contact with the girls than he did. In fact, given the low profile he had chosen to keep in all this, there were some girls he hadn't even met yet and others he had only seen once or twice.

I should send one of the girls an email without them knowing who I really am and see what happens, he said to himself, only half serious. *Be like a secret shopper or undercover boss with my own company.*

Actually, sending such a message to test Sam and make sure he wasn't slacking in sending info over to him for the prescreening procedure he had insisted upon when funding everything wasn't such a bad idea. The only issue was, if Sam realized he was testing him, there might be hell to pay, the implication of distrust hard to ignore.

Do you actually trust him, though?

Sam, as an individual, yes; Sam, when partnered with Kristi, not so much.

So…

He thought about it for nearly a minute and realized it would be in his best interest to send such a message, the threat of implied distrust be damned.

First things first, however, he had to set up an email account and then type up a message, one that would bluntly specify what it was he wanted with the girl he had chosen from the site.

What if you get a reply with a time and place to meet the girl?

Fuck, just the thought sent an angry chill down his spine, one that seemed to settle within his bowels and make him regret the coffee he had downed that morning.

Not long after that, having paid a visit to the bathroom, he wondered what would happen if he did get approved to see one of the girls. Technically, if he paid for it, he wouldn't be taking advantage of them like a pimp, so…

No.

Though he didn't think there was anything wrong with it, he didn't want to actually pay for sex. Something about going that route just felt off to him, as if he were admitting failure in trying to achieve such an end result in the real world and had given in. Plus, if he did it once, he wouldn't have any qualms about doing it a second and third time, and eventually would grow so fond of how easy it was to get sexual satisfaction when in the form of a business transaction that he would probably stop pursuing female relationships altogether.

Unless it all starts to feel so humdrum and meaningless that you need the relationship aspect to get any thrill from having sex?

Hell, having such a thing happen might actually make whatever relationship he found himself in seem better and more rewarding.

He shook his head at the attempt of justification for seeing one of the girls, justification that could easily guide his hand into not even paying for things and stepping into the pimp shoes he so desperately wanted to avoid.

Just send the email.

Thirty minutes later, he did, from a new Gmail account with a fake name, age, and address entered into the information section. He even used a web service to create a fake phone number, one that allowed people to leave him a message right on his account that he could listen to later on his laptop. Once that was done, body so worked up from expressing so many sexual desires in the message, he couldn't help but spend the next ten minutes jerking off. He used a picture of Isabella, one that was part of a set that had been taken while setting up the prostitution gig, the initial idea having been to create a second, password-protected website that displayed the girls in their real profession, thus allowing the approved clients to get a better idea of who each girl was, what they looked like in sexual attire, and what services they performed.

In the end, the three had been forced to abandon the secondary site idea, the skills required to build such a thing with the level of security required to prevent hacking and potential discovery by investigators beyond their abilities. And bringing in someone with the know-how to do such work had seemed risky, the potential for blackmail once all was said and done a fear none of them could dismiss. Fortunately, everything seemed to work fine without it. The men, once approved, didn't seem to have any problems in choosing a girl to spend time with, their fantasies and desires easily accommodated through a series of messages with Kristi.

15

Stacy waited a long time for the group to leave the house, her assumption that things would be over quickly, given the sex she had heard while in the overgrowth, seemingly incorrect. Of course, given the camera tripod she had seen being carried inside, sex itself might not have been what the men had paid for. Instead, they were making porn, porn that required the hiring of girls outside of the legal channels because of the activities involved and the ages desired. If so, this setup was even bigger than she originally thought.

A few texts went back and forth during her wait, disappointment that Alan hadn't really uncovered much beyond being able to add a couple more addresses to the list of houses bringing her down.

Not his fault. He did all he could.

Plus, she had uncovered quite a bit herself.

It's still not enough.

You need proof.

You need—

Two figures emerged from the house and walked to the second car, one carrying the bags and tripod toward the trunk while the other went to the driver-side door. Less than two minutes later, they were gone, the car having taken a right onto the main road up ahead.

So... she silently said as if face-to-face with the man and girl, her word implying a question on when they would be leaving.

Twenty minutes was the answer, the time seeming to last twice that as she stared at the house, waiting, a silent cry of *FINALLY* echoing within her mind as both emerged, the girl swishing her skirt back and forth as she walked while the man moved quickly to the driver-side door.

And then, once they were gone, she continued to wait, a realization that she should make sure they weren't simply going out for a snack or something unfolding as she reached for her door handle.

Initially, another twenty minutes seemed like a good idea, but then, after eight minutes, she decided ten was enough, and then nine, her impatience getting the better of her.

No one returned as she walked up to the house, her body taking on an "I totally belong" look as she strolled down the sidewalk and turned toward the house beyond the pine trees.

The front door, as expected, was locked.

The back too.

Pulling her debit card, she went back to the front door and after looking at it for several seconds, slid the card into the narrow gap between the frame and door, scenes from movies and TV shows of such procedures playing across her mind.

The card hit something and stopped.

The lock?

Has to be.

She pushed down with the card while twisting the knob. Nothing. The lock stayed in place.

She pulled the card out and looked at it, questions about what she was doing wrong unfolding.

No answers followed.

She tried again, this time easing the card directly at the lock rather than from an angle above. As before, she twisted the knob when the card hit the lock, and, as before, nothing happened.

"Fuck," she muttered, frustration building.

She tried again, card going directly at the lock once more, this time with force from the beginning rather than a hesitant, probing approach.

The door opened.

Startled, she stared and then, realizing it had worked,

stepped inside, dismay at how easy it had actually been arriving.

Now what?

The question was answered by taking a walk through the place, head swiveling back and forth as she soaked everything in.

Other than the unmistakable smell of semen-infused-latex, one that sat atop a heavier, more established smell of staleness, nothing really jumped out at her upon the first walk-through. The place was obviously a crash pad, one stocked with secondhand furniture and a sense of disinterest when things like spills occurred, plaster peeled, or trash was left about. This wasn't to say the place was heaped with rotting garbage or home to civilizations of mold, just that it appeared a quick wipe with a paper towel rather than a scrubbing of the area with cleaner and a sponge was used if something spilled, and things like empty beer cans and bags from chips and fast-food places were left about until someone realized it would be best to toss it all out during a visit.

On the second pass, she noticed an abundance of extension cords, some still plugged in, others just heaped in coils in the far corner. Why so many would be needed was a mystery, but the fact that they were there seemed important and thus picture worthy.

Equally picture worthy was what she saw when she looked inside a plastic Jewel bag that was sitting next to an old recliner. Condoms. No specific size, style, or brand seemed to hold dominance within the bag, which in turn made her wonder if one of the men who had shown up had access to a free supply at a health clinic somewhere.

Was it left here by mistake?

What if they come back?

The thought earned a moment of consideration followed by a quick stroll to the front window to see if anyone was pulling up outside. No one was and, in reality, even if someone did discover they had left the bag behind, chances were good they would just grab it the next time they were here.

If they even come back, she said to herself, a realization that her assumptions about how exactly this location worked could be off.

Not that it mattered at that particular moment, the only thing of importance being to gather as much information as possible. Later, with the pictures before them, she and Alan could speculate on how exactly the place worked.

And once you get a video camera in here...

She looked around, eyes trying to spot a suitable location for a nanny cam, but after several seconds decided to think about it later.

With that, she headed into one of the two bedrooms at the rear of the house, both of which had beds, the first looking fairly standard with sheets and a bedspread, the second, nothing but a stained mattress.

Blood? she wondered, sudden thoughts and concerns about what else might be going on in this house entering her mind.

She took a picture and sent it to Alan.

After that, she went to the dresser that sat beneath a boarded-up window and looked inside. Rubber sheets were in one, plastic sheets in another. The third had more condoms, many of them the familiar Trojan brand, though the styles and sizes were varied.

Her phone buzzed.

LOOKS LIKE BLOOD TO ME, Alan said. Then, before she could reply, HOW'D YOU GET INSIDE?

DEBIT CARD.

WOW.

She smiled and, when nothing else arrived, tucked the phone away. A moment later, after getting on her hands and knees to peek under the bed, she pulled the phone back out and snapped a picture of the thin piece of nylon cord that had been tied around the leg of the bed.

Each of the bed legs had a piece of cord, all of which had obviously been used to tie someone spread-eagle to the bed. Whether or not it had been someone underage, she could not tell, but once the picture was posted, she wouldn't hesitate to suggest such a thing, a statement on the rope length and how it had most likely been used to secure someone who had not yet finished growing into a standard-sized adult being made.

Nothing else really jumped out at her within the room, so she backed up into the doorway and took another picture, this one capturing both the bed with the rope on it and the boarded-up window.

LOOKS LIKE THEY KEPT SOMEONE PRISONER IN HERE, she typed with the picture and sent to Alan.

OMG! Alan replied. BE CAREFUL!

DON'T WORRY, THEY'RE LONG GONE.

I hope.

In the bathroom, she found a shower that had hard-water stains all over the sliding door and a towel that reeked of mildew, thanks to whoever had left it balled up in the corner after using it. A disgusting toothbrush was also present in an equally disgusting plastic cup that had been left on the sink, and the inside of the toilet, well…she hoped the stains were from hard water and rust, rather than what it looked like.

From the bathroom, she checked out the kitchen, which was pretty bare, and then, after finding the light switch on the wall next to the door, went down into the cellar that stood next to the pantry, the wooden stair boards announcing her approach with every step to anyone that might be below.

No one was there, at least, no one that she could see, the stairway light only reaching so far into the unfinished cellar.

Dangling just beyond the light was a string.

She gave it a tug…

…and jumped back with a cry as the light revealed a person standing before her in the corner, eyes directly upon her.

16

FINISHED WITH THE FIRST, WAITING ON THE SECOND, Amanda texted to Emily before heading into the bathroom to take a shower, a thought on how, if the situation were reversed and she was the one that needed to be picked up, she would like to be kept informed guiding her hand.

No reply awaited her when stepping from the shower eleven minutes later, which probably meant Emily was still in her own scene. Later, while on her knees with a dick in her mouth, Amanda would probably hear the faint buzz of the phone, a message letting her know Emily was finished arriving.

Encased in a towel, Amanda went to one of the windows to peek out at the neighborhood, eyes looking for the car that had been following them earlier.

It wasn't out there.

Though fading, she still felt a bit of apprehension about the situation, apprehension that had gotten a boost earlier when she thought she saw the car pulling into the gas station on Army Trail Road. Whether or not it truly was the same car with the same driver was a mystery, but just seeing one that was similar enough to catch her attention had caused her heart to start racing as she made her own turn.

Why would someone follow us?

Several possibilities arrived, none of them very pleasing to the mind.

She sighed.

If he was following her, and if he was out there now watching from an unseen vantage point, there was nothing she could really do about it. Later, if she saw him again while driving home or maybe parked somewhere by any of the houses, she could report his information to the boss. Until then…

…just try to relax and give the new guy a fantastic scene.

Speaking of which…

She needed to get dressed, her wardrobe choice for the new guy being a red teddy with stockings hooked to garters, and red panties, all beneath a fitted blazer and skirt. She also had a nice pair of heels that she would quickly put on to answer the door, relief that she didn't have to wear such things all night long while pacing a street corner still present after all these months.

Dressed, she approached the full-length mirror that was hooked to the back of the closet door in the master bedroom and inspected herself, mind trying to push away what she had seen on the scale the other day.

Easier said than done, she said to herself, the new tightness she felt in the jacket not helping.

Tears threatened.

Don't! You look fine.

The statement was true; she did look fine, but for how much longer? If she kept gaining weight, there would come a point where she was no longer appealing to the guys that hired her, especially those who were expecting the skinny girl from the pictures they had taken in the beginning. Once that happened…

This time the tears did start to fall, causing her makeup to run. Such a look was okay after the scene, the gagging from a blow-job, if given, often causing such streaks, but before it began…nope.

She headed into the bathroom to fix herself and then, once that was finished, went to the window to check the area again before heading downstairs to wait.

Eight minutes later, the doorbell rang.

She took a deep breath and went to answer it, feet slipping into the heels while her hands smoothed down her skirt.

Here we go.

She answered the door.

17

"Oh my god," Stacy said while letting out a weak laugh, adrenaline racing.

The figure, which was wearing a fading wedding dress, was a life-sized mannequin, one whose head had been twisted to look directly at the stairs.

As a joke?

To spook anyone who comes down here?

If so, it had worked, her scream still vibrating within her ears while her heart pounded against her rib cage.

She took a deep breath and turned to look at the other side of the cellar, the boxes and plastic containers stacked behind the mannequin of no real concern to her. Later, if nothing else caught her attention, she would give them a peek to see if anything interesting was inside, but now, she didn't really care.

What the...

More mannequins, some with clothes on, others bare, a few with dildos glued on, were placed in various positions, some paired up sexually, along the far wall amid more boxes. Beyond that, pushed into the corner, was a tattered mattress, a balled-up blanket sitting at the foot of it.

She walked up to the mattress, eyes looking for blood or other signs of foul play, but nothing really jumped out at her...until she saw the ring in the wall. It had been drilled in at about chest height, right above the mattress. Others stretched the entire wall, most chest level like the first one above the mattress, two others near the floor, and one was way up toward the ceiling, just reachable if she were to stand on her tippy-toes.

For chaining up children?

If so, where had they all gone? And was the place still in use, given that so much stuff had been pushed up against the walls?

And what about the mattress?

Maybe there used to be more?

In her mind, she could see a line of mattresses along the wall, children and teens able to sit upon them or even lie down while also secured to the rings by lengths of chain, their young minds awaiting some horrific fate.

Maybe to be auctioned off to sick fucks with money who enjoyed youthful flesh in the bedroom?

A chill tickled her bowels.

Could such a thing have really taken place? Beneath the noses of all those around here?

Sadly, she knew the answer was *yes*. Things like that happened all the time, the unaware public often shocked when the horror was finally revealed to them. Questions of how they couldn't know about it would then follow, dismay and anger present within the words even though they too would have probably been oblivious to it had it unfolded near them. In fact, an unspoken recognition of that was probably what upset everyone the most. The knowledge that the idea that one should be able to easily spot such evil individuals, and the evil things they were engaged in, was a falsehood, thus making their condemnation of those who failed in seeing this something that might really be directed inward.

The question of whether or not such things were still taking place entered her thoughts once again, an answer of "probably not" slowly unfolding. Instead, something else was, something that could be just as bad yet didn't seem to require imprisonment within the cellar.

And the mannequins?

Her mind couldn't even begin to speculate upon them, the only obvious thing being that someone had had a lot of fun positioning them. That could have been a simple act of boredom, however, one that had no real significance to everything else that was going on within the house.

But why are they even here?

Had someone grabbed them on a whim when a local store was closing?

If so, had the clothing items been on them already when taken, or had someone actually spent time dressing them? The latter possibility added an extra layer of creepiness to everything, though she guessed boredom could have been the sole cause of that as well.

Whatever the answer was, speculating upon it now wasn't going to get her anywhere, so she pushed the thoughts from her mind and snapped several more pictures, her attempts at capturing everything she saw within one or two photos not going well and forcing a focus on each individual element.

After that, she started typing up a message to Alan with a picture of the mattress, one that conveyed her thoughts on the possibility that children had been kept prisoner here, but then she hesitated to send it due to the possibility that Alan might want to get the police involved, even though no children were here now.

At some point they will need to know about this place, she told herself.

But it would be better once there are actually children here.

Doing a raid now would just result in alerting whoever used this place for such things—if they still did use it—that they had been discovered, which in turn would lead to them closing up shop. The children, wherever they were, would not benefit from such a thing.

So rather than sending the picture with the text, she simply sent the picture.

He didn't reply.

She then sent another, this one of the mannequins, the word CREEPY added to it.

Still no reply.

THIS PLACE IS EASY TO GET INTO, she typed in a third message, this one without any pictures. I THINK WE COULD GET A COUPLE CAMERAS IN WITHOUT ANY TROUBLE AND SEE WHAT HAPPENS.

Once sent, she tucked the phone into her pocket and started for the stairs, which was when she heard the front door open and footsteps echo across the floor above.

Oh fuck! her mind cried, body quickly racing across the cellar to switch off the light.

Darkness settled in but didn't disappear completely, not with the stairway light still on. Unfortunately, she couldn't get to that one, not without climbing the steps.

Heart racing once again, and this time for good reason, she carefully moved along a wall until she was in the corner, tucked behind the boxes and the first mannequin she had seen, ears listening as whoever was upstairs walked around.

"Jesus Christ," a voice echoed. More words followed, but she wasn't able to make them out.

The steps moved toward the kitchen area and then, without warning, she heard the door open.

Breath held, Stacy waited and then let out a sigh as the stairway light was switched off. Unfortunately, the footsteps that followed were not those of the person leaving. Instead, they took a path into one of the back bedrooms, the nice furnished one being her guess, and stopped. The sound of a phone conversation followed, one that got quite heated for a moment as the guy on this end told whoever was on the other that they had left the place a mess.

Her phone buzzed.

She pulled it out.

GOOD IDEA, Alan said. HEY, WHAT'S THE ADDRESS?

She didn't know the exact address but did have the picture of the street sign and pulled it up.

Up above, footsteps walked from the bedroom to the kitchen, the stairway door opening once again, the words, "You're sure you didn't go down there?" reaching her ears.

Stacy froze.

The stairway light came back on.

Fuck!

Knowing the glow from the phone would give her away, she quickly stuffed it into her pocket without sending the picture.

"Okay," the voice at the top of the stairs said. "I'll check."

Oh god!

Wooden steps groaned as the man began his descent into the cellar, Stacy just able to make out his figure in the light of the stairway and the fact that he was holding something that resembled a gun.

18

HEY, I'M HERE, Amanda texted moments after pulling up into the driveway of the house on Swift Road, exhaustion from the two scenes making it so she just wanted to get back home, shower, and climb into bed.

Emily didn't come out.

Amanda waited, frustration building that Emily wasn't ready despite the "on my way" text that had been sent fifteen minutes earlier.

Concern followed, a realization that Emily hadn't replied to any of her messages since being dropped off entering into her mind.

Maybe her phone died…

Though plausible, Amanda didn't really believe this to be the case. At the same time, she didn't want to think of any other possibilities, not when she had made her fears of this place known earlier.

Maybe she fell asleep?

Exhaustion from a scene, coupled with waiting to be picked up, could easily cause one to drift away while resting the body. It had happened to her several times in the past.

But would it happen here?

Not with me.

Emily was probably a different story, the conversation earlier proving she didn't really have any fears of this place.

Amanda sighed.

One minute came and went, followed by a second, third, and then fourth minute.

No Emily.

Another minute.

Amanda opened her phone and called, the phone ringing on the other end but never being picked up.

She ended the call without leaving a message.

Another five minutes came and went.

She called again.

No answer.

Go ring the bell.

Though she really didn't want to get out of the car, she knew she had no choice and let out a heavy sigh while stepping from the vehicle.

Ten seconds later, she was at the door, her fingers pushing the doorbell once, then twice, and then over and over again several times.

No answer.

Now what? she asked herself, concern growing.

Call the boss?

She did and, *surprise, surprise,* didn't get an answer.

She tucked the phone into her pocket and looked down at the door handle, hesitation growing.

Don't, her mind urged.

I have to, another part said.

If Emily were hurt and needed help, Amanda would never forgive herself for not going inside. However, if someone else were inside, waiting for her to enter and then hurt her…

She would go in for you.

Would she?

Yes, she would.

Amanda tried the door.

It opened, hinges squealing.

She shivered.

Nothing happened.

The front hall was completely empty and, once the squeal of the hinges faded, silent.

Amanda waited, ears trying to hear something that could give her a clue.

Nothing.

The place seemed empty.

But it probably isn't, her mind warned, right hand gripping the pepper spray she always carried, index finger ready to unleash the wretched mix into anyone that sprang out upon her.

"Emily?" she called.

No answer.

She stepped into the house, eyes scanning both sides of the front hallway.

No one came at her.

She took a deep breath and headed to the right, pepper-spray nozzle held at the ready as she rounded the first corner.

Nothing.

Slowly, she crept across the room toward the next corner,

which led into the short rear hallway. Four doors were present, two leading into bedrooms, one into the bathroom, and the final one into the small laundry area. All were closed.

She checked the bedrooms.

Nothing.

The bathroom.

Nothing.

She turned to the laundry one, her gut telling her she didn't want to open it, not with the faint smell of poop that was seeping out.

You have to.

She put a hand on the knob but didn't turn it right away, an attempt at preparing herself for what she was about to see unfolding.

Open it.

She did, the door bumping something that shifted a bit, but not enough for the door to open all the way.

Blood!

It stood out upon the fake-tile squares of the floor, a thick smear that could only have come from a serious wound.

Seal broken, the smell of poop engulfed her. Piss was present as well.

Don't, her mind cried as she gave the door a good shove, one that allowed for three more inches of open space between the frame and door.

Fingertips were in the blood, the rest of the hand still unseen.

Unable to stop herself, Amanda squeezed her upper body through the opening and then gasped as her eyes locked on Emily's frozen gaze, eyes wide, lips broken, face completely battered.

Further down, her bowels could be seen protruding from a hole in her abdomen, almost as if someone had slit her open and reached inside to pull a chunk free.

Amanda gagged.

No air!

She couldn't breathe.

Get out!

Everything swayed as she pulled her body back through the gap and tried to get to the front door, her legs growing heavy and useless within two steps, her body crashing down onto the floor in the hallway cutout.

Darkness followed.

19

"Come out, come out, wherever you are," the man taunted from the bottom of the steps, gun pointed at a downward angle as he scanned the dark cellar.

Heart racing, Stacy stayed as still as possible, her body folded in upon itself by the first mannequin she had seen, balanced on her toes, ready to spring up and run if given the chance.

The man looked directly at her, eyes obviously trying to focus into the darkness. Why he didn't simply walk over and pull the string on the light was a mystery.

He probably will in a moment.

And when he does…

Given the sudden brightness and the momentary confusion as his eyes adjusted, she might have a chance at escape.

The trouble was the gun that he held.

Two years earlier, she had written an article talking about guns and how, unless someone practiced regularly, the average person couldn't even hit a figure coming at them from five feet away. The question was, did this guy practice regularly? Even if he didn't, her article had simply addressed the averages, something that always left room for chance and luck.

The man shifted his eyes a bit, and while they were no longer looking directly at her, they were still looking in her corner.

"I know you're down here," he said.

Stacy stayed quiet.

"You left the light on," he continued. "And Robert and his boys say they didn't come down here with the girl, so…"

He wants me to talk.

Why?

No answer arrived, nor would one.

Get ready…

The man waited several seconds and then moved toward where the light cord dangled, his hand reaching up to tug at it.

Stacy jumped up and ran to the right, wrapping around toward the stairs.

"Gotcha!" the man shouted, voice seemingly excited.

Stacy expected him to come after her, but instead he simply twisted back toward the stairs and went to cut her off, his arms swinging out and connecting with her chest as she sprang upward onto the steps.

The blow was solid and knocked her back, her legs fighting for balance as she crashed into the cement wall, head bouncing against it with a painful *thunk.*

And then a fist held her by the hair, fingers twisting upward, roots straining.

"*Gahhhh!*" she cried against the pain, unable to help herself, hands reaching up to try to pull his fingers free.

"Don't," he said and slapped at her hands with his gun, all while continuing to hold her hair. "You'll hurt your—"

She grabbed the gun by the barrel and twisted, another scream leaving her lips.

Seemingly startled, the man released her hair and grabbed at the gun with his other hand, which was when she let go and watched as he tumbled backward, his legs tangling within themselves as he fought and failed to keep his balance.

Stacy ran up the steps.

"Stop!" the man shouted. "I'll shoot."

Stacy ignored the demand and continued toward the door.

No gunshot echoed.

She slowed in the kitchen, hand throwing the door shut behind her, and then turned toward the front door.

Behind her, the stairway boards squealed as the man came up them, his body closing the gap quickly.

Stacy reached the front door and twisted the knob—only it didn't work.

Panicked, she flipped the lock and pulled it again, the handle turning without a problem, yet still not allowing the door to open.

Deadbolt!

She grabbed the lever between her fingers and threw it into the open position while pulling with her other hand.

The door opened…

…and then slammed shut as the man threw his body into hers, the weight crushing her once the door was firmly in place.

"Bitch!" he shouted into her ear, a hand grabbing her hair once again.

She kicked back at him with her heel, trying to connect with his shin, and then, without warning, saw thousands of yellow explosions within the darkness of her mind as her head was slammed into the wooden door by her hair.

After that, nothing really worked.

She was simply there, watching herself from inside her own mind, an awareness of being dragged across the floor entering her thoughts but not really processed.

The same was true of the ropes he used to bind her wrists,

ones that caused her to mumble something about the tightness.

He laughed and just pulled harder at the knot, making them even tighter. After that, she felt a hand on her right boob, squeezing it once before letting go and leaving the area, a statement leaving his lips about returning later once she was fully awake again and could enjoy things.

20

Alan had a reply to his email inquiry about seeing Isabella waiting for him when he got home, instructions on bringing a "processing fee" to the real estate office in the morning present. A phone number if he should have questions about anything was also present, one that was different from the number publicly listed for the real estate agency. Nothing about sex was in the message, everything coded in such a way as to allow for deniability should the email be revealed to the public, while still being obvious to someone like him who had a pretty good idea what was going on.

Knowing she would want to hear about it right away, Alan typed up a message for Stacy.

No reply followed, though he wasn't concerned by this, given that she probably was on the road.

Or maybe still in the house? his mind questioned while looking at some of the pictures she had sent him, the last of which had arrived about forty minutes earlier.

Looking through the boxes?

Or going through a desk in a room?

Or a crawl space?

The possibilities were endless, given everything a house like that could contain. He just hoped she didn't lose track of the time and made sure to leave before the guy came home — if it was actually his house.

If not his, then whose?

From everything he had gathered based on what Stacy had said, the location wasn't one that the real estate company owned, which was probably why the girl had been dropped off with the guy rather than being brought to the location herself. The question was why not use one of their own houses? He also wondered if this was common. Did the girls do house calls if the client desired?

Such an option had not been given to him, but then again, he was just getting started. Maybe after presenting his "processing fee" things would be different. Maybe then all the secrets of this thing would be opened to him.

We'll just have to wait and see.

He yawned and then flipped on the TV to see what AMC was showing that evening, his hope for a movie he enjoyed going unfulfilled as he recognized *The Walking Dead*.

Further disappointment was revealed when he checked their website. Nothing that appealed to him was playing until later in the week.

Hoping for something, he went through the channels but once again couldn't find anything that appealed to him, which, given how close it was to Halloween, seemed strange. As a kid, once Halloween was near, it felt as if every station had something creepy playing. Now, they just stuck with their regular programming. It was sad.

Of course, given his vast collection of DVD and VHS films, he had just about everything he wanted to watch within reach. Popping in one of his own movies wasn't appealing though. He wanted to see them on TV, probably because that was how he had originally watched them and wanted to relive the feel. He wanted to be a kid again, sitting on the couch while everyone else was asleep, watching *Friday the 13th* on Joe Bob Briggs' *MonsterVision*, eyes wide with fear, heart racing, and mind wondering a dozen *what-ifs*.

He sighed and tried flipping through the channels once

again, even though he knew nothing was on, finger eventually settling on an all-day news station.

21

"So, let me see if I understand this," Mr. Woodman said while handing her a first-aid ice pack he had had in his trunk. "Emily got a call about doing a scene shortly after you received a call about a same-day addition?"

Amanda nodded, the ice pack held against her right ear, which must have hit the coffee table when she fainted earlier.

"Did you speak to that caller at all?"

She shook her head and then added a weak, "But..."

"But what?" he asked.

She shook her head again. "Never mind, it's nothing."

"I think it's something," he said and then, when she looked away, gently took hold of her chin to turn her face back toward him. "Amanda."

"It's just...my call was from Mrs. Woodman. It was a real client."

"Oh, I know that," Mr. Woodman said. "That young man was pretty anxious to scene with you, but today was the only day that worked for him until next weekend, so we reluctantly gave you the back-to-back setup. Nothing was scheduled for Emily though."

Amanda nodded.

"Something else?"

"Um...no..."

"Amanda," he said.

"It's just, well...I heard the ringtone of the call that came to..." She couldn't say Emily's name. "... *her* and it was the same one that always plays when your...when Mrs. Woodman calls."

Mr. Woodman didn't reply to that right away, his stare forcing her to look away for a moment and then back at him.

"You sure?" he asked.

Amanda nodded.

"Maybe she has that ringtone set as the default for when no other ringtone has been set for the caller?"

"She doesn't," Amanda said, though she wasn't actually certain of this. "And it was Mrs. Woodman for sure because they talked about doing the porn films on Tuesday."

"Porn films?" he asked.

"Yeah," Amanda said, a sudden realization that Mr. Woodman had no idea what she was talking about appearing.

Mr. Woodman thought about that for several seconds and then asked, "You didn't happen to find her phone, did you?"

Amanda shook her head and muttered, "No."

"Okay."

"But I didn't...well...I didn't really look around in that room at all or anything." She looked away while saying this, a sense of shame unfolding at the lack of aid she had tried to give Emily.

But she was dead, her mind said. *There was nothing you could have done to help.*

Still, she should have tried something.

"That's okay," Mr. Woodman said, a hand now caressing her head.

Though it was meant to be a soothing gesture, Amanda was not comforted by it. In fact, she wanted it gone and, after a second, pulled away a bit.

"I'm sure I'll find the phone," Mr. Woodman said, hand returning to his lap. "Now, you said you messaged her a few times, but that she didn't reply at all."

Amanda nodded and then let out a heavy sigh, her body feeling as if it could crumple at any moment due to her exhaustion.

"Okay." He stared at her for a few seconds and then said, "I don't want you trying to drive back by yourself in this state, so I'm going to have Kristi come get you and bring you home."

"Mrs. Woodman?" Amanda asked, not really liking that idea.

"Something wrong?" he asked.

"No." She shook her head. "Nothing. That's fine."

He eyed her for a moment and then said, "If you're uncomfortable with her or know something that you think might upset me, you can tell me. I'd rather know the truth than be stuck believing a lie."

She shook her head again and said, "I just want to get back home and rest."

"I totally understand," he said and then asked if she wanted anything to drink.

"Water," Amanda said.

"Okay."

Relief arrived as he disappeared around the corner but then was quickly dashed when she looked toward the room where Emily was. An image of her body sprawled against the washing machine, head twisted toward the door, appeared.

And then he was back, a bottle of water and a can of Coke in his hand. "Probably best if you have a bit of soda too," he said. "Help get your sugars back up after everything that's happened."

Amanda accepted both, a thought on how the sugar from the Coke was probably a moot point, given all the time that had already passed, going unvoiced.

It tasted good.

While she was sipping the Coke, he called his wife and explained the situation and then listened for several seconds, nodding repeatedly. "Okay," he said at the end. "You're right. That's probably best."

He turned back to Amanda. "I'm actually going to take you back, and she's going to meet us there and then come back here with me."

"Okay."

"So let me just go move my car onto the street, so we can get your car out of the driveway."

Amanda nodded and took another sip of Coke, a second bout of relief arriving at the fact that she wouldn't have to ride with Mrs. Woodman. She wasn't sure why, but something about the boss lady had always rubbed her the wrong way. She just seemed manipulative. Amanda had noticed it about two days after she had finished her withdrawal in their back bedroom, body still weak yet functioning enough to recognize traits within her caregivers. The fact that she sensed resentment leveled her way from Mrs. Woodman added to her discomfort with the lady. It had been obvious from the first interaction between them that Mrs. Woodman did not like her, nor thought much of her. She also hadn't liked it when Mr. Woodman was alone with her and always seemed to find a way of being present when the two were together.

Footsteps echoed outside the door, Mr. Woodman having finished moving the car.

Amanda stood up, ice pack set aside, and quickly grabbed the couch arm as the room spun.

"You okay?" Mr. Woodman asked.

"Fine," she said, a brief memory of the confusion she had felt upon regaining consciousness after fainting—and the dizziness that had followed as she tried to stand—arriving. Once that settled, she reached over for her Coke, took a long swig, and then moved toward the door.

Guilt at leaving while Emily was still in the laundry room unfolded within her, a sense that she was abandoning her friend hard to deny.

She's dead.

Nothing you can do for her.

Neither argument was able to displace the guilt as she sat down on the passenger seat, the relief she felt at being free of the house only making it worse.

A few seconds later, while Mr. Woodman adjusted the seat to fit his larger build, Amanda pulled down the sun visor to look in the vanity mirror, curiosity about whether or not the bump from the coffee table was visible getting the better of her.

The guy that was following us!

She gasped.

"What is it?" Mr. Woodman asked.

"I just remembered something. There was a guy in a car following us from the house, one who actually turned away before we got here, so we both figured it was just a coincidence. Now though...well..." She wasn't sure what else to say. *Could it still have been a coincidence?*

"Would you be able to recognize the driver if you saw him again?"

"Um...I don't know." She took a deep breath. "Emily was the one that actually noticed him and was watching since I was driving."

Now that she was out of the house, saying Emily's name seemed easier for some reason.

"Do you know what kind of car it was?"

"It was red, a...um...Saturn, I—" She gasped as the car came to a sudden stop, seatbelt holding firm as her body tried to slam into the dashboard.

"Sorry," he muttered. "Your brakes are way tighter than mine."

"It's okay." She took a deep breath and then sighed as the seatbelt loosened its hold.

Once an opening appeared, Mr. Woodman turned right onto Army Trail Road and then quickly got over into the left-turn lane.

"You said it was a red Saturn?" he asked while easing the car to a stop at the light.

"Yeah, I think so."

"And it followed you from the house?"

"Yeah." More memories surfaced. "And I might have seen it at one of the houses the other night when doing a scene. I thought he was simply writing down the phone number on the sign, but now…I'm not so sure."

"Would you recognize the car if you saw it again?" he asked.

"I think so."

"Okay. If you see it, call me right away, and if for some reason I don't answer, call Kristi."

Amanda nodded and then said, "I will."

"Okay."

Silence followed, during which Amanda stared out the window, mind once again replaying the moments of confusion as she had awakened upon the floor of the house after fainting. Nothing had made much sense to her during the initial moments of consciousness, but then, as her mind settled, an image of Emily entered her thoughts. Fear came with it, fear that whoever had committed such a heinous act was still present in the house and would do the same to her.

She had to get away.

She had to get into the car and—

Trying to stand had nullified the thoughts of fleeing, her only focus being to stay balanced as the room shifted back and forth. After that, clarity arrived.

No one was in the house.

If they had been, they would have killed her as she lay on the floor, or secured her somehow so she couldn't get away once she did regain consciousness. Neither had happened.

Need to call someone.

Need to tell them about Emily.

"How's Vicky doing?"

The question came out of nowhere and for a moment, she couldn't answer.

"She adjusting to everything?" he added.

"Um…I guess," Amanda said. Hesitation hit. Then, "Honestly, she and I don't really get along all that well."

"Oh, why not?"

She's a little brat. Keeping that to herself, Amanda said, "I'm not really sure. Guess we just don't click." She shrugged.

"Ah, I see," he said. "Well, hopefully things will settle. How did she and Emily get along?"

"I don't really know. I kept my distance."

He nodded.

Questions about the girl, her age, her background, and the type of clients she was seeing bounced around within her mind, the desire for answers helping to keep the thoughts of Emily and her mutilated body at a distance.

Unsure how to proceed with such questions, she simply said, "I saw the marks on her butt and legs from the coat hanger."

No reply.

"How bad was her situation before you rescued her?"

"If you saw the marks and the scars, I think you already have a pretty good idea on that," he said.

Amanda nodded and then when he didn't continue said, "She actually seems proud of them. The marks."

"That's just a defense mechanism." The light changed and he made the left turn. "You see it a lot in girls who have been prostituted out and abused for as long as she has. Or even just with those who have been abused."

"Yeah," Amanda said. She had already known it was a defense mechanism but didn't feel the need to voice it, especially since he wasn't being condescending or anything. "Hard to believe things like that can happen, especially in this day and age."

"Sadly, most people don't believe it can happen, which is why it does. Ignorance of the possibility leads to ignorance of the reality."

They came to a stop at the next light.

Silence arrived once again and stayed with them until the light turned green.

"I'm worried," Amanda said.

"About?" he asked.

"I…" She hesitated, unsure how to explain herself. "I just don't want this all to end, and now with what happened to Emily…" She shook her head.

"Ah, don't worry. We're not going to let anything happen."

"But what about Emily? Won't people wonder what happened to her and eventually figure everything out?"

"Who would? Aside from some of the classes that she almost never actually attended, there really is no real-world connection. She is pretty much off the grid. You all are. The only people who cared about her were you, me, Riley, and a few of the other girls she was roommates with before we moved her into the house you two have been staying in. She had no family, and the guy who used to pimp her…well…he'll probably never again utter her name, let alone inquire about her."

Amanda thought about that, questions on what might have happened to Matt after she was free of him entering her mind yet going unasked. Instead she said, "So she wasn't going to class?"

"Nope."

"Then where did she go when she had class?"

"Don't know. Was kind of hoping you might have an answer. Do you know if she was seeing anyone on the side?"

"No, not really." She considered voicing the suspicions she held but then didn't due to the fear that he might grow upset that she'd never brought it up before. After all, if rules were being broken or were suspected of being broken, they were supposed to say something.

"Okay."

Though she couldn't be sure, Amanda thought she sensed relief in his voice when acknowledging her statement, which seemed odd. Then again, maybe she was simply reading too much into a simple change of tone.

22

"So, how many guys did you fuck today?" Vicky asked once Mr. and Mrs. Woodman had driven away, a Mountain Dew in her hand.

She still wore the yellow dress that Mrs. Woodman had insisted she wear earlier, the innocence it tried to project giving Amanda the creeps.

"One?" Vicky continued. "Two?"

Amanda just stared at her, mind trying to get away from what had happened that afternoon yet not really wanting to jump on the topic of Vicky's scene.

"I fucked and sucked two myself, and it was for a movie. Well, several movies, actually." She took another sip of her soda.

"Wait, what?"

"It was for several little movies," Vicky said in response. "In some I was a little girl who wanted to learn about sex from her daddy. In another a Sunday school teacher was showing me how to clean my body of sin by sucking his penis and smearing the cum all over me. We then did some tied-up stuff where I had been kidnapped by perverts and fucked over and over again on a bed."

Amanda listened to all this, disgust growing.

"The only thing they were upset by," Vicky continued, "was

that I only had one outfit."

"Huh? Why?"

"*Because*," she said, the word coming out like a *duh*, "they didn't want the same dress in all the videos."

"Oh."

"So I think they're going to film me again soon. Especially since they said I'm like one of the best kids they ever worked with."

One of the best kids!

"The only thing they said is that I totally need to work on making it look like I'm not enjoying myself during the kidnap and rape videos." She took another sip. "It was funny because they said if I couldn't make it look like I was horrified by what was happening, they'd do a scene where I was fucked in the butt by a big cock. Guess they don't know that I've done that like a gazillion times."

She took a final sip of her Mountain Dew and set the empty can on the counter.

"You know, when they first took me from my mom, I didn't realize I'd be doing movies and things. It's pretty cool." She wiped at her mouth. "Do you think that's what they took me for, or am I going to be seeing guys too like you and Emily?"

"I don't—" Amanda started.

"Hey, where is Emily? I really want to tell her about the movies."

"Um...she...um...Emily..." She shook her head, unsure how to tell the teen that Emily was dead.

Vicky, however, seemed to sense what Amanda was trying to say and said, "Oh no, what happened?" while putting a hand to her mouth.

Amanda told her and then watched as the girl completely broke, the sadness that overwhelmed her something that she had not expected at all. Equally unexpected was the sudden embrace that Vicky required, her body nearly knocking Amanda over as the young girl plowed into her, arms out, seeking comfort.

23

He heard the buzz in his sleep and slowly opened his eyes, ears catching the menu music for the season two *X-Files* DVD he had put in while going to bed.

On his phone, a notification light was blinking.

He reached over and grabbed it.

Stacy had finally replied to his earlier inquiry on whether or not she was okay.

SORRY, PHONE WAS DEAD, the message read. BUT ALL IS WELL. GOOD JOB WITH THE GIRL. THAT'LL BE FUN. TTYL <3

Relief arrived.

Not long after that, the *X-Files* episode playing again, he was asleep, the images that played across his mind an odd mix that he wouldn't remember upon waking.

Monday

October 28, 2013

1

Stacy awoke thinking she had slept on her hands, the numbness similar to the type she often felt after having zonked out while watching TV on the couch, hands cradling her head. In reality, her hands were bound behind her back with thin cords of rope, a fact that became known when she tried to shift herself.

Panic arrived.

She tried to scream but couldn't due to the cloth that had been balled up in her mouth, which now threatened to tickle her tonsils and cause her to gag. Tape also sealed her lips, thus making it impossible for her to push the cloth free.

Something was playing in the other room, something with the sounds of sex. Hearing that, she remembered the man that had come here after the men had finished up with the girl, and how she had gotten slammed up against the door while trying to flee.

Panic growing, she shifted again, her body trying to figure out a way of freeing her hands.

Springs within the bed squealed.

The sound in the other room stopped.

Fuck!

She stayed still while he listened, her hope being that he would ignore the sound and go back to watching his TV.

Footsteps echoed.

"Awww, did someone finally wake up?" a voice questioned from the hallway.

The door opened slowly, the darkness of the room retreating as light from beyond eased its way in.

Stacy closed her eyes, feigning sleep.

The guy chuckled and then flipped on the room light, the brightness of which she could see beyond her lids.

"You're not sleeping," he said.

She waited, eyes still closed.

And then she couldn't breathe, his fingers pinching her nostrils shut.

Eyes wide, she struggled against him while trying to suck in a breath with her mouth. Cloth went down her throat.

A heavy gag followed.

He laughed again and then released her nose so she could breathe—only her body didn't acknowledge the release right away and still struggled against the cloth and tape.

Seemingly unfazed by her panic and the fact that she could die if she did end up vomiting while gagged like this, the man took a seat on the bed next to her and began to fondle her breasts.

"I made some calls about you while you were sleeping," he said, hand finding the bottom of her sweatshirt and slipping up inside. A second later, it was gently caressing the fabric of her bra, fingers trying to firm up her nipple. "Read some of your articles too."

Despite her disgust, the nipple he was toying with did firm up, the pleasurable tingle she felt when his fingertip made circles around the base horrifying.

"Robert's a bit worried and has some questions for you, but he won't be here until morning." He continued making circles around the nipple and then, after a few seconds, moved over to the other one. "I'm not worried at all though. If you were part of something official, or if anyone knew what you were up to, your backup would have had police here by now."

The other nipple became erect.

"Oh, and I let your friend Alan know that you were okay, since he was asking." He grinned. "What're you two, like boyfriend girlfriend or something?"

She just stared at him.

"You two sure text a lot, only he wanted to let you know that he was going to be seeing some girl, so I don't know."

Alan had been approved.

Learning this should have been a monumental moment, but now, obviously, it didn't really matter.

Nothing did.

"Anyway, if he somehow knows where you are, it'll be a while before he comes to see if you're still here, and by then, Robert will have learned what he needs to know and figured out what to do with you, and I'll be back home, so until then, let us enjoy this short period of time we have together." He punctuated the statement by ripping free the bra beneath her sweatshirt, the fabric digging into her flesh before snapping free.

She then watched in horror as he got off the bed and took off his boxer shorts, penis protruding outward from the tangled jungle of sweaty pubic hair.

"Like what you see?" he asked.

She turned her head away from him.

"Oh no you don't," he said and stepped close so he could grab her hair and twist her face back around. Then, holding her face in place, he rubbed his penis against her cheek, pre-cum clinging to her flesh. "Ah, yes, you like that, don't you?"

She tried pulling away again, which resulted in him force-fully lifting her up from the bed by her hair into a sitting position and then slapping her across the face, hard.

The gag muffled her cry.

He let her fall back down and went to undo her pants, her feet catching him off guard as she kicked out at him, heel slamming him in the forearm.

"Bitch!" he cried.

She waited for another attempt at her pants, her hope being to get him in the testicles this time.

He stayed where he was, eyes glaring at her.

She glared back.

He licked his lips and then said, "You do that again, and I'll make you pay for it."

Had she been able to reply, she would have told him to go fuck himself. At least, this was what she visualized herself doing, a visualization that was attempting to keep her fear at bay.

He's going to fuck you.

And then that Robert guy is probably going to kill you.

The two thoughts, which were completely unwelcome, chilled her.

And then the first became realized, his movement toward her so fast that she didn't even get a chance to strike, his hands pulling her pants free with a roughness that once again caused fabric to dig in before tearing.

No! No! No!

Her panties were next, his hands ripping them from her body as if they were made of tissue paper.

And then...

In reality, it didn't last long, but in her mind, it was an eternity, the pressure of his overweight body squishing her into the bed and causing her bound hands to scream, while his midsection squirmed against her, his penis poking in and out with tiny thrusts, given his inability to properly flex himself back and forth.

His ejaculation arrived with a snort and then, once his composure was regained, he stood up upon shaking legs and used what was left of her panties to clean himself off, his fingers at one point squeezing a glob of semen onto his hand so that he could wipe it on her face.

She did not resist the action.

In fact, she didn't move at all, the shock of what had just transpired too much for her mind to process.

2

"Morning!"

Alan jumped, coffee sloshing all over his hand, which then caused him to try to jerk his hand away from the heat, which only caused more to slosh out upon him.

He swore while dropping the cup in the sink.

"Oh, honey, I'm sorry," his mother said. "Here, put it under the water."

"I got it," he snapped, blocking her from the sink and turning the water on with his left hand while his right went under the faucet.

"Remember, not too cold," she said. "Room temp is the best for—"

"Mom, please!"

She stopped and simply stood there for a second and then, needing something to do so she didn't feel helpless, grabbed some paper towels to soak up the coffee that had spilled.

"You scared me," Alan said, stating the obvious, hand turning off the water.

"Are you sure that was long enough?" she asked, soiled towels in hand.

"It wasn't bad. I think the creamer probably cooled it down." He shook his hand dry and reached for the coffee mug.

"I'm sorry. I thought you knew I was there," she said. "Normally you do."

"Yeah, I'm still half asleep and totally lost in thought."

"Oh," she uttered with a nod, lips squeezed tight against her desire to ask him what the thought had been. A yawn followed, one that he mirrored.

He fixed himself a new cup of coffee and then held the carafe out so he could pour some for her. Seeing this, she quickly got herself a mug and let him fill it.

"Thank you," she said, taking a sip.

Alan took a tiny sip himself, taste buds checking to make sure his ratio of cream to coffee was correct.

"So, why're you so tired?" she asked.

He shrugged and while yawning said, "Don't know."

"Was your stomach bad?"

"No, I slept the entire night, so…" He shrugged a second time. "Just a long weekend, I guess."

She thought about this. "Okay, well, I'm going to go take a shower. What time you leaving for class, seven forty?"

"Yeah."

"Okay," she said again, nodding, and turned to leave the kitchen. Then she stopped and asked, "Hey, will you be home for dinner?"

"Um…don't know." He thought about the trip to the real estate office and how afterward he would probably meet up with Stacy to fill her in on what that process had been like. "I'll let you know later once I know for sure."

"Hmm, okay."

He went downstairs but then came back up about seven minutes later to get a second cup of coffee. His mother was in the shower by then, so it was a quick trip, one that carried with it thoughts of Stacy and his newfound concern over the text she had sent him last night. He hadn't realized it at the time, probably due to being half asleep, but the text did not sound like her at all, especially the TTYL <3 part.

3

Amanda didn't really feel like going to class that morning but knew it would be better than sitting at home, mind dwelling upon what had happened. In fact, the idea of getting out and waiting in the quiet morning hallways was so appealing that she actually left early.

The one downside was leaving Vicky to wake up all alone. Hopefully, the girl would remember that Amanda had class and that her being gone didn't mean anything sinister had happened.

A couple chairs were actually sitting in the hallway outside the classroom, something that happened from time to time.

Amanda took one and waited, eyes closed as she relished the calmness. It was nice...for a moment...her mind betraying the peacefulness by bringing about a memory of finding Emily.

Sadness hit, again.

Last night, while in bed, she had cried, the emotions coming on without warning.

Now it happened again.

She wiped her eyes, clearing them of the moisture that threatened to fall.

Coming here was a bad idea, she said, a sudden fear that she would break down in the middle of class arriving. *Should have just stayed home.*

No, coming here is better.

Once class starts, it will take your mind off it.

She wiped her eyes again and then, having felt some tears actually fall, rubbed her cheek, sleeve trying to soak up the moisture before it left the white salty residue upon her skin.

"You okay?" a voice asked.

She looked up and saw a young man from her class, his approach having gone unnoticed.

"Yeah, I'm okay," she said and wiped at her face. She then gave him a smile.

His face changed, almost as if her smile had startled him, and then went back to that of a concerned classmate, one who she knew was always quiet and seemingly self-absorbed.

He took a seat across from her.

"You were in the army?" she asked, unsure why she was trying to engage him. Something about the look he had given her brought it about.

"What?" he asked, puzzled, and then, without needing to be directed to it, looked down at his sweatshirt, which read US ARMY across the chest. "Oh right, yes, I was." He let out a weak chuckle. "Caught me off guard for a moment."

"Oops, my bad."

"No worries." He smiled.

"How long were you in?" she asked.

"Just over ten years."

"Really? Ten years! Wow!" He didn't look old enough to have been in for ten years, even with the two- to three-day stubble that covered his chin and cheeks. "I would never have guessed that."

"How come?" he asked, an inquisitive smile distorting his face.

"I don't know," she said and then hesitated. "I guess, well…this is going to come out wrong, so please don't be offended, but, well, you just don't carry that military vibe."

He laughed.

She waited and then when no reply followed said, "I really hope that wasn't disrespectful or anything."

"Oh, no, don't worry. I didn't look like the military type even when in the military, so…" He held up his hands in an "it is what it is" gesture and then let them fall. "By the way, I'm Alan."

"Amanda," she said.

He nodded and then checked something on his phone while two girls walked by. By the time they passed, he returned his attention to her, the phone tucked away, and asked, "So, Amanda, what do you do when not a student?"

"What do you mean?" she asked.

"Are you a full-time student that just goes to school, or do you work too?"

"Oh, I work too. Can't afford not too, it seems." She let out a fake laugh. "Just the book for this class would have wiped out my savings if I had to rely on that."

"Tell me about it," he said. "And of course they didn't have any used ones we could buy since we needed the new updated edition."

"Right!" Amanda cried. "I was literally speechless when I saw the price appear on the display screen in the bookstore. I had a brand-new math book too, and it was almost three hundred dollars!"

"And even if you keep it in perfect condition, they'll only give you like thirty dollars, if that, when you try to sell it back, yet they will sell it themselves next semester for around two hundred. It's ridiculous."

A few more students walked by, many of them arriving for an eight o'clock class two doors down. As far as the earth science class went, she and Alan were the only two waiting thus far.

"Maybe I'll just hang on to them," Amanda said. "I have some friends that will probably take this and the math class soon, so I can pass the books on to them."

"Yeah, if a new slightly updated edition isn't required by then," Alan said. "So, what is it you do when not in class?"

She eyed him for a moment, a question about why he was so interested entering her mind.

Hope he isn't trying to work in a proposal to start dating or something.

Though he is cute…

"I'm in real estate," she said.

"Ohhh, cool," he said. "Sounds like a good job for a college student, what with classes and being able to set up your own appointments."

"Yeah," Amanda said. "Well, my boss sets up my appointments, but she knows my schedule, so nothing ever overlaps."

"That's good."

Mentioning Mrs. Woodman brought to mind the phone call Emily had received yesterday and the question of whether or not it had really been their boss on the phone fixing that last-minute scene change.

Two more students walked up and waited by the door, each one kind of nodding to them before finding a spot to lean against the wall. A few seconds later, a third student appeared and took the seat next to Amanda, a statement on how it was *"way too early to be up"* leaving her lips.

No one replied.

Amanda checked the time on her phone and saw that class was supposed to start in two minutes, yet the professor wasn't even there yet.

More students arrived, none of them really saying much.

And then the professor showed up, a question about how everyone's weekend was leaving her lips as she unlocked the door.

A few students voiced replies.

Amanda did not.

Alan stayed quiet as well, his attention once again on his phone.

Something about him…

Amanda couldn't put her finger on it but knew something

was there. Whatever it was, however, had decided to stay hidden within her mind for the moment.

4

"Go ahead," Alan said as Amanda walked up to the door, his hand motioning her to go first.

"Thanks," she said with an awkward smile and stepped into the classroom, feet taking her to a spot on the left side near the weather and volcano posters.

Alan followed for a moment, his own feet taking him to his typical back-row seat, one that would allow him easy access to the door should his bowels decide to act up. He also didn't like having anyone behind him ever, his eyes always wanting to see what was going on with the people in his vicinity.

Though it was two minutes past the start time, the professor didn't get the class going right away, a comment on how it was Monday and some were probably running a bit late being voiced.

Alan didn't mind the delay and used it to type up a message to Stacy, his amazement that he had been sharing a class with one of the girls they had been watching hard to shake. He had to tell someone, and she was really the only one to tell.

After that, he checked the picture he had saved from the real estate site once again, one that he had actually looked at briefly while talking to Amanda in the hallway, her weak smile while crying having triggered the sudden recognition.

Disbelief arrived.

Not at the fact that she was one of the girls, since that was now undeniable, but at how the two had been crossing paths every Monday and Wednesday since late August. It was unreal.

Three students hurried into the class, relief washing over them when they realized it hadn't started yet.

Alan looked at his phone, concern over the lack of a reply

from Stacy arriving. That plus the oddity of the message she had sent last night had him worried.

Did something happen?

Did someone come back to the house while she was inside, someone who then sent a message to him with her phone to make him think everything was okay?

The more he thought about it, the more likely that scenario became.

Frustration and fear arrived, the former toward himself for not realizing how *off* the message had sounded when it arrived, the latter toward what might have happened to her between then and now.

Could still be happening…

Jesus Christ, what if she told them all about him, not just who he was but where he lived…

The fact that they could plainly see he was involved by the texts he had sent talking about the girls and setting up cameras in the location she was at would give them prompting for such questions, and once they started to inflict pain, she would talk.

"Okay, let's get started," the professor said.

Shit, what do I do?

A part of him didn't want to sit there listening to a lecture, not when he knew Stacy was probably suffering, but another part of him didn't really know what he could do even if he were free. It wasn't like she had told him where she was, just that she had followed the guy and girl to a house in Joliet.

"How many of you have ever visited Yellowstone?" the professor asked, the question leading into a discussion on super volcanoes.

5

Stacy was still in a state of shock when the man entered the room during the midmorning hours, his body odor the first thing her mind really processed as it tried to focus on the moment rather than what had happened.

He didn't say anything at first, his eyes gazing upon her body, starting with her face, which brought about a tiny grin, and then down to the nakedness beneath her sweatshirt, which brought a huge smile.

"I enjoyed myself last night," he said. "Your warm juicy pussy felt so great around my hard blood-filled cock."

Stacy felt tears in her eyes and suddenly wanted to vomit.

"I wish Robert and his crew had left their camera stuff yesterday." He stepped forward and took a seat next to her, springs squealing, his hand caressing her bare leg. "We could have captured the beautiful moment on video so that we could enjoy the connection over and over again for years to come."

Gooseflesh sprang up upon her leg where he touched it, followed by a knee-jerk twitch as her leg tried to get away from him.

"Well, *I* could enjoy it for years to come," he corrected, seemingly unfazed by her attempts to get her legs away from him. "After this morning, Robert may not let me keep you, and even if he does, I know it won't be a long-term thing."

The pressure on her leg grew more pronounced as his caressing became more aggressive, and then his hand shifted to the area between her legs, fingers struggling to get into the opening as she squeezed her thighs shut.

"*No!*" she screamed, the sound audible beyond the gag, and while it might not have been recognizable as an actual word, anyone with sense would know what it meant.

He didn't or just didn't care, his hands getting more and more forceful as she fought him until he had had enough and flipped her down onto her stomach, one hand pressing down on her leg while the other looped a cord around her ankle.

Thin rope tore into her skin as she fought against the restraint, anger at herself for not trying to escape during the night when she had simply been tied on the bed, not to it, entering her thoughts.

And then those thoughts went away as he climbed up on top of her, his hands reaching under her stomach to lift her body up into a bent-over position, her face pressed into the mattress as it supported the upper part of her body.

Though numb and nearly useless from being bound all night long, Stacy tried to grab hold of him with her hands, her hope being to pulp his testicles with a fist.

Instead, all she managed to do was grab part of her own sweatshirt, fingers barely even able to hold on to that, let alone squeeze anything.

His penis poked her, first on the right side of her inner thigh, then the left, then in the space between the two holes before finding the opening and thrusting in, a cry of, *"Oh yeah, baby!"* echoing from his lips.

Stacy screamed against the gag, something that he probably interpreted as a cry of pleasure, all while tears sprang from her eyes.

Springs squealed as the thrusting took on rhythm, his grunts clubbing her eardrums while his dirty hands pulled her body into his own over and over again, the stench of his body engulfing them.

And then he came, his semen shooting up into her body with one final thrust, his fingers pressed into her flesh as he held her tight.

The smell of his ejaculate mixed with his body odor.

"Wow," he mumbled softly as he released her, his own body oozing forward so that he could lie next to her, an arm coming to rest upon her shoulders as she slid back into a facedown, lying on her check and stomach position. "That was the most amazing fuck ever, even better than last night."

Tears, which had been falling the entire time, grew in their intensity, the mattress beneath her eyes completely soaked by the time they dried up.

And then there was a knock on the front door, one that caused her captor to jump up and fumble around for his pants, statements of *"Shit! Shit! Shit!"* echoing.

Stacy twisted herself as he left the room, body managing to get up onto her left side so that she was no longer facedown.

"Hey, Robert, my man, what's happening?" her captor said.

"Where is she?" Robert said.

"Back bedroom, resting."

Footsteps echoed.

"Want anything to drink? Got stuff in the—"

"No."

The door opened, the man she had followed the day before stepping in.

"Jesus," he muttered, a grimace at the smell distorting his face. He then turned to her captor and said, "I can't do this in here. Bring her downstairs."

6

Amanda saw that she had missed a call from Mrs. Woodman while on break, the silent mode she had put the phone on during the lecture having kept her unaware of the call attempt until she gave it a quick glance while in the bathroom.

Why would she call?

She knows I have class this morning.

Concerned, Amanda headed over to an area that wasn't populated with loitering students and called Mrs. Woodman back, an apology for missing the call leaving her lips along with a statement on being in class.

"Just wanted to make you aware that I have you down for a

scene tomorrow afternoon with Caroline and Isabella," Mrs. Woodman said. "They'll pick you up since they have to come your way anyway."

The film that Emily was supposed to do!

"Is that for the porn video?" Amanda asked.

"Um…yes," Mrs. Woodman said. It was the first time Amanda had ever heard her stumble over words, almost as if she had been startled by the question. "Did one of them already call you?"

"Emily told me about it after you called yesterday," Amanda said. *And then I told your husband, who seemed surprised by the videos.*

For a moment, nothing but the sounds of breathing on the other end could be heard, and then, "I see. Well, then you already know what to expect."

"I do, and…" She hesitated. "I really can't do that scene."

"Excuse me?" Mrs. Woodman questioned, voice changing a bit to one that sounded on the verge of an outburst.

"Sorry, I can't do that scene," Amanda repeated. "I really can't do work like that, not with the career field I'm hoping to enter once I'm finished with college." She tried sounding professional with her statement and, thankfully, managed to keep the anxiety she felt at saying *no* out of her voice.

"College that we're paying for," Mrs. Woodman said.

"Um…yeah," Amanda said, eyes looking at the clock and realizing she was going to be missing some of that "college that they paid for" if she didn't get back into her class soon. "So, as you yourself told me, we can get a good foundation under us and make something of our lives."

Mrs. Woodman snorted and then said, "You can't refuse an assignment."

"But starring in porn wasn't what I signed up for." Anxiety

was present this time, hand threatening to shake.

"You signed up to fuck guys for pay, something that is illegal, but won't fuck guys for pay in front of a camera, which is legal?"

"Something that might haunt me for the rest of my life and make it so I can't get a job working with kids who've been abused."

"You actually think you'll make it through school and work such a job?" Mrs. Woodman snapped, voice so loud that it echoed from the phone. *"You're a whore, nothing more, and always will be."*

Startled, Amanda didn't know how to reply.

"And one who is on the verge of losing the best gig she could ever hope to get," Mrs. Woodman continued.

"But—" Amanda started, lip quivering.

"I'll give you till noon to decide what you want to do." *Click!*

Amanda stared at the phone, horrified, and then, without warning, burst into tears, a blind dash to the restroom occurring as she tried to shield her face from anyone who happened to look her way.

7

For the first time ever, Alan skipped out on a class, a decision to leave during the break having arrived shortly after it began, given that he was unable to focus on anything the professor was saying.

Of course, visualizing himself doing something to help Stacy—if she was actually in trouble—was easier than doing it for real, uncertainty about what he should or even could do getting the better of him once he was in the car.

Check her apartment.

See if anything is amiss.

All his concerns had been focused on her having been interrupted while at the house down in Joliet, but really, something could have happened at her place. That was, after all, the location of the first attack, so...

In his mind, he pictured her body sprawled upon the floor, blood having oozed out from various wounds, but then shook the thought away, a realization unfolding that he probably wouldn't have received any messages from someone using her phone if he had simply killed her. Why try to make it seem like she was okay if she was dead? It didn't make sense. Such tactics would only be used if someone wanted to hide the fact that she was alive and in trouble.

Unless they're crazy.

Rules of logic didn't really apply once the "C" word came into play.

But are they crazy?

Everything seemed too well calculated.

Of course, thinking things through to the best outcome didn't necessarily nullify the possibility that they were crazy, but it made it far more likely that the craziness would be more like an undercurrent than a tidal wave. Both were dangerous and destructive, but at least with a tidal wave one could see it coming and run. With an undercurrent, one might not notice it until it was too late.

In the end, he decided to check her place, mostly so he could confirm she wasn't there. After that, if he couldn't figure out anything to go on in a timely manner, he would give the police a call and let them know what had happened.

8

Stacy wanted to make a break for it once her legs were released but didn't get the chance, her actions somehow anticipated and prevented by a hand that instantly grabbed her hair the moment her legs were free.

With that, she was pulled from the bed, her feet barely getting hold of the floor, and marched toward the cellar door, legs threatening to give out due to a numbness that quickly spread throughout both.

"Don't even try it," he laughed when she did finally stumble, a yank on her hair to keep her upright forcing a scream against the gag. "You're not gonna fool me."

The next stumble elicited the same type of response, minus the words, followed by a second grip on her arms as he marched her down the stairs.

Robert was waiting at the bottom.

"Okay, I got her from here," Robert said, taking hold of her shirtfront. "Go visit your mother and I'll call you when I'm done."

"But I wanna help," he said.

"No."

"Why not?"

"I said NO!"

Her captor mumbled something that sounded like "no fair" under his breath and headed back up the stairs, door slamming in frustration once he was beyond it.

"Fucking retard," Robert said and walked her over to the mattress in the corner. "Sit down."

Stacy did, angry at herself for complying so easily. Oddly enough, fear wasn't really present, her mind thinking the worst of the worst had already happened—twice.

"His mom still owns this place even though she's in some sort of assisted living community type of apartment complex, and he managed to get her to name him the legal resident, sort of like a caretaker, not that he gives the place any care as you can probably see." He shook his head. "I do most of the cleaning myself when I'm not pressed for time. And all these mannequins that he dresses up and takes pictures of…I just don't know."

The simple statement, as if the two were on equal footing in a break room or something, caught her off guard.

"He isn't actually retarded though, at least not in the clinical sense." He opened a duffel bag that Stacy hadn't noticed, one that had been set atop a stack of boxes so that it was easy to reach into. "He's just...well...odd." He pulled out a coil of rope and set it down, followed by a knife secured in a sheath. "You should hear him go on and on about how he was *discovered* by a *Hollywood talent scout* while going door-to-door selling magazines for his junior high school and auditioned right in the man's basement." He shook his head. "And he doesn't really seem to be able to think, if that makes sense." Another object came out of the bag, one that he clicked to bring about a flame, which resulted in a nod of satisfaction. "It's more like he simply does stuff, as if driven by pure instinct."

Having seen the knife and lighter, Stacy no longer really processed his words and instead felt a growing sense of terror, one that made her rethink her earlier thought on how the worst had already happened.

"He has actually cut holes in some of the mannequins, though I'm not sure if he goes so far as to fuck them himself." A pair of pliers came out. "Most of the time he just has them fucking each other when not forcing kids on them."

Stacy shifted her gaze toward the mannequin with the dildo but didn't really focus on it, her eyes only wanting to see what was being pulled from the bag.

A roll of duct tape came next.

"All right," Robert said. "I think that's all we really need to get started. Let's get that tape off so we can have us a little talk."

The gentleness of his words were not mirrored by the force he used to pull the tape off her mouth, her lips feeling as if an entire layer of flesh had been ripped free.

He then pulled out the cloth that had been balled up, looked at it for a moment, and said, "Ah, Vicky's panties from yesterday. She must've forgotten them somehow." He held them up for her to see. "Mickey Mouse." He shook his head. "Is it just me, or do you think Kristi Woodman was trying way too hard to give her a little girl feel?"

Stacy didn't reply.

He waited and then turned back to the bag and said, "Oops, forgot the clippers." He pulled them free and showed them to her. "Bought them for my wife last year when she was in her 'I'm going to grow us fresh veggies' phase, but I don't think she ever used them." He set them down next to the other items he had pulled free and turned back to her. "I'm really hoping you and I can talk freely without my having to use all this stuff."

Stacy shivered.

"I'm not, by nature, a violent person..." He paused and looked up at an angle for a moment. "Or maybe by nature I am a violent person but am able to suppress it." He shook his head. "I don't know. Nature and nurture debates can go on forever. Anyway, I don't really like violence or hurting people, especially women, so if you can simply answer my questions without giving me a hard time, we'll both be much happier in the end. Okay?"

Stacy nodded.

"Wonderful. I'm happy to hear that. So, from what I understand, you're a reporter that's looking into Kristi's little escort business, which, sadly, has led you into my little video business?"

Stacy didn't say anything.

"Oh, Stacy, I thought we had an understanding here." Leaving his tools where they sat, he took a few steps toward her. "I have all day and, as much as I dislike being here in this filth-ridden child molestation pad, I have no problem stringing you up by your wrists for an hour or two while I go upstairs and read the book I brought. With your hands behind your back and all your body weight held by them, you'll be in agony for every second of the ordeal, one which I will film as well so I can sell it to my snuff fans."

He waited.

She still didn't say anything.

"Okay, very well." He turned and went for the coil of rope he had brought.

Tell him! she thought, mind wondering what the point of being silent was, especially after saying she would tell him what he wanted to know. *You already gave into your fear and—*

"Yes, I'm a reporter, and yes, I'm looking into the escort thing with the real estate girls, which has led me here."

"Ah, thank you for confirming that." He grabbed the coil of rope. "Unfortunately, if you're stubborn with that simple introductory question, I'm thinking you're going to be even more stubborn with the real ones, so…"

He grabbed her by the shoulder and twisted her so that she was facedown on the mattress, the force of his actions so startling after how gentle his voice had been that she cried out in surprise rather than anger.

She then fought against him, trying to squirm out of his grip so he couldn't connect the rope to her bound wrists.

A knee in her back put an end to her struggles.

Once the second rope was secured, the knee went away.

A moment later, she heard the sound of a step stool moving across the concrete, which he positioned close to her so he could thread the rope through the cross beams in the ceiling.

She shifted a bit to watch.

Do it, her mind cried as he climbed to the top of the stool, hand reaching up to thread the rope.

Her heel kicked the stool perfectly, a cry of fury echoing from her lips, and while the force wasn't enough to topple the stool, his reaction to the kick worked to her advantage as he shifted himself in anticipation of it toppling.

A second cry left her lips, this one as her shoulders were

yanked upward, the man actually holding the rope as the step stool collapsed, his own scream mixing with hers to create a horrific echo.

Fortunately, his grip only held for a moment, her shoulders relieved of the tension, allowing her to fall back onto the mattress.

Another scream left his lips, one that was muffled by the sounds of the step stool and his body hitting the concrete at the same time.

Unsure what type of damage was done from the fall, Stacy quickly pushed herself from the mattress into a sitting position and then attempted to bounce herself onto her feet, only to fall back onto her arms, a spring in the mattress catching and tearing her left hand.

Gritting her teeth, she rolled herself onto her knees and then up onto her feet, eyes watching Robert as he clutched at his leg, which looked as if it had folded at a bad angle.

Get the knife!

She was halfway to it when her arms were pulled back and her body forced to stop, Robert having managed to grab the rope end that still dangled down from the beams above.

He pulled.

Stacy screamed.

His position wasn't one that would allow him the leverage to yank her off her feet, but that would change as soon as he got back on his, so rather than allowing him to get the upper hand again, she ran toward him and kicked him as hard as she could in the face, her toenail actually nailing him square in the eye, the delicate ball of tissue deflating as the jagged edge of her nail pierced it.

The most wretched scream she had ever heard left his lips, one that was, to her relief, muffled a bit by his hands as they went up to grab his face.

Get the knife.

She did and then, once the blade was free of the sheath, struggled to find a way to cut the thin cords that bound her wrists while leaving the flesh around them intact.

9

As expected, Stacy wasn't at her place. In fact, no one was at any of the apartments, the parking lot completely empty.

Seeing this, Alan almost didn't even bother going up to her door, but then, thinking that maybe there was some clue inside if she had been taken from this place (or her body), he parked and went up. After all, if they were sending him texts as if she were okay, why not take the car as well to make it look like she had gone somewhere.

Feels empty, he noted while at the door.

He tried the knob.

It was locked.

He jiggled it a bit to see if it would open, the gap between the frame and door edge, added to the fact that someone had been waiting inside the other day, making him think the place was fairly easy to get into.

It didn't open.

He pulled out a credit card, looked around a bit to make sure no one was watching, and slipped it into the door.

Nothing.

Five attempts later, the door was still locked, and his credit card had a busted-up edge where he had continued to jab at the lock.

And here Stacy said it was easy.

He sighed.

Now what?

No answer arrived.

One thing he did know: standing at her door would get him nowhere, so he went back down to his car.

Sitting at home will accomplish just as much.

Head over to the real estate office?

Probably should get money first.

He had no idea how much a "processing fee" would cost but figured it would be pretty substantial. He also knew that setting up such a thing, and therefore having hard evidence of the prostitution gig before he got the police involved, would be better than simply calling them now and hoping they would be able to piece things together from what he had so far.

Might even be able to find out the address she went to, he said to himself but then remembered something Stacy had said about how it didn't seem to be one of the real estate places.

He sighed.

I'm stuck.

The police were his only option.

They had the manpower and resources necessary when it came to finding a missing person. He did not.

But they don't always find them.

Especially when there is so little to go on.

10

Stacy ended up creating a disturbing display in her attempt to free her wrists, the knife handle fitting perfectly within one of the mannequin pubic holes Robert had mentioned, a masturbation fleshlight inside to hold the handle, blade twisted upward so that she could slice away the thin strands of rope.

It worked, the only damage to her wrists being from the ropes that had secured them all night long.

Robert lay on the ground still, hands holding his face, a pathetic wet sobbing type of sound slipping from him.

"Hey," she snapped, foot nudging him, knife held ready, fingers secure around its handle despite the numbness that still plagued her hand, the holding of an object actually seeming to help keep the pins-and-needles sensation at bay.

He pulled away from her, his movement revealing a stain of smeared goo where chunks had been pulled free as she removed her toe from his eye socket, one tiny strand still holding a piece of what had been the cornea.

Stacy took a deep breath and then, letting her anger and hatred get the better of her, kicked him in the chest several times while shouting for him to get up.

He screamed and tried crawling away from her, one hand still covering his eye while the other pulled him across the floor.

Stacy watched this, a debate unfolding within on what to do, the desire to kill him for what had happened to her last night and this morning hard to resist.

Cut off his penis!

No.

Such a horrific act would be better suited for "the retard" as Robert had called him, whom she could hopefully catch unaware upon his return later. With Robert, she wanted answers.

And her phone.

Does he have it?

No answer arrived, not in her mind, nor from his mouth after several more kicks tried to bring the information forth.

Gotta do better.

Kicking him is so… She didn't know what it was, but it didn't seem very effective.

She went to the duffel bag and found a pair of handcuffs in the side pocket along with a key.

"Hey," she said again, handcuffs in one hand, knife in the other. "Look at me."

He did, hand still covering half his face.

"Crawl over to the post by the stairs, and lock your hands behind your back." She tossed the handcuffs toward the post and watched as they skidded across the floor.

He did as instructed, much to her surprise, the satisfying sound of the handcuffs clicking shut reaching her ears.

Once that was done, she set the knife down so she could look through the entire bag, hoping to see the phone tucked away somewhere amid all the horrific items he had brought along to extract information.

Nothing.

She turned back toward Robert, his body sitting against the post, ruined face hard to look at now that it was fully displayed.

"Where's my phone?"

"Rusty probably has it," Robert said, a sense of defeat present within his words. "He likes keeping souvenirs."

"And he's waiting for you to call?"

He shrugged. "Maybe, or he might come back on his own. Probably all depends on if his mother made him anything for lunch."

His mother. Cooking lunch for him like a little kid after everything he had done to her this morning.

Anger flared.

She took a deep breath and then asked, "What's her role in all this?"

"I told you, she owns the place."

"And what, rents it out to perverts like you to film child porn?"

"She doesn't know the details, and Rusty's too dumb to realize there's anything wrong with what we do."

"But not you," she said, moving closer. "You know it's wrong."

He shrugged. "I'm just a producer filling a niche that will always have a demand for content. If they don't buy my videos, they'll buy others."

She remembered how he had stepped outside yesterday while the sex was taking place and wondered if he ever took part in the sex or simply filmed it.

Does it matter?

No.

"The men that were here with you, who are they?"

"My cameraman and a guy with a huge dick who's so obsessed with sex that he'll fuck any girl I find for free, just as long as his face isn't showing."

Stacy nodded, which caused the room to tilt a bit, a realization that she hadn't had anything to eat or drink in over twenty-four hours unfolding.

Deep breath.

"Would it be too much to ask for you to put a cigarette in my mouth?" he requested.

The question caught her off guard.

"The pack and my lighter are in my coat pocket over there." He needlessly tried to point toward the boxes with a shoulder.

"Only if you tell me about Kristi and the girls," Stacy said.

"What do you want to know?" he asked.

"What is your connection? How did you come to work with her and that young girl?"

"I asked her," he said.

"You what?"

"I went to her office, told her who I was and what I did, and asked her if I could film her girls, specifically any of the children she and her husband had taken." He shrugged and then winced. "I could really use that cigarette now."

Stacy walked over to his jacket and found the pack with the lighter. Once it was in hand, she walked halfway across the room and then stopped. "How did you find out about her girls?"

"A friend of a friend," he said, eye following the pack. "It's no secret what they do, at least not with the people I know, and shit, her husband pretty much advertises their services with everyone he ever arrested while working vice."

Stacy didn't reply.

"What, you didn't know her husband was once a cop?" Robert asked, an odd grin appearing.

Not liking that he had caught her off guard like that, Stacy pulled a cigarette from the pack and lit it, the memories of smoking during her younger days returning full force, as did that indescribable moment of bliss that always arrived with the first puff.

And then her lungs rebelled, eyes watering as the organs panicked.

She tried to hide the discomfort but couldn't and eventually coughed up the mouthful of smoke she had inhaled.

Without warning, Robert sprang up from the floor and charged her, his hands having never been cuffed.

Twisting, Stacy dropped the cigarette pack and shifted the knife back to her right hand just as he grabbed for it with his left and swung at her head with the right, his fist weighted by the cuffs he held.

The blow caught her just below the ear, which hurt but wasn't a knockout strike by any means. In fact, it only served to enrage her, the adrenaline that had been fading from her body rebounding.

Bending her wrist backward, he tried getting her to drop the knife, blood actually bubbling from his eye socket as he exerted himself.

Holding tight, Stacy tried to ignore the pain he was causing and then, as he leaned in closer, head butted his bubbling socket.

His grip loosened but did not break, so she reached up with her left hand and shoved her fingers into the gooey opening.

He screamed.

Her knife hand was free.

Holding his face once again, he turned a bit as she went to the left, his good eye trying to track her, and then let out an odd gasp as she plunged the blade into his belly.

Stunned, he looked down, free hand moving toward where the knife had pulled free, something pinkish poking out, blood seeping from the edges. Several seconds later, he crumpled to his knees, an attempt at walking toward the stairs failing after the first two steps.

Stacy waited, knife still at the ready.

Moving slowly, Robert slithered halfway across the floor toward the mattress before giving up and rolling onto his side, knees pulled up toward his chest.

He's in a lot of pain, she said to herself.

Good, another voice said.

A debate on whether or not to finish him off began to play out within her mind. In the end, she didn't do anything to quicken his departure, her only action before going upstairs being to grab his wallet and phone, the latter having a nasty crack across the screen.

From his fall? she asked herself.

Though it seemed likely, there was no way to tell for sure. Not that it really mattered. All she cared about was seeing if the phone worked, which it did, and calling Alan.

He didn't pick up.

"Alan, it's me…um, it's Stacy," she said into his voicemail. "Everything's okay now. I don't have my phone, but you can call me back on this one."

She ended the call, looked at Robert again, who was breathing heavily while grinding his teeth, body still folded into the fetal position, and then went upstairs.

In the fridge, she found an unopened bottle of Pepsi, and while she preferred Coke, it tasted like one of the most wonderful beverages she had ever consumed.

Several belches followed.

Bottle in one hand, knife in the other, Stacy started toward the living room, trying to decide if she would wait for Rusty to return or simply flee. During this, she realized she did not have her car keys, which then led her to realize she didn't even have any pants on.

Everything that happened down there... her mind started, dismay that she had not acknowledged her own nakedness during it arriving.

She shook her head, took another swig of the Pepsi, and then headed into the back bedroom to grab her pants, which, thankfully, were still balled up on the floor where Rusty had tossed them.

Thoughts of what he had done surfaced.

She tried pushing them away, knowing now was not the time to focus on it, but couldn't get it out of her head.

11

Something was wrong, but not in a "he needed to go rescue her" type of way. Instead, something had happened to her, the sound of her voice and the statements of being okay *now* making him certain of this.

She was raped.

How exactly he knew this, he did not know, but it was the first thing that entered his mind.

With the thought came horror, both at the general atrocity of such a thing and at how something like that would forever haunt her.

And she will claim differently, but...

He didn't finish the thought.

Up ahead, the real estate office loomed.

Stacy had called him while he was withdrawing four hundred dollars from the ATM, his hope being the daily limit would be enough for the "processing fee" the email had talked about.

Anxiety over what would occur within the office overshadowed the relief he felt that Stacy was "okay." In fact, the anxiety had been so severe that he had stopped at home to change into something more professional looking after going to Stacy's place, his mind knowing there still was no guarantee that he would actually get to see the girls until after he got signed up with one. If they didn't like what they saw today, they might say no, all without him having gained any useful information.

12

Stacy waited and waited, but Rusty didn't return, his instructions to leave while Robert was working with her seemingly heeded in a way that she hadn't expected.

During her wait, once the Pepsi was gone, she drank water from the tap and ate crackers that she found in the cupboard, ones that were still sealed so she didn't risk any sort of contamination that could be present, given how gross Rusty was. She also spent some time staring at the bed she had been tied to and fucked upon, a desire to strap him down and mutilate him bringing about a grin that she was unaware of until she caught sight of it in a bedroom mirror.

An hour passed without him returning, Stacy growing more and more weary of being in the house.

She wanted to go home.

She wanted a shower.

She wanted Alan, his arms around her, his strength providing comfort after she had scrubbed herself free of what had been done to her, if such a thing was even possible.

She wanted—

A car door slammed.

She hurried to the window.

One of the guys from the day before was walking up to the house, his fist pounding on the door several times before he gave up and went back to his car.

Questions followed.

Why was he here?

What did he want?

Had it been to film her?

If so, why not arrive with Robert?

So much about this house and the men who came to it was still a mystery to her.

13

"Why wouldn't you want to be in movies?" Vicky asked while squeezing a stream of Hershey's syrup into a tall glass of milk. "It's a lot of fun and you could become famous."

"I don't want to be famous, especially not that way," Amanda said.

"Oh," Vicky said, mind seemingly more focused on watching the milk darken as she twirled the spoon within the glass. "Why not?"

"Because making porn films like that is something you can only do for a couple years, yet it will follow you for the rest of your life."

"What do you mean?" Vicky finished stirring her chocolate milk and took a sip, eyes widening as the chocolaty goodness hit her taste buds.

Amanda sighed. "It's hard to explain, and I don't really want to think about it right now."

"Okay." Vicky started to walk away.

"What sucks is I don't think I have a choice. I need these college classes to get the job I want, but I would never be able to afford college if I had to work a regular minimum-wage job while also renting a place."

Vicky stared at her.

"So I think I have to do the porn film, even though I don't want to and it wasn't really part of the agreement when I signed up."

Well, it wasn't part of what they said I'd be doing after they came to get me from Matt, her mind silently added, the fact being she hadn't actually signed up to work with them. Instead, it had been more of a "you should really come work with us since you'll get better pay, better housing, schooling, and won't have to worry about being arrested anymore," which sounded fantastic.

Vicky took another sip of her chocolate milk, her face, once the joy of the beverage had passed, showing disinterest in what Amanda was saying.

14

The Kristi Homes Real Estate office was located in a small strip of offices not far from North Avenue near the eastern edges of Lombard, one that looked as if it was experiencing a serious decline in upkeep and occupancy.

Inside, the office was a different story, the décor giving a feel of success and complete professionalism in the business of real estate.

Kristi Woodman gave off that vibe as well as she sat behind one of two desks, body clad in a strict yet somehow sensual blazer and skirt.

"Mr. Miller?" she asked, standing as he walked in.

"Yes," Alan said. "Sorry I'm late. I had class this morning."

"Quite all right," Mrs. Woodman said while shaking his hand. She then motioned for him to have a seat.

He took it, one leg crossing over the other, all while his

mind debated whether or not to share the fact that he had a class with Amanda.

No, don't give too much information just yet, he said to himself.

"So, Mr. Miller, I must ask, how did you become aware of our services here?" She crossed her own legs and folded her hands in her lap.

"From one of your girls, actually," he said.

"Really?"

He nodded and decided to use the "sharing a class" information after all, minus the identity. "I have a class with one of them over at the College of DuPage and, admittedly, I was trying to see if she would go out with me, which is how I learned about her career as a real estate agent, which led me to your site, which led me to realize that showing houses wasn't exactly what was being marketed, especially not after I did some research on the girls, several of whom have interesting histories and are not quite old enough to be licensed real estate agents."

"Maybe their interesting history is why I'm trying to help them get back on their feet with an apprenticeship with my company," she said. "I wouldn't be the first person who tried to help rehabilitate lost girls who simply need a second chance at getting a fresh start."

"Actually, I considered that possibility, which is why I went to one of the houses to see how well the girls worked and noted fairly quickly that only men seem to be interested in the houses you have up for sale, and that the showing of them typically lasts an hour to two hours. I also couldn't help but notice that many of the men have families, ones that live in houses that don't seem to be up for sale themselves."

Kristi studied him for several seconds and then said, "Well, you've certainly done your homework."

"I have and really like what I see, which is why I got in contact with you. I'm not the type of person who is interested in a super serious relationship with anyone. I just want to have a good time, and I honestly believe the girls you have working for you would fit the bill."

"And I'm guessing you want to have them fit that bill without actually paying any type of bill yourself, given all the information you've obtained."

"Oh, not at all. I seek pleasure, which means I don't want my presence with them to feel like a chore—something you order them to do to keep me silent." He shook his head. "I've always viewed the laws preventing such businesses to be ridiculous, even detrimental to society, and am willing to pay what is necessary to achieve moments of sexual ecstasy. Especially if the girls are well cared for and willing, which is obviously the case, given that they're going to school and living in a house that is well kept and in a good neighborhood."

Kristi nodded. "I'm happy to hear that."

Alan smiled, all while his racing heart threatened to punch through his chest like an alien baby.

"Might I ask, which girl was it that you were interested in dating?"

Alan shook his head. "I'd rather not say. Rest be assured, it wasn't the one I ended up choosing, my visit to your site making me realize that my interest lay elsewhere when it came to the selection. Just thinking about the pictures I saw and what could unfold once I'm with her..." He let his voice fade as if distracted by the sexual imagery he was alluding to.

"I see," Kristi said, smiling. "Did you bring the processing fee as instructed?"

"I did, though I was not told an amount, so I hope I brought enough."

"Why don't you place what you brought here upon the

desk," Kristi instructed. "I will let you know if it's enough, and we will go from there."

"Sure." Alan pulled four hundred dollars from his pocket and set it down.

Kristi looked at the money as the twenties unfolded themselves but didn't touch it.

Alan waited.

"Okay," Kristi said. "The way things work, you pay by the month to have credits toward my girls, whom you can see once a week. Appointments must be scheduled in advance and desired activities noted, some of which require more credits from your account."

"And do my credits carry over from month to month?" Alan asked.

"Yes."

"And how much do I pay each month?"

"One thousand dollars, which amounts to four scenes a month, one a week, unless, of course, what you desire during one of those scenes involves more than one girl or activities beyond what would be considered 'normal' in the world of sex."

Alan nodded.

"You are also required to show clean test results for an STD panel, which you can have done at the DuPage County Health Department for fifty dollars. The HIV results are usually ready before you leave, and the rest become available the following week. Should you desire to see a girl before all the results are in, you must make a deposit to cover the cost of treatment should they come down with a treatable STD; however, under no circumstances can you see a girl before the HIV results are in. Is that acceptable to you?"

"Um...yes, though how recent of results do you need?" Alan asked. "I was just discharged from the military and have all my medical results on file, and if I had any type of infection or sexually transmitted disease, that would have been noted."

Kristi thought about this for a moment and then said, "Okay, if you have recent paperwork you can show me, I will accept those results, though I will still require a deposit for the treatment should you have something that you are unaware of. That deposit will go toward credits should the girl test negative during her next round of testing."

"Sounds fair." He wasn't just saying this. It honestly did sound fair to him. In fact, the entire setup seemed pretty well laid out and professional, a model for how such establishments should be designed should it become a legalized industry in the near future.

"Great. When do you think you can bring in those results?"

"Um...later this afternoon if you're available," he said, his mind picturing the file cabinet where all his medical records were kept. Recent blood work stuff had to be in there.

"Okay, if you're able to get it here between four and five, I can certainly get everything going on setting up your first scene. The first thousand too, obviously."

"Does any of that"—he pointed toward the four hundred dollars—"go toward my first month?"

"No, but it will allow you to see a girl this week before your monthly credits begin for November and will be used as the deposit toward any treatment that is required should you infect one of my girls."

"Oh, okay, that works for me."

"Excellent. Well..." She stood up. "Hopefully I will be seeing you later this afternoon."

"You will, for sure," Alan said while standing up himself and shaking her hand, an odd sense of accomplishment warming his body.

"Oh, and by the way, you said you were in class this morning," Kristi said.

"Um…yes," he confirmed, somewhat caught off guard.

"With Amanda?" she asked.

Alan had no choice but to nod, a realization that she probably already knew the answer making it dangerous to lie. "Yes."

"Okay. Was just curious."

No, he said to himself. *That was not curiosity.* Something was turning within her mind, something that concerned him. Unfortunately, he couldn't even begin to speculate on what it was and realized he would just have to wait and see. And stay a bit guarded.

16

"I'm glad you've decided to do the video," Mrs. Woodman said. "And I do apologize if any of my comments earlier sounded harsh. I was just frustrated and still quite shaken by what happened yesterday."

You're not really sorry. You're just saying that because you have to, Amanda said to herself. Into the phone, "Okay, well thank you. I'm still shaken too."

"We all are, and hopefully we can all understand and accept that we might be on edge a bit the next few days."

"Yep," Amanda said.

"By the way, I have a very last-minute thing I need you to do this afternoon."

"Oh?"

"I need you to be here at the office by three forty-five at the latest."

"Oh, okay." This was out of the ordinary. "Am I seeing—"

"I will explain everything when you arrive," Mrs. Woodman said. "And you will receive a cash bonus for your time."

"Wow, okay. I'll be there."

"Excellent." With that, Mrs. Woodman ended the call.

Last-minute, just like Emily, Amanda noted to herself, concern suddenly unfolding within her mind.

She sat on the edge of her bed and contemplated this, thoughts on whether or not she should make what she was doing later today known to others just in case something bad did happen crossing her mind.

You could call Mr. Woodman, she told herself but then realized that might cause drama if he then spoke to his wife.

What about the other one?

Early on, when she had first been "hired" to work with the real estate girls, there had been a second guy involved in everything, one who had pulled back quite a bit it seemed. His name had been Riley, and for some reason, she had always felt comfortable around him, more so than with Kristi or Sam.

But there is probably a reason you never see him these days, she said to herself. *And calling him might really fuck everything up.*

Despite the thought, she did stare at his number for several seconds, finger coming very close to hitting the call button.

In the end, she didn't, though the thought did stick with her as she looked in her closet for an office-appropriate outfit to wear that afternoon.

After that, she went to take a shower, during which she once again pondered what exactly would be taking place at the office. Never before had she been asked to go there like this, at least not for what sounded like a scene. It was odd. But maybe others had?

Not Emily, she would have said something.

Or would she?

Emily did have secrets, of this there was no question, but the extent of those secrets was a mystery. Now, given what had happened, she wondered if any of them had played a part. Take the party the other night. Had something that occurred there led to what had happened yesterday? And what was Mrs. Woodman's involvement? Had she simply set up a scene that went bad, or was there more at play?

No answers arrived as she ran the razor over her pubic mound, the steadiness of her hand while doing this in complete contrast to how her mind felt.

Bring your pepper spray.

Would such a thing have helped Emily?

Again, no answer arrived, but she did think having had one of the canisters wouldn't have hurt. Naturally, this led to her feeling guilty about never having shared any of them with Emily, her fear of Emily saying something and getting her in trouble always leading toward her secrecy on such items.

Nothing bad is going to happen, she told herself.

Not at the office.

That was one upside about this unusual request: she couldn't for the life of her picture something horrible happening at the office. Concern was still present though, simply because it was such an unusual request. Something weird was going on and she didn't like that. It made her uncomfortable.

17

Stacy decided she couldn't wait at the house any longer and headed to her car, a moment of fear arriving as she stepped through the front door due to the idea entering her mind that Rusty would return just as she was walking down the sidewalk and jump her.

It didn't happen.

He still has your phone and your wallet, she noted once she was in her car, though, honestly, she wasn't too concerned by this, given that he knew who she was anyway.

She twisted the key and listened as the engine groaned, all while staring at the house.

Why did you walk up to it?

Why did you go inside?

Why did you—

Over and over she asked herself, the focus of the questions so intense that she didn't even realize she had started to drive until someone honked at her to go once a light turned green. And then she was on I-55, the distance between her and the house growing greater and greater with each passing second, all while she felt as if her mind were still stuck inside.

Rusty will find Robert soon.

And then he will come after you.

Whether or not this would actually happen, she did not know, but the fear that it would was present.

At the Weber Road exit she pulled off so she wouldn't have to go through the tolls on I-355 again, her thoughts on this bringing about thoughts about how she had followed the man and girl the day before. Only twenty-four hours had passed since that moment, yet it felt as if years had come and gone during that period.

What will happen when Rusty finds Robert?

Will word get out to Kristi Woodman and her husband?

Did the two even known she was there?

Speculation on this last question put all the other questions on hold, speculation that eventually caused her to lean toward an answer of *no* on whether or not they had been notified. The reason for this was simple: Robert wouldn't want to lose his access to the girls; thus he wouldn't have shared that his porn-video-making operation had been uncovered. It wouldn't matter that he had put an end to the one that had discovered it; just the fact that it had been discovered would have caused unease with Kristi Woodman.

Then again, it was because of her that his own operation had been discovered, which he had seemed to be aware of, so maybe he would have told Kristi. In fact, he might have tried to use his capture and elimination of the "reporter threat" to his advantage when negotiating deals when hiring out the girls for his films.

She crossed Seventy-Fifth Street while thinking about this, the sound of the phone buzzing suddenly filling the car.

The caller was named Mindy, the display picture showing a cute little girl wearing a white bonnet and holding a basket with brightly colored eggs inside.

Not long after the buzzing stopped, a notification that a voicemail was present arrived.

Wait, she told herself, a desire to listen to it right then and there almost getting the better of her. *You're almost home.*

Five minutes later, while stopped for the light at Ogden Avenue, she nearly gave in again but, thankfully, didn't. If she had, the cop, who she hadn't even realized was behind her until she looked in the mirror as the light turned green, would have surely pulled her over, the use of a cell phone while driving, even when waiting at a stoplight, no longer lawful in the state of Illinois. Once that happened, her arrival home would be delayed quite a bit, her lack of a driver's license raising eyebrows to the point where she might be taken to the police station.

Not long after that, she was pulling into the parking spot behind her apartment, an odd sense of exhaustion hitting hard and making it nearly impossible to climb the stairs.

Once inside, she took a seat on the couch, body completely drained, so much so that she didn't even have enough energy to get into the shower.

Alan.

She called him and told him she was home. "I can't talk right now, too exhausted, but...well...can you please come over?"

"I'm on my way," he said.

She sighed with relief and leaned back on the couch, eyes struggling to stay open.

Don't!

Stay awake!

The two statements, shouted within her mind, did get her eyes to widen but only for a few minutes, the weight of her lids causing them to fall shut once again long before Alan arrived.

18

Medical records in hand, Alan headed back out to his car and drove over to the Chase Bank on Naperville Road, where he went inside and withdrew a thousand dollars from his savings account. After that, he drove over to Stacy's place, relief at seeing her car in the parking lot flowing through him.

The door was locked.

He knocked.

Nothing.

He knocked again, fist pounding the old wooden door three times, all while calling out, "Stacy, you okay?"

This time, the door opened, barely, Stacy peering out through the two-inch gap at him for several seconds before allowing him to enter.

And then she was hugging him, her arms squeezing him in a way that reminded him of the embraces that often followed firefights in Iraq and Afghanistan. The first had occurred in 2003, after a harrowing battle along a road through a neighborhood that sat between two bridges. Saddam's forces had set up a perfect choke point, one that Alan's convoy filtered into without much thought. Shots had been fired at them several times leading up to that point but had done nothing to prepare them for the sheer velocity of gunfire and rockets that were unleashed upon them that day, or the destruction such things could do to the bodies of friends.

Tears followed, her face pressed against him in a way that he had not anticipated.

Unsure what to say, he simply went on holding her, his right hand rubbing her upper back while his left cradled her lower back.

Five minutes came and went, the moisture from her tears having dampened his shirt to the point where he could feel it on his skin.

"Sorry," she muttered at about the five-minute mark, body slowly easing away from him. "I don't know what happened."

"You have nothing to be sorry for," Alan said, looking around the room for a box of tissues he could bring to her.

No boxes were visible.

Stacy, obviously aware of what he was looking for, said, "I don't have any," and after a second, rubbed at her eyes with the bottom of her shirt.

Alan watched her do this, his mind trying to think of something else to say, when, without warning, she ripped the shirt from her body, followed by her pants, and ran into the bathroom, the clothing left behind on the floor.

The sound of the shower filled the apartment, the pipes groaning with protest as the water raced through them.

Alan waited, eyes occasionally going to the clothes on the floor, a debate over whether or not he should do something with them beginning to unfold.

Yes, he finally decided, a search of the kitchen revealing a collection of plastic shopping bags in a drawer near the floor.

He put the clothes into one, tied the ends shut, and set it by the door. After that, he went to the couch and took a seat, questions about what exactly had happened to her going through his mind, but not getting much of an answer beyond the idea that she had been raped.

She probably won't say anything.

Should I say something?

No, not today.

Maybe not ever.

All he could really do was make himself available to her should she need to talk, or if not talk, be comforted by his presence.

The shower ended, probably due to the hot water cutting out.

Alan waited.

And waited.

On the coffee table, a phone with a cracked screen came to life, a call from someone named Rusty arriving.

Alan did not answer it.

After five cycles the buzzing stopped.

Alan waited, but no alert about a voicemail appeared.

Whoever Rusty was, he did not feel the need to leave a message.

Another minute passed before Stacy left the bathroom, steam billowing out as she wordlessly went down the hall to her bedroom and closed the door.

Alan continued to wait, knowing she was doing things on her own schedule, and any attempts by him to interfere with it could be met with resentment.

You will have to leave eventually, he noted to himself, eyes looking at his own phone to check the time.

He didn't want to keep Kristi Woodman waiting.

Stacy will understand.

The only problem was he really didn't want to leave her by herself this afternoon, not after what had happened. Sure, it would be for only an hour or two, but even that short bit of time, when in the mind of a person who had gone through something traumatic and wasn't in a good headspace during it, could feel like an eternity.

The bedroom door opened.

Alan stood up.

Stacy walked back into the main room, body clad in pants and a long-sleeved sweatshirt, wet hair hanging down and dampening her shoulders, face looking completely worn rather than refreshed from the shower.

She looked at Alan, probably wondering if he had been standing the entire time, and shifted her gaze to the floor.

Alan waited and then, even though he already knew the answer, asked, "Are you okay?"

Stacy looked at him again and then, much to his surprise, let out a small laugh.

"I know, it's a ridiculous question, but..." He pointed his palms toward the ceiling in an "I didn't know what else to say" gesture.

"It really is, and if anyone else had asked me that I'd probably lose my mind and never let them hear the end of it, but with you..." She stopped, lip starting to quiver again. She took a deep breath, fighting the onrush of emotion, and said, "You know what happened." It was not really a question, just a statement.

"Yes," he said with a nod.

"Twice," she said. "Both this morning...I was tied down to the bed."

He waited.

"He was...gross. Dirty and unwashed and smelled bad, and he got on me, and...and...*fucked me.*" Disgust spread across her face. "I can still feel his body on me wiggling around while he...while his..." She shook her head and sat down on the couch, looking at the floor.

Alan stayed on his feet for a few seconds and then sat down next to her, arm hesitantly reaching out to hold her.

As before, she welcomed the embrace and leaned into him, her fight for control over her emotions failing once again.

"I shouldn't have gone into that house," she said through her tears. "I should have just stayed outside and noted who went in and with what."

Alan knew that such thoughts would be with her for a long time, and while nothing would change what had happened, the repeated questioning of her actions would help her mind come to terms with what had happened.

"I should have—" The rest of her statement was lost as tears overwhelmed her, face once again pressed into him, his chest feeling the wetness of her lips and the dampness from her eyes.

Feeling helpless, Alan went on holding her, his mind and body knowing this was all he really could do.

19

Wearing a blouse, jacket, skirt, stockings, and heels, Amanda drove to the real estate office, a series of questions about what exactly was going on still occupying her mind. Mixed in with the questions were memories of her first visits to the real estate office. She had gone there several times during her first couple of weeks of work, after the withdrawal period, the purpose being so she could get familiar with the office and the real estate process should anyone ever question her on the legitimacy of it. Naturally, a sense of nostalgia for the past arrived with these memories, though, honestly, she wasn't sure why.

Maybe because it was all so new and sounded so great?

The real estate escort setup had seemed like a fresh start, one that would surely get her pointed in the right direction so that her life wasn't wasted, something that she had felt was impossible while living in the one-room, roach-ridden dump with Matt, body broken from the abuse and drugs.

Now...

You can still make something of yourself, just as long as you play ball with Mrs. Woodman.

Play ball, but be wary at the same time.

She did not trust Mrs. Woodman. Never had and never

would. In the beginning, however, she had been less questioning of things, mostly because she didn't feel that Mrs. Woodman would harm her. Make decisions that weren't always in her favor, yes. Purposely do something that would hurt her, no. Now, after what had happened to Emily and the phone call she had gotten this morning while at school, she wasn't so sure.

As expected, no one but Mrs. Woodman was at the real estate office, the "by appointment only" statement on all the signs and the front door of the office keeping people away.

Has she ever actually sold a house?

No answered followed, mostly because she didn't care enough to dwell upon it as she stepped inside, the electronic *ding* as the door opened echoing across the office.

"Amanda?" Mrs. Woodman called from the back room.

"Yes," Amanda replied and started back, feet stopping as Mrs. Woodman entered through the cutout that led into the back.

"Excellent. Nice and early. That's something I've always admired about you."

Amanda smiled and then asked, "So, what am I doing today?" She shifted a bit, feet not enjoying the heels, and then pulled at the blouse sleeve beneath the cuff of her jacket, which had slid up a bit.

"I have a young man coming in who you might recognize, one who I want you to suck off."

"Oh? Um…here?"

"Yes."

"Why?"

"Because I don't really trust him and want to make sure the reason he has contacted us truly is because he wants to pay for our services."

"Oh…okay." *Still doesn't make much sense, but…* Well, money was money, and doing something like this was far better than the video stuff she had to do tomorrow. "When does he get here?"

"Sometime between four and five."

Amanda nodded and then glanced over at one of the chairs in the office, the desire to get off her feet growing.

Mrs. Woodman motioned toward the seat, as if giving Amanda permission to sit.

Amanda took it.

"By the way, did you have a fellow student at school trying to ask you out for the last couple of weeks?" Mrs. Woodman asked.

"Um…no," Amanda said, a puzzled look crossing her face.

Mrs. Woodman stared at her.

"Honest, no one has been trying to ask me out, and even if they were, they wouldn't get very far. I know the rules." Panic was present in her voice, the type that often had appeared back when she was with Matt and feared she had somehow displeased him without meaning to.

Mrs. Woodman continued to stare at her without reply.

Amanda, growing more and more uneasy, began to fidget with her skirt. She also felt sweat beginning to ooze from her skin, the moisture soaking into her blouse in such a way that she decided to leave her jacket on while giving the blowjob.

And if he wants to fuck me?

Bend over so he can flip up the skirt.

20

Alan arrived at the real estate office at four twenty, a horrible sense of having abandoned Stacy stuck in his head, despite the fact that Stacy had pretty much pushed him from the apartment once she learned of his appointment that afternoon.

"Everything that's happened, it will all be for nothing if you don't follow through with Kristi Woodman and learn about the girls," Stacy had said.

Though he didn't agree—mostly because he never bought into the idea that something was made worthwhile by a certain outcome, especially something as horrible as being raped—Alan had nodded with her statement and headed out, a promise to give her a call once he was finished leaving his lips.

As before, the parking lot was pretty much empty, save for a new vehicle, which he recognized right away as being the one he had followed the day before.

One of the girls is here.

Or maybe more than one?

But why?

No answer arrived from within his mind, but he knew one was sure to appear once he was inside.

Taking a deep breath, he stepped out of his car and walked up to the entrance, the hesitation in his mind not filtering down to his limbs as he pulled open the door and entered the office.

As before, Kristi Woodman was sitting behind her desk, pretending to work on something, her eyes looking up at him as he entered, a fake smile on her face.

"Ah, Mr. Miller, glad you could make it back," she said.

"Glad to be back," Alan replied.

She motioned toward the chairs once again, fake smile still in place.

Alan took a seat while setting the folder and envelope down on the desktop.

Mrs. Woodman picked up the envelope and peeked inside and then opened up the folder.

Several seconds passed.

"Okay, everything seems in order." Mrs. Woodman stood. "Now, if you don't mind, I have a little 'welcome' surprise for you in back."

"Oh..." Alan said, hesitation arriving as a red warning flag was raised inside his mind. "I don't actually have much time right now."

"Nonsense," Mrs. Woodman said with a wave of her hand. "You have time for this." She motioned for him to get up. "Come on, you'll love it."

Alan stood and followed Mrs. Woodman, his mind on full alert and ready to react should some kind of trap be sprung.

She led him through the arched wall cutout.

Amanda was waiting.

Alan stopped, startled.

Amanda did a double take as well, eyes going from him to Mrs. Woodman and then back to him.

"I believe you two know each other," Mrs. Woodman said. "From school."

"Y-yes," Amanda said.

"We have…um…earth science together," Alan said.

"And you have been interested in dating Amanda," Mrs. Woodman said, "which is how you learned about our little operation here."

"No…well…she wasn't the one that…" He was all jumbled up. "I didn't realize Amanda was a part of this until this morning when we were talking. I recognized her from the website. She wasn't the one that I…the one that made me realize what was going on."

"Oh, I see," Mrs. Woodman said. "And here I thought this would be an excellent surprise for you."

Alan knew the "surprise" she alluded to was not actually what she had had in mind, and that she was far more cunning and conniving—*and dangerous!*—than he had initially perceived.

"Anyway, I hope you have time enough for Amanda to give you a proper welcome into our company," Mrs. Woodman said. "I'll be in front if you need me."

"You don't want to join in?" Alan asked, his thinking being that someone who truly was interested in what he was supposed to be interested in would assume that all the women in the company were a part of this, even the boss, and thus eager to have sex with the clients.

It took several seconds, but eventually Mrs. Woodman grinned and said, "I don't think you can afford time with me."

Amanda stepped close while Mrs. Woodman said this, a hand touching his chest, and said, "What's the matter, soldier boy, don't think I have what it takes to please you?"

Alan felt his body shiver as her hand teased the nerve endings all the way down to his groin, her body pressing up into his once the hand had cleared the chest area, breasts actually causing him to back up into the wall for support.

She smiled, hand cupping his penis though his pants, and said, "Oh my, maybe I *will* need a hand with this."

The sound of his zipper going down followed, her body still pressed into his while her hands slipped into his boxers to find him, both just lightly brushing his growing manhood as they went further down to tease the areas of skin that surrounded it and then briefly tickled his testicles.

And then her entire body was sliding down toward it, mouth ready to welcome him as Mrs. Woodman had instructed.

21

"Sounded like he enjoyed himself," Mrs. Woodman said after Alan Miller had left.

Amanda nodded, hand rubbing the underside of her lip where semen had dribbled, the size of the load he had shot into her mouth one that she had not been able to swallow in a single gulp.

"Missed a spot," Mrs. Woodman added, finger pointing to the right side of her jacket.

Sure enough, a dollop of cum stood right where her breast caused the jacket to bulge outward.

"Here." Mrs. Woodman handed her a paper towel.

"Thanks," Amanda replied and began dabbing at the stain, prior experience telling her she would need to have it dry cleaned. Then, "Why did you have me here if Isabella is the one he had originally chosen?"

"I think you know," she said.

"No, I really don't."

"Well, it doesn't matter. What does is we have another client who obviously enjoys what we offer, one who will hopefully be with us for a long time."

Amanda knew there was more to it than that but couldn't figure out what it was. "So, am I done?"

"No...not quite," Mrs. Woodman said.

Amanda waited.

"I need you to—" Her phone buzzed.

Amanda continued to dab at the semen, her goal being to make it so the dry cleaners wouldn't know what it was when it went in.

"What?" Mrs. Woodman snapped into the phone. "Jesus Christ, you can't be serious!"

Amanda looked up at her.

Mrs. Woodman looked back, covered the phone for a moment, and said, "You can go. Never mind about tonight." She then turned her attention back to the phone and said, "Okay, where do you want to meet?"

Puzzled, Amanda started toward the front of the shop but then hesitated, a thought about the money Mrs. Woodman had said she would receive for today entering her mind.

Don't. Just go!

No, I earned it.

She turned back toward Mrs. Woodman, who gave her a "what?" look while she listened to whatever was being said.

"My money," Amanda said.

Mrs. Woodman stared at her for a moment and then something seemed to click within her face. "Over there," she said and waved toward her desk.

Amanda nodded and went over to the desk, eyes spotting the money envelope that sat next to the keyboard.

A few seconds later, she was back in her car, money envelope sitting in her purse atop the canister of pepper spray, mind trying to piece together what had just happened, both with the guy from school and with the phone call that had arrived.

How did he know? she wondered, thoughts drifting back to that morning when the two had been talking. *And what was all that stuff she said about him wanting to date me?*

It didn't make sense.

And coming here to suck his cock?

Why would she have me do that?

Mrs. Woodman had said it was because she didn't trust him, but, honestly, in Amanda's mind, that made this little side job even more bizarre because if trust was an issue, why had she allowed him to come here and pay for sex?

And why with me?

Obviously, Mrs. Woodman had been expecting something more to unfold once the two were together, something that would answer a question she carried.

Had it been answered?

And was that answer worth the risk?

Amanda had no idea. One thing she did know: the phone call had come at the perfect time because Mrs. Woodman had been planning something more for her, something that probably didn't involve an actual client, given that she just pretty much said "forget about it" once the call arrived. Now if she could just figure out what the call was about, she would be more comfortable with things.

22

"How'd it go?" Stacy asked, mind and body trying to mask the anxiety she had displayed the entire time he was gone, a horrible certainty that Rusty, or someone else, would show up having plagued her mind.

"Great," Alan said while rubbing at his cheek. "They've accepted me and are going to work me in with Isabella later in the week."

Something was off, but Stacy couldn't figure out what. She also had a sense that he had showered before coming over here, which was odd, given how perceptive he typically was toward how others were feeling and would have known she needed him.

"I also found out I actually have a class with one of the girls," Alan added.

"One of them is a student?" Stacy asked.

Alan nodded. "I think several of them are."

"Wow, that's..." She shook her head, unsure what to think about that. One thing was for sure, taking classes, living in nice houses, and having a new car was not how she had initially pictured the day-to-day life of these girls when she had first stumbled upon the real estate prostitution scheme. Nope. In her mind, she had figured the girls would be living in squalor and that every house would have a girl stationed inside, the front door opening and closing every hour or two as one guy left and another showed up.

"Not what you expected?" Alan asked.

"No, not at all."

"Same here," Alan said. "I was kind of envisioning something a bit more...sinister."

Stacy contemplated that for a moment, his statement mirroring her own thoughts, but then said, "Don't forget, we both watched as a transaction was made with a very young-looking girl who was taken to a disgusting house where she was fucked over and over again on camera for a video that is marketed to those who enjoy underage pornography."

And then I was raped and nearly tortured to death!

And I killed a man!

A man who had a daughter who left a message asking when he would be home because he promised to take her to get a pumpkin to carve during her day off from school.

He still deserved to die!

"I won't," Alan said.

Stacy sensed he wanted to say more, but nothing else followed.

He's holding something back, she said to herself, questions about what it might be and ways to get him to talk about it unfolding within her mind.

Resentment followed.

This was her story, and he had agreed to help, which meant whatever he had learned was something he should be telling her. Good or bad, he needed to share his information with her.

And why did he shower?

The question kept popping up within her head, the answer just beyond her reach.

Doesn't matter!

It did, though, only she wasn't sure why at this point.

"Oh, and it seems payment is done monthly, sort of like a subscription to the girls, though it isn't unlimited access," Alan said.

"Really?" she said, frustration fading. "How much?"

"Thousand bucks a month, which allows a guy to see one girl every week."

"You gave her a thousand dollars!" Stacy said, shocked.

Alan nodded.

She'd had no idea it would cost so much, or that Alan would be able to hand over such a sum without it seeming like a big deal.

Maybe it is a big deal; he just doesn't want me to know that. Maybe that is what is off right now?

"I..." she started, voice struggling to bring forth what she wanted to say. "I didn't know you'd have to pay so much."

"Me either, but don't worry. If it helps you break this story and become a world-famous journalist, then it's worth it."

Hearing this flipped a switch, one that triggered a wave of emotion that she hadn't anticipated. "Thank you," she said as it arrived, her arms suddenly enwrapping him. "Thank you so much."

23

The first thing Riley did once he was home that evening was check the old computer in his closet to make sure the money was still present, which it was. After that, he did a careful investigation to see if there was any evidence that Kristi had been in his home once again.

Nothing jumped out at him.

Sadly, this didn't put him at ease, his lack of understanding about why she had been inside the other day plaguing him.

Was she really looking for the money?

What else could it be?

The question that followed, the one asking whether or not Sam was in on whatever she was up to, was what troubled him the most. In fact, it wasn't even the question that troubled him, but the realization that he had reason to ask it.

Frustration and sadness mixed together while he contemplated this, the emotions killing his appetite to the point where he could only manage one tiny slice of the personal margherita-style pizza that he had grabbed from the Buona in Naperville, the boxed meal going into the fridge, where it would probably stay until the hunger returned later that evening.

A check of his email inbox added anger into the mix, the fake web persona he had created having been accepted to see Isabella, a welcome message from Kristi instructing him to arrive at her office tomorrow morning with a processing fee.

He called Sam.

No answer.

He didn't leave a message.

A debate on what to do next followed, his finger hovering over the call button while Kristi's name was highlighted.

And then what?

Ask if they are still screening potential clients?

The answer was obviously *no* since they hadn't sent him this one to run a check on, so what was the point in asking, especially if Kristi would just lie about it? Once that happened, he could tell her he knew it was a lie, but he doubted that would really have much of an impact.

And since Sam is the one that should be sending me the name and information...

His mind couldn't continue with the thought, not when he knew his brother was now keeping him in the dark on things.

How long?

During breakfast the other day, and then again while waiting to see if the pimp showed up at the motel, Sam had offered up several options for how to expand their client base. The question was, had his brother been seeking approval to go forward with such steps, or had such steps already been taken and he wanted to cover his own ass?

Riley shook his head, the answer somewhat obvious.

Sam had been hoping that he would agree to the suggestions, thus making it so he would always assume the new steps had been implemented after the discussion rather than before it without any discussion. Sam wanted him to think he still had a say in what unfolded.

But why?

Was it because of the money or because they were brothers and he wanted to keep that relationship intact?

Maybe both.

Maybe Sam was caught in the middle.

Riley considered this for several minutes, concern growing with each cycle of the minute hand. Kristi would win this tug-of-war over Sam, mostly because Sam would aid in her tugs. Not consciously, but he would do it nonetheless, the simple fact being that when torn between a wife and brother, one would ultimately give in to the wife as a matter of self-preservation. Sam had to live with her, not Riley; thus he would always lean toward keeping her happy over others.

It doesn't always work that way, another part of his mind said, thoughts of his own failed marriage coming into play.

It will with Sam.

Knowing this, he once again considered wiping his hands free of the entire thing. Within seconds, however, his mind brought up the likelihood that doing so would simply lead to them being reckless and nabbed by the authorities. Not long after that, those same authorities would be knocking on his door, Kristi being the type to bring him down just out of spite.

So...

Stop trying to guide things with the promise of funding when money runs low and simply move in and exert your own authority.

Take control.

He could do it, the only problem being the possible reaction Kristi would have. She might not stand aside and instead would do everything she could to ruin him, even if it meant ruining herself in the process.

And then play the victim card.

His phone buzzed, the call coming from his partner.

Not long after that, he was heading back to work, a case his team had been working for two months having had a break, thanks to a simple traffic stop.

24

Alan stayed with Stacy that night, her body held tight against his as she slept. At first, given what had happened to her, he worried about holding her close like this, his fear being that the contact might trigger something within her. Now, however, it felt right.

The same could not be said of her refusal to seek medical attention. He felt such was necessary, as did she, yet even so she refused to go, her fear that the police would then get involved and ruin her journalistic dreams guiding her decision.

Alan had wanted to argue about this, had wanted to pick her up and carry her to the car and then the ER, but in the end he'd respected her decision. He did not respect his decision to respect her decision, though, which was weird. He felt like he was failing her, even though he knew there was really nothing he could do. It was her decision.

You should have been there.

You should have realized something was wrong last night and tried to find her.

Deep down inside, he knew the chance of him having actually been able to locate her before she had been violated was incredibly unlikely, yet even so, the fact that he didn't try until this morning was enough to make him feel wretched.

He was also determined to keep such a thing from happening again, which meant he was going to do whatever it took to help her finish her story.

And if the guy that raped her shows up here...

He let the thought fade without a specific mental visualization, his mind both comforted and a little bit chilled in knowing he would make it so the guy could never do what he did to Stacy (or anyone else) ever again. What exactly this meant, his mind did not speculate upon, but removing him from the world of the living was not off the table.

Tuesday,
October 29, 2013

1

"I just need to swing by my sister-in-law's place really fast," Riley said to his partner as he drove them toward the apartment of a young mother they needed to speak with, one who had a truck-driving boyfriend suspected of taking part in the shipment of drugs from Mexico to Chicago.

"Oh? Business or pleasure?" his partner asked.

He has absolutely no idea that her business is pleasure, Riley said to himself. Out loud, "With her, it's never pleasure."

"Ha, so you've said." He laughed. "Expecting any drama?"

"Of course, which is why I want to talk to her while she's at work rather than at home," Riley said. In reality, he just wanted to make her think that the reason the guy from his fake profile didn't show up this morning was because he saw a vehicle in the parking lot, one that had a very official "undercover police" look to it. Kristi would be pissed with him, which is what he wanted, though, honestly, he wasn't sure why. "It cool with you?"

"Yeah, no problem."

"Great, thanks."

Not long after that, Riley was pulling their unmarked car into the battered parking lot that housed the Kristi Homes Real Estate office, a mental image appearing of a picture he had once seen of Kristi standing outside the office with her parents, who had helped her get started with her business several years ago, smiling.

Had she known what would happen?

The answer was no, the young bright-eyed Kristi—the twenty-four-year-old who had done so well in the late nineties working for a Naperville-based real estate company that she had been able to put the commissions she received toward her own company—would never have dreamed of what would unfold in the country following that amazing real estate boom. Nor would she have known she would one day be running a prostitution scheme from the business she had longed to own. It was a bit tragic.

"You want me to just hang here?" his partner asked.

"Yeah, if you don't mind," Riley said, hand shifting the vehicle to park. "This won't take long."

"'Kay." He sipped his coffee, which they had gotten from a Dunkin' Donuts stop fifteen minutes earlier, the closure of several Caribou Coffee joints in the Chicago suburbs earlier that year having forced them into helping add credibility to the cop-and-donut-shop cliché. "Good luck."

"Thanks," Riley said and stepped out from the vehicle, body taking a moment to compose itself before walking up to the door, which, when opened, announced his entry.

Hearing the door announcement, Kristi came out from the back room, body clad in one of her expensive custom-made skirted suit outfits—Sam always complained about how much she spent on them—and then halted abruptly upon seeing him.

"What're you doing here?" she asked.

"Nothing really. My partner and I were in the area on a case, so I thought I'd drop by." He took a seat in one of the leather chairs. "How's business going?"

"It's not, thanks to you."

"What's that supposed to mean?"

"You know what it means. All your little rules and making

the girls go to school and then not allowing Sam to find more girls, even though we have several bedrooms going unused." She crossed her arms.

"My 'little rules'?" Riley said, crossing his own arms. "You didn't seem to mind my 'little rules' when you needed my money to get things started."

"The money you stole from a drug dealer," she spat.

Riley shrugged. "Money is money. I had it, you didn't." He paused. "In fact, I still have some of it, and you still don't, so—" He glimpsed a shadow moving along the wall beyond the cutout.

Someone's here!

"Who's back there?" Riley asked.

"No one. I'm—"

Riley stood up and started toward the back room.

"Hey!" Kristi snapped and tried to block his path.

Riley, being gentle but also firm, moved her out of the way and headed into the back where, much to his surprise, he found Isabella standing in the middle of the room, her body, like Kristi's, clad in a tailor-made business outfit as if she truly were ready to show houses to a perspective buyer.

"Oh, Isabella..." Riley started, his thoughts completely jumbled up now. "I didn't know...what're you doing here?"

"Um..." Isabella started and then looked at Kristi.

Riley looked at Kristi as well.

"We had some things that needed to be discussed, and since I had no one else to watch the office, she came here," Kristi said.

Riley knew it was a lie. Her body gave it away while speaking, as did his knowledge of who was supposed to show up during this period of time. What this all meant, he didn't know, but he doubted it would be something that he approved of.

Rather than pursue the lie, however, he turned back to Isabella and asked, "Everything going well?"

Isabella nodded.

"And the girls you're rooming with? Everything going well with them?"

She nodded again.

"And school?"

A third nod, though this one a bit more hesitant, and then, "Didn't do so good on my history paper."

"Oh, what happened?"

She shrugged. "Don't know. My teacher said I didn't document my sources right, so…" She shrugged again. "He wants me to come in so he can show me how to do it correctly, so I don't fail another paper and the class."

"Oh, well, that shouldn't be a difficult thing to fix. I had trouble with citing sources my first year in college too." He turned back to Kristi, her pissy look making him smile. "Well, I suppose I should let you two get back to whatever it was you were working on."

Kristi didn't reply to this.

"Oh and…" He turned back toward Isabella. "If you ever need help with anything or have any concerns about anything, please don't hesitate to call me. I know I've been kind of distant from all of you lately, but now I'll be around again. A lot. Okay?"

Isabella smiled. "Okay."

He turned back toward Kristi, her face having somehow obtained an even greater level of pissed-offness, and said, "Well, catch you later."

Again, no reply.

He walked past her and headed back out to the unmarked car, door announcing his departure as he left the office.

"How'd it go?" his partner asked.

"Better than expected," Riley said. "Apparently she has a new girl working for her who is…" He stopped and started backing out of the spot.

"Who is what?"

"Ah, never mind. You're married and don't want to hear about hot college girls."

"Says who!"

"Your wife, for one, I'm sure."

2

Though she could have gone back to the house to check Facebook, Amanda headed into the college library instead, a secret hope of bumping into Alan while walking the hallways guiding her.

No Alan.

A check of his profile also showed that he had yet to accept her friend request, which she had sent last night, a two-hour debate on the idea having taken place within her mind before she finally decided to do it.

At least he hasn't said no…

The thought didn't comfort her all that much, given that Alan probably had not seen it yet; thus a rejection could still be heading her way.

No…he'll accept it, a part of her mind countered. *He'll…*

Her phone buzzed.

It was Isabella.

She ignored the call, finger refreshing the computer screen to see if the request had been accepted.

Still pending…

She refreshed the screen again.

No change.

Another buzz from her phone alerted her to a voicemail.

Another refresh.

Nothing.

No acceptance, no messages, no notifications.

She sighed and closed down the computer, thoughts on why she had become hooked on Alan arriving. It wasn't a romantic attachment, though she did have to admit that she had felt an interesting tingle while pressed up against him, one that had triggered an aggressiveness that she wasn't used to displaying with her clients. No. Something else was guiding her interest in him, something that she couldn't really put a finger on.

Why now?

The question had popped up several times after she had arrived back at the house last night, no answer ever arriving.

It was weird. She had been seeing him in class for two months yet never really gave him much thought, but now, after talking for a bit before class and meeting up unexpectedly for a blowjob, she couldn't get him out of her thoughts.

Why?

Still no answer.

Though she knew she was being silly, she punched her student ID number back into the computer and logged onto Facebook once again.

A notification!

It was a game request.

She went over to Alan's profile.

The friend request was still pending.

She sighed.

Go home.

Rather than give in, she stayed at the computer and looked through the public portions of Alan's profile. Not much was in there, but this didn't necessarily mean he wasn't that active on the site, just that he didn't make things public.

Twenty minutes came and went.

Her phone buzzed again, this time with a call from Mrs. Woodman.

No message was left.

You really have to go, she told herself and once again shut everything down on the computer.

Thirty seconds later, she was in the hallway, hitting the call button on her phone.

Isabella picked up after two rings.

"Sorry," Amanda said. "Got stuck in class."

"No problem. Just wondering where you are. Me and Caroline are at your place right now. Our thing today got bumped up by an hour. But no one's here."

"Vicky's not there?" Amanda asked, cutting her off.

"Who?"

"Vicky, the new girl."

"Oh, no, no one's here. Maybe she and Emily went somewhere?"

She doesn't know about Emily.

No one does.

Just you and Vicky.

And now Vicky's gone.

Or is she?

A visualization of someone sneaking inside and stabbing Vicky to death played across her mind, her bloody body crumpled in one of the bedrooms or on the floor of the living room.

"Amanda?" Isabella asked.

"Yeah, I'm here," Amanda said, voice pushing the imagery away. "Sorry."

"It's okay. You on your way?"

"Um…yeah, be there in like ten minutes."

"Okay, great."

The two disconnected.

3

"How long did I sleep?" Stacy asked, right hand accepting the mug of coffee Alan had made her.

"Almost twelve hours," Alan said. It was well after ten in the morning.

She sipped the coffee. "Don't you have class?"

"I did, but…" He hadn't wanted to leave her alone, not after everything she had been through. And waking up alone after such a thing…that could be pretty traumatic. Thus he had stayed. "Just didn't feel like going today."

She took another sip.

Alan looked at his empty hands, and though he was completely coffeed out, he wished he had his own mug to sip just so he wasn't simply standing there.

"How'd you sleep?" he asked after several seconds, the question completely pointless.

She shrugged. "Pretty good, I guess. Didn't wake up once and don't think I had any dreams."

"Ah, that's good."

"Yeah."

She took another sip, the silence returning.

"Are you hungry?" Alan asked. "I could make us something, or we could go somewhere?"

The mention of food seemed to trigger something within her, and before he knew it, she was pretty much pushing them toward the car.

Not long after that, they were sitting in a booth at the Egg'lectic Cafe, a new mug of coffee before her, a glass of orange juice before him.

"No coffee?" she asked.

"No, I drank like an entire pot this morning while you were sleeping."

"Really?" She sipped hers. "When did you wake up?"

"Like six something."

"Wow, I didn't even feel you get up."

"I was careful, didn't want to wake you." He smiled.

She smiled back.

More silence, then, "Thanks for staying."

"You're welcome."

Judy came by to take their order, which for Alan consisted of a simple two-egg breakfast with hash browns, bacon, and toast. Stacy ordered twice as much.

"Almost two days without food," she mumbled after Judy had left with the order, a slight look of embarrassment creeping upon her face. "Sooo hungry!"

"Ah, I bet," Alan said, memories of going without food for days filling his mind, as well as what typically happened once food was finally an option. "Just don't make yourself sick."

"I won't," she said and took another sip of coffee. "So, what did you do all morning while I was sleeping?"

Though the question was projected toward him as if nothing more than innocent curiosity, Alan could tell she was actually concerned by his "unsupervised" time in her apartment. Knowing her, this was simply a result of the control she carried over her own space, and not because anything was there that she didn't want him to know about.

"Not much really, just tried to get more familiar with my phone," he said with a shrug. "I still have trouble with it."

"What do you mean?"

"Well, okay, I can call and text and take pictures and send emails and whatnot, but trying to use the web..." He shook his head. "I just can't get used to the sites when on the phone and how they're laid out differently. Throws me off."

"Which sites?"

"Well, Facebook for one. It's hard for me to navigate."

"Really?"

"Yeah…well…for me at least." He shrugged. "I might just be too used to using computers."

"Maybe you have a weird setting turned on," she suggested, eyes looking toward the kitchen as Judy came out with food, anticipation obvious. Disappointment followed as she watched it go to another table. Then, "Here, let me see your phone."

"Okay." Alan handed it over.

She looked at it for a moment, her finger clicking things, and then said, "Huh, looks normal to me."

"See, I'm just smart phone dumb," he said with a smile.

"Nah, you just need to get used to it. Spend a month at my place with a shitty web connection and you'll grow so savvy with this that you'll start using it over the laptop even when the connection is solid."

Did she just suggest we move in together?

"By the way, do you want to accept a friend request from Amanda Wesson?" Stacy asked.

"Amanda who?"

"Amanda Wesson." She turned the phone toward him so he could see her picture. "You don't have any friends in common. Probably one of those whores that try to get men to email them or click their webcam links. I did a story on this a while back. Want me to deny it for you?"

"Um…" he muttered while she twisted the phone back toward herself, her finger getting ready to press the screen. "No, no, no!"

He reached for the phone.

"You know her?" she asked while handing it back, head twisting toward the kitchen again.

"I think so," he said, fingers struggling to enlarge the profile photo. *Is it her?* "I think it's one of the girls from the real estate thing."

"Seriously?"

"Yeah. Amanda." *It is her!* "The one I actually have a class with." He took a moment to locate the accept button and pressed it.

"Wow, is she the one you're signed up with?" She looked at the kitchen again and this time smiled as Judy carried a tray of food toward them.

"No, well…um…Isabella is the one I'm signed up with," he said, hands moving a few items to make room for the plates. "But Amanda's the only one I've met in person."

"Huh, I wonder if they friend everyone who hires them." She leaned back as a tray of food was set before her, then a second one with side items, and a third with the pancakes. "Or if she just has a thing for you."

Alan shrugged, an odd feeling of discomfort settling in with this topic. "You know, I kind of caught her in a vulnerable moment yesterday and we had a nice talk, all before I realized who she was, so that might be part of it."

"But she knows you know what she does now?" Stacy asked.

Alan nodded as a plate was set before him, one that looked incredibly boring opposite Stacy's spread. "She was at the office when I went in to make the payment, though I had figured it out while talking to her earlier."

"Everything look okay?" Judy asked.

Alan looked at his plate and then Stacy's and nodded.

"Yep," Stacy said, a forkful of food already heading toward her mouth.

"Okay, enjoy."

"Thanks," Alan said, fork breaking open the yolk on one of his eggs so he could dip his toast in.

"I wonder if she'll talk to you about how she got involved in all this," Stacy said. "I mean, if she's friending you on Facebook and hanging out with you before class, then chances are she feels some sort of connection, which you could totally use to your advantage."

"Hmm," Alan voiced, unsure how to reply to that. The idea of getting close to someone to the point where they would confide in him, simply so he could use what they said to his advantage—well, Stacy's advantage—didn't sit well with him.

Especially if they reach out to you without prompting.

But maybe you can help her by helping Stacy expose what is going on?

"Or," Stacy continued, a mouthful of crispy potatoes distorting her words, "they want *her* to get close to learn more about *you.*"

"What do you mean?" Alan asked, even though he knew exactly what she meant.

"Didn't you say that they know you sort of stumbled upon this thing rather than being recommended to it by an existing client?"

"I did." He tore a chunk of soft toast from the piece on his side plate and dipped it into the yolk.

"Well, maybe they're concerned by that and want to make sure you're legit." She forked a triangle of syrup-soaked pancake into her mouth, chewed for a moment, and swallowed. "That's why it will be good once you've been with one of the girls. That'll make them realize you're serious about them."

Alan thought about this and wondered if the blowjob at the office had been a test. If so, had he passed?

But why do it there?

Why allow such an obvious connection between the real estate company and the prostitution?

The risk involved in having the sexual act performed there led him to think it was unlikely that they had been testing him.

Well, at least not in the way Stacy thinks.

Instead, if anything were being tested, it had probably been to see what type of reaction he and Amanda shared when face-to-face, his earlier explanation to Kristi Woodman about how he had learned about the prostitution setup having triggered some sort of concern.

Does she still think Amanda was the one I supposedly followed?

Was it more of a test on her?

If so, he hoped he had helped alleviate Kristi Woodman's suspicions to the point where she no longer suspected Amanda of doing something wrong. He also hoped he and Stacy were doing the right thing in opening the door on this thing.

Stacy was raped by a guy who is a part of a group that uses underage girls for videos that he hires from Kristi Woodman, he reminded himself. *Doesn't matter how many of the girls in the company are there willingly and enjoy what they are doing. The fact that they have some for the purpose of such videos needs to end.*

And the guy that raped Stacy...

He watched her eating for a moment, the thought going unfinished as he allowed relief over her escape from the situation to enter his mind.

4

Isabella and Caroline were waiting in their car when Amanda pulled up, her coworkers having had the forethought to park on the street rather than in the driveway so they didn't block Amanda when she got back.

Mrs. Woodman never does that.

Speaking of which...

Amanda placed a call to the bitch, knowing that a failure to return her missed call could be used against her, the thin ice she was on after her hesitation to do the video followed by accidently taking the thousand dollars from the desk the day before beginning to crack.

"Kristi Woodman," Mrs. Woodman said after two rings.

"Hi, it's Amanda. I missed your call." In the mirror, she saw Isabella and Caroline walking up the driveway.

"Yes, first, I wanted you to know that I have Vicky with me for a last-minute scene. Second, there has been a change in plans, and Isabella and Caroline will be meeting you at your place when you're done with class."

"Oh, okay, they're here now actually. I just got back."

"Okay, then go get yourself ready. They'll tell you what outfits to bring." With that, Mrs. Woodman ended the call.

Amanda stepped out of the car and greeted the two girls, neither of whom she really knew all that well. Emily had, all of them having lived together in the first house for a while before Emily had been moved to this one back when Amanda had been hired. In fact, she and Caroline had been really good friends, it seemed, which made the question about how Emily was doing a bit difficult for Amanda to answer. On the one hand, she wanted to tell the truth; on the other, she didn't want to have to tell Caroline what had happened.

"She's good, really busy these days," Amanda said.

"Yeah, that's what Kristi said. Kind of bummed. Was looking forward to working with her again. She and I used to double up on guys all the time, had an amazing rhythm." She chuckled. "This one time—"

"We should probably get going," Isabella said. "You two can talk in the car while on our way."

"Oops, sorry," Caroline said. "Let's go pick out some stuff for you to wear."

Amanda nodded.

The three went inside, Amanda somewhat relieved that she had actually showered and set her hair before class, all on the chance that she would run into Alan. At the same time, she felt a bit ridiculous about having done it, especially since he was a client.

One that didn't even pick you…

And the reason he found out about all this was because he wanted to date someone else…

These two thoughts aside, something had happened yesterday. She had felt a spark that she couldn't deny, one she was certain he had felt as well.

"Oh wow, this is your room!" Caroline said.

"Yep," Amanda said, embarrassment at how messy it was unfolding within. Not only had she showered and put her hair up this morning, she had also fretted over what to wear, the result being several outfits tossed aside in frustration.

"It's huge."

"Really?" Amanda asked. It seemed pretty standard to her, similar in size to the room she'd had while growing up.

"Totally," Caroline said, hand sliding open Amanda's closet. "The rooms at our place are like cupboards compared to this."

"They're not that small," Isabella said, shaking her head. "But they aren't as big as this one, that's for sure. Okay, you have a school uniform?"

"I do," Amanda said and went to her dresser where the skirt was.

Caroline pulled out a white blouse and handed it to Isabella. After that, she pulled out a simple sundress and then a formal black cocktail dress, both of which she handed over.

"And something red," Isabella said.

"I have—" Amanda started.

"Here," Caroline said, pulling out a red dress that she had only ever tried on.

Amanda wondered if she could still wear it, given how tight she remembered it being back in August.

"Okay, and we need corsets and teddies," Isabella said.

"Why so much?" Amanda asked.

"They're going to be filming us all day and said we need different outfits for each scene."

"I thought it was just us giving blowjobs to several guys?"

"That's just one scene. We're doing several."

"Oh." She watched as Caroline pulled out five of her corset-like tops, garters swinging as she handed them over to Isabella, who then passed them over to her. "And you two are cool with doing this?"

"You kidding?" Caroline asked. "If this goes well and we start to get known, we could make our own videos and keep all the money. Fuck, have you ever seen what some of those girls are making with just webcam videos? Guys pay by the minute to watch them fucking themselves with a dildo, no cocks needed."

"But how many of those girls don't really make anything?" Amanda asked. "I mean, sure, some are making it big, but for every one of them, aren't there like hundreds, if not thousands of girls who aren't making much at all?"

"Yeah, but that's because they don't know what they're doing and aren't appealing."

Isabella nodded and then added, "And they don't have the experience we have. Tell her about that lady we read about."

"Which one?"

"The one who used to be a teacher in Kansas."

"Oh yeah, one day she and her husband decided to put a webcam up in their bedroom. She'd be blindfolded and he'd wear a mask so no one knew who they were, and he'd fuck her from behind while she looked at the webcam. Next thing they knew, they were making enough for her to quit teaching."

"They're making like twenty to thirty grand a month."

"Wow," Amanda said, realizing nothing she could say

would change their thoughts on how successful they would be. "So, we ready?"

Isabella looked at all the outfits they had grabbed. "Um…yeah, this will work."

"Should she grab more skirts?" Caroline asked.

"No, we're good."

"Okay."

They started toward the door.

"Wait," Amanda said. "You're just going to carry it all out like this?"

Caroline looked at Isabella and then back at Amanda and said, "Why not?"

"Um…because my neighbors might see us walking out and wonder what we're doing," Amanda said.

"No one's going to care," Caroline said and started out the door.

We're supposed to be discreet!

Are they always like this?

The fears she had felt the other day at how easily all this could crumble began to arrive once again, and for a moment she actually considered protesting their lack of discretion.

But then she realized that even the bosses were starting to lighten up on the procedures they had put in place, the fact that she had given a blowjob at the office for Alan after he had handed over money proof of this.

And Caroline was once raped.

And Emily was killed.

And we're doing videos.

And Vicky is…

Fuck it!

She followed the two down the stairs and out to the car, the outfits they carried completely visible, garter straps blowing in the wind as they crossed the yard.

5

Stacy looked at was left on her plates, embarrassment unfolding at how little she had actually been able to eat once the food had started to hit her stomach.

Alan, however, didn't seem to care and simply said, "Now you have lunch for later since that all reheats well."

"That's true," Stacy said. She took a sip of coffee. "So, what are your plans for today?"

"I don't know, was kind of wondering what you'd be do-ing." He toyed with a bit of bacon for a moment before tossing it in his mouth.

She shrugged. "Just some research for a story. Got a few lit-tle pieces I need to finish so I can pay the rent next week." *If they accept them*, she silently added.

"Do you want me to stay while you do that?" he asked.

She shook her head. "I'd love to have you there, but I don't want to become dependent on it. You already missed class for me, and I know you have stuff you need to do to get your Halloween display up, so..."

"You sure?"

No! her mind cried, the idea of being alone in her apartment not something she even wanted to think about, but she knew she had to do it. "Yep, I'll be fine."

What if Rusty shows up?

He won't.

Well, not during the day...maybe.

She had no idea what that crazy motherfucker would do, but she had a feeling he would, at some point, come for her.

So go for him first.

She looked at Alan while thinking this, a sip of coffee masking the look of contemplation she knew her face carried, and wondered what he would think of such a plan.

He'd want you to call the police.

And he would probably call them himself if he knew I was going down there again.

Kristi Woodman's husband!

You going to tell Alan about him?

Not yet. First, she wanted to see what she could dig up on the guy, the fact that she had not given him much thought until now somewhat embarrassing.

What if the police are involved?

Former coworkers from when he was on the force?

If true, Alan really needed to know, yet even so, she could not bring herself to tell him yet. Later, once she had a few more details, ones that went beyond being a simple statement from a bloodied pedophile.

While she was thinking this, Judy brought them the check and a box for Stacy's leftovers.

"Ready?" Alan asked once she had forked everything from the plates into the box.

"Yep."

With that, they stood up and headed to the counter to pay and then out to the car. Five minutes later, they were parked outside her place, Alan insisting he come up to make sure everything was okay before heading home, Stacy pretending like such an act was unnecessary when really she wanted nothing more than for him to not only check the place out, but stay.

6

Leaving Stacy alone felt weird yet was also something that needed to be done, so he tried not to think of it as him abandoning her and instead as a necessary step toward her recovery from what had happened.

As if anyone can truly recover from such a thing.

Nothing you can do.

Actually, being there for her when needed was something, letting her know she wasn't alone—such knowledge and understanding could do wonders for one's mental state after such a horrific experience.

Well, at least this was true of those who had been through combat and witnessed horrors many people couldn't even fathom. Someone who had been raped…he didn't really know.

He headed to the Spirit Halloween store while thinking about this, the excitement he should have felt—had been looking forward to feeling for a month—nowhere to be found as he browsed the shelves for items that would be necessary for his frightening display.

Not long after that, his checking account down another sixty dollars, he headed home with the items he had purchased, mind going over the mental blueprints that he had been slowly but surely working on for the last month.

House empty, he made himself a pot of tea, Puttabong again, and flipped on AMC to see what horror movie they were showing. As before, it wasn't something he wanted to watch, so rather than letting it play, he went and got *The People Under the Stairs*, which he watched while drinking the tea and unloading all his supplies.

Fool and Alice were talking with Roach in her room when he paused his viewing of the movie, tea finished, and took everything outside. The spiderweb was the first thing he set up, the twisted branches of the crab apple tree by the front door and the low bushes that sat right below it allowing him to create a giant pyramid-like web that would look incredibly spooky in the dark, especially with the strobe light going beneath it.

Once that was up, he began anchoring several tombstones in the yard, all at crooked angles, some of which also had rotting arms reaching up near the base as if zombies were on the rise.

He was positioning one of these, fingers growing numb from the unseasonable chill, when a car slowly pulled into the cul-de-sac and cautiously approached the house.

Alan stood.

The car, which despite looking pretty worn seemed to be running smoothly, pulled in behind Alan's car and stopped. Inside sat a man, one who was soon struggling to get out through the door, his overweight body looking as if it had been inside while the vehicle was in production and only now realized the door width would not be sufficient.

Alan waited, eyes noting a gun on the belt as the suit coat was caught on something before falling back in place.

Police officer? Alan wondered, an image of the man trying to chase down someone who had stolen something a bit worrisome, especially when contemplating tax-dollar money going toward the paycheck.

"Mr. Miller?" the man asked, voice seeming to carry relief that he was now out of the vehicle.

"Yes," Alan said, hand brushing off some leaves from his pants.

"My name is Walter Doyle. I'm a state licensed private investigator." He pulled out his identification. "May I have a moment of your time?"

"Um...sure." Alan motioned him toward the front porch where two chairs were waiting. From there, once he knew what it was they would be discussing, he would let him inside, if necessary. Until then, the porch was fine.

"Quite a display you're setting up," the investigator noted. "Going to scare the crap out of the kids."

"That's the goal," Alan said. "So, what brings you here?"

"Just some questions," the detective said. Then without warning, "Are you in the market for a new house, Mr. Miller?"

"What?" Alan asked.

"A house, one like this, only with you listed as the owner rather than your mother."

Alan stared at the investigator for a moment, a red flag going up.

He has done research on me.

Why?

More important, who was paying for it?

"Maybe," Alan said. "Who wants to know?"

"Actually, no one. I just noticed that you seemed to be interested in a couple different houses this past weekend, so much so that you actually paid a visit to the real estate office yesterday that manages those locations."

"Really? And you noticed this because you are also interested in those houses?"

Mr. Doyle shook his head. "Not the houses, but what goes on inside. And it isn't really me that is interested, but the wife of a man who I've followed to a couple of the locations that you seem to be watching."

Alan nodded.

"And you visited the office of the company that owns the houses yesterday, so the only conclusion I can reach is that you're interested in purchasing one of the houses."

Alan didn't reply.

"By the way," Mr. Doyle continued, "do you find it odd that the Kristi Homes Real Estate company only represents houses that the company owns? Most real estate companies simply represent owners and their houses and aren't really in the buying and reselling of them."

Again, Alan didn't reply, at least not right away, the fact that he had been observed without being aware of it disconcerting. It also made him realize that despite how unprofessional Mr. Doyle appeared, he was pretty legit when it came to this work and obviously knew what was going on. Because of this, he finally asked, "Is that the only thing you find odd about this company?"

"My goodness, no."

Alan waited, but when nothing else followed, asked, "So, I take it you've informed your client of her husband's indiscretion?"

Mr. Doyle nodded. "I have."

"And you've explained what is going on with the real estate company?"

"No, that didn't seem necessary. I just showed her evidence that her husband was having an affair with a young lady that worked in real estate. Officially, that's what my notes say within the file."

"And unofficially?"

"Unofficially, it didn't take long for me to figure out what was going on or to notice that I wasn't the only one watching the houses."

"And now you've come to me for…" Alan asked.

Mr. Doyle shrugged. "Curiosity."

Alan nodded. "You want to know why I was watching the houses."

"Yes."

Alan didn't reply right away, thoughts on whether or not he could actually trust this man bouncing around inside his head. On the one hand, everything he said made sense. Private investigators were often hired by spouses who suspected their significant others of cheating. On the other, given how common such a thing was, it would be easy for someone like Kristi Woodman to hire someone to portray a private investigator, one who would then try to use the fake investigation story to learn more about him. After all, every-thing Mr. Doyle had just said was stuff he had shared with Kristi Homes, so it would be easy for Mr. Doyle to claim he witnessed him watching the houses.

"Which houses did you see me outside of?" Alan asked.

Mr. Doyle sighed and then pulled out a set of car keys from his jacket pocket. "There's a file folder on the front seat. Could you go grab it?"

Surprised, Alan took the keys and walked to the car, body moving in such a way that he could keep an eye on Mr. Doyle as he sat by the unlocked front door.

ALAN MILLER was written on the tab of the file folder, startling him. He had figured it would be a file for the case the in-vestigator had been working on, not one solely dedicated to him.

File folder in hand, the smell of cigar smoke from within the car clinging to it, Alan walked back up to the porch, where he handed over the keys.

"May I?" Alan asked while indicating the file that was still in his hands.

Mr. Doyle nodded.

Alan opened the file.

Inside, a picture of himself in uniform greeted him, one that had been taken after he had made it into Special Forces. Beyond that was a page of notes detailing observations that had been made of his actions during the last four days, followed by notes on information that must have been gathered through various research channels. Within the notes, paper-clipped to one of the rear pages, was an-other photograph, this one of him actually sitting in his car watching one of the houses.

"So..." Alan started, eyes going from the notes to Mr. Doyle. "Honestly, I don't even know what to say beyond asking, why?"

Mr. Doyle put his hands up. "Like I said a few moments

ago, curiosity. When I followed my client's husband for the first time, I had no idea what to expect and was pretty surprised when he pulled up to a house that was for sale. I also wondered if maybe her suspicions about his odd behavior were correct, but the theory on what exactly was going on incorrect. It wasn't until the following week, when he went to that house again and stayed for a couple hours with the agent, that I started to suspect something. During the third visit, I saw you."

"And…"

"And I kind of wondered if maybe my client wasn't the only one who suspected a significant other of cheating."

"Ah, okay," Alan said. "So, you figured maybe I was a boyfriend of the girl working the real estate job."

"Exactly."

Alan nodded but then said, "I still don't understand why you had to look into all this," while lifting the file folder.

"When you work as an investigator, you never know what information will prove important and what won't. As it turns out, doing a little research on you didn't really provide anything necessary in proving to my client that her husband was cheating on her, but it did open up an interesting sidenote on what was going on, especially when coupled with my viewing of the real estate website and my research on a few of the young ladies who were being displayed upon it."

Alan thought about all this and then asked, "So you're done with the case then?"

"Yep."

"And you're not going to report what is going on to the authorities?"

"Undecided on that," he said. "That's why I'm here. I wanted to talk to you about it."

"Oh?" Alan asked, his surprise genuine. "Why?"

"Like I said, I'm curious about you and why you're involved in all this. Admittedly, your background is a large factor in this. Seems we both had similar beginnings to our adulthood. You were in the sandbox; I was in the jungle."

"Vietnam?"

Mr. Doyle nodded.

"Special Forces?"

Another nod, then, "Only in my day, we weren't looked upon too fondly."

"Snake eaters."

"Yep." His eyes drifted for a moment, not in where they looked but in what they saw, which Alan felt was probably an event that had taken place back in the jungles of Southeast Asia.

Or when he got back home?

Being spit on and called names...

A gust of wind swept across the neighborhood while he was contemplating this, tearing hundreds of dry leaves from the trees.

A chill followed, and for a moment Alan considered asking Mr. Doyle inside. Mr. Doyle, however, seemed fine, probably because of all the fat insulating his body, so Alan decided not to voice the suggestion.

"Tell me, what is your purpose in all this?" Mr. Doyle asked, eyes once again focused on the present.

"Honestly, I'm just helping a friend."

"A friend?" Mr. Doyle asked. "One of the girls?"

"No, a reporter friend, one who stumbled upon this real estate scheme when doing a story on the local real estate market." He paused for a moment. "She needed help getting close to the girls."

"I see, and you're what, posing as a john?"

Alan didn't really like the term since it felt kind of seedy, which didn't seem to fit with what was going on, but he didn't dispute it either and said, "I guess."

"And by doing this, what do you hope to learn? You already know their secret."

"She wants personal details, life stories on the girls and whatnot. This story is kind of a *make or break* moment for her, so she doesn't want to jump the gun on releasing it."

Mr. Doyle nodded.

"Basically, she's worried that people will read the story and not feel anything, their minds shrugging it off as another simple prostitution thing."

"And she thinks that having sob stories on the girls and why they became prostitutes will change that?"

"You don't?" Alan asked.

"I have no idea," he admitted. "Do you?"

Alan shrugged. "I don't know."

"Yet you're willing to do all this to find out," he noted. "Must be a pretty special girl."

Alan wasn't sure how to reply to that.

"You're bored too, aren't you?" Mr. Doyle added.

"Yeah," Alan admitted after nearly a minute.

"And you can't really talk about that because no one would understand."

"Yeah," Alan said again. Then, "It's not the fighting or the killing that I miss, though that had an odd sort of appeal to it as well, but the sense of being a part of something that few will even understand. A part of something that felt important, but not in the 'we're fighting for freedom' bullshit that everyone always voices."

"I know what you mean," Mr. Doyle said. "For me, the secrecy was a big part of it, and even though we were looked upon as if we were crazy, especially when going out into the jungle in a small team on a simple seek-and-destroy mission, there was a sense of respect that seemed to ooze from the regular grunts." He sighed. "In today's military, I'm guessing that respect was even more noticeable."

"It was," Alan said, a sudden longing to experience it again hitting hard.

"But of course you can't tell people this, not without them looking at you as a crazy war junkie."

"Right!"

Another gust of wind raced across the land, more leaves carried upon it to the ground, where they would eventually be bagged up or left to rot beneath a layer of snow.

"Have you considered going into law enforcement?"

"A bit, but with my disease, I'm not sure if I'd be able to."

Alan expected a question on what his disease was to follow, but that didn't happen. Instead, "True, though just remember, being a police office in a squad car isn't the only way you can work law enforcement." He handed over a business card. "And with that, I must be going. I have a meeting soon with another prospective client." He pointed to something on the card. "My number, if you need anything."

"Oh, thanks." Alan looked at the card, surprised to see his office was just over in Naperville, which wasn't far.

"And please be careful with this story you're helping your friend with. I didn't look too deeply into things, but I do know Kristi Woodman's husband, Samuel Woodman, isn't a person you would want to cross."

"Why's that?" Alan asked.

"The guy is a former police officer who spent quite a bit of time undercover for the city of Chicago. I wasn't able to get much, but from what I did look into, it appears that his actions while undercover may not have been officially condoned, which may have led to his early retirement."

A police officer who worked undercover, Alan said to himself. *If Stacy knew about that this entire time...*

Alan wasn't sure how he was going to respond if that was the case, but he did know that her not telling him crossed a line.

"So if you do continue forward with this, just remember, this guy probably has access to things most pimps would not if he still has friends on the force, and he could easily learn everything there is to know about you."

"But I can hurt him too," Alan said. "A decorated police officer who helps his wife run a prostitution ring through her real estate company…that would draw a lot of attention if released to the media."

"Yes, it would, which is why this guy might not take any chances once he figures out what it is you're up to."

Alan hadn't thought about that.

7

"What did you do?" Sam demanded, voice echoing from the phone to the point where Riley was forced to pull it from his ear.

"What do you mean?" Riley asked, a half-eaten taco sitting on the wrapper in his lap, sour cream oozing from the back. Had it been a bit warmer out, he would have eaten the taco on the trunk of his car, but given the chill in the air and the wind, he had decided the risk to his pants and the upholstery in the car was justified.

"Kristi says you ruined everything today," Sam said.

"Really? And how exactly did I manage that?"

"She says you went to her office just as a potential client was supposed to show up for an interview and that he never showed after that. And then you sexually harassed Isabella."

"I did what?" Riley asked.

"You sexually harassed Isabella."

"Are you fucking kidding me," Riley laughed. "I didn't even know she was at the office until just before I was going to leave, and then I only asked how she was doing with the clients and school."

"That's not what Kristi says."

Riley shook his head. "Okay, and what, may I ask, is your lovely wife saying I said?"

"She wouldn't go into details, given how angry she was, but she told me to tell you to stay away from her office and that she doesn't think you should be around the girls anymore because you might upset them to the point where they'll quit."

"Sam, I didn't do anything like that, and you know it!"

"Why would Kristi make something like that up?"

"Seriously?" Riley asked. *How many times have we been over this?*

"Seriously, why would she?" Sam pressed. "Kristi hates drama and does everything she can to avoid it."

"Sam, do you honestly believe that?"

Sam didn't reply.

"Sam?" Riley asked.

"Just stop, okay," Sam said. "I know you don't like her and that she has pretty much given up on ever being accepted by you, but you know what? I love her and am going to spend the rest of my life with her, so you need to accept that."

Again, Riley didn't know how to reply to this. He couldn't even wrap his mind around it. What had happened to his brother? How could he be so blind? It was crazy.

And they are running things.

And not in the way we all decided upon in the beginning.

"Sam, are you still sending me names for the background checks on potential clients?" Riley asked.

"Of course," Sam said.

"Really? Because I haven't gotten any from you in over two weeks."

"That's because we aren't getting any new clients, thanks to all your rules."

Riley sighed.

"What?" Sam asked, the sound of the sigh having reached him.

"I gotta go," Riley said. "You and Kristi…" He didn't know what to say. "Well, good luck." He disconnected the call.

Sam texted him less than a minute later while Riley was tossing out the taco, which was no longer appetizing to him, a question on what the "good luck" comment was supposed to mean.

Riley didn't respond.

Another text followed a few minutes later, one that prompted him to put Sam's number in the blocked category on his phone, thus making it so nothing would get through to him. This, in turn, would make it so Riley wouldn't be tempted to reply, something that he couldn't help himself from doing whenever he knew a text was present.

Not long after that, the stoplights between the taco shack and his office having been in his favor, Riley was walking back into work, an evening of paperwork awaiting him. He also needed to get a surveillance operation authorized on an Aurora storage locker that was, according to the girl they had interviewed earlier, being used to store bricks of marijuana and guns.

8

Amanda had never before been on a porn set, yet even without any experience behind her, she could tell what they were doing was incredibly amateurish and did not carry with it any artistic quality whatsoever, which in her mind eliminated any possibility of future stardom for her two coworkers. Not that they recognized this at all, their minds seeming to think the presence of the two Best Buy-bought digital cameras and a homemade stage light was enough to make this "director" the Steven Spielberg of the porn world. In reality, the director and his cameramen had simply found a way of getting girls to fuck them without having to worry about the whole dating thing and then made money from it. It was pathetic.

"You guys have a website?" Amanda asked at one point, a glass of water from the sink helping to wash out the taste of semen from a blowjob she had just performed upon the one named Luke.

"We're still working on it," the one with the main camera said. His name was Patrick. "Right now we put the videos up on Clips4Sale."

"Oh, what's that?"

"It's a giant site full of videos that producers like us upload. They do all the work maintaining the site and bringing in traffic, and people like us just set up our own storefront and upload the videos." He pointed toward Isabella and said, "Would you be cool with being handcuffed and forced to deep throat?"

"Sure," she said. "No problem."

"You won't puke or anything, will you?"

"No way."

"Okay, great. I mean, I know there is a market for that stuff if you do end up puking, but I don't watch them and can't stand to see stuff like that, so..." He shrugged and turned back toward Amanda. "It's great. The site, they take a forty-percent cut from each video you sell, so the rest, sixty percent, goes right into your pocket."

"And how much do you sell the videos for?"

"Um, it all depends. These ones we're doing today will all be between five and ten minutes, so probably between five and ten bucks for a video. The site likes it if you match the price to the minutes, though you can go lower with longer videos." He thought for a second while Isabella was getting ready and then said, "After her, could you two both give Dean a blowjob at the same time, and at some point during it start to argue over who gets the cum and sort of fight over getting your mouth on the cock?"

"No sweat," Caroline said with a smile.

"Just don't jerk it back and forth too hard," Dean said from the corner, the laugh doing little to mask the concern he actually had.

"Wouldn't dream of it, sweetheart," Caroline said.

"Okay," Patrick announced. "Quiet on the set."

Amanda rolled her eyes.

With that, everyone watched as Isabella had her hands handcuffed behind her back and acted as if she didn't want the penis her ski-masked captor pulled out to go into her mouth. In it went, however, the sound of wet, muffled gags filling the room as he repeatedly forced it down her throat while holding her by the hair.

Eight minutes later, he pulled his penis out and shot the load all over her tear-streaked face.

"Wow, fantastic!" Patrick said. Then, "Luke, can you go fuck her mouth now and then come hold the camera for a bit and film me doing it? We'll really milk this position and sell this one as a full video and a three-part series. Isabella, stay right where you are, okay?"

Isabella agreed, not that she had much choice with her wrists handcuffed to the post.

Patrick filmed as Luke grabbed Isabella and thrust himself down her throat, the gags this time sounding pretty wretched. Nine minutes later, his load dripping from her mouth onto her clothes, he took the camera from Patrick and began filming. Patrick lasted just over six minutes, the gags and panic Isabella projected much more intense.

"What a trooper," Patrick said afterward while unlocking her wrists so she could go clean herself up. He then turned back to Amanda and said, "Perk of being the director, when something incredibly hot gets me going, I can totally jump in."

"And just wait," Luke said. "He'll be all over you once you have that schoolgirl skirt on."

"I can't wait," Amanda mumbled and then got down on her knees before Dean, Caroline at her side.

"So here's the deal, after one of you gets the cum in your mouth, whoever that turns out to be, I want the other to look all sad as if she is going to start to cry, which then will lead the other to kiss her and swap the cum. Guys love videos like that."

With that, Amanda and Caroline began sucking, Dean seeming to enjoy himself up until the tugging moment began. After that, he lost the buildup that had been developing and required another seven minutes of gentle sucking to get it back.

Amanda managed to get the mouthful, a finger pressing into that magic area of flesh between his testicles and butt to get him off.

Caroline gave her the pouty look.

The two then kissed, Amanda pushing the glob of semen into her mouth.

Caroline swallowed it, a look of pleasure dancing across her face, one that she faked so well that even Amanda had a difficult time realizing it was forced.

"Okay, great. Let's give the blowjobs a rest for a bit, let your mouths recover." Patrick looked around a moment. "Where'd Isabella go?"

Amanda and Caroline exchanged glances and then looked toward the hallway that led to the bathroom.

"Can one of you go check on her, make sure she's okay?" Patrick asked.

"Sure," Amanda said and started down the hallway.

Behind her, she heard Patrick start to discuss what they would do next, a question to the guys on whether or not they had a few more cumshots in them being asked.

Amanda didn't hear the replies as she headed upstairs, the first bathroom having been empty.

Isabella was upstairs, not in the bathroom, but in a bedroom, sitting against the wall with her knees pressed against her chest, arms wrapped tight around them.

"You okay?" Amanda asked.

It was a ridiculous question, yet all she could think to say while standing there.

Isabella looked at her for a moment and then went back to looking at the floor.

Amanda moved in close and knelt down next to her. "What is it?"

"The handcuffs," she said, voice barely above a whisper. "I thought it'd be okay, but it wasn't."

Amanda waited, sensing more.

"They used to handcuff me like that to a post in the basement and let men fuck my mouth for twenty-five bucks. All day and all night."

"Who did?" Amanda asked.

Isabella didn't answer.

Amanda put a hand on her, Isabella's body flinching for a moment. "It's okay."

Tears started to fall.

"They once forgot about me down there too. They were so high that they passed out, and I couldn't get away from the post for nearly two days, with rats and...and...guys who found me and...none of them seemed to care that I had shit myself and had spoiled spunk all over my clothes and in my hair."

The tears became more pronounced.

"Hey," Caroline called up the steps. *"Everything okay?"*

"Give us a minute!" Amanda replied.

"I should get back down there," Isabella said, wiping away the tears.

"No, you stay right there," Amanda insisted. "We've given them like fifteen videos so far, all without a break, so they can wait a bit."

Isabella wiped more tears away and started to stand.

Amanda stood with her and again suggested they wait.

"I don't want them to get upset with us," Isabella said, pushing away Amanda's hands. "Working with them could be our ticket out of—"

"Girl, you and Caroline could do the same exact thing all by yourselves with a video camera and a light from Target."

"But the editing and website stuff, we don't know how to do that."

"Didn't you hear what he said? All you do is upload them, probably like putting videos on YouTube."

"Yeah?" Isabella questioned.

"Hey!" Caroline said from the hallway. "You two okay?"

"We're fine," Amanda said. "Just needed a quick break."

"Okay, cool. So, um, they're going to film me in a moment, so why don't you two stay up here until they tell you to come down. Don't want to ruin the shot by walking in or talking or anything."

"Yep, will do."

"Great, oh, and when you do come down, they want us all to put on school uniforms for a spanking and butt-fucking video."

"Okay, got it."

Caroline grinned, twisted, and headed back toward the stairs, a shouted statement of, "They're cool, just needed five!" leaving her lips.

Amanda turned back to Isabella and motioned her to the chair, which she took, face still looking as if it was about to break.

"I never was handcuffed to a post in a basement for blowjobs," Amanda said, "but my ex did once get me so high that I woke up the next day covered in piss, shit, and cum. I was like the centerpiece of some gangbang party. I don't know how much he charged for them to use me, but whatever it was, I never saw any of it."

"How old were you?" Isabella asked.

"Twenty-one."

Isabella contemplated that. "I was fifteen."

"Fifteen?" *Jesus. I was a freshman in high school then.* Giving blowjobs at that age, that was just something she and her friends had joked about, the actual sensations involved completely unknown to them.

"Yeah, twenty-five bucks to have my mouth used over and over again so my parents could buy smack, and now, less than two years later, men pay big bucks for me to pleasure them!" She shook her head. "American dream."

"You're only seventeen?" Amanda asked.

"Yeah."

"But..." Amanda didn't know what to say. The guys downstairs, they had taken photos of their IDs and had them all sign model release forms, all to verify that they each were over eighteen years old. "How old is Caroline?"

"I don't know, seventeen, maybe eighteen." Isabella sighed. "You're gonna tell them, aren't you?"

Amanda thought about it for a second, a question about whether or not it would do any good unfolding, and then, "No, but...well...do Kristi and Sam know how old you are?"

Isabella shrugged.

Amanda didn't know what to say.

"Does it really bother you?" Isabella asked, her recovery from the handcuff flashback seemingly complete.

"A bit," she admitted. "But only because I was told everyone was over eighteen in the beginning."

"You asked?"

"Well, not in the beginning, but once I was clean and they explained to me what was going on and how I could work for them if I wanted, yeah, I did."

"Why?"

"Because I was worried about moments like this," Amanda said.

"What do you mean?"

"Do you realize, if the police were to walk in right now and find out you two are underage, that I'd be arrested not just for prostitution but for having sex with a minor?"

"Really?"

"Yeah."

Isabella actually contemplated this for several seconds before eventually saying, "Well, just tell them you thought I was an adult. Everyone else does." She started toward the doorway.

"Wait, are you sure you want to keep filming?" Amanda asked.

"Yeah."

"You're sure you're okay?"

"YEAH!"

Amanda sighed.

"What the fuck's wrong with you?" Isabella asked, anger suddenly present.

"Nothing, just surprised." *How can you go from completely broken down in the corner to bouncing back up and eagerly wanting to get in front of the camera again, knowing you're going to be butt fucked?*

Isabella stared at her for about ten seconds and then headed toward the stairs.

Amanda didn't follow right away, thoughts of what Isabella had gone through as a kid and how those events had shaped her into someone who could just bounce back like this dominating her mind.

Being handcuffed to a post in a basement for days by your parents, covered in filth and forced to suck cocks.

Shit, even without the two-day "they forgot about me because they were high" period, the fact that Isabella's own parents sold her body so they could buy drugs was almost impossible for Amanda to comprehend.

Did the same thing happen to Caroline?

And what about Vicky?

From there her thoughts shifted over to Emily and some of the discussions they'd had, ones that had sometimes lasted well into the night when neither could sleep.

Though often abused by her various pimps, it had seemed like Emily had had a pretty solid foundation while growing up, one that had been similar to Amanda's. Neither one of them had been "forced" into prostitution, just sort of edged in that direction.

If I had never fallen in love with Matt…

She shook the thought away.

"Amanda, you coming?" Isabella asked.

"Yeah," Amanda said and started toward the stairs.

Are you going to continue doing sex scenes knowing they are both underage?

The answer was yes, though only because she feared what would happen if she said something about it to the men. Well, actually, she didn't fear what they would do, but what Kristi and Sam would do after they learned what she had done.

"Everything okay?" Patrick asked as Amanda returned to the main room.

"Yeah," Amanda lied, watching as Isabella changed into a school uniform.

Caroline was already wearing her own, garters visible beneath the skirt and blouse opened in a way that would never be condoned at a real Catholic school.

"Great, well, once you're changed, we'll begin. Do you need to do any type of…um…cleaning before we start?"

"Here's the thing, I actually don't do anal stuff," Amanda said.

"What? But your boss said—" he started.

"My boss originally was going to have another girl here but needed me at the last moment. Guess she forgot about your anal request. I can do everything else, just not that."

"Oh, I see…well…" He was obviously caught off guard by this, so much so that he didn't say anything for several seconds.

"Pat, you don't have to have all three of them doing it," Luke said. "She could suck on us to lube us up before we dive in. Would save on K-Y."

"Yeah," Patrick said, his disappointment still evident. "Okay."

Isabella glared at her.

Amanda glared back.

Five minutes later, homemade stage light shining upon them, Best Buy cameras rolling, Amanda was on her knees lubing up the men with her mouth while Isabella and Caroline were bent over on the floor, knees pressed into the carpet with their butts held high and ready.

9

Alan spent the next three hours finishing his display, the final third of that being used to create a life-sized dummy for the chair in the corner by the door. Come Halloween night, Alan would take the place of the masked dummy, his own shirt stuffed with a pillow to give it an unnatural bulge beneath the dark cloak he would be wearing while the fake rubber hands stuck out from his sleeves. In the dark, with the strobe light going and his head leaning against the wall at an odd angle, no one would realize he was real until he sprang up as they approached the candy bowl. It would be fantastic.

Though focused on the work, his mind did stray toward the conversation he'd had with the private investigator, which then led to thoughts of Stacy and what she might be keeping from him.

Maybe keep this from her?

No, he had to tell her about Kristi's husband and his possible connections to the law-enforcement world. He had to tell her how dangerous this thing could—

She already knows that, he said to himself, images of her being tied down and fucked flowing through his mind.

Memories from their first night back together and the attack that had unfolded within her apartment followed.

Was that been Kristi's husband?

As before, the idea of attacking her for what little she knew seemed foolish, given that it had actually helped her confirm her suspicions, but that didn't mean someone like Samuel Woodman wouldn't do it, especially if they had felt she knew more than she actually did. Plus, the more he thought about it, the more he felt that the attack hadn't been meant to silence her in a "stop what you're doing or else" kind of way, but in a "you can't report on us because you're dead" one.

The question was, if killing her had been the original intent, why hadn't they tried again?

10

Stacy spent the better part of the afternoon trying to learn as much as she could about Samuel Woodman, and while there was plenty of information out there about him, there was very little that actually felt useful to her. Then again, anything that would seem useful for her story probably wouldn't be public, not if he was still able to walk around as a free man; therefore, searching the web for anything beyond general information was probably pointless.

Footsteps!

On the stairway.

Panicked, she went to the kitchen to grab a knife and then hurried toward the front door, feet catching and almost tripping over a shoe that she had carelessly kicked from her foot upon arriving home after breakfast.

No peephole was present in her door, and the only window looking out at the small wooden landing was at eye level in the middle of the door, a flimsy curtain hanging over it. Not wanting to give herself away, she simply stared at the curtain, eyes waiting to see if a figure appeared before the door blocking the light that filtered in.

Nothing.

Even the sounds, which she had been sure were footsteps upon the aging wooden planks, had stopped.

Heart racing, she waited, knife held at the ready, wishing it were a gun, even though she wasn't really any good with one.

Seconds turned to minutes, the third of which saw her risking a deep breath, one that she was sure could be heard beyond the door.

A gust of wind sped its way between the brick buildings surrounding the parking lot, the sound easily masking the steps of the person on the stairway.

Sweat slickened her palm.

She momentarily switched the knife to her left hand and wiped her right against her leg. While doing this she heard the phone on the table by her laptop buzz with a phone call.

Ignoring the call, she stayed by the door, desperately wanting to peek through the curtain.

No!

Fifteen seconds later, she did, eyes taking a moment to adjust to the glare on the glass before seeing that no one was there.

Another gust of wind raced through the parking lot, a few dried leaves and several other tiny pieces of discarded trash carried upon it.

Stacy opened the door.

Both the landing and stairway were empty, as was the parking lot.

You're losing it, her mind said.

No, someone was there, another part countered.

Concerned, both by the idea that she was losing it and that someone had been there, Stacy stepped back into her apartment, knife switched to her left once again so she could pull the door shut and lock it. With that secure, she headed over to the phone to see who had called, the caller ID saying the name Travis.

You shouldn't keep the phone.

Eventually, the guy's wife was going to report him missing, if she hadn't already, and the police might try to track him down using the GPS software within the device.

Assuming they don't find his body first, the reporter part of her brain injected.

So far, such a discovery hadn't happened, unless, that was, it had gone unreported by the local media, which seemed unlikely. Most likely, Rusty and the others who were involved with the events inside that house had covered everything up, their twisted minds having enough sense to know that any police investigation into the death would be disastrous for them. Self-preservation was key.

And you're a threat to that.

They will come after you.

Her grip on the knife tightened.

Let them come.

The empowerment she felt from this inner statement lasted

until sunset, at which point she grew incredibly uneasy.

Call Alan.

No.

She didn't want to become dependent on his company to get through the night.

Go to the house in Joliet.

Kill Rusty.

As appealing as the idea was, she knew that doing so could put her in jail for the rest of her life. Yesterday, while still in the house, a self-defense argument would have worked, but now, nearly a day and half later, and with her actually going to him, that wouldn't be the case. She would have to wait for him to come to her.

Or call the police.

No.

That just wasn't an option. After all, what was the point of surviving such an ordeal if the life that followed would be one of dodging collection agents and fighting off depression, all while the only dream she had ever had crept further and further away with each passing day?

She closed her eyes and felt Rusty on top of her, penis poking at her as it tried to find her opening.

Tears and anger erupted.

She had to make that moment worth something; she had to use it to get rid of her current reality.

She had to —

A *bleep!* sound signaling a Facebook notification echoed from her laptop.

Curious, she went over to it and saw the message was from Alan, a statement of WE REALLY NEED TO TALK present.

11

"We're going to get in trouble," Isabella said as they drove Amanda home. "They paid good money for our time, and you pretty much said *fuck you* with your *no anal* bullshit."

"Oh, give me a break!" Amanda said. "With you two getting pounded and me sucking them off, they didn't give a shit. We gave them tons of new videos to upload on that stupid site, and everyone is supposed to know that I don't do anything anal anyway."

"Why not?" Isabella demanded.

"I just don't!" Amanda snapped.

"Such a poor delicate girl," Caroline said. "Did someone hurt your butt when you were younger?"

"No," Amanda said. She had tried anal sex once, with Matt at his insistence before he had turned her into a whore, and it had caused her to shit herself. Since then, she refused to allow anything up her butt EVER, the humiliation of that moment far too great to risk a second experience.

How many times was I fucked like that while high?

No answer arrived.

"I bet her daddy fucked her up the butt," Caroline said.

"Probably right," Isabella replied.

"Probably came home drunk one night and went to her bed instead of Mommy's bed and put it right up there."

"Yep."

Amanda wanted to reply but didn't, the anger she felt at the statement far too great to risk opening her mouth, especially this close to the house.

"Oooh, I bet that's it, isn't it?" Caroline said, turning in her seat to look at her. "Or maybe you encouraged it and liked it so much that you want to savor the moment and don't want anyone else to ever interfere with the memory."

Amanda hit her, hard, a backhanded blow that smashed her knuckles right into the side of Caroline's mouth, splitting her lip.

Blood bubbled.

"Bitch!" Caroline cried after the shock wore off. A hand reached out to grab her.

Amanda grabbed her hand and twisted it, the angle such that she could probably break bones if she used the car seat as brace while pulling.

"Stop! Stop! *Stop!*" Caroline begged.

"Don't ever talk about my father like that!" Amanda said, voice firm yet controlled, her hand having applied just enough pressure to make Caroline think she was about to break her wrist.

"*Okay!*" Caroline cried.

Isabella, stunned, just continued to drive, eyes staying on the road, eventually pulling the car up along the front yard of the house, tire bouncing off the curb.

Amanda waited until the car stopped to let go of Caroline's hand and then, without saying a word, grabbed her clothes and left the car.

Isabella didn't wait for her to get inside before pulling away, her foot hitting the gas hard enough for the engine to be heard in all the houses up and down the quiet neighborhood street.

Vicky wasn't back yet.

No one was there.

Relishing the sudden silence, Amanda headed upstairs to put her clothes away—as in, thrown on the bed—and then headed to the bathroom to take a shower.

Once done with that, she went back to her room and opened up her computer, a moment of excitement appearing when she saw that Alan Miller had accepted her friend request.

She also discovered she had been right; much of his profile was hidden from the public. Now that they were friends, however, she was able to see everything, the most interesting posts, to her at least, being the pictures of him while in the military.

Still wrapped in her towel despite being dry enough to put

her pajamas on, she spent the next fifteen minutes sitting at the desk typing up a message to Alan, her mind seemingly stuck on each word as she composed the sentences, a statement on how it was really nice meeting him the other day and that she looked forward to seeing him again finally coming together.

Hesitation about sending it followed, though she wasn't sure why. In fact, she had no idea why she felt the way she did about Alan, the attraction something that she had not experienced with anyone since her early days with Matt.

Even more bizarre was that she had not really given him any thought during the time they had shared together in class up until yesterday, yet now he seemed to dominate her thoughts—more so than Matt ever had during the beginning days of their relationship.

Is he experiencing the same thing?

Has he even thought of me at all?

Fear that he would think her nothing more than a whore who could suck his dick when desired plagued her mind and brought about the question of whether or not his compassion yesterday in the hallway had been genuine. After all, he had apparently known who she was due to his interest in another one of the girls from the site, something that Mrs. Woodman had been eager to learn more about yesterday. But did that necessarily mean she couldn't trust his actions? Did it mean there had been an ulterior motive?

She leaned toward an answer of no simply because he had already been scheduled to see Kristi that day; therefore their encounter hadn't had any influence on that.

And the moment at the real estate office, that had simply been due to Kristi wanting to find out if the two had something going on behind her back. Both of them had been surprised and a bit apprehensive, until the intimacy had actually begun, and then...

A longing to share that moment of closeness returned. It wasn't necessarily a longing for the act she had performed upon him, but the connection she had felt while doing it, one that she was sure could arrive with them just being close.

He had to have felt it too, she said to herself, almost as a reassurance. *How could he not?*

The thought didn't shake the fear that he hadn't, or the fear that he would say no if she asked to hang out, which she realized was her real hesitation in sending the message. It wasn't a question she was going to include in this message, but one she wanted to ask after seeing his reply—if he replied. Earning that reply was in question, however, and if she didn't get one...

That was the fear.

Once she sent her message, she would be waiting on him, longing for him to reply, which might not happen at all.

He accepted the friend request.

But that doesn't mean anything.

Yes it does.

Her phone buzzed.

In fact, she had a missed call that she'd been unaware of, one that must have arrived while she was in the shower.

KRISTI WOODMAN.

Fuck!

"Hello?" she asked.

"Amanda?" Kristi said.

"Yes."

"I'm on my way back with Vicky and want to speak with you about something. We should be there in about fifteen minutes."

"Okay." She wanted to ask what it was about, even though she was pretty sure she knew. Isabella and Caroline had said something to Kristi, and now Amanda was going to get a lecture.

Nothing else was said.

Amanda returned her attention back to the message, read it over three more times, changed the wording in the final sentence, and hit send.

Heavy sigh.

She then closed the laptop and went to get dressed, the idea of putting her pajamas on now set aside, given the visit. She wasn't going to doll herself up completely, but she was going to be presentable, pants and a sweater being the final choice after about five minutes of staring at her selection.

Dressed, she opened her laptop again to see if Alan had replied, her heartbeat quickening as Facebook loaded up.

No reply.

He hadn't even seen the message yet, the little check mark indication that would be present if he had not there.

At least that was something, the lack of a check mark following the lack of a reply a bit of a relief since she didn't have to contemplate the idea that he had seen it and chosen not to reply. Such a situation would be hard to deal with.

From the message screen she went back to his profile and looked at a few more pictures, but the longing it was creating to see him was too much at the moment, so she shut everything down again and went downstairs to await Kristi Woodman, who pulled into the driveway four minutes later.

12

"You didn't know at all?" Alan asked, watching her face, looking for signs of dishonesty from her.

"No, I never even considered it," Stacy said. "I promise you, yesterday was the first time I heard about it, and then I didn't even verify it until today."

"Why didn't you tell me yesterday?" Alan asked and then regretted it and the harshness that was present in his voice.

"Sorry, but I was a little distraught yesterday," Stacy snapped.

Alan held up his hands, palms outward, and apologized. "I'm a little overwhelmed by all this," he added. "Having that private investigator show up and finding out there may be police connections to all this"—he shook his head—"all after you were raped and nearly killed."

Stacy didn't reply to that.

Alan considered going silent as well but then asked, "What are we doing here?"

"What do you mean?" she asked.

"Setting up appointments, hiring these girls, following them...I just don't understand what this is all going to contribute to your story and how it's going to make you the big world-renowned journalist you've always dreamed of being."

"I told you, I want the readers to know what these girls are like and why they're involved in this."

"But you already have so much. You could easily start to achieve the success you dream of by offering this story to the public and then continuing with it as we learn more and more. It doesn't all have to be one epic tome."

She shook her head. "Once the story breaks, that's the end. Everyone will be talking about it, and there will be no access to the girls because it will all be shut down."

"No access to the girls through appointments and sex at the houses, but they'll still be around," he said. "Hell, most of them go to school right down the road, so I doubt they're going to just vanish."

"And how do you suppose they're going to be paying for school once the jig is up? And where are they going to live?"

Alan hadn't really thought about that.

"That house we've watched, the one where they live, is

owned by Kristi Homes Real Estate, and while I'm not too familiar with how things work when prostitution is involved, I'm pretty sure the police will be able to seize the property due to it being used in a criminal enterprise."

"And throw the girls out on the street?" Alan asked.

"Probably," Stacy said with a sigh.

"You know what, there's a second story."

"What?"

"First you write about how the girls are victims of a prostitution business. Then you write about how they are victims of society as it turns its back on them after the business is dismantled."

"But are they really victims right now?" Stacy asked.

Alan took a moment to think about this, the term "victim" difficult to apply, given that the girls were going to college, had a great place to live and a car, and seemed, from what he'd seen of Amanda, very well kept. "Not victims so much in the typical sense, but most certainly trapped within a system, one that society feels is wrong. In fact, society will go so far as to dismantle it, all in the name of what's best for the girls, but then will fail to offer up any secondary opportunities."

Stacy thought about that.

"What you need to do is make sure people don't forget about the girls, make sure they don't just assume all these girls were released back to happy families or something, finally free from the sexual slavery everyone will envision."

"But we still need to learn everything we can about the girls before I can do that, especially if they're all going to scatter after this."

Alan nodded. "I think I'll be able to find out quite a bit about Amanda, especially after she friended me on Facebook."

"Okay, just remember to be careful with how you go about it," Stacy cautioned. "Don't be too aggressive, and don't let them realize you're asking questions." She paused. "Well, don't make it seem like all you're doing is asking questions."

"I know what you mean," Alan said. "I won't be interrogating her."

"And find out if there has been any drama or abuse within this thing. Or if any of the girls are disgruntled."

Alan nodded. "Don't worry. I'll get everything you need to know. In the meantime, you should start writing the story if you haven't yet. Start getting it all down on paper and—"

"Alan, I know how to write."

"I know. I'm sorry."

13

Stacy locked the door after Alan left, the desire to ask him to stay going unvoiced as their conversation came to its natural conclusion. Resentment followed, both at the fact that he hadn't offered to stay and because he had given her writing advice, the latter of which irked her to no end.

How many articles has he written?

How many has he published?

She then took in her surroundings and realized she couldn't really blame him for thinking she needed advice. After all, her place didn't exactly scream success.

But I used to be successful!

And he knew me back then!

She'd had an apartment in Lisle, up in the Four Lakes, a place that was so nice it had its own ski hill during the winter and a beach on its own lake right in the middle of the suburbs. The two used to spend hours walking the grounds, talking, all between visits to her bed, or the floor, or up against the door. It was—

The doorknob jiggled and then there was a heavy knock.

Stacy turned, a sudden hope that he had decided to stay

without having to be asked unfolding as she headed to the door and threw the latch.

14

Alan got stopped by a train on his way home from Stacy's place, his mind going over what they had talked about while waiting for the graffiti-scarred cars to rumble by as they carried their coal shipments toward the city.

She's scared of failure, he told himself.

That was why she hadn't written the article yet. She wanted to, wanted to see it in print all across the globe, but also knew that the moment she sent it out was the moment that it could fail, so she was doing everything she could to postpone it — to postpone the lack of control she would have once it was out there.

With most of her articles, such a fear did not exist, but with this one, given how big the story could be and the impact it could have, it did. After all, it wasn't every day that a story of an illegal prostitution ring centered in the suburbs fell into a struggling reporter's lap; thus Stacy was going to do everything she could to make sure the story was perfect before she released it to the masses, before she relinquished control over it.

Coal cars continued to rumble by, the train seemingly endless.

Behind him, cars began stacking up.

Alan studied them in the mirror, curiosity and boredom guiding his eyes. He then went to his phone, finger clicking away at the buttons to pull up Facebook, his unfamiliarity with the mobile version of the web once again making him feel as if he had never before visited the site.

New message, he noted and fumbled around before he managed to pull it up.

From Amanda.

The train ended.

He set the phone back in his cupholder and got ready to cross the tracks, only to watch as the gates stayed down and another train, this one going the opposite way on the second set of tracks, began to rumble by.

Alan sighed, shifted the car to park, and started to read the message.

15

"How did the videos go?" Mrs. Woodman asked once the two were seated in the family room, a momentary look of judgment at how poorly the room had been kept showing upon her face.

"They were fine," Amanda said, voice cautious. "They got quite a few videos to add to the site they use." She paused for a moment and then added, "I think they'll make a lot of money with what we did today and that it was worth the price they paid."

Mrs. Woodman nodded.

Amanda waited. She had no idea where Mrs. Woodman was going with this and didn't want to direct the focus to her refusal to do any anal scenes if that wasn't the original intention of this visit.

"Samuel and I, we've been thinking that branching out into our own adult video market while cutting down on the escort side would be a worthwhile endeavor, given that it would be, for one, legal, and two, an enterprise that would continue to generate income after the sex since multiple people would be buying and download-ing the videos."

"I see," Amanda said, still guarded, the idea that Mrs. Woodman wanted to consult with her on such an idea seeming off.

"Is that something you would be okay with doing?" she asked. "I know you didn't want to be associated with such videos, but now it seems that since you'll be appearing on screen in these ones anyway, your reservations about it from this point forward would be somewhat silly."

"They would be," Amanda agreed.

"Okay, good. I'm glad we are on the same page with that." She looked around for a moment and then leaned in close. "Now, I need to ask a favor of you, one that is very important. Do you remember Riley, Samuel's brother who was still a part of everything when you started?"

"Yes," Amanda said.

"Well, early on there were several little conflicts with him over how we were going to run this thing, his view being that we were way too conservative in our approach. Now, I believe much of this has to do with his desire to recoup the investment he made in this setup, one that he kept insisting upon making so that we could get several of you girls up and running at once and have several houses at our disposal to cut down on being noticed by the community. He also didn't like that we were serious about all of you going to college and getting an education. He thought that idea was ludicrous and a waste of money. I think a big part of all this is because he is jealous that Samuel and I ended up together rather than me and him. He has never forgiven Samuel for stealing me from him, as he puts it. Anyway, Samuel and I had to pull back from him two months ago while also making sure to pay back his investment so that he didn't cause trouble, which, unfortunately, he is in a position to do. What we didn't realize was that his willingness to pull back was a bit too cooperative and we should have kept an eye on things. Turns out, he pulled back from us but not all of you, though I'm not sure if he approached you at all about doing scenes that he set up?"

Amanda shook her head.

"Okay. I know with Caroline and Isabella, who he has had relations with, and Emily, he set up scenes for them to engage in, ones with men who were not vetted properly and which were solely so that he could pocket chunks of money. Meanwhile, Caroline, thinking nothing unusual, was struck down for several weeks with an STD, which is gone now, thankfully, and Emily had a scene set up that resulted in her being killed. He also set up scenes with guys who used to frequent other such establishments, which has now caused them to want to put us out of business, since you all are far more appealing than the ones they market." She shook her head. "It's a mess."

"Wow," was all Amanda could say, the question of what exactly the favor was going to be going unasked.

"Wow is right. It's really sad when a family has a split like this, especially between two brothers who were so close while growing up. Samuel is..." She shook her head. "He's so distraught that nothing seems to cheer him up these days, and I have a feeling he's getting ready to throw in the towel."

"You mean let his brother take over everything?"

"That, and just give up on life."

Amanda wasn't sure what to say to that and simply projected a solemn look toward her boss, all while continuing to wonder what the favor was going to be.

"You never heard anything about this from Emily?" Mrs. Woodman asked.

"No, nothing. She went out a lot, but I figured it was just because she was the type to easily make friends and was always out having fun with them." Once said, she thought about her own suspicions of Emily moonlighting and wondered if her outings truly were scenes that had been set up by Riley. She also wondered why she was continuing to protect Emily from Kristi and Sam.

Because deep down inside, you don't believe a word Kristi is saying.

Well, that wasn't entirely true. She believed Mrs. Woodman but also knew the woman was manipulative and out to serve her own needs; thus she had no idea how much of what she was hearing had been tweaked and twisted.

She also was a bit surprised by the idea that Riley Woodman would be doing such things, yet also knew that she had only met him a few times and had no idea what type of person he really was. Even so, what she was hearing now didn't seem to fit the personality she had interacted with during those times together. He had also always seemed genuinely interested in how she was doing with her classes, whereas Kristi never asked about them and had given her the impression that she didn't think highly of the schooling the girls were receiving.

Something isn't right about all this.

"So, what I need you to do is let me know if he approaches you and Vicky about anything, or if any of the other girls do. We have a good thing going here, as you have mentioned to Samuel, and it will get even better once we start generating royalties from videos every day, so we really don't want it all falling apart."

"I will."

"Good." Kristi smiled.

"So, that scene that Emily did the other day…that was set up by Riley?"

Mrs. Woodman didn't answer right away and when she did, she simply said, "Yes."

Amanda nodded, though only with the understanding that she was lying. Now the question was, had all of this been a lie, and if so, why? Something was going on.

"Do you know who the guy was that she saw?" Amanda asked.

"Unfortunately, no, which is why I'm letting you know not to agree to do any scenes that Riley tries to set up or let him even talk with you at all. If he comes around, be sure to tell either me or Samuel, and if you notice anyone else paying too much attention to you or Vicky or any of the houses, be sure to let us know."

"Okay, I will."

With that, Mrs. Woodman stood up and started toward the door, only to turn and say, "Oh, I will also be bringing some new girls by either tomorrow or the next day and should have a scene for you tomorrow night."

"A video one or a normal scene?"

"Normal scene. New guy. I will have more details later."

"Okay." Amanda followed her to the door, making sure to lock it once Mrs. Woodman had pulled out of the driveway. From there, she headed up the stairs to see how Vicky was doing.

16

Stacy knew she had made a huge mistake the moment she twisted the knob, but by then it was too late, her body unable to hold the door shut as it was thrown open, the force knocking her backward into the room, where she tripped over her shoe once again and, this time, crashed down onto the floor.

Get up! she screamed at herself as Rusty stepped inside, her limbs taking far too long to heed the command.

A booted foot caught her in the chest, forcing the air from her lungs.

She crumpled back down on the floor.

"Did you think I'd just leave you alone after what you did?" Rusty asked before kicking her again, a laugh at the sound she made following. "Well, did you?"

Even if she had wanted to, Stacy couldn't reply, her chest feeling as if it had caved in against itself, her lungs unable to take in an entire mouthful of air.

A hand grabbed her by the hair and pulled, the roots straining as she was lifted off the ground and slammed into the wall.

And then he was pressed against her, his body holding her to the wall, his penis poking her through her pants, his eyes inches from hers, and the smell of his last meal flowing into her nostrils.

"You left a mess for me to clean," Rusty said, voice nearly a growl. "I had to chop up my best friend and put the pieces in a Target Dumpster."

She squirmed, face trying to get away from his without much luck.

"And now he can't bring anymore girls to my place, and the money he used to give me to film there is gone!" Spittle landed on her and dripped down her cheek. "So now you're going to come live with me and help replace what you ruined."

She kneed him in the balls, the upward force enough to crush his testicles.

A scream echoed in her face, and then she was falling, his hands and body unable to hold her as he stumbled backward.

He tripped, the shoe that had caught her feet twice that day catching his and causing him to fall backward, his head thumping against the side table with a sickening crunch.

Stacy was on her knees, a hand to her chest, eyes staring at him.

He groaned and then sat up, his movements awkward.

"Bitch," he mumbled and started to pull something from beneath his jacket.

A gun!

Seeing that and knowing he probably would use it, Stacy sprang upward and to the left, the pain in her chest endurable as she went for the only weapon she could find.

A moment later darkness engulfed the room as she smashed the lamp against his head, the wooden base holding firm as it met his skull while the vibration from the blow damaged something within the fragile bulb.

Rusty grunted and crumpled to the floor, his lifeless body disappearing into the shadows.

Stacy held the lamp for a moment and then, knowing she needed to check on him and, if necessary, secure him, hurried into the bedroom to grab a bulb from the bedside lamp.

A minute later, bulb in hand, she started twisting the broken bulb free, all while Rusty lay somewhere near her feet, the light from the bathroom doing little to displace the shadows in this part of the room.

Once released, she tossed the broken bulb on the couch and began twisting the good one into place, her fingers fumbling a bit as she tried to fit it into the opening.

A hand grabbed her ankle just as the room was bathed in light, Rusty looking up at her with eyes that didn't seem to have any life in them.

"Fucker!" she snapped and pulled her leg free, his fingers providing no resistance at all once she tugged.

And then he crumpled again, his head hitting the floor with a *thunk*, blood oozing from where she had hit him with the lamp.

Resisting the urge to kick him in the face, she checked his pulse and though he looked horrible, his heartbeat seemed fine, which meant all the damage she had inflicted upon him was probably survivable.

Unless his brain starts to swell...

Did I hit him hard enough to do that?

No answer arrived, though she had a feeling the answer was no, given how hard the skull actually was. With the thought came a desire to hit him again just to see if she could crack it, a desire that she resisted, both because she knew the pain would be pointless if he could not feel it while unconscious and because she didn't want to kill him.

Yes, I do.

No, you don't.

Though typically stronger and more domineering with her

body, the emotional side did not get its way this time, and she resisted the urge to end it for him, the lamp put back on the table, her eyes only now noting the crack that was present in the base.

Rusty moaned.

Hearing this, Stacy took her attention away from the lamp and hobbled into the bathroom, where she threw open the linen closet, eyes seeking out but failing to find the roll of duct tape she knew she had somewhere.

From the linen closet, she went to the kitchen junk drawer, but it wasn't there either, nor was it in the nightstand drawer.

Growing frantic and feeling the pain of the kicks to her chest returning, she went back to the kitchen and dumped the drawer out onto the floor.

No duct tape.

In the bathroom, she pulled almost everything from the shelves, a long-lost lightbulb that she didn't know about falling and shattering.

Coat closet!

She hurried across the apartment, eyes staring at Rusty as she passed, his body still lifeless, and pulled open the door.

The duct tape was on the top shelf, along with several random items that served her no purpose in her day-to-day life, the oddest being a can of paint that she had taken a few brushes from to cover up a discoloration on the bedroom wall a year earlier.

A box cutter was also up there, which she grabbed so she could cut the duct tape once he was secure.

Both items in hand, she walked back over to Rusty, twisted him around so that he was facedown on the floor, and began taping his wrists together.

Now what? she asked.

No answer.

He moaned again.

Unsure what to do, Stacy grabbed him by a foot and dragged him toward the bedroom, her thinking being she would stick him in the closet.

And what, keep him prisoner?

You can't do that.

Letting him go was out of the question as well, and she didn't want to call the police…yet.

Or Alan.

He would not condone this.

Rusty mumbled something and then farted.

Stacy winced at the smell and then wondered if she really wanted him in her closet all night.

Maybe put him in the bathtub.

Taped up and naked so he can't climb out.

And scald him with a blast of hot water when he wakes up.

Several horrific ideas on how to torture him followed, all of which should have been appalling to her reasonable mind yet weren't. She wanted him to pay for what he had done to her, and for what he had done to others, the latter producing several visuals of him doing things with children that may or may not have actually occurred.

Even if they didn't, they probably will if he is left alive.

With that thought, she continued her journey, the idea of putting him into the bathtub better than the closet and requiring a quick turn to the right from where she now stood.

17

I had a great time as well, Alan typed in reply to Amanda's Facebook message, his mind drawing a blank on what else to say once the first sentence was put in place.

A yawn followed.

Class tomorrow.

With Amanda.

He wondered what that would be like.

Awkward at first, but then…

He really had no idea.

One thing he did know: he was attracted to her. In fact, being with her seemed a bit more appealing than being with Stacy, though he wasn't exactly sure why.

Because of Stacy's drive toward success?

Because she only really wanted to get back together with you so you could help her with that success?

Maybe…

The thoughts lingered in the air as he finished typing up the message, his eyes reading it over three times before he hit send.

Once that was done, he waited a while to see if she would reply, but when nothing came, he decided to call it a night and went to bed.

18

What the…?

Riley stared at the thumb drive that was sticking out of his laptop, one that he hadn't even noticed was plugged into place until he got a NEW HARDWARE message on his screen after the boot-up procedure was complete.

Concern arrived.

He moved his mouse cursor over to the new icon and double-clicked it.

Pictures!

Hundreds of them, it seemed, each one containing an image that he didn't want to enlarge but had to in order to figure out what was going on—not with the pictures themselves, that was obvious, but the intent behind them having been left here for him to see.

Vicky.

She and another young-looking girl who he did not recognize were the focus of the pictures, most of which displayed one or both engaged in sexual acts with an unidentifiable male figure.

Oral sex seemed to be the focus, but in some the girls were being fucked as well, both holes used, the penis looking huge when halfway inside the second girl, who was really tiny.

At the very bottom of the folder were three videos, each one showing a preview image of what was contained within.

He clicked on the first.

It opened with Vicky and the unknown girl sitting on a bed, each wearing innocent little dresses, ones that had no sexual appeal whatsoever unless a person was wired to enjoy such youthful displays.

A masked man walked into view, naked, and without saying a word, Vicky and the unknown girl began playing with his penis, first simply touching it and then eventually sucking on it.

Riley felt an erection growing.

Horrified, he closed out of the video and pushed back from the chair, all while his mind reminded him that it was seeing the blowjob, and not the fact that underage teenagers were performing it, that had created the excitement.

Still…

He took a deep breath and got up to walk around, questions about why she would leave this here on his laptop plaguing him.

Is she flaunting the fact that Sam will go get other girls without me? That Sam will do whatever she commands?

Kristi was the type who would love to rub that in his face, of that there was no question, yet even so, this seemed a bit much for that. This seemed—

His mind hit a wall as he stepped into his guest bedroom, the path he was taking throughout the house completely random.

Oh God!

He hurried back to the laptop and enlarged the first picture he could double-click.

Fuck!

He clicked another picture and then another.

Fuck! Fuck! Fuck!

He hurried back to the guest bedroom and started looking around, eyes finding condom wrappers in the small garbage bin and a pair of discarded panties in the corner.

Anger-laced panic unfolded within him.

Not only had Kristi violated his home, *again*; this time she had brought some pervert along to fuck two underage girls in one of his beds.

It was—

He couldn't even wrap his mind around it, his growing anger overpowering everything within his mind and body.

Worst of all, he knew exactly why she had done this. *Blackmail.* Not in its pure form since she had fabricated the situation, yet blackmail nonetheless because she would use the video against him.

That's why the guy's face is never seen.

She wants people to think it's me.

My bedroom, my video, my penis penetrating those poor innocent girls...

It would be a no-brainer for many, an implication that would smear his name beyond the point of recovery even before any investigation took place.

You have to call Sam.

You have to get control of this.

Doubt that it was even possible to get control plagued him.

Kristi would not back down.

This was why he had never gotten close with her. She had revealed her true self to him so early on that he knew she was a psycho who would never give up. It didn't matter the situation, she would fight to win every time, even over something as trivial as if someone liked a movie that she didn't. When that happened, she could not move on until the other person finally agreed that the movie sucked.

And somehow, she found Sam.

He sighed.

Call him.

Two minutes later, he did, only Sam didn't answer.

Riley hesitated as the voicemail instructions unfolded in his ear and then disconnected.

A minute passed.

He called again.

No answer.

He called again.

No answer.

He called five times before the phone was switched off on Sam's end.

He wondered who had turned it off.

Would Sam do that, or had it been Kristi?

Or had Kristi instructed Sam to turn it off?

Does she have that much control over him?

Yes!

Fuck!

Is the money still here?

It took two minutes to answer the question, another yes echoing within his mind. No relief followed.

Wednesday

October 30, 2013

1

Stacy heard a crash followed by something shattering, both of which filtered into an odd dream she was having where she was back in the Joliet house, body under siege from a dozen mannequins that had come to life and were trying to fuck her.

A second later, the reality of her apartment—and who was in her bathroom—returned, and she threw herself from her bed and sprinted down the hallway

Rusty was on the bathroom floor, pain apparent on his face as he lay tangled in the shower curtain, the bar that typically held it in place angled atop him, his wrists and ankles partially free while his mouth was still covered in the tape that she had twisted around his head.

Unsure what to do but knowing she couldn't risk him getting free, Stacy grabbed her hair dryer and smashed it into his ear.

A grunt echoed from behind the tape, followed by a glazed look.

Stacy hesitated, unsure if she should hit him again.

The glazed look began to fade.

Better safe than sorry, she said to herself and shattered the hair dryer above his left ear, pieces of it scattering across the bathroom floor.

After that, she redid the duct-tape binding, adding several

more layers to his wrists and ankles and then some around his upper body, locking his arms in place.

Enough? she asked herself, the roll considerably smaller from what she had started with yesterday.

In answer to her own question, she wrapped the roll around his knees four times, which hopefully would make it impossible for him to wiggle his legs back and forth, weakening the tape around his ankles. From there, she debated whether or not to put him back in the tub, the idea of using the bathroom while he was in there, even while unconscious, unappealing.

Plus, if Alan shows up unexpectedly…

That more than the bathroom privacy issues swayed her, and soon she was dragging him into the bedroom closet, questions about what she would do with him unfolding once again.

You can't kill him.

Though many would probably support her in the act after what he had done to her, a jury might still follow the rules of law and have her incarcerated.

And Alan would never condone it, which, for some reason, was a huge factor. In fact, it was the biggest.

But why?

We aren't even together, just friendly fuck buddies.

Maybe not even that anymore. The idea of having sex with him, or anyone at this point in time, not just unappealing but downright frightening.

Cliché! she shouted at herself.

For good reason! another part of her mind countered.

She thought about having Alan over for sex in an attempt to shift her feelings toward such acts back into a positive light, but she didn't know how successful such a thing would be, or if he would even be on board with it, given that Rusty hadn't used a condom when fucking her.

He'll want you tested.

And he's right about wanting that.

Her mind stayed on this for a while before shifting back to the main issue of having Rusty in her closet. With that, thoughts of torturing him as payback for what he had done to her arrived once again, a desire to fuck his ass with something that would make him regret every moment of penetration he had ever engaged in filling her head.

A yawn followed.

She glanced at her bedside clock.

It wasn't even five thirty in the morning yet.

She looked back at the closet, contemplating different ways of blocking the door so that even if he freed himself, he wouldn't be able to get out unless she opened the door.

Even if you block it with a dresser, he could just break through and tip it over, she noted with a sigh, the flimsy folding doors no match for a person who wanted to get out.

Another yawn arrived.

Not wanting to fall asleep in a bed next to where Rusty was being kept, she retrieved his handgun from the nightstand drawer, grabbed her pillow, and headed toward the couch in the family room.

Sleep arrived within ten minutes.

2

Riley spent much of the night tossing and turning, his mind too worked up to sleep, which eventually forced him to the couch where he lay amid the glow of the TV, scenes from an old *Seinfeld* episode providing a comfortable sense of nostalgia for times long since past.

Sleep arrived…

…and then he woke up, the alarm from his phone just barely reaching his ears from where it sat in the bedroom.

Exhausted and wanting nothing more than to close his eyes, Riley shuffled himself into the bedroom to switch off the alarm and then headed toward the shower, the hot water refreshing his body but not his mind.

What're you going to do?

The question stuck in his head for most of the morning, no answer ever arriving.

3

Amanda nearly overslept and then was in a panic to get ready for class, the knowledge that it was one she would be sharing with Alan nullifying the "go as you are" option, as did her unanswered Facebook question on if he wanted to hang out afterward.

Making things worse, Vicky was actually up when she headed downstairs to leave, face pale, body wrapped in a blanket.

"You okay?" Amanda asked, feet trying to slip into her shoes while she was looking through the wall cutout at the couch where Vicky was curled up.

"I don't feel good," Vicky said.

"How so?" she asked.

Vicky mumbled something that Amanda couldn't hear and then, without warning, threw off the blanket and ran to the first-floor bathroom, the sound of her vomiting filling the air.

Amanda looked up toward the ceiling and took a deep breath, the sounds having caused a horrifying tingle in the back of her throat.

The toilet flushed.

Amanda looked at her phone, winced at the time, started toward the front door, then stopped and walked up to the bathroom door. "Vicky?" she asked.

No answer.

"Vicky?"

Amanda waited, heard the faucet turn on followed by the gurgling of water. Not long after that Vicky stepped out of the bathroom, face still pale, eyes red, cheeks damp.

She looked up at Amanda, lip trembling, and asked, "Will they make me get rid of it?"

"Rid of what?" Amanda asked, and then it clicked. "Oh god, are you sure?"

Vicky nodded, tears falling from her eyes, and then asked again, "Will they make me get rid of it?"

"I…" Her mind drew a blank. "…have no idea. No one has ever gotten"—she didn't want to say the word *pregnant* for some reason—"it hasn't happened before."

Vicky didn't reply to that, tears continuing to fall.

"Are you sure? It could just be a stomach thing?" Amanda asked.

Vicky looked up at her, tears still falling, and asked, "Have you ever been pregnant?"

"No," Amanda said.

"I have, and—" She squeezed her lips together and put a hand to her chest.

Amanda stood where she was, unsure what to do.

The moment passed.

Vicky looked up at her again, lip quivering once more. "Please don't tell them."

"I won't," Amanda said, though deep down inside she knew Kristi and Sam would find out. After all, how did you hide something like this, especially when your body was the main focus of the business you were in?

With that, Vicky walked back to the couch and once again wrapped herself in the blanket.

"Do you need anything?" Amanda asked.

"No," Vicky mumbled and then asked, "you going to

school?"

"I was, but…" *Alan!* "Do you need me to stay?"

Vicky shook her head. "No, I'm just going to rest here until you get back."

"Okay. I…um…if you need anything, call me."

Vicky nodded.

Amanda hesitated again, the idea of leaving Vicky all alone feeling wrong, yet at the same time, she didn't know what else to do and finally reached for her coat.

"Bye," she said while opening the door.

Vicky didn't reply.

Amanda stepped out and pulled the door shut behind her, thoughts about how this was not the first time Vicky had been pregnant plaguing her mind.

And they made her get rid of it!

How old was she?

The questions stuck with her as she drove to class, her mind barely able to contemplate what Vicky's life had been like prior to being brought here. And then a new thought arrived, one that asked how, given her age, had Vicky's previous pimp gotten rid of her child? Had it been an abortion like she had initially assumed, or had she actually carried the child all the way to birth? If the former, who had performed the abortion? And if the latter, who had delivered it and where had the baby gone? Both situations would raise eyebrows if brought to a clinic, which meant…*oh god.*

Amanda shook her head, mind not wanting to go down the path the questions were leading her toward yet unable stop the momentum that was pushing her that way.

4

A pop quiz had awaited the class, one that Alan felt he did pretty well on, given that he hadn't even had to think about the answers.

Unfortunately, the sense of accomplishment he felt from that didn't do much to sway the disappointment he felt about Amanda not being there, a message from her suggesting they hang out after class having greeted him upon signing onto Facebook that morning.

Did something happen? he asked himself while out in the hallway during a break. *Was she forced to go service a client?*

For some reason, he didn't think that was it, though there really was no telling, given how little he knew about her and the escort setup. All he did know was that he had been looking forward to seeing her, both in a "she seems like someone I would love to get to know" and a "this will really help Stacy if I can learn something" way. Yet now it seemed she wasn't going to show.

"Alan."

Alan turned as her voice reached him, surprised that he hadn't seen or sensed her coming down the hallway.

"Hey!" he said. "You made it."

"Only forty minutes late," she said with a huff. "What're you doing out here? Early break today?"

"Um…yeah…well, sort of. We had a pop quiz, and I finished early."

"Oh fuck!" she snapped.

The class had a no-makeup policy on quizzes, one that Alan had always feared, given the plausibility of missing a class one day due to a sudden bowel event. So far, he hadn't missed any, though he had come close once a few weeks back, his body stuck in the bathroom up until the start of class, a debate over whether or not he should simply go home rather than back having nearly swayed him into skipping it.

"You know," Amanda continued, "I've never once missed a class or even been late, yet none of that will matter."

"I know," Alan said, a layer of understanding present in his voice. "It really sucks. Did you oversleep?"

"No! Well, yeah, a bit. I got up way later than normal. But it was my roommate. She's…sick…and I, well, I wanted to make sure she was okay before I left, you know."

"Aw, yeah, that really sucks, but it sounds like you did the right thing. Is it the flu or something? I know they say that's going to be really bad this year and is already starting to hit hard in some areas."

"No, stomach thing." She waved a hand to dismiss the topic. "So, what do you think the chances are of her letting me make up that quiz?"

"A bit better than seeing a Tea Party endorsement of Obamacare, but that probably still isn't all that great," he said.

"Yeah, no, I think I'm totally screwed." She shook her head. "I don't even want to do the rest of class now. Too pissed off at myself."

Alan nodded with understanding and then asked, "You still want to go hang out? Get some coffee or something? My treat."

"Now?" she asked.

"Sure, why not?"

"You don't mind missing the rest of class?"

"It's just a lab after this, one that we'd have a week to make up after hours, so I figure I could do coffee with you now and then we could pair up one afternoon and come in to do that lab as well."

"Oh, smooth," she said.

"Hmm, but not smooth enough for you to not notice how smooth it was, thus nullifying the smoothness?"

"Um…it was borderline until you said that, which has now nullified all the smoothness and made me begin to rethink the idea of coffee."

"Damn, totally shot myself in the foot…again."

"Again?" Amanda asked. "And the first time, did you literally shoot yourself in the foot?"

"Maybe."

"Such a tease," she said and then, taking charge, "Go get your things and take me out for some coffee."

"Yes, ma'am!" he said and headed back into the classroom, where some students had taken their seats once again while others were still out and about in the hallways. "So where should we go?" he asked once he had returned.

"Up to you," she said. "You probably know this area better than me."

"You might be surprised," he said. "When I came back, it had changed so much I wasn't sure I had the right Wheaton."

"Really?"

"Well, no, though it had changed quite a bit. Hmm, let's see. The Caribou in Danada is gone and the Borders bit the dust at some point so..." He put his palms up. "Any ideas?"

"There's a Starbucks over by the library," she said. "I've never been a fan of their coffee, but their chai tea isn't bad."

"Hmm...okay, we could do that," Alan said. He considered asking if she wanted to simply go back to his place but then decided it would be too forward, even if the suggestion was simply for a pot of tea. "I'm not really a fan myself, but if the chai is good, I'm game."

"Great," Amanda said with a smile and shifted her bag.

Alan smiled as well and then motioned toward the hallway. "Shall we?"

"We shall."

With that, the two started walking, feet taking them from the Health and Science wing to the glass walkway that went over the road connecting the north and south parking lot, to the hallway that wrapped around the library.

"Did you know this is actually where the building ended when I was in high school?" Alan said. "The entire Health and Science wing was part of a prairie and marsh project back then, and that technology center wasn't there at all."

"Really?" Amanda asked.

"Yep," Alan said, trying to gauge whether or not she truly was interested in what he was saying. "It was so weird driving by here after I came home, and then walking around inside for the first time back in August…it might as well have been an entirely different college."

"Had you been inside before?"

"Actually, yeah. While growing up my mom would often sign me up for art classes and whatnot. Most were over in the art building, but every now and then something would be in the IC or across the street in the old temp buildings."

"Wow, I bet that was fun," Amanda said. "My parents used to sign me up for art classes too. Not here, of course, but over by where we lived."

Alan sensed something within the comment, a longing for the past. He also realized she had given him a great opening into discussing herself, one that could easily be shifted into focusing on how she had become involved in prostitution. Now he just had to hope they were able to return to that topic following the chai ordering process, their journey to the Starbucks counter having come to an end.

"Just a tea?" Alan asked.

"Umm…do you mind if I get a muffin too?" Amanda asked, a timid ring present within her voice. "Didn't eat any breakfast."

"Not at all. What kind?"

Amanda took a moment to look through the selection and eventually settled on a lemon poppy-seed one.

"Hmm, that sounds good. I'll get one too."

Amanda smiled.

Order placed, Alan pulled out some cash and handed it over

and then turned to Amanda and said, "If you want to find us a nice quiet spot over in the lounge, I'll bring everything over."

"I don't mind waiting with you here," Amanda said.

"Okay, that works too," Alan said, his own smile appearing.

Together they waited, a natural silence spreading between them, all while the rest of the place carried the sound of blended conversations and media devices.

"Here you are, two chai teas," the girl behind the counter said, handing over the drinks.

"Thanks," Alan said, taking both and handing one over to Amanda, which earned a thanks from her as well.

From there they shifted over to the sugar area, where Alan loaded his tea up with sugar, nutmeg, and a pinch of cinnamon. Amanda simply put in one packet of sugar.

Beverages perfected, the two strolled into the lounge and began looking for a place to sit, their eyes eventually settling upon two cushioned chairs in a corner near a plant and a small table that looked fairly private.

5

"So, you said you used to take art classes," Alan voiced while taking a small sip of his tea.

"I did," Amanda said, her own sip of tea unfolding. "I've always enjoyed drawing and, when I have all the right stuff, painting." She took another sip. "You?"

"I used to draw as a kid, but it wasn't anything special. I had some talent but could never really get behind it in any meaningful way."

"I know what you mean," Amanda said with a nod. "I've always been fairly good at drawing and really enjoy doing it, but I lack that extra step that would make it stand out." She eyed her lemon poppy-seed muffin, wondering if it would be rude to start eating it before he started his. "As a kid though I figured I would be a great artist that would make millions from my artwork, a modern-day female Michelangelo or something." She laughed. "Used to drive my parents crazy."

"How so?" Alan asked.

"They didn't want me going to college for art. Said I needed to pick something that I could fall back on. I disagreed, said that if I didn't have anything to fall back on I'd be forced to succeed." She shook her head. "You know how it is. I took what they were saying to mean I had no talent and no future as an artist, but really all they meant was that I should take steps to secure myself financially so that I could produce my art without the pressure of it having to pay the bills." She sighed at how foolish she had been back then. "Without the pressure of having to work crappy jobs that suck the life out of you and kill any artistic drive you possess because all you want to do once you get home is watch TV and go to bed."

Alan nodded.

Amanda gave him a weak smile, sadness at everything she had lost during the last several years unfolding, and reached for her muffin.

Tears threatened.

Don't cry!

Somehow, her eyes heeded the command.

"What happened?" Alan asked. He reached for his own muffin, pulling off the top portion.

"Well...I fell in love with someone who supported my artistic endeavors and moved in with him, only to learn that he wasn't exactly what he seemed."

Why are you telling him all this?

He nodded.

"So what led you to joining the military?" she asked, shifting the topic before he could ask her any questions about Matt.

"September eleventh, though, honestly, I had been thinking about it before that as well. Ever since I was a sophomore in high school. Just seemed like a path I wanted to take. September eleventh sealed the deal."

"A lot of people joined the military after that," Amanda noted. "I remember seeing people being interviewed on the news that had joined, ones who had never considered such a thing before the attack."

"Yeah," Alan agreed, a somber look appearing. "And most of them ended up in Iraq instead of fighting the terrorists in Afghanistan, which is what they joined up to do. I knew so many soldiers who were upset by this, though many others were brainwashed into thinking Iraq was where the fight needed to be." He shook his head.

"I actually tried to join the military at one point," Amanda said, memories of going to the recruiting office unfolding within her mind. "They wouldn't let me, though. Iraq was ending, and it didn't seem like anything else was going on that they needed a huge army for, so…" She shrugged.

"Yeah, for a while there, when things were really bad in Iraq, they would take anyone, it seemed, even offered huge bonuses that were mind-boggling, but then, around 2007 or 2008, it all started to wind down to the point where they were asking people if they wanted to be discharged early."

"And I tried a little less than two years ago, so they were really, REALLY selective, and having an arrest record was pretty much a deal breaker."

Alan didn't reply.

Amanda felt an awkwardness settling.

So much personal information, so early on…

Then again, you sucked his dick the other day.

Still…

He just seemed so easy to talk to.

Too easy.

"So why were you trying to join the military?" Alan asked.

Amanda shrugged. "Seemed my only option. I needed a fresh start, something that would help get me back on track and provide money for college."

And make it so you could face your parents again.

"Ah, yeah, the military can certainly offer that, though it seems you're on the right track now. I mean, here you are, in college, taking classes, doing pretty well it seems…"

"Yeah," Amanda said. *It seems.*

Once again, silence arrived, only this time it carried an awkwardness within it, one that gnawed at her mind.

"So, how did you—" Alan started but then stopped, eyes looking over her shoulder.

"Amanda?" a voice asked.

Startled, Amanda turned.

Caroline was standing by the chair, a large cup of coffee in her hands, eyes going from her to Alan and then back to her.

6

The tension between the two was undeniable, as was the difference in appearance, Amanda's being fairly conservative, while the second girl's was borderline inappropriate for a classroom setting, her nipples easily visible through the tight pink fabric of her shirt and her leather pants looking as if she needed to lube up her legs in order to pull them up to her waistline. Stiletto heels completed the outfit.

"What're you doing here?" Amanda asked.

"Just waiting for Isabella," the girl said. "She had a private meeting with one of her professors." She turned to Alan. "Hi, I'm Caroline." She reached out a hand.

"Alan," he said. "Nice to meet you."

"So, what're you two doing?" Caroline asked.

"Having tea," Amanda said.

"I see that," Caroline said and smiled, swollen lip distorting her grin. "Mind if I join you, or is this like a private conversation?"

Amanda glared at her and then looked at him and said, "We actually should be getting back to class. Have a lab that is going to be starting soon."

"Oh, boohoo," Caroline said and gave a pouty look. "It's not every day I run into cute guys here, but I suppose *finders keepers*, right?"

Amanda didn't reply.

Caroline waited and then said, "Well, it was nice meeting you, and if you ever want to hang out, just ask Amanda for my number. I'm sure she'll be a doll and let you know how to get in touch with me."

"Shall we?" Amanda said while standing, a desperate look pointed his way.

"Yep," Alan said and grabbed his tea. He turned to Caroline. "It was nice meeting you too." With that, Amanda started walking away, which forced Alan to take several steps to catch up with her. "Everything okay?" he asked.

She waited until they were around a corner and said, "Sorry, she and I don't get along at all, and her only intention just then was to get between us."

"It's okay," Alan said. "I could totally tell she was trying to instigate something there." This was a bit of a stretch, but if it put Amanda at ease, then he would go along with it. "She part of the real estate thing?" he asked, even though he already knew the answer.

"Yeah," Amanda said. "And she has absolutely no shame when it comes to flaunting herself and her services. Her and Isabella both. I wouldn't be surprised if this meeting she is having with a professor right now is an attempt to seduce him. She's probably sucking his dick as we speak."

Alan wasn't sure how to reply to that and masked his hesitation with a sip of his tea.

Amanda took her own sip, followed by a heavy sigh. "Sorry."

"Nothing you need to apologize for."

"It's just, well, I was really enjoying talking with you and then she…" Amanda shook her head.

"No reason we have to stop just because she made an appearance," Alan said. "We can go find another place to sit. Plenty of lounges here, as well as places we could go if you would rather not stay here."

Amanda thought about that for a moment and said, "Actually, there is a place not far from here where I know we wouldn't be interrupted. It's…well…it's one of the houses we use to…well…you know how all this works."

"I do, and if you're comfortable with that, I don't have a problem with it."

"Okay, let's do that then, just…"

Alan waited.

She hesitated.

"Just what?" Alan asked.

"I…um…I friended you because I really like talking with you and felt a connection that I hadn't felt with anyone in a long time. I just want you to know that. It wasn't so that I would make money from you or anything. Yesterday was…I had no idea Kristi was having me meet you at the office, or that you knew what I did for a living while we were talking the other day."

"I like talking to you too," Alan said. "And I have no problem with what you do to make a living. Honest. And yesterday, it doesn't change anything." He hesitated. "You were amazing and I really enjoyed myself, but I also don't want that to create any awkwardness."

"Thank you," she said and then surprised him by reaching out and hugging him, which he returned, their bodies tight.

Guilt followed.

You're lying to her.

Am I?

The answer was a partial yes, because, honestly, he did feel a connection with her, yet he was also using her to learn about the real estate setup. It wasn't right. At the same time, he knew that even without the real estate thing, he would spend time with her, the personality she presented him with one that he enjoyed being near. She also carried with her a strength that he admired, one that he hoped he displayed as well.

The embrace broke.

"So, you want me to drive, or should we meet there?" Alan asked.

"I can drive," Amanda said. "It isn't far at all, and if you want, we can pick up some food or have something delivered...if you're hungry."

"It's up to you," Alan said.

"Okay, I could use some lunch, especially since I forgot my muffin back there."

"Don't worry, it wasn't that good," Alan said. "We'll order some real food. My treat."

"You sure?"

"Yeah."

With that, the two started toward the exit, Amanda leading the way to her car.

7

"Dude, you okay?" his partner asked once they were back in the hallway, Riley rubbing at his eyes while a yawn stretched his face.

"Yeah, I'm fine," Riley said. He sipped at a cup of burnt coffee.

"You sure, because you look like shit and you literally fell asleep back there."

"I know. Couple of rough days." Riley yawned again. "Last night…" He shook his head. "Just got a lot on my mind."

"Yeah, well, maybe you should go home and try to clear that mind, because we can't fuck this up. Can you imagine how much fun a defense lawyer would have if they found out you fell asleep during an interview?"

Riley didn't know how to reply to this, mostly because he knew his partner was correct. Unfortunately, he also knew that going home and resting wasn't the answer. He needed to fix the situation with Kristi. He needed—

Buzz!

He felt it against his hip, his personal cell phone.

"So?" his partner asked.

"I think you're right. I'll cut out early today and see if I can get some rest, though only if you really don't mind."

"Dude, I'd rather you be home resting than walking around like the living dead here, so go on, get some sleep, and call in tomorrow if need be. Lord knows you have the sick time available. Might as well put it to use finally."

Riley nodded. "Yeah, okay, that's probably best."

Who texted me?

He desperately wanted to check the phone but not while in the company of his partner, so without any further discussion, just a simple, "I'll let you know about tomorrow," Riley headed to his desk to clear it for the day and checked his phone.

It was from Sam and read: I THINK WE HAVE A PROBLEM.

No shit! Riley said to himself while shaking his head. In reply, he typed: WHAT IS IT?

CAN WE MEET?

FINE. WHEN AND WHERE?

YOU ON LUNCH SOON?

Rather than explain that he was going home for the day, Riley simply typed: YEAH.

OK. LET ME KNOW WHERE YOU WANT TO DO LUNCH AND I'LL SEE YOU THERE.

JUST COME TO MY PLACE.

OK.

Nothing else followed.

Twenty-five minutes later, Riley was pulling into his driveway, Sam already there sitting in his own car.

"Waiting long?" Riley asked.

"Ten minutes, tops," Sam said. "Was in the area."

"Well, you should have let yourself in. Kristi always does."

Sam shook his head. "Are we going to start that shit, because if we are, I'll just say *forget it* and take care of this problem on my own."

"Sam! She filmed child porn in my bedroom."

"She…" Sam started but couldn't seem to get the words out. "What do you mean?"

"What do I mean?" Riley demanded. "What I mean is this, I came home yesterday and found pictures and videos of Vicky and some other young girl I didn't even know about having sex with an unknown guy in my bedroom. So if you think that is me *starting shit,* then I really think you and I will have to go our separate ways."

Sam didn't reply for nearly a minute and then said, "Show me."

Riley did.

Sam looked at the photos for several minutes.

"Well?" Riley asked.

Sam sighed. "I'll take care of this."

Riley waited for more, but nothing else was said, and then Sam closed out of the folder.

"That's it?" Riley asked.

"What?" Sam asked.

"You'll take care of it?"

"What else do you expect me to say?"

"How about we start with you telling me who the hell that girl is and when you felt it was okay to simply pick her up without even discussing it with me," Riley suggested. "And then, once you explain that, you can tell me who this guy is and what type of scenes are being set up with Vicky and this new girl, because the way they're dressed, it almost looks like they are being marketed as children."

"You knew we were seeking to get more girls," Sam said. "So what's the big deal about getting a new one?"

"We were looking at some who were supposed to be in their late teens, early twenties. *Adults.* This girl looks even younger than Vicky, who is far too young already."

"So what was I supposed to do once I had her? Turn her over to child services? Maybe you don't remember, but I tried that once before."

Riley hadn't forgotten. And it hadn't just been one girl. During his career, Sam had turned over hundreds of girls to child services, most of whom had ended up back on the streets. There was one case in particular, however, that haunted him, one that, given his actions following the girl's death three weeks later, had ended his career. After that, Sam had decided it was time to create his own system, one that would truly help the girls rather than continuing the cycle that always ended with them back on the street.

But having them film porn!

That is going too far.

Fuck, just having them hired out to guys willing to pay for sex with them is going too far.

"Well?" Sam urged.

"Why did you pick her up without telling me?" Riley asked, shifting things a bit.

"Because Kristi was all over my ass about not getting any new girls the other night and bitching and moaning about needing to make more money and how you weren't keeping up your end of the deal, so I finally said fuck it and did a shakedown on a pimp."

"Without telling me?" Riley said in an attempt to bring that point back to the forefront.

"Yeah, because then you'd give me shit too. It never ends. She urges me to get things so that we're making enough to live the good life while constantly bitching about you, all while you want to make sure we keep things so hush-hush that we never even have a chance of appearing on anyone's radar, all while bitching about her. In the end, I can't help but say *fuck it* and do whatever it takes to shut both of you up! With her, that means doing what she asks, and with you, lately, that means not even saying anything."

Riley didn't know how to reply to that, a desire to stress the possibility of being caught and sent to jail going unfulfilled since Sam was aware of such consequences, even if it seemed like he wasn't.

"Okay," he finally said. "Let's cool down for a moment and take a look at things. First, you had no idea that Kristi took these pictures and videos in my place and left them here for me to find? Or why?"

"That's right," Sam said. "And I *will* discuss that with her at length tonight. That I can promise you. First, however, something has come up that could really pose a problem. Well, two things actually."

"What?"

"First, I think that reporter managed to slip one by us. His name is Alan Miller. He kind of came to us differently than most, popped into the office unannounced and said he had figured out that the girls were prostitutes after trying to date one of them and getting the cold shoulder. He also befriended Amanda to the point where they became Facebook friends, which is how I realized he is also friends with Stacy Collins, the reporter that hounded Kristi."

"Wait, how did he find out they were prostitutes?" Riley asked. Seemed a bit of a leap to go from being rejected by a girl he was trying to date to coming into the office to talk to Kristi.

"Well, he claims he followed the one he was trying to date to one of the houses and watched as a guy came to visit for two hours. Said he did that several times and it all clicked together, especially after looking at the website. It's all bullshit though, a story he and Stacy Collins put together prior to his heading over to the office."

"And you're sure he and Stacy are friends?" Riley asked. "Maybe she figured out who he was and sent him a friend request out of the blue?"

"Him, but none of the other men that see our girls?" Sam asked.

Riley didn't reply to that, especially since it would be difficult for her to figure out enough information on one of the clients to the point where she could friend them on Facebook. Unless…

"Could she have maybe confronted him after he saw one of the girls?" Riley asked.

"That's the thing: he hasn't seen any of the girls yet. This literally all unfolded on Monday when he arrived at the office. So how would she even know about him unless they already knew each other?"

Riley nodded. "Okay, good point."

"Plus, I did some research on the web and discovered that she wrote a human interest story on him back in 2008, and her Facebook profile has pictures of them together from that year as well."

Riley nodded a second time, concern building, and said, "So obviously they've known each other for quite some time, and now you think she has recruited him into helping her break open the prostitution setup."

"I do," Sam said.

"What does he do?"

"Nothing. He's a student at the college, which is how he met up and became friends with Amanda. Caroline actually called Kristi to say the two were hanging out together today, drinking coffee, and then went somewhere in Amanda's car. She suspected her of moonlighting and was trying to get her in trouble, but I...well...I don't like the idea that they are hanging out and talking on Facebook all the time, not with his connection to Stacy."

"A real honest-to-god student, or did he simply start hanging out there to get at the girls?" Riley asked.

"No, an honest-to-god student. From what I gathered after looking at the public stuff on his Facebook profile, and from what he told Kristi, he was a soldier who just got out of the military recently and decided to go to college."

"Okay and when did the reporter start looking into things?" Riley asked.

"Mid-September."

"So he was in the class with Amanda before the reporter even got involved."

"Yeah."

"Do you think he and Amanda became friends naturally, or is he just working her to learn more about the girls and what they do?"

"That I don't know," Sam said and then after pausing for

several seconds, "And it really doesn't matter, does it? I mean, either way, having him this close to things is dangerous, especially given his friendship with Amanda."

"It is," Riley agreed. The question of what they could do about it followed but went unvoiced, fear of what Sam would suggest unfolding.

"We need to know more about this Alan Miller," Sam said after a minute. "I had a friend run a search on him and found out he served in Iraq, was wounded, and was awarded a Bronze Star. After that, in late 2008 early 2009 he became a Green Beret and saw service in Afghanistan before being medically discharged."

"You had a friend run a search on him?"

"Yeah, guy I used to work with. Told him Kristi was a bit apprehensive about a guy who was interested in buying a house, given she couldn't get much from his credit report, so he did me a favor."

"Sam, what're you thinking?" Riley demanded. "You can't just have friends running backgrounds on potential clients! That's..." He didn't know what to say. "I could have done that!"

"Dude, it wasn't a big deal. They do stuff like that for me all the time, and given how anal you've been about this entire thing, I didn't want you to get all panicked about this guy and his connection to Stacy."

"Yet here you are telling me about it," Riley noted.

"Yeah, well, something really bad happened the other day, something that you need to know about, so I figured you needed all the details on everything that has happened this week."

Riley didn't like the sudden concern he saw on his brother's face and asked, "What happened?"

8

Should have just killed him, Stacy said to herself while struggling to put the shower curtain back in place, the constant concern over Rusty getting free mixed with her now being chargeable for unlawful imprisonment getting the better of her. *At least it would have been considered self-defense.*

Metal bar in place, Stacy released her hold upon it and stepped back, eyes watching for any sign of collapse, all while her ears were constantly tuned in for sounds from the bedroom closet.

All seemed well.

And then the curtain rod fell.

"Fuck!" she snapped.

That had been her third attempt.

She had no idea what she was doing wrong but knew that whatever it was, she would be unable to overcome it on her own, which meant she would need someone to come into her apartment.

But who?

Though he would not approve of her having imprisoned Rusty, Alan was still the best choice simply because he knew the situation. If she called someone like her landlord, and he uncovered Rusty, it would all be over. He would call the police. No question about it. Everyone but Alan would.

Now?

Is he still in class?

The two had talked about his class schedule but hadn't really gone into detail about it, so she really had no idea what the time periods were or which class he would be in right now. One thing she did know: he didn't stay in any class beyond one in the afternoon, which meant, no matter what, he would be ending soon if in one.

What the hell.

She pulled out her phone, which she had retrieved from Rusty's car, and sent Alan a message asking if he were free and wanted to come over.

NEED HELP WITH SOMETHING, she added after a few seconds.

Nothing followed.

She waited, mind unable to focus on anything but the phone now that she had reached out to him.

Five minutes passed with no reply and then ten, at which point she decided to pop in a DVD to kill time. She chose *Blood Diamond*, not so much because she enjoyed the story, but because she really liked the Maddy character. Going overseas and reporting on such things had always been something Stacy envisioned herself doing yet never could figure out how.

Ten minutes later, before the Maddy character even made an appearance, she switched off the DVD, the question of why she wasn't doing something productive filling her head.

Get up and get some answers.

Despair followed, her mind unable to figure out what to do, the events of the past several days weighing upon her in ways she had never experienced before.

And now you have Rusty locked in the closet.

What are you going to do about him?

What were they going to do with you? she asked herself a moment later. *What did they do with all the others they had trapped down there?*

Anger replaced the despair.

Make him talk.

Make him give you answers.

Make him pay!

Thoughts echoing, she headed into the kitchen to get a knife and then, once that was in her hand, headed toward the bedroom.

9

"What do you mean gutted?" Riley asked, a mix of horror and anger building within at the news that Emily had not only been killed, but that Sam and Kristi had kept this from him for three days.

"Stomach slit open and intestines pulled out while she was still alive," Sam said, voice solemn, "after she was fucked raw by three men."

Riley didn't know what to say to this, his mind trying to figure out how something like that could happen, and then, after a moment, he asked, "Three men? How do you know it was three men?"

"They left us videos and pictures of it on her phone, one after another." He shook his head. "It's awful. They must've spent over an hour fucking her, taking turns, laughing at the blood after they tore her rectum and at her pain as they continued to use that hole. At one point one of the men tried to hold her butt open with his fingers while the guy with the camera zoomed in to show the tear and the blood, and then they went back to using her again and again and again, after which they slit open her stomach and reached in to pull out her intestines."

"Jesus," was all Riley could say.

"I've never…" Sam started and then simply shook his head. "The final video on the phone had a message from one of the guys stating that this was payback for stealing one of their girls."

"Did they say which girl?"

"No, and what's worse, they said that they would take our girls one by one if we didn't start paying them weekly. They want the money put in an envelope and left in one of our house mailboxes once a week, a message with which house coming the night before, and pretty much said that if we try any countermeasures, our girls will suffer for it."

"And you've known about this for three days without saying anything to me?"

"We were trying to figure out who it was so that we could

stop them without you freaking out," Sam said. "Given everything that has been going on, it seemed you were on the verge of losing it and putting an end to everything, so..." He shrugged. "I don't know. I just thought I could take care of this quietly."

"And by yourself," Riley said, voice a bit harsh.

"Yeah, well, who is it that spent most of their career busting people like this?" Sam asked, a bitter ring present. "Not to mention nearly a year of his life working undercover within a prostitution group where things like this happened on a weekly basis."

Riley didn't reply.

Sam waited.

"Sorry, you're right, but even so you still should have said something. I mean, they killed her. One of our girls is dead and the others have been threatened. Everything we've worked toward—the progress we've made in the lives of these girls is all at risk now."

"I know," Sam muttered, eyes looking toward the floor.

"And on top of it, Kristi is fucking around, making porn videos in my house after we agreed not to do such things, even with the girls that are of age for such things."

"Riley, I—"

"Sam," Riley said, cutting him off. "What is she thinking? I mean, I know you said you would talk to her, which is great, but why the fuck are we even having to react to something like that in the first place? What is going on in her head?"

"I don't know, but come on. I said I will talk to her about that, so let's leave that alone and focus on this threat. Like you said, they killed Emily." He paused, hands spread out in a "come on" gesture. "Okay?"

Riley sighed. "Okay." Then, "But..."

"But what?" Sam asked.

Riley shook his head. "I just don't know. We got the reporter and her friend looking into things, we have someone who has decided to try to extort money from us, and"—he hesitated—"and it seems Kristi has found at least one person who enjoys having sex with minors who could easily fuck us over should the police ever investigate him for something, or if he simply wants to try to get more bang for his buck with the threat of blackmail."

"Your point?" Sam asked after a few seconds.

"I don't know," Riley admitted. "Maybe we should shut things down for a bit."

Sam shook his head. "Kristi wouldn't go for that."

Riley sighed. "What does she suggest?"

"We keep letting the girls service customers as if nothing is amiss, all while making it seem like we are going to pay the fuckers what they want, so we can figure out who they are and...well...put an end to their threat."

"And how are we going to do that?"

"What do you mean?"

"Figure out who they are? It's not like we can gather trace evidence from the scene and try to match it with someone from the database, not without raising several eyebrows, and if we do follow their instructions on where to put the money and then grab whoever picks it up, someone else will simply be sent out to carry out their threat to kill more of the girls."

"Yeah, it's a risk, but what choice do we have? We can't just put an end to the scenes. How would we support the girls if we did that? And what about the men who have credits toward the girls still? Just this week three of them have paid for the next month of scenes, and last week two paid up for a month."

"But—"

"And it seems pretty unlikely that whoever is doing this will just throw up their hands and quit if the girls aren't doing scenes. It's not like they offered us the choice of shutting down."

Sam had a point.

"So what we need to do is carry out business as usual, wait for them to direct us to a house where to leave the money, and then make sure to make a countermove once they grab it. While doing that, Kristi is going to be keeping an eye out for any new clients that are similar to the men in the videos. One had a nasty scar on their lower back, probably from being stabbed at some point, so she will keep an eye out for such scars when dealing with clients."

"How would she even see the scar?" Riley asked.

"She has devised a setup where new clients can see a girl in the back room of her office. A one-time welcome scene with a girl of our choosing that is secretly filmed, so we can study the video and see if a scar is present or if the guy behaves like one of the men from the videos."

Riley shook his head.

"What?" Sam asked.

"Sam, these guys aren't going to be setting up scenes. We'd be paying them with their own money if they did that, and what would the point of it be? They obviously are already able to get at the girls. If anything, we just need to have the girls let us know if they encounter anyone with a scar similar to the one you saw on the video."

"And how're they going to encounter such a scar outside of a scene setting? It's on the guy's lower back."

"I don't know, but I can tell you this, having the girls do scenes in the back of the office is a really bad idea." He put up his hands. "I'm not going to tell you to have her stop doing that because it's pretty clear she's going to do what she wants when she wants, but it won't net anything worthwhile. Instead, it's just going to provide another hold for law enforcement should they start looking into things, though, honestly, I don't think we'd be able to hide anything even if they did."

"What do you mean?"

"Well, obviously we must be pretty easy to uncover and infiltrate. I mean, a reporter who doesn't really have any significant stories to her name figured it out and managed to get her friend involved with the girls, and now Emily is dead because some pimp we ticked off figured out where to find her. Of course, maybe none of this would have happened if you two would have actually been having me do backgrounds on the people who were interested in the scenes like we had agreed upon."

"What're you talking about?" Sam said. "I send you the info on every guy who approaches us."

"Really? Then why was I able to create a fake name online and get him accepted to meet with Kristi to set up a scene?"

"What name?"

Riley told him.

Sam pulled out his phone and checked something. "Fuck."

"What?" Then before he could reply, "Did she not send you the info to send to me?"

Sam didn't reply.

"Shit, Sam, we had a system set up, one that would have kept things going smoothly and now, because she isn't following it properly, we have the reporter, the reporter's friend, and Emily is dead."

"Hey, the reporter figured things out on her own. That had nothing to do with Kristi."

"Jesus Christ, that had everything to do with Kristi and the way she reacted when the reporter asked her questions."

"Yeah, well, you'd get defensive too if someone called you without warning and started talking about the prostitutes you had working for you who weren't old enough to have real estate licenses."

"Okay, maybe you're right. That whole thing was fucked up from the beginning."

"It was," Sam agreed.

They both went silent for a moment, then, "Sam, have you considered the possibility that Kristi is setting up scenes without telling us anything? Setting up scenes that are posing a risk to the girls and us."

Again, Sam didn't reply.

"Sam, was Emily attacked during what was supposed to be a standard scene?"

Sam hesitated and then, "According to Amanda, yes. When I asked Kristi about it, however, she said that Emily was not scheduled for anything and that she must have agreed to do the scene herself."

"And who do you believe?"

"Amanda," he said after nearly a minute. "Emily's phone confirmed it."

Riley sensed there was more, but Sam did not continue, so he asked, "Something else?"

"No...well...yeah, sort of. Emily was seeing someone. Her phone confirmed that too."

"And..." Riley asked.

"She was texting him about their videos and whether or not they were making enough for them to get a place yet."

"Videos? As in porn?"

"Seems that way."

"Jesus, has he tried contacting her since she was killed?"

"Yeah, that's how I discovered their message history."

"Shit, he's going to start to wonder if something happened to her."

"There's more."

"What?"

"See for yourself." With that, Sam pulled a phone from his pocket, its pink case stained with blood, hit a button on the bottom to turn on the screen, and then took a second to scroll through it before handing it over.

Riley silently grimaced at handling the bloody phone and momentarily thought about how they were totally fucking up evidence, but then he pushed both things from his head and looked at the screen.

YOUR BOSS HAS GIVEN ME THE OK TO FILM YOUR COWORKERS, Patrick's text said.

GREAT! JUST REMEMBER, DON'T SAY ANYTHING ABOUT WHAT YOU AND I DO. I COULD GET IN BIG TROUBLE.

DON'T WORRY. MUM'S THE WORD. BY THE WAY, THAT BJ VIDEO WE DID LAST THURSDAY IS AVERAGING FIFTEEN DOWNLOADS A DAY AND YOUR STUDIO IS CURRENTLY IN THE TOP 50 IN BOTH THE AMATEUR AND BLOWJOB CATEGORIES.

REALLY! WOW! THAT MEANS WE WILL BE ABLE TO GET A PLACE SOON.

YEAH.

BUT ONLY IF YOU KEEP YOUR MOUTH SHUT. IF THEY FIND OUT, I'M TOTALLY FUCKED AND NOT IN A GOOD WAY.

BABE, DON'T WORRY.

OKAY, I WON'T.

GOTTA RUN, TALK TO YOU TOMORROW.

OKAY, LOVE YA!

LOVE YA TOO. SWEET DREAMS.

The messages were from Saturday night. On Sunday, Emily had sent a message asking: WHY DID YOU CHOOSE TO HAVE ME IN THE VIDEOS WITH THE OTHER GIRLS? I DIDN'T WANT THERE TO BE A CONNECTION TO US LIKE THAT AND I DON'T WANT TO SEE YOU FUCKING THEM!

YOUR BOSS SUGGESTED YOU WOULD BE GOOD FOR THEM. I FIGURED IT WOULD BE WEIRD IF I SAID NO.

Later Patrick asked: YOU OKAY? DO YOU WANT ME TO CANCEL WITH THE OTHER GIRLS?

Still no reply.

COME ON, TALK TO ME. I HONESTLY DIDN'T THINK IT WAS GOING TO BE A PROBLEM. I DON'T HAVE TO FILM THE OTHERS. THE VIDEOS YOU AND I DO ARE GREAT.

Later that same day: SO, I GUESS I'LL SEE YOU TOMOR-ROW THEN? BTW, YOUR STUDIO MADE IT INTO THE TOP TEN IN THE AMATEUR CATEGORY. WE MADE OVER TWO HUN-DRED DOLLARS JUST LAST NIGHT.

The final message read: YOU DIDN'T SHOW UP TODAY. THEY HAD US WORK WITH A GIRL NAMED AMANDA IN-STEAD WHO MENTIONED THAT YOU WERE SICK. I'M SORRY TO HEAR THAT. IS THAT WHY YOU AREN'T REPLYING? DO YOU NEED ANYTHING? I MISS YOU AND LOVE YOU.

"Wow," Riley said.

"Yeah, you almost feel sorry for him toward the end. Here he thinks she is pissed at him and is all worked up over it, when really she's dead."

"Did you know she was doing videos?" Riley asked.

"No, I had no idea. No one did."

"Not Emily, Kristi!"

"Oh, no." His voice changed. "And she doesn't know that I know yet. Wasn't sure how to talk to her about it."

"Well, I don't know what to say. Everything is totally fucked up." He shook his head, anger continuing to grow. "You and I, we need to have a sit-down with her."

"I'll talk to her," Sam said.

"No, *we'll* talk to her. From here on out I'm involved in every decision that is made."

Sam shook his head. "She's not going to like that."

"Yeah, well, I don't give a fuck."

Sam didn't reply to that.

10

"Here's the deal, you answer the questions to my satisfaction, and I won't stick this thin little teensy-weensy blade down your peehole," Stacy said, eyes noting a look of fear on Rusty's face as she touched the tip of the vegetable knife to the head of his penis, her left hand forced to endure a moment of contact with his manhood so she could threaten it with the blade. "Understand?"

He nodded, his mouth still sealed with tape.

"Good," she said, face somehow hiding the disgust she felt at being face-to-face with his pathetic penis. "Oh, and I hope you understand how much restraint I'm showing. Without it, I would simply stab this pathetic little organ over and over again until there was nothing left but a bloody stump, at which point I would turn my attention to your butthole and make it run red."

No reaction.

"Or maybe I should just start with the butthole," she said, knife ever so slightly sliding down his shaft, through the hairy mess, and into the puckered-up circle of pink flesh, blade easily slipping inside.

His breathing quickened, fear once again present.

She smiled and then, unable to hold back, slowly slipped the blade in further, feeling a bit of resistance as the blade caught up against something within.

Eyes wide, Rusty lifted his head from the bed and tried to say something against the tape, all while Stacy continued to smile and said, "Oooh, you like this, don't you! Should I go deeper?"

He shook his head.

"You sure?" she eased it in some more. "But I can tell you're just oozing with pleasure!"

He jerked his head back and forth while screaming something against the gag.

"Oooo-kayyyy, I won't," she said and pulled the knife free, the blade having maybe gone in two inches, if that. "But if you don't tell me what I want to know"—she ever so slightly took hold of his penis and slipped the tip into the hole—"it goes all the way down. You understand?"

He nodded again.

"Great!" She released his penis and took the knife away. "I'm going to take that tape off, and we're going to talk. If you shout or say anything other than the answers to my questions, I'm going to cut out your tongue, cook it, and make you eat it, along with whatever is left of your cock after I spend several hours peeling the flesh from it. No second chances. Got it?"

He nodded again.

"Good." She leaned forward and ripped the tape free, her fingers failing to get it in one quick yank, his pain evident and somewhat pleasing.

"Oh, poor baby, did that hurt?" she asked.

He glared at her.

She grabbed his penis and squeezed, knife threatening. "I asked you a question!"

His glare continued for several more seconds, at which point she pressed the blade against his flesh.

"No," he said. "It didn't hurt."

"I think it did, which means you just lied," she said, fingers pinching a piece of flesh and pulling it outward so she could poke the knife blade through it.

He screamed.

Stacy winced at the sound, fear of how far it might carry overriding the joy she felt at inflicting pain upon him.

Tossing the knife aside, she grabbed a pillow and slammed it into his face, muffling him, all while down below he twisted back and forth, thighs squeezing together to try to dull the pain.

Not much blood was present, but the blood that was there managed to splatter her bedspread, which was something she hadn't even thought about when deciding to use the bed as her info-gathering platform. In fact, she hadn't thought much about this setup at all, the realization that it was unsuitable for what she had hoped to do finally arriving.

Down below, he kept twisting his lower body back and forth, legs kicking all over the place.

"Stop!" she snapped, lifting the pillow.

"Fucking cunt!" he screamed. "I'm going to—"

She put the pillow back on his face, arms pressing down as hard as she could, his body continuing to fight.

This isn't going to work!

It's—

Yellow spots exploded across her darkened mind, the impact of his knee feeling like a hammer to the head, one that knocked her off the bed and across her nightstand as she attempted to get away from the attack.

Pain followed, something from the nightstand sticking her in the back before she slipped butt-first between the nightstand and the wall, body getting wedged and then falling to the left as she was pushed out from the crevice and into the open area between the bed and the closet door.

Dazed but conscious, she watched as Rusty got up off the bed, his naked lower half taking a moment to balance his upper half as he stood for the first time since his entrance into the apartment, the duct tape that still encircled his arms and wrists making it difficult for him to maneuver himself into a position to open the bedroom door.

Stop him!

She started to stand, room spinning from the blow, mind determined to prevent his escape.

Spotting her, Rusty suddenly decided against opening the door and came at her, right foot hitting her just below her left boob, ribs cracking and lungs feeling as if they had been forced free of air.

"Cunt-faced bitch!" he cried. "I'm going to fuck the shit out of you now!" He kicked her again. "I'm going to shove my dick so far up your ass that my cum will squirt out your mouth! I'm going to—"

She threw herself upon his leg as he tried to kick her again, her chest, back, and head screaming with pain from the movement yet somehow fighting through it.

With his upper body bound, Rusty was unable to keep his balance and fell backward, head just missing the corner of the dresser by inches.

He screamed for help, and she attempted to muffle him with her hands.

He bit her, his teeth snagging the flesh from her knuckles as she pulled free, her own cry entering the air.

He grinned, blood dotting his mouth, and then grimaced as he tried to twist.

Do something!

He bucked, trying to throw her off, a look of agony on his face.

Unsure what to do, she grabbed his testicles and squeezed, a satisfying pop vibrating against her palm.

Rusty looked as if he was going to scream again, but before any sound could leave his mouth, his eyes rolled backward as his body slumped.

Stunned, Stacy stared at him for several seconds, breathing deeply yet carefully due to the pain in her chest, and then, before he could wake up, forced herself to her feet, hands using the bed for balance until she was confident in her ability to walk, and went in search of the duct tape.

11

The two ordered Chinese food from Lu's on Roosevelt Road in Glen Ellyn, which, if Alan wasn't mistaken, was in the storefront that used to house a Blockbuster he'd frequented as a teen.

"There was also one in Danada I used to like," Alan said. "Not far from a Chinese place called Café Jasmine that my mom and I loved, but they didn't have a very good horror section, so I would go to this one instead. That was, until I discovered Hollywood Video down the street and convinced my mom to set me up an account there with her credit card. They had everything, it seemed."

"Blockbuster and Hollywood Video," Amanda said with a shake of her head. "I still can't believe they're all gone. My mom would get me videos from them when I was a kid and then rack up fines when she forgot to return them."

"Ha ha, yeah, my mom did that too. We also would always forget to rewind things, though I can't remember if there was a fee for that at Blockbuster." He paused, marveling over the memories. "It's amazing how much everything has changed."

Amanda nodded.

Alan waited, unsure where to go from there.

"So..." Amanda said, obviously experiencing a similar struggle.

Alan smiled.

"What?" Amanda asked, her own smile breaking.

"Our random moments of awkwardness," Alan said. "It's funny, especially considering what we've already done and the things we have both seen."

"I don't know if I've seen all that much, nothing like what you have at least, what with being in a war and everything." Her smile faded.

Alan nodded, concerned that he had taken a misstep in getting her to open up even more than she already had, but then said, "Well, I've seen some things that no one will ever understand, but I can tell by your eyes that I'm not alone in this. You have seen and experienced things as well, things that most, not even myself, can't even comprehend."

"Yeah," Amanda agreed.

"But we don't have to dwell upon any of that right now. Instead, since I'm in the market, why don't you show me around and tell me about this house."

Amanda laughed. "Are you really in the market for a house?"

"Kind of, though maybe a condo would be the best choice to begin with," he admitted.

"What're you in now?" she asked.

"My mother's basement."

"Seriously?"

"Yep."

"Wow, I don't know if I could do that. My parents—" She simply shook her head.

"Thankfully, it isn't all that bad. She always gives me my space, and while sometimes she can be a bit inquisitive and involved in the things I'm doing, it's not in a 'I want to know what you're doing every second of every day' kind of way, but more of a 'I'm bored and would really like to be a part of your activities' thing. She never does any of the 'you're under my roof so you have to live by my rules' bullshit."

"That's good. Mine would never be that way. I could move back in at forty and they would treat me like a kid and give me a curfew and a no-guys rule—it would be ridiculous."

"I knew several soldiers who had parents like that. They'd come back from leave with horror stories. Actually, they were talking about it on the radio the other day since so many adults have been forced to move back in with their parents in recent years." He checked his phone, which had buzzed, and saw that it was from Stacy.

"Everything okay?" Amanda asked.

"Oh yeah, just a friend asking what I'm doing."

"Ah, female friend?"

"Maybe. How'd you guess?"

"Can just tell. You seem like the type of guy that women like to have as a friend, one that is easy to talk to and feels safe since you view us as more than a potential sexual companion."

Alan wasn't sure how to reply to that.

"Sorry," she said, a sense of awkwardness arriving once more.

"Don't be sorry," Alan said. "I think you're probably right. I've always gotten along better with women than men. I have no idea why, though maybe it has something to do with it just being me and my mom while growing up." He shrugged.

Relief appeared on her face.

He looked around.

She followed his gaze.

"I have a question, and it's totally out of left field," Alan said.

"Oh, okay."

"Do you and your coworkers actually sell houses too, or is it all just a front?"

"It's all just a front," she said. "Mrs. Woodman, our boss and her husband, they sell houses, though I don't know if they have sold any since I've been here, but the rest of us, we just act the part so we can go from house to house without anyone asking questions—though it sounds like it didn't fool you."

"It didn't, but..." He shrugged, momentarily unsure what

else to say on that. "I'm a bit more observant than most."

Amanda nodded.

"And that sounded kind of self-appreciating, didn't it?" Alan added.

"A bit, but I don't mind. Plus, it's true, right? I mean, most don't really pay attention to things unless it directly impacts them; you, however, seem to absorb the things around you."

"I do."

"And I'm guessing it was helpful in the military?"

"It was." He paused, trying to figure out a way to redirect things so he could gather more information without sounding like he wanted information. And then it clicked. "I have a question," he said.

"Oh, okay."

"I have a female friend who might actually be interested in working for Mrs. Woodman. If I set up a meeting for her, do you think Mrs. Woodman would hire her? I mean, what is the process for you to get hired? How did you get involved?"

"She wants to be a prostitute?" Amanda asked.

"Uh-huh. Well, she has often said, 'I have a body guys want, so what's wrong with profiting from it?' So she really wants to do something with her body, especially since she is in her twenties and knows it is only a matter of time before her looks and figure begin to fade. And she loves having sex. So..." He shrugged.

"Is she any good?" Amanda asked.

"What do you mean?" Alan replied, the question catching him off guard.

"A female friend that talks to you about wanting to profit from her sexuality, one who you know loves having sex." She grinned. "If you two haven't had sex..." She shook her head. "I'm not even going to speculate on that. You two have had sex, plain and simple." She laughed. "Right?"

"You got me." He put his hands up in mock surrender. "So, do you think you'd be able to talk with her and let her know about all this and whether or not it would be something she would want to do?"

"Sure, though I can't make any promises that Kristi would hire her," Amanda cautioned.

"Of course not, and she'll know that as well," Alan said, heart pumping as a possible meeting between Amanda and Stacy came together. "Maybe if you could just talk to her, my friend, not Kristi, about what it is you do and the ups and downs, that might give her a better idea of what it would be like and whether or not this is a career path she wants to take."

Amanda considered this for several seconds. "Will she be discreet?"

"Yes, very discreet."

"Because I could get in trouble for talking about this stuff with someone not associated with it—big trouble!"

"Oh, I bet. And she'll understand that as well."

"Hmm," Amanda mumbled while continuing to consider this.

Alan's heartbeat quickened.

"Okay, I'll talk with her," Amanda said.

"Excellent," Alan said, a mixture of excitement and relief flowing through him.

Guilt followed.

He had lied to her.

You had no choice.

Yes, I did.

"You okay?" Amanda asked.

"Um...yeah," Alan said, a mental shake of the head knocking the guilt away. "Any idea when you—"

The doorbell rang, cutting him off.

"Ah, bet that's the food," Amanda said.

"Fantastic," Alan said and stood up, hand going into his pocket for his wallet. "Starving."

"Me too," Amanda said and followed him to the door.

Two minutes later, they were carrying bags to the kitchen, Amanda making a statement of, "I hope there's silverware in this one."

"Do most of the houses have silverware?" Alan asked, wondering how far the furnishing of the houses actually went.

"Some do, some don't," she said while pulling open a drawer. "All depends on how often the place is used and what we add to it during our visits." She pulled open a second drawer, the sound of loose silverware echoing from within. "Ta-da!"

"Phew," Alan said. "I've never gotten the hang of chopsticks and would have made a total fool of myself."

"You're not the only one," Amanda admitted. She handed him a fork and then went in search of plates, two of which she found quickly in a cupboard to the right of the sink. From there she opened the fridge and said, "Shit, we should have ordered some soda or something. All we have here is one can of Coke that I brought like three weeks ago and never drank."

"You can have it," Alan said.

"You sure? We could always share it."

"That works too."

"Great. We'll share." With that, the two headed back into the family room, food, plates, silverware, and the can of Coke in hand.

12

HEY, GOOD NEWS, Alan's text said. ONE OF THE GIRLS IS GO-ING TO TALK WITH YOU. YOU JUST HAVE TO PRETEND LIKE YOU ARE INTERESTED IN WORKING WITH THEM.

ARE YOU SERIOUS? Stacy typed back, the ice pack she had been holding to the side of her face momentarily forgotten, as was the pain from the knee that had struck her. WHEN?

TONIGHT IF YOU'RE FREE.

I AM!

GREAT. I'LL LET YOU KNOW WHEN AND WHERE IN A BIT.

OKAY! Stacy typed and then waited for his reply, her thinking being it would arrive fairly quickly.

It didn't.

A minute passed.

Then two.

Then three.

Still she waited, frustration growing, her mind demanding to know why he would say "in a bit" if he really meant later that day.

Five minutes came and went.

At the ten-minute mark she got up and took the melting ice pack into the kitchen, her mind sure that upon her return she would see a text had arrived.

No text.

Fuck it, she said to herself and went back to watching *Blood Diamond,* only to hit the pause button a few minutes later due to her stomach, which was growing hungry, her lack of eating that day finally catching up with her.

Is he with one of the girls right now? she asked herself while walking to the fridge, already knowing she wouldn't find anything within that she wanted but going through the routine anyway.

If he is, he's probably buying her lunch.

He's too generous!

As expected, nothing good was in the fridge.

Unsure what to do, she headed back to the couch, her desire

to continue with *Blood Diamond* no longer present. Once she had finished this story and had a guarantee that her days of pointless articles about grocery store openings and kids fighting city hall over their illegal tree houses were over, she would watch it again, a newfound joy at being able to identify with the Maddy character rather than aspiring to be like her unfolding. Until then...

She checked her phone again.

Nothing.

Relax, the meeting isn't until tonight and can't happen without you.

She took a deep breath and then shifted her focus to the idea that she had to pretend to be interested in becoming a prostitute. From there, her focus shifted to what she should wear for the meeting.

Should I look like a whore?

Could I even pull that off?

The question stuck with her for a long time, her mind eventually settling upon a decision to dress in normal everyday attire for the meeting, her thinking being that she didn't want to overdo the impression, which might be suspicious.

13

"All finished?" Amanda asked, motioning toward his plate.

"Yep," Alan said with a smile, hand moving away so she could take it. "Can't believe I ate so much."

"Same here," Amanda said. "And yet look how much is left."

"I know, right?"

Together they had eaten about half of what they had ordered, the rest still sitting in the tall round plastic containers the two meals had arrived in. A large box of rice was present as well, though it only contained enough for one more helping.

Plates in hand, Amanda walked to the kitchen to wash them.

Alan followed with the leftovers and asked, "Do you want to take this home to your roommates?"

"Um...sure," Amanda said, hands drying the first plate. "Though only if you don't want it."

"Oh no, you can take it. My mom will probably cook something that will have two days' worth of leftovers, and I'd hate to waste either."

"Okay." She smiled. "You can put it right into the fridge then, and I'll be sure to grab it before I go home."

Alan nodded and went over to the fridge while she started rinsing the second plate.

"By the way, where did you want to meet my friend tonight?" Alan asked. "Should she just come here, or did you want to go to a restaurant or something?"

"Um...here should be fine."

"Okay, great."

"Can you do me a favor? Can you come too?"

"Oh...sure, that's not a problem."

"Great, thanks," Amanda said, a sense of relief unfolding. "Given the nature of everything, it'll just make me more comfortable."

"I totally understand." He took the dry plates and put them back into the cupboard. "Actually, I think that'll make her more comfortable as well."

Amanda turned off the faucet.

"And I'll bring some soda and tea and whatever else I can think of to drink."

"Okay, excellent." She smiled again, mind feeling as if this were a party in the making rather than a simple meet and greet for a girl that wanted to become a prostitute. "And—" she began, but then stopped as her phone buzzed with a call in the other room.

Alan followed her.

"My boss," she said while looking at the screen, and then, "Hello?"

"Amanda, where are you?" Kristi asked.

"Having a study lunch with a classmate."

"Oh, okay, well, I just wanted to let you know that I confirmed your scene for this evening. It'll be at four o'clock at the house on Walnut Avenue."

"Four o'clock. Got it. And he's a new guy, right?

"Yep, new guy."

"Okay. Any particular requests I should know about?"

"Just one, he enjoys things to be rough, so don't be worried if he gets a little aggressive."

"Okay, no problem. Anything else?"

"Nope. Oh, I did bring a new girl by the house today named Crystal, so don't be surprised when you get back. She used to be part of the same group Vicky was from, so the two know each other pretty well. Just wanted to give you a heads-up on that."

"How is—" Amanda started but then stopped, remembering that she had promised to keep Vicky's morning sickness a secret.

"How's what?" Mrs. Woodman asked.

"Oh, nothing. I was just going to ask how the new girl is adjusting, but I'm sure she's fine, especially if she and Vicky already know each other. That'll help make the change easier."

"Yep, well, okay. I gotta go. Have a good scene tonight."

"Thanks, I will." Amanda disconnected and looked at the phone for a moment.

"Everything okay?" Alan asked.

"Oh yeah," Amanda said, fake smile appearing. "I just have to go do a scene tonight with a new guy. It's at the house on Walnut Avenue. Kind of last-minute, but shouldn't get in the way with meeting your friend. We could even meet over there if you like rather than here. Just have to make sure not to bump into the client on your way in."

"Walnut Avenue?" Alan asked. "Is that in Wheaton or Glen Ellyn?"

"Oh, it's in Glen Ellyn, on the north side, not far from President Street and Geneva Road. Let me pull up the exact address for you." She fumbled with her phone for several seconds and then read him the street number, which he punched into his own phone. "If you want, I'll call you when I'm done. Shouldn't take more than an hour, maybe two, so if you wanted to bring her by around six or six thirty, that should work. Just don't come up to the front door until you hear from me."

"Okay."

"And don't park right outside the house where he can see you waiting, since that might spook him."

"No problem."

Silence settled.

She looked at Alan, who looked back at her, eyes locking, a sudden longing to kiss him appearing.

Do it! her mind cried.

But...

Now or never!

She stepped forward and leaned in, her lips meeting his without any further hesitation, his own lips accepting them and then, after she probed with her tongue, opening to accept it, all while his arms went around her body to hold her. Several seconds passed before they pulled apart, a longing for more flowing through her yet going unmet. Nothing was said either, each just looking in each other's eyes, words unneeded.

14

"Dude, no, let me talk to her first," Sam said, voice almost a plea. "If we simply show up there, she is going to get defensive, and you know that she doesn't do well in situations like that."

Riley hesitated, his anger toward Kristi at the point where he didn't really care if she was put on the defensive, his only desire being to pummel her with words until she was completely broken and could do nothing but admit that what she had done was a mistake, and that she would cease making decisions on her own and confer with him from that point forward.

And that will never happen.

Instead, she would probably agree to everything with no real intention of following through with her promise—and then become even more reckless as she attempted to do a better job of hiding her actions even deeper so that neither one of them could figure out what she was really up to.

What a mess.

"Okay, you talk to her, but make sure she knows I'm serious about all this and that I want all three of us to sit down and have a meeting before anything else happens. No more new girls, no more videos, no more scenes with new guys that weren't already planned—not until we have a meeting."

"And if she says no?" Sam asked.

"Not an option," Riley said.

Sam sighed, exhaustion evident. "Okay, I'll do my best."

Riley nodded, concern for his brother suddenly present. "Are you okay?" Riley asked.

Sam stared at him for several seconds and then shook his head. "Man, I don't know," he admitted. "This whole thing. I just wish...well...I don't know. It's not going the way I thought it would, that's all."

"Yeah," Riley agreed.

"But at least we're helping these girls, right?" Sam asked. "I mean, in the end, they're all better off, right?"

"Not Emily," Riley said.

Sam looked down, the momentary hurt on his face making Riley regret the comment.

Nothing else was said for nearly a minute and then, "Well, I'm going to head back and talk to Kristi and see if anything new has come in."

"Okay, keep me posted."

"Yep."

With that, Sam headed out.

Riley watched him go, mind mercifully free of thoughts for several minutes before the enormity of the events that had unfolded that week came crashing back.

Fucking Kristi.

If she had followed the protocol they had set in place, one that required the background checks on the clients prior to allowing them to even make a payment toward seeing the girls, chances were they would have realized something wasn't adding up about the client. But no, she had simply said *yes* without any research, much the way she had with the fake profile he had set up, and now one of their girls was dead.

Frustrated, he headed into the kitchen to get something to drink and then back into the family room, his eyes coming upon the bloody phone that Sam had handed to him earlier.

Horror at what had happened to Emily followed.

It wasn't just her death, but the fact that the poor girl had never really had much of a life beyond her teen years, her entire adult existence up until that point being one of having her body used over and over again by men who cared nothing for her.

Did Patrick care for her?

He powered up Emily's phone once again and looked down at the conversation boxes he and Sam had read earlier, his finger scrolling back beyond what they had focused on so he could see what their early interactions had been like.

Unfortunately, nothing significant jumped out at him, the two having apparently met back in August when Emily was starting her classes, the first text from Patrick being a reply to a message she had typed that read: TEST! TEST! IT'S ME, THE PRETTY GIRL SITTING NEXT TO YOU. DID YOU GET MY MESSAGE?

Patrick's reply: 10-4, MESSAGE RECEIVED, CONNECTION ESTABLISHED, NUMBER NOW SAVED ALONG WITH PICTURE OF SAID PRETTY GIRL.

From there, the two had texted each other fairly often, mostly in a random chitchat type of way, until the end of September, when Patrick asked her what she thought of the footage he had sent.

IT'S HOT, Emily replied. Then in the next text box, BUT I THINK WE NEED AT LEAST TWO CAMERAS SO THAT YOU CAN SPLICE TOGETHER SCENES FROM DIFFERENT ANGLES. JUST HAVING THE ONE VIEWPOINT FROM THE TRIPOD GETS KIND OF DULL AFTER A FEW MINUTES.

YEP! I TOTALLY AGREE. YOU WANT TO COME WITH ME TO GET ANOTHER CAMERA?

SURE! :) Then in another text box, TODAY?

YEP.

GREAT! CAN'T WAIT.

Not much more was said about the videos for the rest of the week, though it wasn't for a lack of talking. Instead, the focus simply shifted to that of two young adults who were enjoying the company they shared with each other, a discussion on what movie they should see that weekend unfolding, followed by a statement of how Patrick didn't care what they saw as long as they saw it together.

AWWWW! Emily had replied back, the text punctuated by several heart icons.

Young love, Riley said to himself, a new sense of sadness at what Emily had lost unfolding.

From there he switched over to her video folder, mind dreading what he was going to find but knowing he had to watch it. He had to see what had unfolded and see if he could figure out any clues as to who the attackers might have been, only…

No videos.

The last video entry within the folder was a candid interview with Vicky, who was wearing a ridiculous yellow dress that made her look even younger than her sixteen years, Emily asking if she was excited about the prospect of her first scene with the company.

Riley exited the clip before hearing what Vicky had to say, eyes staring at the video icons, mind trying to figure out where the ones he was looking for were.

Did Sam delete them?

Am I missing something?

He started going through the videos one by one, most being silly little clips that Emily had taken of things that unfolded around the house with her and Amanda or while on the road, one of the earliest videos showing excitement over finding a bunch of ducks at Lake Foxcroft that wanted to be fed. Others were of her and Patrick, Emily pretending to be a behind-the-scenes reporter doing an interview about the upcoming porn shoot they were going to do, her hand, at one point, holding the phone in such a way as to try to get a comment from Patrick's penis, which she stated was the star of the show. An off-angled clip of her sucking on it for a few seconds while she held the camera to video the act followed, her lips eventually leaving the penis so she could turn back to the camera and say, "Well, maybe we'll hear more from him later once he's given his performance, available for download at Amateur Emily's Blowjobs and More."

Phone in hand, Riley went to his computer and did a Google

search for the porn site Emily had mentioned, the first search result directing him to a storefront on the Clips4Sale website. Over a hundred videos were already present, most of them looking to be five- to ten-minute blowjob and handjob clips, the occasional straight sex and anal video present as well. One, which had what was probably a user-created congratulatory note rather than one the site generated for such clips, mentioned that it was a bestseller in the Amateur and Blowjob categories. It was titled *Three Dicks, One Girl—Can She Find Room for All Three at Once?* and had a cover image of Emily dressed as a cute girl next door looking with wide-eyed surprise at three penises, her hands on her cheeks while her mouth was giving an "oh my" impression.

Riley clicked the preview button and saw a ten-second clip of Emily looking at the penises of three naked guys, a cut-off statement about figuring out where each would go beginning to unfold around the seven-second mark.

Three men, he noted, though obviously they were not the same three men who had butchered her. Instead, they were probably friends of Patrick who eagerly agreed to have sex with Emily in exchange for the two being able to put the video up for sale.

Bookmarking the site, he turned his attention back to the phone, his thinking being there had to be something on it that would help him understand what had unfolded and hopefully give some clue as to who was responsible.

Nothing jumped out at him.

And he could not find the videos Sam had talked about.

Frustrated and unsure what else to do, he went about exploring the phone, eyes looking into the picture folder for several seconds before he shifted over to the text message folder, his thinking being that the latter would be quicker to process.

Nothing.

Stumped, he went to the call history folder, but again nothing caught his attention.

And maybe nothing will, he said to himself.

But what about the videos?

Sam had said they were on the phone, which meant...*what?*

Did he lie?

Why would he do that?

He went back to the video screen to see if there was some option he was unaware of, but once again he couldn't find any videos of her being killed.

Would Sam have deleted them?

If so, why?

Something wasn't adding up.

He went back to the picture folder and carefully started scrolling through it, his eyes glancing over each row to see if anything within the icons jumped out at him.

Nothing.

Like the videos, most of the pictures were simple spur-of-the-moment snapshots of things that really weren't all that significant—shots of the food she was eating and outfits she was trying on. Others were selfies of her and Patrick, one of which showed him grabbing her boob, another her kissing his cheek, all of them showing a couple that looked happy.

Thoughts of how he and his ex-wife had been like that at one point early in their relationship entered his mind, memories unfolding of them taking photos of themselves with the old disposable cameras while on their honeymoon.

A desire to relive those moments hit, along with sadness for what they had lost.

Losing his wife had been painful, especially since he knew there had been nothing he could do to stop her from leaving, the love she had once felt for him gone.

And now Patrick is experiencing that as well.

Only he had no idea what had actually happened, likely thinking he had screwed up and ruined a good thing simply because he had chosen her to be in the videos with the other girls.

Thinking about the young man brought to mind the silence Riley had been met with when trying to talk to his wife after she had left and how he had gone days replaying conversations they'd had, each word analyzed as if it were something he had to write a paper on for school.

You should tell him.

He also needed to speak with Amanda, find out if she knew of anything that had been going on in Emily's life, something that might not have seemed significant until now.

First things first, however, he called Sam, who, upon hearing the question about the video clips, said, "I didn't delete them. They should be there, last videos in the folder."

"Well, they aren't," Riley said. "I looked at every video in that folder, and there are no videos like you described."

Sam didn't reply.

"So?" Riley asked.

"What?"

"Where are the videos?"

"How the fuck should I know? They were there last time I looked at the phone."

"Which was when?"

Again, Sam didn't reply.

"Sam, did Kristi have access to the phone?"

"I suppose," Sam said. "Wasn't like I locked it up or anything."

"So she may have deleted the videos."

"Why would she do that?"

"I don't know," Riley admitted, "but if you didn't delete them and if she was the only other one with access..." He didn't have to continue.

Silence.

"Sam?" Riley asked.

"I'll talk to her," Sam said.

Riley shook his head, but rather than pressing any further, simply said, "Okay."

"Anything else?"

"No, just keep me posted."

"Yep."

Nothing else was said.

Riley went back to looking at the phone, finger hitting a few buttons so he could find the contact information for Patrick. Once that was done, he entered it into his own phone and hit call.

"Hello?" a voice asked after two rings.

"Hi, is this Patrick?"

"Yes," Patrick said, caution evident in his voice.

"Patrick, my name is Riley Woodman. I'm one of the founders of..." He stumbled, unsure how to present himself. "I understand you hired some of our girls for some videos and have been working with Emily for quite some time."

"I did," he said. "Is everything okay with Emily? I haven't heard from her in several days."

"Emily is...well...I think we should talk about Emily. Are you able to get together with me this afternoon?"

He hesitated. "I guess."

"Maybe somewhere at the college?"

"Okay," he said. "Like now?"

"Yeah, if that works for you. I can be there in fifteen minutes."

"I...okay." More hesitation. "Did something happen to Emily?"

Riley didn't know how to reply and simply said, "Yes, I'm

sorry…I…um…I know you two were close."

He didn't reply to that.

Riley waited a moment, unsure how to proceed.

"Was she in trouble?" Patrick asked.

"What?"

"Was she in trouble?" he repeated.

"I don't understand what you mean. In trouble with who?"

"With you, with her job. She said she worried that she was going to get in trouble because she and I were seeing each other. She said that wasn't allowed."

"As far as I know, she wasn't in trouble at all." He had also not been aware of any rules against being in relationships. In the beginning, they had made sure the girls knew not to take any side jobs with the men they did scenes with, and that relationships with those men were forbidden simply because of the complications that could arise, but as far as dating someone not involved in the prostitution setup, he had never suggested any rules against that, nor had Sam ever mentioned anything about it. "You were not a client, so the relationship you two shared would have been fine."

"I see."

Riley could tell the young man was not convinced, which meant that Kristi must have made it pretty clear to the girls that they were not allowed to date, period.

"I'm going to head over to the college now. Will you be there?" Riley asked.

"Yeah, but how do I know who you are?"

"Just wait for me in the cafeteria. I'll find you. My name is Riley."

"Okay."

"And Patrick?"

"Yes?"

"I really need to find out what happened to Emily, so any

information you may have, even if you don't think it is important, might be. So please don't hold anything back. I promise nothing you say will get any of the other girls in trouble."

"Okay."

With that the two disconnected, Riley quickly heading to his car.

15

Once home, Alan found himself unable to think about anything beyond his time with Amanda, his mind hitting a wall every time he tried to branch out to another subject. Within these thoughts was a layer of regret, a sense of betrayal toward her, due to the lies he had spoken fouling up what should have been a perfect moment of two people coming together and enjoying each other's company. Guilt about his attraction and what it might mean to Stacy was also present, but not to the same extent as the betrayal toward Amanda since Stacy and he weren't really together, just friends who liked having sex with each other, which meant each had to be prepared for something like this to unfold.

But she's a prostitute...

So what?

She's sweet and generous and liked being with you, and you with her.

Having lunch and talking had been nice, the sense of connection he felt toward her running deeper than anything he had ever experienced with anyone else before.

And she felt it too.

Of this, there was no question.

And then it had ended, her having to go back home so she could get ready for a scene with a new guy, him needing to get back home so he could shower and get himself ready for the meeting afterward—not that there was anything he really needed to do for that other than show up with Stacy.

All three of us together…

Amanda knowing I've had sex with Stacy, me knowing I've had sex with one and gotten a blowjob from another, Stacy probably sensing I have feelings for Amanda…

Once planted, he couldn't help but think about how awkward the entire situation could become, and how the possibility for drama was present.

That said, he knew Stacy could push all of that aside, given her desire to get the story; thus he probably didn't have anything to worry about. Not now, at least. Later, if he continued spending time with Amanda, which he hoped would be the case, Stacy might start to grow upset, but that wasn't something he needed to worry about at the moment. They would deal with that if it occurred. Now all he needed to do was help her finish this story, all while making sure he didn't destroy the connection he and Amanda now shared.

One week, he said to himself, mind startled at how much had happened. *All because you opened that email.*

All because you saved her life that evening after having dinner.

Did I really save it?

Was he planning on killing her?

As before, when contemplating this question, he leaned toward the answer of *yes* and then wondered why no other attempts had followed. Was it simply because no other moment had presented itself, or something else? Had his interference in their attempt caused them to step back and rethink what they were doing?

He made himself a pot of tea while thinking about this, this time with first-flush leaves from the new Longview Darjeeling estate. Once ready, he took the pot and his tea mug into the family room to watch TV while relaxing, AMC finally showing a horror movie he wanted to watch, his mind and body eventually drifting away into a world of sleep while leaning back in the chair.

16

"I don't really remember whose idea it was," Patrick said. "We kind of just started talking about it one night and then the next thing you know, we're making videos and uploading them." He shrugged. "Two months ago I never would have ever dreamed of being involved in porn, but now…well…I have ads out on modeling sites, dating sites, Craigslist, and flyers all over the work boards here."

Riley nodded. "I know what you mean." *More than you will ever realize.* Then, "They let you put up flyers here?"

"Well, the flyers just call for girls who want to model and have a phone number and email address for details. I've had plenty of calls, but only three girls actually agreed to be filmed once they found out what it entailed, and one of them only wanted to do handjob work, due to safety concerns. She also wouldn't take her clothes off."

"I see. And this site is different than the one you and Emily were doing?"

"Yeah, well, same site, different storefront. Emily's was just focused on her and had her name on it. The other one is for all the other girls, though I'm open to doing individual stores for girls as well if they want."

Riley considered that for a moment, realizing that the last part of his statement was a bit of a proposition, Patrick probably considering having all the girls that worked for him starting up their own storefronts as a way of bringing in more revenue.

"And if you did individual stores, would you share the profits, or just pay a modeling fee to the girls who have the stores?"

"I could go either way. If the girls want a percentage of the profits, they would just have to have their name on the storefront as well as listed as an owner. That way they can carry some of the tax burden."

"Is that how you and Emily did it?" he asked, trying to redirect without it seeming like a redirect.

"No, she and I...we kind of fumbled our way into it, and all the money was coming to me and I was splitting it with her. We only actually ever cashed one check since they pay once a month, and that one was nothing compared to the one we'll be getting this month." He considered his own words for a moment, eyes glistening. "I...I can't believe she's gone."

Riley waited a moment. "Did she ever say anything to you about being worried that someone was going to hurt her?"

He shook his head. "Her only concern was that she would get in trouble for doing the videos. Keeping that secret was always important, which is why I never was allowed to pick her up. Shit, she never even told me where she lived—said that if a guy was seen coming to the house by anyone, she would get in serious trouble."

"And it sounds like you two were planning to move in together with the money from the videos?" Riley asked.

"Um...that was an idea she was fond of, but I...well...I didn't really know if that was something I wanted. I mean, don't get me wrong, I was in love with her and really liked what we were doing, but I also knew it had a superficial element to it, especially once we started doing the videos because that became our focus rather than spending time enjoying each other's company."

Riley nodded but then said, "Well, she also enjoyed your company. That was evident to me from the phone conversations and the pictures she had of you two together."

"Yeah...it's just that for the last several weeks she seemed so focused on making tons of money from the videos and getting an apartment. Every time we got together, it was for videos. I'd suggest we go do something, maybe like see a movie or walk in the forest preserve, but she never really wanted to do that anymore. Except once she did like the idea of the forest preserve only because she figured her fans would enjoy a point-of-view blowjob video in the woods."

"I think she was eager to make money simply so she could get out on her own. Did she ever tell you about what it was like for her as a kid?"

"Not really."

"Well, from what I know, at the age of fourteen she fled an abusive stepfather who frequently molested her, only to end up working the streets. For five years, she was passed around from one pimp to the next, all of whom had her working every night, until eventually we found her and suggested she come work for us. At first, she refused because she was terrified of getting in trouble with the pimp, but we managed to help her make the right decision and got her cleaned up."

Memories of Sam shattering the right shin of Emily's pimp with a ball-peen hammer arrived, the pimp's screams for mercy falling upon deaf ears.

He shuddered.

Similar screams had echoed when they forcefully rescued Amanda, Isabella, Sophia, and Vicky, Sam making sure that it would be quite some time before any of their pimps could walk again without pain.

"What do you mean by 'cleaned up'?" Patrick asked.

"Her pimp kept her strung out on heroin, which is fairly common in the sex trade. Rather than giving her money, he just gave her a fix, which also made it so he didn't have to feed her much because food isn't something you really think about when doped up. She also had chlamydia and syphilis, both of which had gone untreated for so long that she never would have been able to have children."

Patrick's face became very pale.

"Don't worry," Riley said. "We got all that cleared up before she started working, and all the men she saw were tested."

Caroline still got sick.

Was that from one of our guys, or was she moonlighting?

"Of course, if you want to be on the safe side, it's not a bad idea to get tested, especially if you are having sex with all the different girls you hire. It's only fifty bucks at the DuPage County Health Department and would save you legal fees if you passed something on to a girl you hired who might be able to file a lawsuit."

Patrick nodded.

Riley looked around, eyes noting the few students who were sitting down to eat meals, questions about how some of them were paying for school entering his thoughts and whether or not the females would willingly take part in the videos Patrick was making in order to get the education they needed to survive in this world.

"The videos you make, what is the process like? Do you simply film them and upload them to that site, or does it involve quite a bit of computer know-how with websites and code?"

"It's fairly easy," Patrick said. "A few clicks of the button and the videos go up. The tricky part is making them stand out. Just setting up a camera and filming can be dull. People will still buy them, but if you want to make serious money and make the top-ten categories, it has to have a professional look to it, which means different camera angles, proper lighting, and a good chemistry between those that are being filmed."

"And the fact that it's illegal to film such stuff in Illinois?" Riley asked.

"Oh please, those laws are so vague as to be almost meaningless, like the ones that state you can still be hanged for stealing a pig in Utah." He shook his head. "Did you know it's illegal to film porn videos that involve bondage and penetration if all four limbs are restrained, yet how many videos of stuff like that are out there? And anal and oral sex? Both are illegal in many states, yet how many people engage in it?"

"But they do still bust people for selling this stuff."

"They bust people who sell it by mail and then, with that charge already in place, rack up other charges for the content infractions so that they can get a sentence worth the time and money of the courts. My stuff is all Internet based. I wouldn't be able to make a profit if I sold it through the mail and had to pay shipping costs. That's the great thing about the Internet. It's totally eliminating costs within the creative fields and making it so people like me and authors and musicians can get their stuff in front of an audience without having to make deals with the big studios and publishers and whatnot."

This sounds familiar.

"I have a question," Riley said. "I know you have been filming our girls and, with the exception of the videos you made with Emily, this week was the first time you filmed them with the consent of Kristi. Right?"

"Yeah."

"And it was just you hiring the girls for the films, rather than a deal where we are part owners of the studio and take home some of the profits."

"Yeah."

Riley waited a moment and then asked, "When did you first broach the subject of hiring the girls to Kristi?"

"Um, like last week."

"And was there talk about doing a partnership deal at all?"

"Nope, we just talked about what it would cost for me to hire some of the girls for a day."

"Okay." Something wanted to click within his mind, but he wasn't sure what. Rather than dwell upon it, however, he asked, "Did Kristi agree right away, or did she get back to you?"

"It took her a few days. I approached her last Wednesday at

her office, and it wasn't until the weekend that she agreed."

Riley thought about that. "Did she ask you how you found out about the girls?"

"Yeah, I told her one of the girls had replied to a flyer I posted and said that several of her coworkers might be interested in doing videos."

"Did you tell her which girl replied?" Riley asked.

"No. Emily said that could be tricky and didn't want anyone getting in trouble. She figured that once Kristi knew I was interested in hiring some girls for videos that she would probably let the details of how I found out about them slide a bit."

Riley didn't think she would, yet at the same time he knew she had not had him look into Patrick's background at all, nor mentioned the situation. Sam had, but more of a "maybe it would be a good idea if we started filming the girls" way, which meant he probably knew Kristi would go ahead with it even if he had said no, thus hadn't wanted to give too many details about it until he knew what his thoughts on it were. When Riley had said no, Sam had decided not to share anything. The question was, what other things was he holding back?

"Can I ask you a question?"

"Go ahead," Riley said, thoughts returning to the present situation.

"Do you think I'm in danger?"

Riley thought about that for a moment and then shook his head. "No, I wouldn't think so."

"You sure? Because it seems to me that if you all rescued girls like Emily from abusive pimps, some of the pimps might not be content with simply letting things go. And if one of them killed Emily, then there's a chance they also know about the videos and might think I'm a part of your setup."

17

The blissful satisfaction that had enveloped Amanda following her time with Alan came to an abrupt end as she walked back into the main house. Vicky pounced on her as she entered from the garage, excitement having completely erased the wretched look of illness that had plagued her that morning.

"She and I used to work together in the city," Vicky said, leading her by the hand up the stairs and toward the back bedroom. "We were the two favorites, and guys had to pay a special price to spend time with us."

They entered the bedroom, Amanda's eyes coming upon a girl who couldn't have been more than fourteen, fifteen at the oldest, her body clad only in a teddy and stockings, garter straps dangling, hairless pubic region completely visible.

"We're trying on the new outfits they brought us today," Vicky said, hand motioning toward the various pieces of lingerie and clothing items scattered upon the bed. "It's all ours. We didn't take anything from your closet."

Amanda didn't know what to say.

"Hi," the new girl said, a nervous smile spreading across her face. "I'm Crystal."

"Hi," Amanda managed, horror at what was unfolding preventing any other words from forming.

"Are you...um...our head girl?" Crystal asked and then, when Amanda didn't reply, turned toward Vicky.

"No, no," Vicky said. "I told you, there's no head girl here and no punishments. We're all equal and just live here and wait for Kristi, or Sam, or the other guy to pick us up and bring us where we need to go. Remember the other day when we made the videos with Kristi and the other guy? It's always like that."

"Oh yeah? Cool." She turned back to the mirror and then asked, "Can you help me with these?" while trying to fasten a garter strap.

"Sure," Vicky said, walking over.

Amanda watched for a moment and then, without saying a word, turned and headed toward her own bedroom, right hand carefully closing the door behind her in an attempt to add a barrier between her and them.

Disgust arrived.

Fear was present as well, fear that everything was going to come to an end. In fact, for her, it had to come to an end. She *could not* be a part of this, not with so many underage girls involved.

But what are you going to do?

How are you going to pay for college?

No answers appeared, but then after a few minutes, thoughts of the webcam stuff Isabella and Caroline had been talking about the day before did enter her mind. Whether or not such a thing was really a viable possibility was beyond her, but it was something to think about. Girls did make money from such things, so with that and maybe a part-time job, if she could find one, and student aid, she might be able to stay in school.

But this is so much better.

This gives me time to actually study and do homework and have a life.

Anger appeared, as did a sense of injustice, her mind feeling as if she had been given a teasing glimpse of how great things could be, and then had it yanked away. For three months, ever since they had cleared the drugs from her system, she had felt as if she was finally back on track with her life, but now, well, it was all going to end.

No, it's not.

You can just go at it alone.

It didn't even have to be a webcam thing. She could tell some of her regulars that she was going to see them on the side, at a cheaper rate, just as long as they didn't tell anyone. And maybe the girl that Alan was going to introduce her to that evening would want to start something with her, something that would help her profit from her body but not throw her into the middle of a setup that was now plagued with underage sex and child pornography.

She sat on her bed and looked around the room while thinking this, thoughts about how she could secretly move all her stuff from here into a new place unfolding. She could even take the car and sell it for cash to someone who moved such things, which she could then use to get a cheap apartment, one that she could share with Alan's friend.

It could work.

Or it could fail miserably and leave you worse off than if you stayed here.

But you can't stay here.

Not with those two girls being sold for videos and to men who enjoy having sex with them.

No.

She wished Emily were there.

She wished—

"Amanda?" Vicky called.

Fuck. "Yeah?" Amanda replied.

"Can we ask you something?"

Amanda sighed and said, "Sure," and then, once they were in the room, both now dressed in outfits that looked completely inappropriate for their ages, "What is it?"

"We were wondering, with tomorrow being Halloween and everything, would we be able to...well...could we maybe carve jack-o'-lanterns and go trick-or-treating?"

Startled, Amanda didn't know what to say at first, then seeing the pleading look in their eyes, especially Crystal's, said, "Of course, you two can do whatever you want." She then realized why they were asking and added, "We could probably go get some pumpkins in the morning." She thought about Sunny Acres in West Chicago, which was where she went as a kid. "And I know just the place to get them."

Crystal smiled.

Vicky turned to her and said, "See, told you this place was great."

With that, the two headed back into Vicky's room, music suddenly echoing, all while Amanda wondered if maybe this place wasn't so bad after all, given that it had taken those two from a horrible situation and put them into one that allowed them to enjoy things like pumpkin carving and trick-or-treating.

Maybe it isn't, but you can't be a part of it.

She sighed and then, knowing she had to get ready for that evening, headed into the bathroom to take a shower, her mind switching gears while under the hot spray and focusing on Alan. Today with him…it had been one of the greatest days of her life, one that she wanted to relive over and over again.

Fifteen minutes later, hot water losing its edge, she switched off the shower spray, dried off, and headed back into her room, a decision unfolding on what to wear that evening for the scene and the meeting following it.

18

Come on, pick up, Riley pleaded while sitting in his car, phone pressed to his ear with his left hand while his right switched on the ignition.

Four rings in, right before the voicemail would have been activated, Sam answered with a, "Hey, what's up?"

Riley backed up out of his parking spot and said, "I meant to ask earlier, where and when did you get the new girl?"

"You mean Crystal?" Sam asked.

Is there more than one new girl? "Um…yeah."

"Believe it or not, from Mr. Right."

"*Mr. Right!* Seriously? When did you go back to him?"

"On Monday. I wanted to find out if it was him, or if he knew who it was that had sent those guys to kill Emily. I figured he may have been pissed enough to go after us, given what we did to him after we grabbed Vicky. I had no idea he would be up and running again, and this time with several girls, so I took the girls, all the cash he had, all his dope, and busted up his hand since he promised us he would never again market teen girls to pervs."

"You took more than one girl?" Riley asked, startled.

"Yeah, but Crystal was the only one that wasn't doped to the gills, so the others are detoxing."

"And Mr. Right?" Riley asked. "What did you do"—he caught sight of the flashing lights in his rearview mirror as he headed toward the stoplight at Park Boulevard—"aw fuck!"

"What?" Sam asked.

"A college cop is trying to pull me over!"

"What're you doing at the college?" Sam asked.

"I was talking to Patrick, the guy that Emily was seeing." He pulled along College Avenue, his blinkers going.

"What for?" Sam asked.

"I wanted to find out if he knew anything, to see if Emily had been threatened or was scared." He rolled down his window and then pulled out his badge and ID. "All I learned is that she was really, *really* trying to make it so she no longer had to work for us and could support herself on the videos they were doing. Was probably going to succeed as—"

"Sir, please put the phone down," the female officer instructed.

Riley looked up at her, handed his ID through the window, and said, "I'm a state detective working a case."

"Here at the college?" she asked.

"Yes, one that involved a possible transaction in your parking lot," he said.

"And you didn't notify us?" she noted.

"It was very last-minute. I followed someone here from their home after watching them put a shipment of drugs in their trunk from a storage locker, but whoever their buyer was never showed up, so they left."

"With no backup?"

"Like I said, it was last-minute and I didn't really have time to get my team out here. I was watching them on my day off, after getting a hunch."

"And if that truly is the case, I'm sure you'll be able to get the ticket I'm going to write you for talking on the phone while driving voided through the proper channels. In the meantime, I'm going to ask that you end your call, put your phone down, turn off the engine, and wait here while I write the ticket."

"But—" he started.

"Sir, I'm not going to ask you again. Put the phone down and keep your hands on the wheel where I can see them."

Jesus Christ! "Sam, I'll call you back."

"Yep," Sam said.

Riley ended the call, put his hands on the wheel, and waited.

Several minutes later, the officer returned with Riley's ID and a ticket and said, "I watched you leave the school and get in your car, which means you were not following anyone or watching as a possible drug deal went down."

Riley didn't reply.

"I don't know what you were doing here, but I suggest you think up a better lie if you're ever pulled over by a fellow officer when in violation of the state traffic laws. Have a good day."

Riley, totally pissed off, headed back toward his house. Once there, he tried to call Sam back, only to have the phone go directly to voicemail, which seemed odd, given that they had just been speaking.

Did the phone die?

Is he on with someone else?

Unsure what to do, he paced his house for several minutes, eyes checking to see if anything had been disturbed, before trying to call Sam again. This time the phone rang several times before going to voicemail.

"Sam, give me a call when you can. I want to know more about what happened with Mr. Right."

After that, he began pacing again, thoughts of the current situation making it impossible for him to sit down, a sense that he needed to act present.

19

HEY, I'M ON MY WAY TO THE SCENE NOW *WISH IT WAS YOU* SO GIVE ME LIKE AN HOUR AND A HALF AND I SHOULD BE FINISHED.

Alan read the text and, to his surprise, felt a twinge of jealousy at the fact that another guy would be having sex with Amanda. At the same time, the *wish it was you* part put a smile on his face, which was nice.

I wish it was me too, he said to himself and then typed up a quick reply, one that expressed hope that all went well.

THANKS! she said, a smiley face following the word.

"That Stacy?" his mother asked from the couch where she was reading, her ear having heard the buzz of the phone as well as his fingers typing up a reply.

"Nope, girl named Amanda that I have a class with. Two of us had lunch today."

"Oh," she perked up a bit at that. "Lunch date?"

"Um…" Alan hesitated. "Sort of, I guess, though it didn't start out that way. Funny how that works." He shrugged. "Anyway, she's working right now, but I'm going to go see her afterward."

"Twice in one day," she said, smiling. "Sounds like it got serious fast."

He shrugged a second time and then said a silent, *Oh great!* when she put her book down and twisted toward him.

"So, what does she do?"

"She's a prostitute," he said, eyes focused on his book.

"Alan!" she laughed. "Come on."

"Well, officially, she's a real estate agent, but secretly she's a prostitute that uses the houses to see her clients."

She shook her head and went back to her book.

Alan grinned.

A few seconds later, "Wait, real estate agent? Are you looking for a place to live?"

"No, not really. Want to finish school first."

"Ah, okay." She seemed relieved.

Of course, the finish school statement wasn't completely true. Once his general education courses were done, he would probably head out to the Northern Illinois University in DeKalb or the University of Illinois in Urbana-Champaign to finish the second half of his schooling, which would mean he would have to get a place near the campus. He wouldn't be buying anything in either location, however, and his mom's place would still be considered his official residence.

"What time you seeing her?" she asked.

"Um…in like an hour and a half," Alan said. "She's showing a house right now, so I have to wait until that's finished." He typed up a message to Stacy while talking and then said, "She's going to text me when she's done."

"Okay."

Alan sent the message he had typed.

"Will you be home tonight?" his mother asked.

"Good question. I have no idea."

She shook her head.

Alan smiled.

His phone buzzed.

OKAY, Stacy replied. LET ME KNOW WHEN YOU'RE ON YOUR WAY TO PICK ME UP.

WILL DO, Alan texted back and then returned to his book, hand reaching for his mug of tea while his eyes sought out the last sentence he had read.

20

It had been about a week since Amanda's last visit to the house on Walnut Avenue, so once inside, she took a moment to look around to see if anything had changed since her last client.

Nothing had.

The house, which was one of the better-furnished places, looked pretty much the same, the only change being the contents of the fridge.

They'll have to bring something if they want anything to drink, she said to herself, surprise at the lack of beverages entering her mind. Last time there had been an entire case of Coke, now, nothing. The fridge was completely bare.

She texted Alan, giving him a heads-up on the beverage situation, which earned a reply stating he would grab some Cokes and water.

OKAY! GREAT! she typed back.

Headlights swept across the front room, something that could only happen if someone had pulled into the driveway.

She checked the clock at the top of her message screen.

Fifteen minutes early.

Fuck!

Physically, she was ready; mentally, however, she liked spending time before the scene relaxing and composing her mind.

Nothing you can do about it now, she said to herself and headed toward the door, hand needlessly adjusting her skirt and jacket before stepping into her heels and reaching for the knob.

Deep breath.

"Hello," she said with a perfect smile, hand opening the door before he even had a chance to knock. "You're a bit early."

"My apologies," he said. "I haven't been to this location yet and was worried I might have trouble finding it in the dark."

"Oh, so you've been with us before?" Amanda questioned while closing the door, her mind suddenly remembering that Mrs. Woodman had said he was a new client.

"I have," he said, "though it's been a while, and the girl I used to see doesn't seem to work here anymore, so..." He spread his hands and then turned his head to the left to look at something in the dining room. "What's that?"

Amanda turned to follow his line of sight, which was when he hit her, fist striking her right below the eye, her feet unable to keep her body balanced as one of her heels twisted out from under her.

Stunned, she rolled onto her stomach and started crawling down the hallway, her only goal being to get away from him.

"Now where do you think you're going?" he asked, voice seemingly amused.

She continued to crawl, eyes spotting her purse, which still carried all four of her tiny pepper spray bottles, his early arrival having prevented her distribution of them.

He grabbed her foot and pulled, her body sliding back toward him across the tiles, hands unable to hook on anything to stop her progress.

"That's better," he said and, without warning, had a chunk of her hair in his hands, her scalp screaming as he lifted her upper body from the tiles, the pain unlike anything she had ever felt before.

Her feet kicking, he began dragging her down the hallway toward the kitchen, her hands attempting to ease the strain by grabbing hold of his wrist.

Purse! her mind screamed, one hand reaching for it while the other continued to hold the wrists, fingers just managing to snag a strap.

"Oh, no you don't," he said, his left hand grabbing the opposite strap and pulling, their journey down the hallway momentarily halted as he tried to rip the bag away from her.

Locking her fingers, she refused to let go, his frustration evident as he released her hair and grabbed the strap with both hands, her own body hitting the floor, her right arm cushioning the fall and then reaching toward the purse as well.

"Let go!" he demanded and gave the purse a savage yank, her body sliding across the floor a bit before she managed to stop herself and pull the other way.

The purse tore, the cheap design unable to withstand the impromptu tug-of-war, items from within scattering everywhere.

"Ah, this what you were looking for," he taunted while reaching for her phone.

In answer to his question, she grabbed one of the tiny cans of pepper spray that had rolled her way and shot a burst toward his face.

Startled, he stumbled away from the spray, his back hitting the corner of a wall cutout that led into the kitchen, body quickly twisting around it to disappear within.

Amanda waited for several seconds, finger on the trigger,

and then glanced toward the floor for her car keys, left hand snatching them, the dark I LOVE CATS keychain easily visible against the cream-colored tiles.

Kitchen to dining room to—

She spun around toward the dining room cutout just as he came through it, her finger pressing the spray trigger, the burst hitting him in the chest a second before he tackled her, the wretched pepper and cinnamon mist invading her lungs as she cried out from the collision, both their bodies crashing through the spray to the floor.

"Bitch!" he gasped, his voice hoarse from the spray, tears and snot starting to ooze and landing on her face, all while her own eyes and nose also began to flow.

And then she couldn't breathe, not from the spray, though that was making it almost impossible to see, but from his hands, which took hold of her throat, fingers squeezing without mercy.

No thoughts entered her mind; she simply reacted, her left hand making a fist with the keys and swinging it at his face. Given her position, and the fact that it was her left arm, she didn't have much force behind it, yet the blow still seemed to have an effect, especially once the pepper spray residue entered the gashes she created on the side of his cheek, the keys acting like dull claws against his skin, catching and tearing rather than piercing and slicing.

Though obviously in pain, he didn't release his hold on her throat, her consciousness beginning to waver, all while her key-fist continued to rip at his face, his head twisting left and right with each attack, trying to minimize the damage and protect his eyes, snot and tears oozing.

And then her right hand joined in and grabbed his throat, fingers trying to juice his Adam's apple.

It worked, his hands releasing the hold on her throat to protect his own.

She gasped, lungs attempting to get air, throat feeling as if a straw had been inserted that she now had to breathe through, the tiny trickle nowhere near what her body wanted.

"Bitch!" he said, voice raw, more snot falling upon her.

Unable to see clearly, she swung the key-fist toward the voice but didn't hit anything, and then she felt hands upon her leg, trying to grip her ankle.

Screaming, she jerked her leg back and then kicked it toward him as hard as she could, heel hitting him. Where exactly she did not know, the simple fact that she was connecting with him enough for her to kick with the other foot as well, mind actually noting the sensation of a garter strap coming undone and snapping back as she lashed out.

The second kick didn't hit anything, and then the hand was back, this time gripping her ankle firmly.

She kicked with her right again, directing it toward her ankle, hitting the fingers that held it, a satisfying cry echoing.

During this, her vision started to clear, the tears from the pain and her frequent blinks having forced the pepper irritant away. Not that it was completely gone, the burn still intense, but enough was removed so that she could make out his figure and guide her kicks toward him, his groin being her primary target.

And then her hand was on the pepper spray canister once more, finger pressing the trigger, a burst of spray arcing his way, her own eyes safely behind it this time so as not to be affected.

He screamed, the cry turning into a horrific gag.

She shot him again, the stream actually hitting his mouth area.

Hands on his face, an odd slobbering sound echoing, he dropped to his knees, body slumping back against the front door.

In pain, lungs heaving for air, throat feeling swollen, and her eyes and nose raw, Amanda crawled backward toward the kitchen, unsure what to do until she saw her phone sitting where the man had dropped it.

Not really thinking about it, she brought up Alan's number and hit call, a "Hello, Amanda?" reaching her ears after two rings.

"Help me!" she cried, voice sounding wretched. "PLEASE!"

21

"What happened?" his mother kept asking as Alan raced around the house looking for his keys.

"I don't know!" he shouted for the third time. "Okay? I just don't know." Then, frustrated, "Where are my keys?"

"Did you—" she started but then stopped, probably knowing nothing she could say would help.

He found them a few seconds later, in the pocket of the pants he had stripped from his body after he had gotten home from being with Amanda.

Keys in hand, he hurried out to his car, a quick apology to his mother for shouting at her leaving his lips as he went through the door.

22

Riley wasn't sure what, if anything, he would find, but he knew he could not spend the evening simply sitting in his house waiting for Sam to call—not after everything he had learned today—and decided to head up to the house on Swift Road to take a look around. Unfortunately, given the time, traffic was not on his side, especially on President Street, where a stoplight, two commuter trains, and a stop sign all conspired to make a mile stretch seem ten times longer than it was.

Eighteen minutes, he groaned to himself at one point while watching passengers from the second commuter train disembark, their work-clothes-clad bodies flooding the street as they walked toward the different parking lots, their minds seemingly unconcerned with the fact that they were blocking traffic.

Horns blared, but the pedestrians didn't seem to care, their bodies continuing to flood the breach that had been created while the gates were still down and the road free of traffic.

Six minutes came and went before the crowd of pedestrians cleared, at which point traffic began to move again, only to come to a stop when the light beyond the tracks turned red.

Riley slammed a fist against his dashboard and then looked down at his phone, hands making sure to keep it below the sight lines into his car while checking to see if he had received any messages.

Nothing.

The light turned green.

Come on, come on, come on, he chanted to himself, his only goal at the moment being to get beyond the tracks so as not to be stopped by another commuter train full of business people from the city.

He made it, though just barely, the lights of the gates beginning to flash as he crossed them.

The relief was short-lived, the traffic he faced once he was on Geneva Road heading toward Swift Road mind-numbing, all thanks to a series of lights with left-turn arrows far too short to accommodate the volume of traffic present. Making it even worse, several of the lights did not have left-turn lanes, thus forcing traffic that just wanted to cross the intersection to stop as the lead vehicles waited for openings in the oncoming traffic to make their left turns.

Beyond that, once he was on Swift Road, things cleared up enough that the drive felt reasonable for that time of day, yet the relief at this wasn't enough to calm him, his body completely on edge from the traffic madness he had faced, questions on how and why anyone would subject themselves to it on a daily basis flowing through his mind.

And then he was at the house, hands maneuvering his vehicle into and then out of the driveway so he could point himself southbound once again and park on the street.

Once that was done, he stepped out and stared at the house, visualizations of the horror that might have unfolded within once Emily had entered playing across his mind.

Were they waiting for her, or did they arrive after she got there, one of them acting like a client before subduing her and letting the others in?

Nothing he could see from the outside would give him an answer to the question. Chances were nothing inside would either, though hopefully some answers would arrive, one being whether or not Sam had cleaned the place.

If not...

Riley didn't even want to contemplate how horrible going inside would be if he hadn't, just the presence of blood on the floor over a period of days enough to attract flies and other insects.

Now or never, he said, a good portion of his mind liking the never idea but knowing it wasn't really an option.

With that, he headed to the front door, only to discover the hide-a-key was no longer hiding a key.

Fuck!

After everything he had gone through on the road, he would be damned if he was turned away due to a locked door. One way or another, he was getting inside.

No lock-release tool, his mind noted, such items being of the type that one had to sign for, which in turn required information on why it would be used. And picking locks with the standard lock-picking tools was never a skill he had mastered.

Breaking through a window, however, was, and since he knew the house didn't have an alarm system nor could be seen from any of the surrounding houses, given the location and overgrowth, he had no problem shattering the window in the back with a rock.

Two minutes later, glass cleared from the windowsill, he climbed through into the back bedroom, joints creaking at the unfamiliar movements, his body stumbling forward into the queen-size bed that sat in the middle of the room just as a wretched smell hit, renewing his earlier concern over what he would be facing as he came upon the laundry area and viewed the crime scene.

23

"When I went to get the knife from the kitchen, he left," Amanda said. "I saw him pulling out in his car and he—"

Tears followed, her face pressed in his chest much in the way that Stacy's had been the other day after she had escaped the house in Joliet.

And like that day with Stacy, he simply held Amanda, his hand rubbing her back, an *"It's okay, now"* statement leaving his lips several times.

"He...he..." Amanda said, face once again pulled away from his chest. "...was going to kill me."

Alan wasn't sure how to reply to that and simply said, "He's gone."

"But..." she started and didn't continue, face pressing into his chest once again.

Alan's phone buzzed.

Amanda, probably feeling it through his jacket, asked, "That your friend?"

"Yeah," he said after looking at the screen. "Want to re-schedule our meeting?"

She looked at him for a moment, eyes and nose red, a large bruise darkening on the side of her face, another appearing on her throat, and actually laughed. "No, let's meet! I can tell her all about how wonderful working the sex trade can be."

Alan grinned and said, "Let's get out of here, okay?"

She nodded.

Five minutes later, after gathering all her things, they were sitting in his car, both agreeing that given her current state, driving herself would be a bad idea.

"I can help you with the car later on or even tomorrow," Alan said.

"Okay." Then, after a few seconds, "I..." She swallowed. "I don't want to go back to my place, but...." She hesitated. "I also don't want to leave Vicky and Crystal all alone." She shook her head. "I don't know what to do."

Alan thought about this for several seconds and then said, "Right now, let's just go to my place. I can make us some tea, and you can get all cleaned up, and then after that, we can figure out what the next step is."

"Okay."

He thought about his mother but then figured he could worry about that once they got there, mind trying to remember if he'd told Amanda that he lived with her or if he had glossed over it.

24

HEY, ARE WE STILL ON FOR TONIGHT OR WHAT? Stacy typed up, her first message that had asked what was going on having received no answer.

Once sent, she waited, feet pacing back and forth across her apartment.

SORRY, Alan replied two minutes later. AMANDA WAS ATTACKED BY HER CLIENT TONIGHT. I'M WITH HER RIGHT NOW. SHE'S IN SHOCK. I'LL KEEP YOU UPDATED.

Attacked! Stacy said to herself. *Holy fuck.*

OK, she typed. Then, YOU STILL AT THAT HOUSE?

NO, I TOOK HER BACK TO MY PLACE FOR A WHILE. NOT SURE WHAT WE'RE GOING TO DO. SHE'S IN THE SHOWER RIGHT NOW.

His place?

In the shower?

She wasn't sure why, but hearing this caused an odd hollow sensation to develop.

Stop! she shouted at herself, determined not to be jealous or to act like a girl with a crush.

Unfortunately, the determination did little to shake the hollow feeling. In fact, it only made it worse.

Maybe you should go over there, a part of her mind suggested.

No, another part said.

Best to simply wait to hear from him, his text stating that he would let her know what was going on. Once he did that, once the girl was calmed down after the attack, maybe they would all be able to get together. Or if she went back home, maybe she and Alan could get together.

Or maybe they are going to stay together...

Maybe they've had sex and he likes her better...

She shook her head, needing to get rid of such thoughts.

25

Riley spent nearly an hour in the house on Swift Road, eyes trying to spot traces of where the events described by Sam had unfolded, the tiny laundry room in the center of the house seemingly the only place where it looked like a murder had unfolded, the floor in that room still showing signs of blood despite the cleanup attempt Sam had made. That was also the only room in the house other than the kitchen and bathroom that didn't have carpeting, the lack of bloodstains upon the grungy cream-colored fabric of those rooms making him think the laundry room was where everything had unfolded.

The only problem was that there wasn't enough room in there for three men to have raped her repeatedly. In fact, there was barely enough room in there for two people to move around. And filming something while in there…no way. The space was not big enough to provide the distance a phone would need to capture what was going on. Riley proved this to himself by trying to take a bit of video with Emily's phone and discovering that there simply wasn't an angle where one could successfully capture anything within.

Did they fuck her elsewhere in the house, film it, and then take her into the laundry room to kill her?

Riley decided to ask Sam, a simple text presenting the question being sent off. No answer followed, which again puzzled him.

What could he be up to?

Especially if he has girls going through withdrawal at his place?

Actually, that might explain it.

If Sam was busy with two girls who were puking and shitting all over the place while experiencing some of the worst pain of their lives due to their bodies not getting the desired heroin fix, then he could see him not being able to answer.

But this long?

That seems odd.

Equally odd was the appearance of the house beyond the tiny laundry room. It all seemed untouched. Both beds were made and unused, one actually feeling grimy with dust, the couches in the family room were straight, the decorative pillows set in their proper spots, the coffee table was lined up correctly, and the carpet was free of footprints—something that could not have happened if several men had been traipsing around within the laundry room as Emily bled out.

And what did Sam do with the body?

Disposing of such a thing so that it would not be found was not easy, even if one was experienced in law enforcement and knew what tripped up people most when it came to hiding such things.

A thought occurred.

He headed into the garage.

Inside was a Deepfreeze, one that Sam had actually joked about possibly containing a body while the two had visited the house following the foreclosure purchase to see if there was anything within they needed to remove before sending clients there.

No body had been present then, much to their relief, but now…

Taking a deep breath, he lifted the lid, expecting to see the frozen remains of Emily, her crystallized eyes staring back at him.

Empty.

Relief arrived once again, only this time it was short-lived.

What did Sam do with the body?

26

"I put a towel in there for you, and there's fresh soap and a clean washcloth and, um, oh, I have an extra bathrobe if you want that for after and—"

"Mom, I think she has everything she needs," Alan said, carefully cutting her off. To Amanda, "Take as long as you need, okay? Don't worry about using up water or anything, and once you're done, I'll have some tea for us and we can sit and relax."

"Thank you," Amanda said, voice barely above a whisper, tears lining her eyes. "For everything."

Alan, unsure how to reply, simply nodded and gave her arm a reassuring rub.

Lips trembling, Amanda turned from Alan and headed into the bathroom, carefully closing the door behind her.

Alan waited until he heard the shower and then headed back into the family room where his mother stood, hands fidgeting.

"Poor girl. You sure she's going to be okay?"

"I think so," Alan said. "She's tougher than she looks, and..." He didn't know what else to say.

"She wasn't...well...the man didn't...you know..."

Alan shook his head. "I don't think so. Sounds like she fought him off tooth and nail."

She thought about that for several seconds and then said, "Maybe we should still take her to the emergency room, have her checked out. Those bruises..."

Alan was shaking his head. "No emergency room, no police."

"But—"

"Mom, it's her decision."

"But after something like—"

"Mom," he said, voice soft but firm. "After what she just went through, the last thing she needs is for us to push her into doing something she doesn't want to do. Trust me. It's best to let her wrap her mind around what happened. Once she calms down, she'll probably realize that it's in her best interest to contact the police and go get looked at by the emergency room, but until then, she needs to process what happened in her own way and make her own decisions."

"Okay, I suppose you're right," she said, though whether she really did agree was doubtful. "So, is she going to stay here tonight?"

"Don't know," Alan admitted, his own mind having been wondering that for a while now. "Earlier she mentioned wanting to get back to her place so her roommates wouldn't worry, but, well, we'll see what she says after her shower."

"Should I make up the spare bedroom just in case?"

"Um...that's not a bad idea," Alan said. In his mind, he wondered if the question had simply been an attempt to see if the two would share a bed that night, should Amanda decide to stay.

"And while you do that, I'll make some tea."

27

Though she knew her body was badly battered, seeing herself in the bathroom mirror before getting into the shower was a shock, her red irritated eyes, swollen cheek, bruised neck, and disheveled clothing making it look as if she had been put through an office-building gang-style beat-in initiation. An odd sense of embarrassment was present as well, her eyes having been unaware that two of her garter straps could be seen dangling beneath the hem of her skirt, the clasps having been ripped free from the stocking, which had also been torn and slipped down to her knee in the struggle, all while the stocking on the other leg was still held in place and only suffered one tiny tear. Her teddy and cleavage were visible as well, her shirt having lost two buttons during the fight.

Amanda stared at herself for several seconds and then sighed, puzzled by her own concern over what his mother had thought of her appearance, considering what she had just been through. After that, she stripped the clothing from her body so she could get into the shower, steam already billowing from the hot water within.

Once under that spray, all thoughts vanished, the hot water encasing her in a way that seemed to shed the horror and violence of the last hour. It wasn't a complete fix, however, just a momentary relief, the fact being that what she had gone through, and what could have happened, would be plaguing her mind for days, weeks, and maybe even months. Right now though, it was gone from her mind, her only care in the world being how wonderful the hot water felt.

28

Alan couldn't decide which tea to make, his mind stuck between the

Glenburn and Puttabong estate leaves.

"Which one did I try?" his mother asked, hovering.

"You've had both," he said.

"But which one was the one that tasted really smooth and had a bit of sweetness to it?"

"Um...you said that about both of them," he said, frustrated.

"Well then, either one should be fine—if she's a tea drinker. If not, she might not like either of them, even if they are brewed perfectly."

Alan knew she was right, yet even so gave her a look that said, *You're not helping.* A second later, "I'll just do the Glenburn." Why he chose that one, he didn't know, but it suddenly seemed the right choice.

Through the wall, he heard the shower cut off.

Crap.

She was going to be out before the tea was ready.

Using a measuring spoon, he scooped out three helpings of leaves into the teapot strainer and then waited, the water still not boiling.

A minute passed.

Amanda was still in the bathroom.

On the stove, the water in the kettle was growing aggravated yet still wasn't boiling.

Thirty seconds passed, the water finally boiling, Amanda still in the bathroom.

Alan pulled the kettle from the burner and then retrieved an ice cube from the freezer, his fingers carefully slipping it through the spout of the kettle.

His mother watched as he did this, shaking her head.

"What?" he asked. "You don't want the water actually boiling or else it scorches the tea."

She just smiled.

Alan took hold of the kettle and carefully poured the water into the teapot and then set a timer.

"OCD alert!" his mother said, following it with a fake cough.

"Hey, you use a timer when cooking," Alan said. "This is the same."

"I didn't say anything," she teased.

Alan shook his head.

Down the hall, he heard the bathroom door open.

"Um...excuse me, Mrs. Miller?" Amanda asked.

"Yeah?" his mother said while turning to head down the hallway.

Whatever it was that Amanda needed, Alan could not hear, the two talking low enough so as not to allow their voices to carry into the kitchen, which was fine with him as he finished brewing the tea.

Not long after that, Amanda appeared, body encased in a red bathrobe, a look of exhaustion present despite the smile she projected his way when he motioned toward the glass teapot and said, "Perfect timing."

29

ANY NEWS? Stacy asked.

No reply.

Growing antsy, Stacy started pacing the apartment once again, her mind and body unable to keep still.

Are they having sex?

Did you manage to hook him up with a whore?

It seemed, given how fucked up her life always became, that such a situation would fit in with how things typically unfolded for her.

They're not having sex, not with his mom there.

But they could go somewhere else.

Yeah, because sex is what every girl wants after being attacked and nearly killed.

She shook her head, frustrated at how she was reacting to this situation.

Calm down.

Easier said than done!

She checked her phone.

Still no reply.

Fuck!

Why won't he respond?

STOP!

She put the phone down on the coffee table and headed toward the bedroom, steps slowing as she neared the door.

No sounds appeared.

Rusty was not doing anything within the closet, probably due to the pain he was still in from having his penis pierced and his testicle crushed.

Horror at her own actions arrived, as did a memory of what it had felt like when the testicle actually burst, her palm having sensed an odd *pop!* as her fist squeezed.

Turn your head and cough...

She smiled at her own wit and entered the bedroom, feet still moving carefully to keep her presence unknown as she stepped up to the closet.

Rusty was curled up on the floor, mouth, arms, and legs completely taped up, limp penis fully exposed, blood present but no longer oozing from where she had pierced the flesh, one testicle discolored from the fluids that had pooled within.

Several seconds passed, during which Stacy considered waking him up and asking more questions, the late hour and surrounding apartment vacancies nullifying the danger from any screams that would echo.

But will he really tell me anything?

Does he even know anything?

Earlier Rusty had said something about not being able to get any more girls now that Robert was gone, which indicated that Robert was the one with the connections. However, she also clearly remembered Robert using the words "child molestation pad" the other day before getting ready to torture her, which seemed to display a sense of disgust toward the house and Rusty.

Could they both be telling the truth?

Were some of the girls that Robert brought to Rusty's place ones that he was able to leave behind once the cameras stopped rolling?

If so, why the disgust from Robert?

Was it because he simply was in it for the business, while Rusty and the others were there for the sex?

Ask him.

Make him talk.

"Hey!" she snapped, kicking him. "Wake up."

Rusty opened his eyes and stared at her, nothing present within them, which to her was a sign of contempt, given that she wanted to see fear. She wanted him to question what was about to unfold, to tremble with terror at what she might do to him. Instead, he simply stared at her and then, to her shock, pissed all over himself.

"Jesus Christ!" she said, grabbing his ankles and pulling him from the closet, her initial reaction being one of preventing the bloody urine from soaking into the carpet, which of course was a fruitless endeavor, given how much carpet there was between the closet and the bathroom.

Anger followed, as did disgust.

Don't! her mind said as she was about to kick him again,

thinking how pissing himself might have been an attempt at provoking her into a senseless rampage. After all, being kicked into unconsciousness would be better than suffering through a calculated mutilation of his genitals, and if that truly had been his motivation behind pissing himself, then it was a satisfying display of fear.

No, it's not, the other part of her mind countered. *I want to see the fear on his face, not pooling on the floor.*

What if the pee was out of fear, something he couldn't even control?

And the blood in it!

What if…

She shook the thoughts away and knelt down beside Rusty, her eyes boring into his for several seconds before saying, "In a minute, once I clean up that little mess you just made, I'm going to take the tape off your mouth and ask you some questions, and this time I'm going to get some answers. If I don't…well…let's just say I've been fantasizing all afternoon about the wonderful little things I can do to that pathetic penis" —she grabbed the organ in question while talking, earning a wretched look of pain—"and now, given that this area is pretty much empty of people, I can finally make some of them a reality without having to worry about your screams bringing the police." She smiled, gave the penis an upward tug that pulled at his busted testicle, and then released him. "Just something for you to think about while I clean."

His eyes, which had been blank up until that moment, were now wet with pain and glistening with fear, a sight that she relished for several seconds before heading into the kitchen to grab some paper towels.

Five minutes later, she returned to the bathroom, the smell of piss from what had soaked his legs hitting her nose.

You should put him in the bathtub, stop up the drain, and make him soak in whatever fluids he expels.

And then what, bathe in the sink?

She shook her head.

If she had a place with two bathrooms and a week or two to keep him, then maybe—*MAYBE!*—she could do something like that. With just the one bathroom, limited time, and the probability that her sadistic desires toward Rusty would fade as more time passed, she would stick with the simplicity of the bathroom floor and the veggie knife.

And my hands! she thought as she once again ripped the tape from his mouth, a chunk of flesh from his lower lip pulling free.

"So, ready to talk?" Stacy asked.

He glared at her, lips pressed tight.

"Silence is not an option," Stacy said and reached down to grip the discolored testicle.

"Don't!" he cried, body trying to pull away as she neared his battered manhood. "Please!"

"Then answer the question!" she snapped, fingers touching but not gripping the testicle.

"Yes!"

"Yes, what?" she demanded.

"I'll answer your questions!" he shouted.

"Good." She took her hand away.

Rusty sighed, tears welling in his eyes while sweat oozed from his pores.

"How often did Robert bring girls to your place?"

"Whenever he had them," Rusty said.

"And was it just for films, or did he sometimes just go there to fuck them?

"Robert never fucked anyone; he was just there to film."

"Never?"

Rusty shook his head.

Oddly enough, she believed him, yet even so she reached

down toward his testicle while asking, "So you're telling me that despite having access to all these girls all the time, he would never ever have sex with them?"

"NEVER!" Rusty shouted, body trying to shift away from her hand. "IT WAS ALL BUSINESS FOR HIM!"

"And what about you?" she demanded, fingers slipping around and taking hold. "Did you fuck the girls?"

"Yes! But only if he said it was okay! Or...*oh god, please don't!*"

Stacy loosened her hold but did not remove her hand. "Or what?"

"Or if I knew he wouldn't find out!" Rusty cried. "Sometimes he would leave them there for a while to be picked up after the videos, so I'd have fun with them!"

"Picked up?" she asked.

"By people who wanted them, if they were available!"

"What do you mean by available?" she asked, fingers tightening again, her mind not liking where this was going.

"*No, no, no!*" he screamed, body clenching. "*DON'T!*"

"Tell me what available means!" she demanded.

"Ones that didn't already belong to anyone, runaways, girls from the street!"

"And what? He sold them?"

"To people that would take care of them!"

"To perverts and pedophiles!"

"To people that would value them!"

"To people that would fuck them senseless!"

"Better than being on the street!"

Stacy, unable to control herself, squeezed.

Rusty screamed.

"I know you said he was going to be rough, but he flat out attacked me," Amanda said, phone held tightly against her ear, voice unsteady. "He punched me in the face and then started dragging me by the hair down the hallway!" She listened for a moment, anger appearing. "What? No! I thought he was going to kill me." She listened again. "He started choking me after he knocked me down again and then—" She stopped and listened and sighed. "No, I had a friend come and pick me up. I was so shaken I couldn't drive." She listened some more. "Yeah, I'll be back tonight with the car." She listened again. "No, you don't have to go get it. Like I said, we're right down the street, and I have the keys so…fine, I'll think about it." She shook her head. "Okay, bye."

"You in trouble?" Alan asked, Amanda's side of the conversation having led him to believe that she had just been chewed out for what had happened.

"Sort of," Amanda said with a heavy sigh. "Kristi says I overreacted to his aggression and that since she told me he was going to be rough, I should have anticipated the roughness and not freaked out." The anger appeared again. "Excuse me if I'm wrong, but since when does being punched in the face and dragged by the hair fall into what one should expect when hearing the term 'rough sex'?" She shook her head. "And now she wants me to meet him again because he feels he didn't get what he paid for and should get an extra scene for free, given the pain I caused him and the scar he'll probably have from when I hit him in the face with my keys."

"That's crazy," Alan said.

"Tell me about it," Amanda said. She took a sip of her tea, eyes brightening a bit. "Oh wow, this is good."

"Ah, I'm glad you like it." Personally, he thought it was too strong, but then again, he had tasted it when brewed perfectly, and she had not, which meant that this cup would taste completely different and be far more flavorful than the store-bought stuff she was used to.

"What kind is it?" she asked.

"It's a first flush from the Glenburn Estate in the Darjeeling region of India," he said.

"Yeah, so, I have no idea what that means," she said with a smile, one that faded quickly.

"Ha, that's okay, most don't. It's just one of the many different estates in India that grows tea in the Darjeeling region, which, as you can guess, is where Darjeeling tea comes from. Each one has a different flavor and quality to it, depending on the elevation, rains, and growing style. This one happens to be one of my favorites of the first flushes."

"And what exactly does first flush mean?" She took another sip.

"Oh, just that the leaves were picked during the spring. Second-flush ones are picked during the summer. They have a darker color when brewed and a stronger, denser flavor."

"I see."

"First flushes from the Darjeeling estates are considered the finest, most sought after of all the teas," he added.

She took another sip. "I had no idea there were different types. I always just bought the purple box from the store." She let out a weak laugh and took another sip. "I really like this though. Are you able to buy it around here, or do you have to order it online?"

"Online," he said. "Places like Teavana will sometimes carry a Darjeeling tea at a price that'll make you think it's from one of the finer estates, but it isn't, and the taste leaves much to be desired."

She took another sip and then motioned toward the pot. "Is it okay if I have some more?"

"By all means," he said.

"Thanks." She topped off her mug, added some sugar, took

a sip, sighed with pleasure, and then without warning said, "Fuck, I'm so pissed off right now. How can she be mad at me? After what happened to Emily, I thought I was going to be killed and simply defended myself! And to think she wants me to see the guy again after all that to make up for everything…ugh, I didn't even know how to respond to that."

"Yeah," Alan said, his own mind shifting back to the attack, a new thought building. "So he called your boss himself to tell her what happened?"

Amanda nodded.

"Which means he didn't fear her reaction at all and probably knew she would take his side."

Amanda nodded a second time.

"So, what if his call wasn't actually to complain about what happened, but to let her know that you had gotten away."

"Gotten away?" she asked.

"Yeah. What if the scene was set up with the sole intention of you being attacked and killed?"

Amanda stared at him for a moment, understanding appearing. "Oh my god," she whispered, hand going to her mouth, eyes wide. "And Emily! Maybe he was the same one that killed her. Maybe Kristi set that up as well!"

Alan nodded. "The question is, why?"

"Because she's a fucking bitch!" Amanda snapped and then a bit more calmly, "She and I have clashed quite a bit, especially over doing videos and the fact that several of the girls are under-age—well no, I never actually said anything to her about that, just about doing the videos, so…" She sat down, a puzzled expression appearing, and shook her head. "I'm not sure why she would go so far as to have me…to send him."

"What about your coworker Emily?" he asked. "Can you think of any reason Kristi would want her killed?"

Amanda thought about it for a moment and then shook her head. "I think Emily was seeing guys on the side, which was against the rules, but…" She shook her head. "I don't understand how that would lead to Kristi having her killed either."

"Yeah, not unless she had threatened to do something drastic like talk to the police or something," Alan said.

"And I don't think it would have been that. Emily wouldn't have gone to the police." She sipped her tea. "But there has to be a reason, especially since Emily was really popular with the regulars."

"Maybe her popularity was the problem if she was seeing guys on her own. Maybe your boss feared she would steal them."

"Hmm, maybe."

"And there's always the possibility that she threatened to go to the police for some reason. People threaten things all the time with no intention of following through with it."

"Yeah…maybe," she started but then gave a slight shake of the head. "Honestly, though, I really don't think it was that. I would have gotten some wind of it. She and I may have butted heads from time to time, but we also confided in each other quite a bit, so…" She shrugged. "I really don't know."

"Okay," Alan voiced. Even though he wanted to project an idea, wanted to put something out there that would make her cry, "THAT'S IT!", he knew the likelihood of doing so was almost non-existent. He just didn't know enough to provide theories that were tailored to this specific situation. Instead, he asked, "Is Kristi the type to fly off the handle and overreact to things?"

"Oh yeah, she'll totally lose it if things don't go the way she planned, or if someone questions her decisions." She took another sip of tea, her second cup nearly finished. "I put up a bit of a fuss about being in a porn video the other day, given that I didn't want it following me around for the rest of my life, and she threw a hissy fit, and then of course acted like my best friend once I agreed to do it."

"Okay, so that makes me think the reason she could have wanted you attacked and Emily killed could be something that wouldn't really make sense to us, something that she just lost her cool on and overreacted to."

"Could be," Amanda said after thinking about it. "But I also think that there must be something that we don't yet fully understand. It's one thing to lose your cool and scream at a person, but it's another to go so far as to have them killed, and I have to think she would see the extreme in such a thing and actually think it through to the point of knowing it was the best option—in her eyes, of course."

Alan nodded.

"So..." Amanda started and then simply sighed. "I don't know what to think."

"Me either," Alan admitted. "One thing I do know, if he truly was sent there to attack you, then going back to your place isn't a good idea, not when Kristi could easily have him go there and finish what was started."

Amanda thought about this for several seconds and said, "You're probably right, but where would I stay?"

"You can stay here if you like," Alan said. "My mom actually made up the guest bedroom for you if you want to use that, or..." Hesitation hit. "Well, wherever you want. It's up to you."

Amanda smiled and said, "I'll stay here on one condition."

"Oh," Alan voiced. "What's that?"

"You make another pot of tea," she said, smile growing.

"Deal," he replied with a chuckle, his own smile appearing.

"Though do you think it would be okay if we ran by my place so I could grab a few things?"

"No, not at all. Just say when."

"'When,'" she said. And then, growing serious again, "We should probably go get my car as well, so I can bring that back."

"Okay, we can do that too, though, honestly, if you pick it up, you might as well bring it back here so you can use it. I mean, seriously, why leave it with them when you might need it, especially after what happened? It's not like they're going to call the police or anything."

"True…" she said, hesitation evident. "Still doesn't feel right for some reason. I mean, it really isn't my car, but then again, I'm the only one that uses it, and they did just try to have me killed."

31

"Hey, we're not finished yet," Stacy said, hand slapping Rusty's face several times to wake him back up, a slip back into unconsciousness having unfolded as she further pulped his busted testicle.

Slowly, his eyes opened, moisture glistening within from the tears that had developed before passing out.

And then he vomited.

It happened quickly, a look of panic appearing on his face followed by his head twisting to the right, the vomit spewing out upon the discolored tiles.

Seeing this and then smelling it nearly made her sick, her lips squeezed tight as she backed up.

Paper towels, she said to herself and then stared in dismay at how thin the roll had become when cleaning up the piss. Only two sheets were left, the second of them leaving several chunks behind on the cardboard roll, thanks to the glue that held it in place.

No other rolls were in the linen closet, and the sheets she held would do little in the way of soaking up the bile stew that was now cooling on her floor.

Fuck!

She didn't know what to do.

Old shirt?

It really was her only choice, one that she put into play, her actions quick so as not to have to breathe while trying to scoop up the mess.

Unfortunately, the smell didn't go away, not even when she tied a knot in the garbage bag that now contained the mess.

Scented candles?

She had several in the closet, their various origins unknown, four of which she was able to light without a problem, the scents doing well to combat the wretched smell yet not erasing it completely.

You could burn him with the wax once it pools, she said to herself while carrying the garbage bag toward the front door, having decided to take it out to the trash in hopes of ridding the place of the smell. Of course, if she did burn him, it would not be on his body, which he might actually enjoy, but in his eyes, which she could keep open with pieces of tape so that he had to watch as the hot liquid fell into them, the splatter being the last thing he would ever see as it burned through his pupils.

She shivered, the thought of experiencing such a thing sending a chill through her.

He raped you.

And probably dozens of others, many of them children.

Even so, the horror of what she was contemplating was almost too much for her; thus she pushed it away, her mind deciding to keep her brutally focused upon his genitals, which, oddly enough, didn't horrify her—at least not to the same extent that burning out his eyes did. Later, she would probably be haunted by her actions, but now it was everything she could do to hold back and use the mutilation threats as a tool to get answers.

"Be right back, my dear," she called, fingers twisting open the deadbolt lock on the front door. "Don't go anywhere."

Though it was hard to make out, given how hoarse his voice had become, it sounded like he used the words "cunt" and "face" within his reply.

She chuckled, thoughts about how to make him pay for that warming her against the bitter October air as she descended the squeaky staircase, the vomit bag held as far from her body as possible while she headed toward the Dumpster.

Behind you! her mind cried, the presence felt seconds before the arms reached around to grab her.

"NO!" she screamed, arms flailing, fingers trying to find the face of her attacker, the vomit bag having landed somewhere upon the potholed pavement.

A gloved hand struggled to muffle her voice, her teeth clamping down on it without mercy, her own jaw screaming in pain as her gums strained to rip free a chunk.

The attacker, a man, cried out, hand pulling free from her mouth.

Blood dripped, her taste buds filled with the coppery flavor.

"Bitch!" he snapped just as a fist hit her lower back, the blow sending a shockwave throughout her body.

A second blow landed, followed by a third, her body dropping down to its knees, bladder nearly releasing its contents.

Her hand landed upon the vomit bag and, without even thinking about it, she grabbed hold of it by the knot and swung, mind trying yet failing to ignore the pain the movement caused.

The bag struck her attacker in the face, the blow stopping him in his tracks as he instinctively braced himself against what he probably thought was going to be a heavy impact.

Nothing happened.

The bag hit with little effect, the plastic holding strong and failing to spew its contents upon him.

And then he had a hand around her throat, one that felt as if it was going to crush everything within, her attempts at freeing herself no match for his strength.

Several gasps for breath followed, a wretched dry sucking sound echoing against the brick walls that surrounded them.

A heavy blow landed, his other hand striking her across the face, knuckles splitting her lip and busting loose a crown she had gotten in her late teens, all while the other hand continued to squeeze her throat, spots appearing in her field of vision.

More gasps for air echoed, her lungs struggling, her hands frantic.

The spots on her vision grew.

She was losing it.

No! her mind cried, fingernails breaking as they tried to cut through the leather that covered his arms and tear his flesh. *NO! NO! NO!*

"Help me!" she cried, only the words did not echo, her vocal cords unable to produce anything more than a gurgle-like wheeze. *"Please!"*

Another blow smashed her face, this one actually knocking her free from the hold upon her throat.

Cool air flooded her lungs, only to be forced out as a booted foot slammed into her chest.

A second boot then came down on her lower back, smashing it, a soundless scream leaving her lips.

Her spine felt as if it had been crushed, only—thankfully—her legs still had life in them.

Needing to get away, she started to crawl, her goal being the end of the alleyway beyond the parking lot area so she could flag down a driver.

She made it about a foot before a kick to the face knocked all sense from her, her mind going in and out of consciousness as she was carried to a waiting trunk, wrists secured behind her back with handcuffs once she was inside.

32

Unsure what to do, Riley started back toward the Naperville area, the roads finally free of the rush-hour madness. At Geneva Road, however, he hesitated and then, after thinking about it for a moment, took a left and headed toward the house where Emily had lived, a desire unfolding to speak with Amanda to see if she knew anything about the Emily situation.

No one was home.

He rang the bell several times, but no one ever answered. He then punched in the four-digit garage code and discovered the car was gone.

Uncertainty arrived once more.

He looked at his phone.

Still no reply from Sam.

He called.

It went right to voicemail.

Hesitation arrived.

Going inside and looking through their things seemed like an invasion of privacy, but then he had pretty much paid for the house, and if something improper was going on the consequences could land him in jail, so…

Closing the garage behind him, he headed into the house and started looking around.

Nothing jumped out at him on the first floor, the place simply looking like a house where several college girls lived.

Only one college girl now, he noted to himself and headed up toward the bedrooms, uncertainty about who lived in which room unfolding.

33

"What do you think, like forty-five minutes?" Alan asked.

Amanda nodded. "Yeah, if that." She slipped on her shoes,

realizing for the first time that she had left her heels back at the house after the attack. *Not to mention several items from my purse and the clothes I had brought to wear for the meeting.* "I don't need to grab much."

"Okay," Alan's mom said.

"And we'll call if something holds us up," Alan added.

"Okay," she said again.

With that, the two headed into the garage where Alan's car was waiting and then, once inside, backed out of the driveway and into the cul-de-sac. From there, Alan made two right turns and then a left, the car quickly coming upon the College of DuPage.

"Wow, you really are close," Amanda said, eyes watching as students who had finished up with some night classes were waiting to pull out at the light, mind wondering if she would be doing the same in the near future, her mind and body almost too exhausted for classes after working various shifts at several different fast-food places simply so she could afford to continue with her education.

Shit, who are you kidding? You'd never be able to afford school with such jobs, let alone a car that would take you to and from it.

This once again led to thoughts on the webcam potential, as well as the idea of creating her own business with Alan's friend.

And maybe more porn videos.

Ones that you would control.

All she would have to do was open up her own page on the site the guys had told them about yesterday, the one that would pay a percentage of every video sold.

Alan said something that she didn't catch.

"What?" she asked, mind returning to the current task.

"Oh, nothing, I was just saying something about how you're close too, that's all."

"Oh yeah, I really am," she agreed, watching as he slowed for the turn that would connect them to the road her place was on, suddenly realizing she hadn't provided any directions at all.

And then he was in her driveway, car coming to a stop.

"How did you know where I live?" she asked.

"What?"

"How did you know this was my house?" she asked.

"I—"

It all clicked. "You're the one that followed us the other day!"

"Yeah, but I can—"

"The day Emily was killed!"

"But it isn't what you—"

His words were a blur as she fought against the seatbelt and then the door, a sense that he was going to grab her and pull her back into the car unfolding.

Instead, he let her get out of the car, his body making no move against her as she headed toward the front door.

"Amanda," he called. "Wait."

She stopped and turned.

Alan had gotten out of the car but wasn't coming toward her, his position by his open door giving no impression of a threat toward her at all.

And he lives with his mother, who put towels out for me and made up a bedroom.

And you had lunch together while all alone, after which he helped you with the dishes.

"Why were you following us?" she asked, the initial fear she had felt moments earlier fading.

"I was trying to help a friend figure out what it was you all were up to, that's all."

"What friend?" she asked, somewhat puzzled.

"The one we had planned on meeting tonight."

"The one that wants to be a prostitute?"

"Yeah, only…" He hesitated. "I need to come clean on something—something that might ruin what we now have."

"What?" she asked, concern returning, though now for a different reason.

He lied to me. About what, she did not know, but it was something, and knowing that was like having an ice pick shoved into her stomach.

"I don't think this is a good place to talk about it. Maybe we should go inside and sit down, or better yet, get everything you need to get and head back to my place."

"I'm not going back to your place until you tell me the truth, whatever it may be." She crossed her arms, a wince escaping at the pain the movement caused.

"Fine, but let's make sure we have some privacy." He motioned toward the house. "Is anyone even home? All the lights are off."

She shifted around and looked at the house, the concern she had felt over what it was he had lied about now shifting to concern over why the house appeared empty.

Where would they have gone?

Especially without a car?

Did someone come to pick them up, or did something happen to them while I was gone?

"Amanda," Alan said, voice displaying his own concern. "Come away from the house right now."

"What is it?" she asked, feet starting to move.

"Someone's by the front window, waiting by the front door."

"What?" She turned toward the window but couldn't see anything. "Where?"

"Amanda," he urged. "Please just listen to me and come away from there right now."

She did, fear now poking at her spine.

Nothing happened.

"Get behind the wheel," Alan said.

"Why?" she asked.

"Just do it, okay."

She did, all while he went around to the passenger side.

"You said you have roommates, correct?" Alan asked once they were both in the car.

"Yes," she said, looking at the house, trying to see what he had seen. Nothing jumped out at her.

"Okay. Pull out and start back toward the main road, going slow. Once you get onto the main road, take a right and come back around and wait for me on the opposite corner."

"What're you going to do?" she asked, hand switching on the ignition and then shifting the car into reverse.

"I'm going to find out who is inside and why they were waiting for you in the dark."

"But—" Amanda started, hand shifting back to drive.

"Don't worry," he said as she started driving down the road, a door ajar warning present on the dashboard. "I'm not going to be reckless. Mostly, I just want to see what happens once they realize you're not coming inside. See if they leave, and what car they go to, and how many there are."

"How are you going—" Before she could finish, he was out of the vehicle, the slow speed making it so he could simply step out and quickly duck between two houses, his body disappearing quickly.

Startled, Amanda almost hit the brakes but then realized that would probably be a signal to anyone that was watching and continued forward as if nothing had happened, foot only touching the brake once she was at the stop sign.

Once there, she took a right and then another right, backtracking around the house so she could park on the opposite side of the street.

34

Riley was twisting the knob of the front door, Emily's laptop slung over his shoulder, ready to leave, when he watched a car slow to a near stop and turn into the driveway of the house.

Shit!

He waited, a decision to slip out and head to his car as they pulled into the garage arriving, only the garage door never opened.

Peering through the front window, he could see the car parked in the driveway, taillights showing that it was still running. And then one of the girls came around the corner, walking toward the front door, only to stop and twist around as a male figure stepped out of the driver side and said something that he couldn't make out.

A few seconds passed, the girl turning once toward the house and then, for some reason, heading back toward the car, this time getting into the driver side while the male headed around to the passenger side.

Confused, Riley watched as they pulled out of the driveway and headed back the way they had come.

Was that Amanda?

Though he couldn't know for sure, his mind leaned toward a yes, given that no other adult-aged female would have been coming here now that Emily was gone.

If it was, then that guy might have been Stacy Collins's friend.

He considered this for a moment, indecision on what to do next arriving.

And then he felt his phone buzz.

WHAT'S UP? Sam asked in a text.

YOU FREE? Riley typed.

NOT RIGHT NOW.

TOMORROW?

MAYBE, WHAT TIME?

NOT SURE, I'LL LET YOU KNOW. WE NEED TO TALK ABOUT WHAT HAPPENED WITH EMILY.

OKAY.

AND HAVE YOU TALKED WITH KRISTI YET?

No reply followed.

And then, through the window in the family room, he saw a figure dart across the yard from the rear of the neighbor's house to the side of this house, positioning itself with a view of the front door.

Shit!

Tucking the phone into his back pocket, he crept back to the window to see if he could see anything.

No one was visible—only he knew someone was there.

The reporter's friend?

The Special Forces guy?

Did he realize someone was inside while the two were in the driveway?

If so, what was he doing now?

And where was Amanda?

Heart racing, Riley stood where he was, not moving a muscle, ears trying to listen to see if he was trying to get inside somehow.

Or maybe he's just waiting in a hiding spot for you to leave to see who you are.

35

HEY, Alan texted Amanda while leaning up against the house. WHAT IS THE CODE FOR THE GARAGE DOOR?

NO! DON'T GO THAT WAY. THEY'LL HEAR YOU!

DON'T WORRY. IT'S JUST A DISTRACTION.

Earlier she had mentioned that the back door was often unlocked. He figured that if he opened the garage door, the attention of those in the house would be upon that, allowing him to slip in through the back unnoticed.

His phone buzzed.

He looked at the four-digit code and then, still uncertain about what to do, waited a bit to see if whoever was in the house decided to leave.

36

Time seemed to slow as Riley stood in the family room waiting to see what happened, his right hand constantly shifting the laptop bag, even though the strap wasn't sliding down his shoulder at all.

And then the garage door started to open.

Fuck!

Without thinking, he hurried toward the back door, only to come face-to-face with the young man as he stepped through it, the two staring at each other in surprise for a moment before the young man hit him in the chest with his forearm and elbow, forcing all the air from his body, and then hooked his foot out from under him.

Panicked, Riley reached for his gun, which he started to pull, the young man grabbing his wrist as he did, the two struggling for a moment, the gun failing to fire as the trigger was squeezed several times, thanks to the safety.

And then Riley felt pain in his wrist like no other as the man somehow twisted him around and pulled, the gun leaving his grip.

"Don't move!"

Riley was flipping back around as the command was given, eyes looking down the barrel of his own gun, body expecting a blast.

Nothing happened.

"Who are you?" the man asked, voice surprisingly calm.

"I'm..." Riley started, lungs having trouble producing enough air to speak. "Riley...Woodman." He tried to take a deep breath, lungs finally able to suck in some air. "I'm...a state police...detective."

"Woodman," the man said. "You're related to Kristi Woodman?"

"Sister-in-law."

The man considered this.

"What are you doing here?"

"Investigating."

"Investigating what?"

He took several more deep breaths, hands struggling to stay up, given his angle on the floor.

"Were you sent here to kill her?" he asked.

Riley looked up in surprise.

"Answer me!" the man demanded while kicking him in the leg.

"No!" Riley cried, hand moving down toward his shin, only to be kicked again.

"Keep your hands up!"

"Fuck, man!" Riley said, rolling over onto his side, laptop pressing into his lower back. "Ease up."

"Get up, slowly."

Riley did.

"Into the other room, onto the couch." He didn't wave the gun as a directional guide, his hands keeping it trained squarely on Riley's chest. "Put the bag by your feet and sit on your hands."

Riley did as instructed, thankful to be off the floor but still not liking the gun situation.

"Okay, you move and I shoot you in the leg, understand," the man said.

"Yes," Riley replied, believing him. With others, he might

have tried calling the bluff, but with this guy…he had no doubt he would squeeze the trigger if the need arose.

The man stared at him for a moment, probably trying to gauge whether or not he could be believed, and then took two steps backward, one hand holding the gun while the other reached into his pocket to pull out his phone.

"Amanda," he said. "Come on back. We have a situation here that I think you should be a part of."

After that, they waited, the sound of a car pulling into the driveway arriving.

37

"What's going on?" Amanda asked, startled by the sight in the family room.

"This is who was in here waiting for you," Alan said, his hand holding a gun on the other Mr. Woodman.

"I wasn't waiting for her," Mr. Woodman said. "I just came to try and find out what happened to Emily."

"Trying to find out with the lights off, by the front door, in an empty house," Alan said.

"No one was home, so I grabbed Emily's computer and was heading out when you two showed up." He took a deep breath, almost as if he was winded. "You two pulled up just as I was leaving, and since I had no idea who you were and what your intentions were, I waited."

Amanda stared at Mr. Woodman for several seconds, then looked at Alan and said, "Alan, it's okay. I believe him."

"You sure," Alan asked, gun not moving.

"Yes."

"Okay." Alan lowered the gun, thumb flicking the safety on.

Mr. Woodman sighed with relief.

Silence followed.

Amanda hesitated, then, "Did you set up the scene that got Emily killed and the one that got Caroline infected with an STD?"

"What?" Mr. Woodman asked.

His reaction was all Amanda needed to confirm her suspicion that Kristi had lied to her the other day. "Mrs. Woodman said you did, said we were not to speak with you if you tried to contact any of us because you were trying to take things over and make all your money back by setting us up with dangerous scenes."

Mr. Woodman shook his head. "I've been trying to prevent HER from setting YOU all up with dangerous scenes. Jesus fucking Christ!" He stood up, anger present.

Alan stepped back and started to raise the pistol.

"Dude, chill," Mr. Woodman said. "I'm not the Taliban!"

Alan seemed startled by the comment.

"Yeah, we know all about you and your military career," Mr. Woodman said. "And about Stacy and your relationship with her, and how you're trying to help her write a story about all this."

"Story?" Amanda asked, concern building. *Is that what he was trying to tell me earlier?*

"Oh, didn't he tell you?" Mr. Woodman asked. "The whole reason he set up a scene and became friends with you was to help his reporter friend write her story about us."

Amanda felt as if she had been kicked in the gut. "Is that the girl you were talking about? The one that you wanted me to meet tonight?"

"Yeah," Alan said.

Amanda, unsure how to reply, felt her lip start to quiver. Tears also threatened.

"A friend that has been attacked and raped while working on this story," Alan added.

"What?" Mr. Woodman asked.

"Actually, she's lucky to be alive," Alan said and then

looked at Amanda.

She looked away.

"When did that happen?" Mr. Woodman said.

"She was attacked last Thursday and then kidnapped and raped repeatedly Sunday night."

Mr. Woodman didn't reply for several seconds, eyes looking down at the floor. "I had no idea."

"Yet you're one of the people running things?" Alan snapped.

"I thought I was, but now…" Mr. Woodman shook his head.

Nothing else was said for several seconds.

"Why were you taking her laptop?" Amanda asked.

"What?" Mr. Woodman asked, genuinely puzzled, and then after a moment, "Oh…I wanted to see if maybe she had anything in here that would help in understanding why she was killed."

Amanda didn't understand how the computer would help him with that.

"Did you know she was dating a guy named Patrick and that the two were making porn videos together that were earning her enough money for her to leave us and do her own thing?"

"No, but…"

"But what?"

"Well, she used to go out a lot, and I did start to wonder if she was moonlighting." She shook her head. "I never even considered the possibility of a boyfriend." Something clicked. "You said his name was Patrick?"

"Yeah, same guy you filmed with the other day."

She nodded.

"When did Kristi have you all start doing videos and seeing clients in the back of her office?"

"This week." She looked at Alan. "Monday was the first time I was instructed to give a blowjob in the back room, and Kristi told me I'd be fired if I didn't do the videos."

"Fired?"

"Yeah, and she said we would all be shifting over to doing videos. She even has Vicky and the new girl Crystal doing them, which is just..." She shook her head, a question about why she was telling him all this unfolding.

Because he's different from Kristi.

Is he really?

Still one of the bosses.

But...

Her mind hit a brick wall.

Sadness and anger at Alan's lies followed.

Everyone always wanted to use her. All her life, she had been nothing but a pawn.

Tears started to fall.

Not wanting to be seen, she turned and started toward her room.

"Amanda?" Alan asked.

"Just leave me alone," she said, stopping momentarily to wipe at her eyes.

"But—" he started.

She waited.

"I'm sorry," he said.

She didn't reply, though she was touched by the apology. It wasn't something she could react to at the moment, however. The hurt was too fresh and the tears too visible. She needed time to process everything.

Wiping her eyes, she continued her exit from the discussion and headed up the stairs toward her room, the tears continuing to cloud her vision as she sat down on her bed.

Thoughts of Alan and whether or not he truly liked her arrived, her thinking being he did and that he was just as tormented by the fact that he had lied as she was.

Maybe we can still be—

An odd cinnamon-like smell caught her nose, one that puzzled her for a moment because she didn't remember having any type of candles or incense in her room.

No!

She twisted around just as his gloved hand was coming down from behind to cover her mouth, the palm missing its mark as she pulled backward but still managing to snag her hair.

A knife appeared, her eyes catching the reflected glint from the blade seconds before it opened part of her throat.

Initially, there was no pain, just a sensation that someone had put a handful of ice against her throat, all while a spray of blood hit her attacker. A wheezing sound followed, the knife having opened her windpipe.

Alan! she tried to call, lips moving but no sound appearing.

Panic set in as she tried to breathe, each gulp causing an odd flutter-like feeling in the opening.

Her legs gave out.

Darkness began to creep in.

And then he was on top of her, his gloved hand putting pressure on the opening, almost as if trying to stop the flow of blood and loss of air.

"There, there, just relax," he whispered, a nasty grin on his face. "We don't want you losing consciousness too quickly."

For a moment, she didn't understand what he was doing, the consciousness he spoke of enough for her to be aware, but not to the point of comprehending everything.

His hand fumbled with something down below.

He's touching me!

No!

Pain arrived as she tried to fight his actions, the realization that he was trying to fuck her as she bled out bringing about a level of horror that she had never before experienced. Her body could not react the way her mind wanted it to, and slowly but surely, a new layer of darkness arrived.

"There we go," he said, penis entering her. "I'm going to send you off to hell with a bang."

Darkness arrived as he started thrusting into her, his wicked smile the last thing her eyes saw.

38

"Do you really have feelings for her?" Riley asked, surprised by the reaction he saw on Alan Miller's face once Amanda had gone upstairs.

Alan didn't answer.

"You do, don't you?" Riley shook his head. "Wow."

"Wow?" Alan asked, a hint of anger present. "What's that supposed to mean?"

"It doesn't mean anything," Riley said, eyes focusing on the gun again. "Just a bit unexpected. Ironic even."

"Why?"

"I don't know." He shrugged. "It just is."

Alan continued to look toward the stairs, obviously hoping that Amanda would come back down.

She didn't.

Riley waited and then, "You know, we were only trying to help these girls."

Alan turned his attention back toward him. "And yourselves," he said.

"Yeah, well, no act is truly altruistic, now is it?" Riley asked. "But it is mutual, the success I mean. Our success is their success and eventually, once they finished their education and had a better financial footing, they would be able to leave all this behind them."

"Really?" Alan asked. "That's what you intended? Let them just walk away once they were ready?"

"It's what we told ourselves, and it's what I intended. And I think it's what my brother truly wanted, but..." He sighed. "His wife just wants money and success. She never saw the horrors that he saw while working, so..."

The ceiling above creaked.

They both looked up, though Riley could tell Alan's attention was still mostly focused on him and whatever threat he generated.

"Look, if you feel *that* strongly about her, go up there and apologize," Riley said.

"I already apologized."

"So go do it again. Show her you don't want to lose her. Girls like to be chased, and given everything she has been through these last few years, feeling wanted and seeing your fear of losing her will mean a lot. More than it would with other girls you have probably been with."

Alan didn't reply.

"Look, for the last several years everyone she has ever met has only wanted to use her, and now she probably feels you did the same, only it's worse than the others since she convinced herself that that wasn't the case."

"Well, that's just the thing. I was just using her in the beginning...sort of...but then something happened and...well...now I just don't know."

Another creak echoed through the ceiling.

Alan looked up again and then turned back toward Riley and asked, "Do you know anything about the scene she was set up to do earlier this evening?"

Riley shook his head. "No, I'm not really kept fully informed on the day-to-day setups the girls have, though given the events lately, I think I'm going to need to be."

"What exactly is your role?"

Riley hesitated.

"One way or another, the story about all this is going to break, so if you want an accurate portrayal of your role in it, you should probably tell me rather than letting Stacy come to her own conclusions based on little tidbits of info."

Riley saw the logic in what he suggested but wasn't ready to start sharing all the details. "What happened tonight?" he asked, shifting things.

"Oh nothing much, except the guy she was set up to see tried to kill her, and then, rather than being sympathetic, your partner Kristi screamed at her about ruining the scene she was supposed to do, and that being sucker punched in the face upon introduction wasn't anything she should have freaked out about because the guy had set up a scene with the specifications of rough sex."

"Are you serious?" Riley asked.

"Yeah. And do you know what I think?"

"What?"

"I think that scene was set up for her to be attacked, given that Amanda told me that she and your partner have had words this week and haven't seen eye to eye on several things."

"And because she was friends with you," Riley muttered.

"What?"

"Oh, well, they both knew about your connection to Stacy, found out through Facebook. My brother told me about it today."

"Fuck!"

"Yeah, so what happened tonight? Seems she held her own against this attacker?"

"Sprayed him with pepper spray, which I guess she has always carried in her purse."

"Pepper spray?" Riley asked, something clicking within his

mind. "Oh shit, I thought that was incense they had burned!" He stood up. "Give me the gun."

"What?"

Rather than argue, he said, "Come on!"

Riley headed toward the stairs, Alan following, their steps heavy as they raced toward the landing.

First door on the right, Riley told himself, memories from earlier guiding him.

He threw open the door just as a figure was turning toward them, his erect penis the first thing Riley's eyes were drawn to.

And then he saw the knife.

And the blood.

"Don't move!" Alan cried, stepping between them, gun leveled at the man.

He moved.

Alan shot him twice in the chest, gunshots causing Riley to jump aside, blast *pinging* his eardrums. He then watched as Alan calmly walked up to the man and put a round in his head, the lack of hesitation on Alan's part shocking.

39

Following the gunshots, which didn't even really register with him, Alan stepped over to Amanda, his mind initially thinking she was in shock from being attacked while in her own room. But then he saw her glazed eyes staring up from her pale face and knew, without needing to check for vital signs, that she was gone.

"He's dead," Riley Woodman said.

"Amanda too," Alan said, his mind blocking off all emotion. "Looks like her throat was cut."

"Shit, seriously?" Riley asked and then stepped over to look. "Oh Jesus."

Alan didn't reply.

"And he was fucking her!"

"Yeah," Alan said. He looked from Amanda to the man then back to Amanda. After that, he checked the gun to make sure it was secure, all while keeping an eye on Riley, who was staring at Amanda, his face quickly losing color.

"Hey, you okay?" Alan asked.

Riley didn't respond.

"Hey," Alan said, snapping his fingers in front of him. "Look at me."

Riley did, a visible tremor appearing.

Alan, knowing what would follow, took hold of him by the arm and guided him toward the bed. "Sit down for a moment before you fall."

Riley did, eyes returning to the man's body, which Alan now focused on, his free hand checking his pockets to see if he could find some ID.

A wallet, phone, and car keys were present.

Alan opened the wallet.

"Stuart McKenzie," Alan read and then looked at Riley. "Know him?"

Riley shook his head.

"Lives in Rolling Meadows," Alan pressed.

"No," Riley said, voice nearly soundless.

Alan nodded and then looked at the phone. "Needs a password."

"Let me see," Riley said.

Alan handed it over and watched as he angled it two different ways, eyes noting how the light reflected off the screen.

"One, three, eight, and nine," he said. "See the wear and tear on the screen protector."

Alan took it and angled it back and forth, the slight wear marks easily visible. "Yeah."

"It's gotta be a combination of those four numbers."

"Or he frequently calls someone with those numbers in it," Alan suggested.

Riley shook his head. "Everyone has speed dial these days."

Alan thought about that and then focused his attention on the numbers, a thought about them representing the year 1983 appearing.

He checked the driver's license.

Sure enough, the man was born in 1983.

A moment later, they had the phone unlocked.

Outside, flashing lights appeared.

"Fuck," Riley said. "Someone called in the gunshots."

"So? It's not like it wasn't justified. He had a knife and had killed her."

"And the fact that you were holding my gun, how am I going to explain that?"

"You tripped on the stairs and I picked it up."

Riley nodded. "And the reason we were running up here?"

"We heard her scream."

The doorbell rang.

"And what were we all doing here?"

"We were going to watch horror movies, you know, since it's almost Halloween, and then she went upstairs to change while we were going to get things ready down there."

"Okay, that actually sounds pretty legit," Riley said. "And nothing about the prostitution."

"Nothing," Alan agreed, though deep down inside he knew there was no hiding it. Once they started looking into Amanda's background, they would figure it all out. He just hoped Stacy could get the jump on revealing everything before that.

Go talk to her after this. Let her know everything is going to unravel soon.

Thursday

October 31, 2013

1

Stacy heard the dry heaves from the unseen girl and nearly vomited herself, her throat swallowing against the sensation several times in an effort to keep the contents of her stomach—or lack thereof—at bay so that she didn't choke to death, the tape that sealed her mouth adding a deadly element to the unpleasant bodily function.

"You okay?" another girl asked.

No vocal reply followed, but given that the second girl didn't repeat the question, Stacy was pretty certain that a nod had been given.

No more dry heaves echoed, nor did a conversation begin, which was what had happened the last time one of the girls had vomited, that episode having been so intense that Kristi Woodman had actually come into the room to tend to the girl.

Questions about who she was and why she was bound up had been asked, Kristi simply telling them that Stacy had tried to ruin things for all of them, so they were going to give her to the girls' old boss as payment for them.

"But he doesn't like old girls," one of them had said.

"Yeah, well, he knows someone that does, a guy that will film her fighting with other girls," Kristi had said.

"You mean Mr. Sullivan!" one of the girls said, shocked.

"Ah, so you know who he is," Kristi said.

"We used to have to go to him if we were bad, not to fight, but to be filmed for his other videos for the guys that like to see us humiliated. I went there once and he made me drink my own piss and locked a plug in my ass for two days and made me lick it off afterward."

"Now see, I'm glad you two are here so that you can share with her stories about Mr. Sullivan and what she can expect." Kristi paused. "Gillian, did you ever visit Mr. Sullivan?"

Gillian didn't reply, but she must have shaken her head because the other girl then said, "That's not true. She's been to him three times, and they told her the next time she went she would stay!"

"Gillian, is that true?"

Gillian didn't reply.

"Well, I hope you know that we don't tolerate misbehavior here either, and if you continue to cause problems like you did for Mr. Right, we're going to punish you as well, and if that doesn't work we will sell you to someone just like Mr. Sullivan."

Gillian began to cry after hearing that, which then caused Kristi to try to comfort her. "There, there, it's okay, don't worry. That's only if you misbehave, which is something you have to choose to do."

"But guys never like me as much as they do the others, so I never make as much money, and then I get in trouble."

"Things will be different here. Our guys are going to love you. Both of you. And they will pay lots of money to spend time with you."

With that, Kristi had left the room, locking it behind her, at which point the girls had started voicing horrific stories about Mr. Sullivan and the things he had girls do. One story, which Stacy hoped was just a rumor, claimed that Mr. Sullivan had once had a girl burned alive in the woods behind his house as if it were a medieval witch hunt, her body being tortured for a confession on custom-made medieval devices so that the videos he made for that client were accurate.

Of course, even if it wasn't true, the horror of what the two girls had been through, and the fact that they had confirmed Kristi's statement about the fighting videos he created, was enough to chill her to the core and make her fear the path she now found herself on.

She had to get free.

Only there didn't seem to be any way to get free, not when it was handcuffs rather than rope that secured her. That, plus the tape they had wrapped around her knees and ankles much the same way she had wrapped tape around Rusty, made it so she couldn't even get up to her feet, let alone run away. Her eyes and mouth were also sealed, Kristi having laughed while wrapping the tape around her head over and over again, all while her husband had tried to tell her that they should put something beneath the tape so that her flesh didn't rip when they pulled it off.

"We'll let them tear it off once we drop her off," Kristi had said.

"But she'll need to have water before then."

"She'll live," Kristi had replied and then, without warning, backhanded Stacy across the face, knuckles striking the same area that Rusty's knee had hit earlier that day.

Tears flowed but went unseen, thanks to the tape.

The same was true with the blood from her busted lip.

Hands then took hold of her from behind, both closing upon her breasts, but not in a "time to fondle my captive" type of way. Instead, he was picking her up off the chair and dragging her somewhere.

"Downstairs?" Sam Woodman asked.

"No," Kristi had replied. "In with the girls."

"But do you want them to see this?"

"I want them to see the consequences of defiance," Kristi said.

With that, Sam had taken her into the room with the two girls, neither of whom asked any questions at the time, probably due to being asleep. After that, through the door, she heard Sam say something about heading back to take care of things at her place, which meant he was going to discover Rusty.

Since that moment, except during the post-vomit conversation about Mr. Sullivan, Stacy had wondered what would unfold once they found Rusty, given that he wasn't a customer but instead had just provided the location for another customer, one that she had killed.

Will I be able to do the same here? she wondered, mind envisioning herself jumping on top of Kristi and smashing her face into the floor over and over again.

No.

Things were going to be different.

Here, they were just holding her; there, they had been fucking and questioning her for information. They had also underestimated her, which she didn't think was going to be the case here. This wasn't to say they thought highly of her, just that they weren't going to risk giving her the opportunity to escape.

And once you're given to this Sullivan guy...

She didn't want to dwell upon that, her future sounding pretty bleak if her transfer into his custody went as planned.

And it will be, unless something happens to prevent it.

Something outside of her control.

Alan.

Last time, he didn't do anything to help you.

Hopefully, this time he would figure out she was missing sooner rather than later.

If he's even thinking about you.

A vision of him with that whore filled her mind's eye, the two fucking each other silly between trips to get food and going to school.

Stop! her mind screamed.

Putting an end to the visions was easier said than done.

2

By the time Alan was finally able to leave Amanda's house, it appeared as if the sun was ready to spring up over the distant horizon and bring about the new day, one that he was not ready for at all. In fact, all he wanted was to crawl into bed, morning classes forgotten, his need for sleep the only priority.

His mother was on the couch, asleep, when he crept into the house, her phone on the coffee table, which had been pulled closer than normal, her ear obviously not wanting to miss the ring if one finally arrived, should she fall asleep while waiting.

At the house, while the police were investigating the situation, Alan had not been allowed to use his phone, an officer actually tasked with the job of watching him between his interviews with the detective that had caught the case. The fact that Riley was a police officer didn't give them much slack, especially since the detective didn't seem to fully accept their answer on how the three knew each other. Alan claimed he knew Amanda, and that Amanda knew Riley, and that she had invited them both over for a movie night. Why the detective didn't buy this, Alan didn't know, but the look on his face and the way he kept asking the same question in different ways solidified his suspicions in Alan's eyes.

"Alan?" he heard his mother ask as he got a glass of water from the kitchen, his movements not stealthy enough to keep from waking her.

"Yep," he said from the kitchen and then downed the water.

"You okay? What happened?"

He walked back into the room, hesitated a moment, and then said, "I brought Amanda back to her house and didn't realize the guy that had attacked her earlier was there waiting for her. He killed her, and then I killed him."

"Oh my god!" She put a hand over her mouth, the look of exhaustion she had carried a moment earlier completely gone now. "Are you okay?"

"I'm fine."

"But—"

"Mom, I'm fine, and I really don't want to talk about it right now. I spent all night talking to the police about what happened and now…" He shook his head. "I'm just exhausted."

"You're sure you're okay though? I mean, killing a person, that's not—"

"Mom, this wasn't the first time I killed someone."

She stopped, considered that for a moment, and nodded. "I know."

Alan didn't say anything after that.

"Do you need anything?" she asked. "Want me to make some coffee, or are you going to try and get some sleep?"

He considered this for several seconds, noting that it was almost completely light out now. Going to bed would completely screw up his sleep cycle. He would almost be better off trying to stay up all day and going to bed at his normal time, a quick nap or two during the day in his reading chair the only moments where his mind could go away for a bit to recharge.

"I suppose I'll take some coffee," he said, decision made.

"Okay. And some bacon and eggs?"

Alan started to say no but then realized that it did sound good and that he really did need to eat something. "Sure, thanks."

She smiled, though beneath it, he could tell she was deeply concerned.

"I'm going to take a shower," he said. "Knock away some of this exhaustion."

"Okay. I'll start making breakfast."

With that, the two parted, Alan wishing things had gone differently with Amanda, especially when he came upon the towel she had used earlier.

Emotion threatened.

This time, he didn't hold it back and let the tears fall. Guilt and anger were present as well. Guilt toward himself for lying to her, anger toward Kristi, who he was fairly certain had ordered the attack on Amanda.

You still have his phone.

It was in his back pocket, his mind having completely forgotten about it until he started taking his pants off and momentarily wondered what the object was.

3

Riley didn't care for the detective in charge of the murder investigation, though only because he knew the detective wasn't buying what Alan and he had said. In fact, he could tell that the detective was going to crack this entire thing wide open.

Fucking Alan!

If he had only fired one round, most would have probably brushed it off as a firecracker or a car backfiring, but two rounds back-to-back, followed by a kill shot to the head...that was just begging for a neighbor to call, which they did.

Could I have done that?

Though he had fired thousands upon thousands of rounds on the range, he had never once had to actually fire at another person. Pull his gun, yes; fire it, no. The closest he had come had been during a bust three years earlier when a young man had reached for something beneath a pillow in the house they had raided, but then thought better of it when he looked down the barrel of Riley's Glock. Hesitation had saved the kid's life, and Riley had been able to return the pistol to its holster with a full clip. Afterward, however, a part of him wished he had fired, especially once he knew a gun had been under the pillow, thus justifying the shooting, simply because he had wanted to know what it was like to have crossed such a line. No one knew this, of course, since sharing such a statement would surely raise eyebrows and quite possibly get him booted from the state police. It also wasn't a desire to kill, just a desire to know what it was like, which was hard to explain.

Would you have been able to do it tonight?

Though he wanted to say yes, the answer was probably a no, given that he hadn't even realized the man was coming toward them with a knife until after Alan had killed him. Instead, he had simply been shocked by the scene.

Good thing he had your gun.

Alan, obviously, was no stranger to killing another human being, his years in Iraq and time with Special Forces having not just honed this ability, but also made it so he could react to a threat quickly and swiftly.

Sadly, neither of them had realized the threat in time to save Amanda, though he was more to blame for that lapse than Alan since he had been in that very room earlier that night.

And smelled the cinnamon.

He shook his head, frustration flowing.

We're fucked.

With Amanda dead and the killer slain, the police would uncover everything. It was only a matter of time.

All because Kristi got greedy and wouldn't follow the protocol we had established.

And Sam turned a blind eye toward her actions.

Or did he?

Riley thought about this for a long time but couldn't come to a solid conclusion. One thing he did know: his brother could not be trusted. And given the events that had unfolded that night, he now wondered if what he had been told about Emily had been true. Was someone trying to extort them by threatening to kill their girls? Or had Kristi and Sam wanted Emily removed due to her relationship with Patrick?

And what about Amanda?

Were her interactions with Alan, who was connected with Stacy, cause for Kristi to have her killed?

And the attack on Stacy that Alan talked about?

Did Kristi plan that as well?

Riley paced his apartment while thinking about all this, a desire to drive over to his brother's place and demand answers unfolding.

No, his mind instructed.

Nothing good would come of that.

Instead—

A thought entered his mind, one concerning Alan and the moments leading up to the police arriving at the house.

Did he ever turn over the cell phone?

If not, they might be able to learn quite a bit about the man and who had sent him.

Or you could let the police handle this and do everything in your power to stay out of jail.

Is that even possible at this point?

No answer, though only because Riley didn't really want to think about it.

A yawn followed.

He decided to go rest his eyes for a bit, the exhaustion he was feeling reaching a point where he could no longer ignore it, his mind and body drained from the drama of the last two days.

4

"Alan?" his mother said, pulling him from a semi-sleep in his reading chair.

"Whoa, what?" he asked, rubbing his eyes, an odd type of panic present.

"I just wanted you to know I'm leaving for work, unless you want me to stay home," she said.

"Oh, um…no, go, I'll be fine." He looked over at his coffee, which he hadn't even sipped at yet, and then toward the kitchen where his mother had been busy finishing up the bacon when he had taken his seat after his shower. "What time is it?"

"After eight. You slept here for over two hours."

He sighed. Earlier, after his shower, he had decided to rest his eyes for a minute or two while she made the eggs, but obviously that minute had grown in length.

"I didn't have the heart to wake you," she admitted.

"Did you end up making the eggs?"

"No. I came in to ask how many you wanted and you were out cold, so I put them back and put the bacon in the fridge after it cooled. All you have to do it microwave it."

"Okay, thanks." He rubbed his eyes again.

"You sure you don't want me to stay?"

"Yeah, I'm probably just going to spend most of the day zonking out while watching horror movies." In truth, he was going to go see Stacy and let her know what had happened and encourage her to get her story finished because now the police were involved and would probably break this thing wide open. "Also need to finish putting together my outfit for tonight."

"Still going to scare all the trick-or-treaters?"

"Yep, been looking forward to it for years."

"Okay. Well, let me know if you need anything."

"Will do." He stood up, body wavering a bit, his exhaustion still present.

"Alan," his mother started.

"Mom, I'm fine," he insisted.

"You can barely stand up."

"I'll be fine."

A little over ten years earlier, he had been up for days while pushing toward Baghdad, and then, in the time that had followed, remembered countless times where he had been forced to stay awake while on operations for two, three, sometimes four days at a time, his body catching little bits of sleep here and there, but never the amount needed for a full recharge. And then there had been selection for Special Forces.

Just thinking about that process sent a shiver down his spine, though oddly enough, the worst part of all hadn't been the rolling in the mud, or what seemed a lifetime of walking in the wilderness with no sleep, but the waiting to see if they called his name after all was said and done, mind not knowing if having his name called was a good or bad thing.

"Okay, well, call me if you need anything," she said. "I'm going to see if I can leave a bit early today. Maybe we can watch *Halloween* tonight after the trick-or-treaters."

"Oh yeah, good idea."

With that, his mother left.

Not wanting to zonk out again right away, Alan headed to the kitchen to make a fresh pot of coffee and then pulled out the phone from last night to see if anything within jumped out at him, the arrival of the police having prevented them from being able to explore the calls and messages. He also noted that he would be able to log onto the guy's Facebook since he had an app on there. In fact, he had five entire screens filled with apps, many of the icons unrecognizable to him.

Start with his texts and calls.

See if there's anything within about Amanda.

Fifteen minutes later, he found what he was looking for, though it wasn't in the form of a text. Instead, the man had a folder on his phone that had pictures in it, the name and address of the person listed in the description.

Emily, the girl that Riley and Amanda had been talking about last night, was the first picture, followed by one of Amanda, one of a young man named Patrick, one of Caroline, who he had met the day before at school, one of a girl named Isabella, who he hadn't met but recognized as the girl he had picked to have sex with, and, lastly, one of himself, which startled him.

No instructions were given concerning those pictured, but knowing that two of them had been killed, Alan didn't have to see anything definitive to know that it was a hit list.

The question was, had the guy been going in order of the pictures' position in the folder? If so, only two of them were dead. If not, all of them could be.

You need to show this to Riley.

Can he really be trusted?

Alan's gut said yes, and while he typically trusted his gut, he knew he needed to be careful. After all, Riley had not been pictured in the phone, so even if he were on the outs with his partners, it didn't necessarily mean he wouldn't still side with them in the end if it meant protecting himself—especially given that his brother was one of those partners.

He also didn't give you any contact information, though maybe that was just due to the craziness of last night.

Thinking about that craziness, he decided to give Stacy a call, the fact that she was not pictured in the phone somewhat puzzling since she had been attacked as well.

No answer.

Too early?

Instructions on leaving a message unfolded.

"Hey, Stacy, it's me. Give me a call when you get this. Something really bad happened last night, and now the police are involved in everything. Bye."

With a message like that, he knew she would call the moment she listened to it.

Maybe just go over there and tell her.

The fact that she hadn't answered nor replied within a minute or two meant that she was most likely still asleep, and while she wasn't the type that liked to be awakened early in the morning, he had a feeling this was a situation where she would be more angry about not being awakened than she would be about being awakened.

5

Numbness was the first thing that registered as Stacy tried to open her eyes, followed by panic at how her lids were stuck in place, the darkness unyielding.

She shifted, her right hand trying to reach for her face, only to be stopped short by the handcuffs that connected her wrists.

Understanding arrived.

The fear of having been blinded at some point while asleep came to an end, the horror of her reality replacing it.

The girls!

Gillian and… No other name appeared within her thoughts.

No sounds echoed either.

The room seemed empty, as did the surrounding house, though how such a situation would be possible she did not know. Could they have taken the girls from the room at some point without her waking up from it? Had her sleep been that deep once it had finally arrived?

Or are they simply sleeping soundlessly?

Shifting around, she attempted to sit up, body struggling to bring her upper half into a position that allowed her butt to scoot under it, her lack of sight and inability to use her hands adding a level of difficulty that seemed impossible to overcome.

No other task or stimulation was present, however, so she kept at it, her body eventually getting herself into a sitting position.

After that, she tried to orient herself in the room, ears listening for the sounds of the outside world—traffic, wind, dogs barking—so that she would know where the outer wall was and have somewhat of an understanding of where the door to the hallway would be. Not that she would be able to open it, her memories of hearing it being locked from the opposite side the night before still strong.

For a moment, no sounds registered, but then, after really focusing, she thought she could hear traffic somewhere in the distance to her right, which meant the outer wall had to be on that side. With that in mind, she carefully scooted herself to the left, body nearly tipping over once, until she found a wall, and then, after taking a moment to rest, scooted herself along the wall until she came to a corner. From there, she scooted along the next wall, bumping a dresser about two feet in. Beyond the dresser was a closet door, which ended at the corner. The next wall, given the coldness she felt when leaning against it, had to be the outer one. Moving along it, she came to the end of a bed that was tucked into the corner, her body tracing the edges of that until she came to a nightstand that sat between that bed and another one that was tucked into the opposite corner. From there she reconnected herself with the first wall she had found, which had a door in it, one that must have been about an inch or two to the left of her original starting point.

Can I open it?

Try as she might, she could not stand, not with her ankles

and knees bound with tape, and thus gave up on attempting that. Instead, she focused on trying to find an edge to the tape with her fingers so that she could pry away at it until her legs were free.

It took several minutes, but eventually she discovered a corner to pick at, one that slowly but surely started to give way.

Why bother? You won't be able to get out of the handcuffs.

Though correct, she didn't let her mind deter her, first, because she was stubborn, especially when arguing with her rational side, and second, because she really had nothing else to do, so it was either lie there and pick at the tape, or simply lie there. She chose to pick at the tape.

6

Stacy wasn't home, the door locked and her car gone, all of which would have been fine and dandy if he hadn't left her a message earlier, one that he knew without a doubt she would have responded to if able.

Something was wrong…again.

Knowing he couldn't open the door with his credit card, the edge still scarred up from the first attempt the other day, he decided to simply throw himself against the door to see what would happen, his thinking being the latch might get knocked out of place within the frame and allow him to enter.

Instead, he found himself with a sore shoulder, which would surely have a large bruise by nightfall.

Now what?

If this had been a typical apartment complex, he could have gone to the main office and tried to persuade them to open the door just to see if she was okay. With this type of apartment, however, he had no idea how to get in contact with the owner and knew that just taking the time to uncover that bit of information would not be worth the effort. With an office, it would have taken about ten minutes at the most to find out if they were going to let him in or tell him to leave. With this situation, he could spend half the day trying to track down the landlord just to get an answer of no.

Not worth it.

Plus, he knew something was wrong and didn't need confirmation of that fact. Instead, he needed to know what the next step should be.

Back at his car, he yawned while contemplating his options, and then, without really thinking about the consequences, started heading toward the real estate agency, a decision arriving to confront Kristi Woodman about what was going on.

Five minutes later, while sitting at a stoplight, he hesitated, thoughts of aborting this plan unfolding.

Indecision gripped him.

He had no idea what to do.

Another yawn arrived.

Up ahead was a shopping center, which he turned into so he could park the car and think a bit.

You should just call the police and tell them about Stacy. After all, they're already involved and should be given all the information possible so that they can put right the wrongs that have unfolded.

He stared at his phone while contemplating this and then went to grab the card the detective had given him, a statement of, *"Give me a call if you should remember anything else,"* arriving with the exchange, the implication that he did have more information and should really share it with them unmistakable.

Card in hand, he switched over to the dial pad of his phone to make the call, but then once again was halted by hesitation.

What about the private investigator?

Maybe he would have some advice.

Alan pulled out Walter Doyle's card, all while his mind told him the guy would simply tell him to call the police.

Still, talking to him might help.

Plus, he was fairly close, the directions on his phone saying he was less than ten minutes away.

But is he in his office?

What if he's out on a case?

Leave a message with his secretary.

If he has one.

You'll know soon enough.

Alan headed toward the office.

7

Riley felt, rather than heard, his phone going off, having failed to remove it from his pocket before falling asleep that morning.

It was the detective from the night before.

For a moment, he thought about dismissing the call, but then he realized it would be better to talk to him and get a sense of the direction he was taking the case.

"Hello?" Riley asked, his ears able to hear how weary his own voice was.

"Trooper Woodman?" the detective asked.

"Yes," Riley said after a few moments, deciding not to correct the detective on his rank. Instead he said, "Officer Robbins, what can I do for you?"

"I'd like to speak to you about the Kristi Homes Real Estate agency and the girls you and your sister-in-law employ."

"I don't employ anyone," Riley said. "That's my sister-in-law's thing."

"Yet you interact with her employees, some of whom have fairly questionable histories."

"Kristi and her husband, who you may have noticed worked undercover in Chicago for many years, felt it would be good to try and give some girls from the city streets a chance at bettering themselves by going to school and showing houses to her perspective clients. I figured befriending the girls they were hiring would help in getting them acquainted with the fresh start, and give them an ear if they needed it."

"Very noble of you," Detective Robbins said. "I suppose that also answers my question on why you all would hire girls like Amanda who had been arrested for prostitution in the past."

"Again, I didn't hire them."

"*Right, right, right,* you were just friendly with them so that they had someone they could trust."

Riley didn't reply, his own skill at interrogation telling him the detective was leaning toward something. What exactly that was, he didn't know, but he didn't want to say something that would then tip him toward something he hadn't already been learning toward.

"Tell me, were you ever worried that some of their former employers might come looking for the girls?"

"It was a concern, yes," Riley said.

"And what about the possibility that some of the girls might resort to their old career while still working their new career?"

"You mean start soliciting guys for money while showing houses?" Riley asked.

"Yes. Or getting in touch with their old contacts and letting them know they now had a place where they could see them if they wanted to have a 'date.'"

Riley waited a moment and then said, "Detective Robbins, have you ever worked within the vice unit of a major city, or had any involvement with girls who are put on the streets by the pimps of these cities, as these girls were?"

"No," Detective Robbins admitted.

"Then let me explain something. In the world of prostitution there are different levels of quality, much like you have within any field of employment. On the upper end, you have the escorts who can make quite a bit of money catering to the wealthy, charging thousands of dollars for their services. On the lower end, you have the girls who are put on the streets giving blowjobs for twenty bucks a pop, who may see two dozen men a night, ones who typically are riddled with disease and kept doped up and live to the ripe old age of thirty, if they're lucky. The girls that are peddled at this lower level are not keeping records of the men they see, nor do they carry address books for making dates."

"And that was the type of level your employees were on before you hired them?" Detective Robbins asked. "The bottom rung of the sex industry?"

"For the most part, yes," Riley said, this time not bothering to correct the statement implying that they worked for him.

"And you managed to bounce them up to the top level."

Riley hesitated for several seconds and then asked, "We what?"

"You helped transform them to the top level of the prostitution world by having them see clients at the houses they were showing."

"Is that what you think my sister-in-law is doing? Someone who has no record of involvement in the world of prostitution suddenly becomes a madam using her real estate company as a front?" Riley was glad this conversation was by phone because in person he probably would have given something away. In fact, he was surprised the detective was conducting this interview on the phone rather than in person.

"Honestly, I don't know, but you have to admit, it is easy to visualize such a situation. And if someone like myself can do that after just a few hours, imagine what someone who previously worked with these girls might have concluded, someone who may have sent someone out to put an end to your sister-in-law's real estate company."

"You think that is why the guy killed Amanda?" Riley asked. "You think he was a pimp taking revenge for stealing his girls?"

"I think, given his connection to the sex trade and the fact that your brother once busted him, that it is very likely this is the impression gained by those that were wondering what you all did with their girls." He waited and then, when Riley didn't say anything, added, "I also think that if you really care about these girls, you should come clean on what is actually going on with them and talk to me."

Riley didn't know how to reply to that, his mind suddenly pulled in several different directions.

Detective Robbins waited.

Finally, Riley said, "I'll think about it."

"Very well, give me a call if you want to talk." With that, the detective disconnected the call.

Riley started to dial his brother's number but then stopped.

Face-to-face, he decided and headed out to his car. Eight minutes later, he switched his journey from one of seeing his brother to discuss things to one of stopping at a McDonald's for an egg bagel sandwich, the realization that someone was following him having made him decide to make it look as if he was simply heading out for breakfast.

Back at home, he ate the bagel while occasionally glancing out his window to look at the car that was now parked on the street, watching his house.

Speculation followed.

Had the call from the detective been an attempt at baiting him? Had he tried to see what he would do once the call was made, therefore adding credibility to the suspicions he carried.

Or was it someone from the sex underworld, someone who

had been sent out by whoever had decided to kill Emily and Amanda?

You need to talk to Sam.

But how?

If he were being followed by the police, the last thing he wanted to do was incriminate himself by interacting with them. That said, he doubted he would escape this unscathed once they did figure out what was really going on.

8

Walter Doyle's office was on the second floor of an old house not far from the downtown area that had been converted into a commercial business location, one that probably didn't receive much foot traffic from those who visited the main shopping district to browse stores and socialize. For those who did manage to venture out this way on foot, it was doubtful they would be drawn into the house once they saw the list of services that were offered within, the private investigation office of Walter Doyle being the most interesting of the five that were displayed.

It was also closed, a sign on the door indicating that Mr. Doyle's hours were by appointment only.

Curious, Alan peered through the window in the door, seeing a small room that contained a desk, couch, two chairs, and a hatstand with a fedora on top, one that obviously was there for show since Mr. Doyle would not have left it behind if it were truly something he wore on a daily basis.

Or maybe he is inside and is simply in the bathroom?

Is there a bathroom?

Alan walked down the hallway he was in and did find a small public bathroom, which made him think there probably wasn't one in Walter's office, though he didn't know for sure.

Back at the door, he knocked.

No one answered.

He knocked again, harder.

Still no answer.

If there was a tiny bathroom in there, and if Walter was in it, he wasn't coming out to the knocks.

Maybe he's stuck? Alan's mind suggested, the memories of Walter's size and how he'd had trouble getting out of the car the other day playing across his mind.

Guilt at how cruel the thought was followed.

Call him.

Alan did, only the phone went right to voicemail.

He left a message explaining who he was and asking Walter to give him a call.

After that, he began to consider his next course of action, during which his phone rang.

He looked at the screen.

It was the detective from the night before.

"Hello?" he asked.

"May I speak to Alan Miller please," the detective instructed.

"This is he."

"Ah, excellent. I was wondering if it would be possible for you to come down to the station to answer some questions about last night."

"Right now?"

"Yes, do you need the address?"

"Um…yes, what is it?"

Detective Robbins gave it to him and then said, "So I'll see you in what, fifteen, twenty minutes?"

"Sure."

"Okay, good."

With that, the call ended.

Alan sighed and headed to his car, thinking it would probably be best to come clean to the detective on what was going on.

9

Freeing her ankles and legs ended up being all she could manage in attempting to rid her body of the tape, her handcuffed wrists unable to slip beyond her feet as she tried to shift them to the front of her body. Without achieving that, she could not reach the tape on her face, which meant she was going to have to try to escape the room without her sight.

It could be worse, she noted to herself.

At least no one here had raped her…yet.

This thought led to the one of being delivered to Mr. Sullivan, which, given what the girls had said, would probably thrust her into a situation that was so horrific she would actually wish for death.

With this thought, she pushed herself to her feet, body using the wall for balance, and then once her legs were stable, went to the bedroom door to try to open it.

The knob would not turn.

Though this had been expected, it still brought her down a bit. It also raised questions about where everyone had gone, the fact that she had been left alone like this for such a long period of time seeming odd to her.

Did they find Rusty?

She remembered Sam and Kristi saying something about going back to her place to destroy any evidence she had left behind.

Had something happened while doing that?

Something that made them take the girls, but leave you?

No, that didn't make sense.

She went to the window while thinking this, body moving slowly due to her lack of vision and hands. Once located again, she put her back to the window and tried lifting it, her wrists able to turn just enough with the handcuff links to take hold of the tiny handle.

It was stuck.

Even if it hadn't been, it seemed doubtful she would have been able to lift it more than a few inches, her arms unable to move very high, given the awkward angle of her upturned hands.

And then what, scream for help?

That wasn't going to happen, not with her head wrapped in the tape.

Can you break it?

Probably not.

Even so, she searched the room for an object she would be able to swing, her hope being it would be weighted enough to break the window without much force, given her limited mobility.

Nothing.

She searched methodically, even going through the drawers, her only discovery being several papers and an old pen.

Even the vomit bucket—or whatever it was Gillian had puked into—was gone, as were the sheets from the bed.

The smell still lingered, however, which was the only assurance she had that she was in the same room. That and the fact that she would have awakened if they had tried to move her.

But why leave me all alone like this?

What happened?

The question was infuriating, so much so that she kicked the wall, the padding of her shoe doing little to soften the blow.

Kick the window!

All she had to do was move the bed about a foot or two so that it was fully beneath the window and then lie on her back to kick it.

What if I cut myself?

Bleeding to death is better than being delivered to that Mr. Sulli-van guy.

Decision made, she moved toward the bed in question and tried to move it, the task more difficult than she had first imagined, given the carpet, which caught the wheels on the bed frame.

It wasn't impossible, however, and soon she had the bed moved enough to where it had to be beneath the window, her exhausted body letting itself twist and scoot upon the bed so that she could confirm this. Once that was done, she lined herself up with the window and got ready to kick it.

10

Riley couldn't take it anymore and decided he was going to find out who it was that was watching his house and why. First things first, he retrieved a pink pistol from his safe in the bedroom, one that he had bought for his wife while they were married in hopes that by having her own gun and becoming familiar with it, she would lose her fear and hatred of the one he carried. Instead, his decision to go pink with the pistol had sent her anger through the roof, her mind twisting it around into him somehow making fun of her and wanting her to be the laughingstock at the firing range if she actually took him up on his offer to join him one day, which, she noted, she would *never, ever* do. Nothing he could say would convince her that he had not been making fun of her, her insistence of this only made worse by the support she received from her girlfriends that she was right. None of them considered the fact that she had loved the pink iPhone he had gotten her back when smart phones were first hitting the market, or the pink laptop she had bought herself a year later. Those items didn't matter at all; the pink gun was an insult, plain and simple, one that resulted in him being exiled to the guest bedroom for a week.

Now, pink gun loaded and holstered beneath his coat, Riley

headed out the back door, hopped the back fence into his neighbor's yard, and headed toward the sidewalk so that he could walk around the block and come at the car from behind. While doing this, he speculated on who might be inside, thoughts of whether or not it was part of a surveillance team put in place by Detective Robbins unfolding.

Could a small suburban city get a surveillance team in place during a twelve-hour period, most of it during the early morning hours?

On Halloween?

He leaned toward an answer of no, especially given that the police department would already be tasked with the need to provide a perception of safety that evening for the trick-or-treaters, which meant a greater presence on the street.

If not the police…

Whoever it was that Sam and Kristi had run afoul of might also have their sights set on him, if, that was, Sam and Kristi had actually run afoul of someone. Given the fact that the man who killed Amanda had been able to get inside the house, all after having set up a scene, Riley couldn't help but wonder if maybe Kristi was the one instigating things.

But why?

What could she be trying to accomplish?

Another question lingered, one that he really didn't want to ask but had to.

What was Sam's role in all this?

If Kristi was behind the events that had unfolded, did Sam know about it?

How could he not know?

This last thought stuck with him as he rounded the corner, the car that had followed him now in sight as it sat on the far side of the street facing his house.

Focus, he told himself.

If it wasn't the police and instead someone associated with the underworld sex trade, chances were they would not react well to him confronting them and probably wouldn't have any issue with putting an end to him right there on the street.

But why would they be watching me?

Why not just kill me and be done with it?

Are they hoping I lead them somewhere, or that they learn something?

Did Sam end up grabbing a girl that they want back but can't find?

With this possibility on his mind, Riley quickly shed his "simple guy out for a stroll" appearance and charged around the car toward the driver's side door, hand grabbing the handle and yanking it open.

Inside, a man who looked as if he needed to lube up before squeezing himself into the car yelped while trying to shift into drive, seemingly forgetting that he would have to start the car first.

"Stop," Riley instructed, pink gun out and aimed at the man, other hand pulling out his ID. "State police."

Without a word, the man lifted his hands into the air, a wretched look of failure present on his face.

"Who are you?" Riley demanded. "And why are you following me?"

The man hesitated before saying, "My name is Walter Doyle and I'm a state-licensed private investigator."

"You're a private investigator?" Riley asked, a serious *what the fuck?* echoing through his head.

"Yes," he said. "Do you want to see my ID?"

"Yes."

The man retrieved it from his jacket pocket and handed it over. Riley examined the ID with one hand while the other continued to aim the pistol. Sure enough, the man was a private investigator; at least, that was what the identification claimed. In truth, Riley had never before seen such an ID, the perception that police detectives and private investigators were frequently crossing paths as they worked similar cases not really accurate, so he had no idea what they were supposed to look like but still figured it was legitimate.

"Are you armed?" Riley asked.

"Yes, it's in my glove box right now." He paused. "Could you lower your gun please? Recuperating from a gunshot is not how I want to spend my holiday season."

Riley looked at him for several seconds and then complied, pink pistol disappearing into the pink holster on his waistband. He then handed the man his ID while asking, "Why are you watching me?"

The man shrugged. "Curiosity."

"Curiosity?" Riley asked.

"Yep, though I must say, when compared to your brother and his wife, your activities are pretty dull. They also don't tease me with trips to fast-food place while I'm trying to lose weight."

Is this guy for real? Riley asked himself. "You've been following my brother and Kristi?"

"Yep."

"Why?" he asked again.

"Like I said, *curiosity*. I'm not working any cases right now, and this whole setup seemed so intriguing that I really wanted to see who was doing what and why."

Riley took a moment to absorb that, his mind thinking it all sounded too implausible to be made up, which meant, oddly enough, that he believed him. Then, "You said you followed my brother and Kristi. Can you tell me what they've been up to?"

"Just that they have been frequent visitors to an old townhouse on the south side, in a neighborhood that I don't particularly enjoy being in during the day and would hate to roll through at night."

Townhouse on the south side!

"What area is that?" Riley asked.

The man told him.

Motherfucker! Riley shouted to himself. *Mr. Right's place.* "You said they've been there frequently?"

"Well, frequently may be an exaggeration, but they've been up there more times during the last few days than would be typical of someone who didn't have an important reason for being there."

Riley considered this and then asked, "You know what type of business is conducted in that area?"

"I do."

"And have you spoken to the authorities about it?"

"Nothing to really report to them, though I've documented everything in the file on this case, which is secure in my office."

"I thought this was just something you were doing out of curiosity," Riley said. "Why do you have a case file?"

"Curiosity or not, it is always important to document your findings."

Behind them, a car drove by, the driver slowing as he passed to see what was going on.

Riley waited a moment and then said, "Well, since you've decided to focus on me now, I can tell you my next destination is going to be that area where my brother and his wife have been visiting, so if you want to follow me there, be my guest."

"Nope. I think I'll pass on that. I've been to that area enough for this lifetime and doubt watching you go in and out will provide me with anything interesting for my file. Besides, I need to go candy shopping for this evening. All the goodies I bought in advance disappeared."

Riley didn't even know how to reply, this little encounter

having taken a serious turn for the bizarre.

"Well, good luck today," the man said. "If you don't mind, I'm going to be on my way."

"Mr. Doyle," Riley said, halting him. "What is it you're really doing here?"

"Did I not just reveal that all to you?" he asked.

"You revealed what you wanted me to hear, but you left something out, something that explains what you're truly doing here, because, with all due respect, this is more than just simple curiosity."

Mr. Doyle didn't reply right away, his face showing signs of contemplation.

Riley waited.

"Very well. Simply put, I'm trying to gauge whether or not a young man who is involved in all this would be someone that I'd like to employ as an assistant."

"A young man?" Riley asked. Then after thinking about it for several seconds, "Do you mean Alan Miller?"

"You know him?" Mr. Doyle said, surprise evident.

"Yes, the 'young man,' as you put it, got the jump on me last night, took my gun, and then ended up killing another man who had just killed Amanda, who, it seems, he had taken a liking to. Shot him twice in the chest and then in the head for good measure, which then caused the police to show up."

Mr. Doyle considered this for a moment and then asked, "The man he killed…was it justified?"

"The man had a knife and had just killed Amanda while raping her. From the standpoint of the police, however, he probably crossed the line when he put the final round in his head. The man was going to die no matter what, but standing over a man and shooting him in the head while wounded…well…that never looks good."

"Was he arrested?" Concern was present.

"No, not last night, but that doesn't mean charges won't be filed at some point in the next day or two."

Mr. Doyle nodded.

"So, you've been investigating this thing simply so you can see how well he does in his investigation of it?" Riley asked. "All without him being aware of it?"

Mr. Doyle shrugged. "He knows I looked into things back when I was hired by a young woman to look into her husband's activities, but he is not aware that I'm still looking into things to see how well he does."

"Why didn't you tell him?"

"Like I said, I haven't made a decision yet on if I want to hire an assistant to work with me, and if I do, I'd like to know what his talents are within such a field before offering him a job."

"But if he doesn't know you're watching him—"

"I'll get to see where his instincts lie and what his natural abilities are. If he knew I was following his investigation, he might overthink his actions."

The reasoning was sound, Riley had to give him that, but at the same time, it also seemed really odd. "You do know people have been killed, right?" Riley asked.

"I do now," Mr. Doyle said.

"So do you think it's really a good idea to keep letting him play amateur detective in a situation that is growing more and more dangerous?"

"With all due respect, this is not the first time this young man has faced a dangerous situation," Mr. Doyle said.

"Yeah, I know, but this isn't a war zone, and he can't call in air strikes if he gets himself into a sticky situation. Shit, just the way he is trained to react to things might get him in trouble. Last night is a perfect example of this. He shot the guy in the head while he was bleeding to death from two chest wounds." Riley couldn't shake that image from his mind, and while he knew the man had deserved it, it still disturbed him.

Mr. Doyle considered this and said, "You're talking as if I have authority over him, as if I can tell him to stop looking into this. Nothing I can say will get him to end his involvement in this, believe me. I suggested it the other day when I first introduced myself to him. He is committed."

"But why?"

"He's helping a friend."

"Yeah," Riley said. "I know, one who seems like she is more trouble than she's worth."

Mr. Doyle didn't reply to that and instead said, "You don't seem all that concerned that so many people have figured out what it is you and your brother and his wife are doing."

"Believe me, I've been nothing but concerned for days, weeks even." He sighed. "Fuck, I've been against this entire thing from the start."

"Then why did you go along with it?" Mr. Doyle asked.

"Because I knew my brother was going to go forward with it," he said, holding back the part about the money and Kristi's threat. "So I figured I might be able to help control things to the point where he actually succeeded in what he was trying to accomplish while also protecting him from those that would want to put an end to it."

"Didn't quite work out that way?"

Riley shook his head.

"And now?"

"Now, I'm fucked. Last night has made sure of that. But, honestly, I don't think it would ever have worked. Eventually things would have crumbled."

And you knew it would, yet went along with it anyway.

Frustration and anger, both at himself and at his brother and Kristi, began to mix together within his body.

"The only thing I can really hope for at this point is that there will be enough mitigating circumstances to keep me from going to jail, though I'm guessing that is just wishful thinking, especially given the growing animosity toward the police the country seems to have these days. Social media has fucked us, the few bad eggs that were caught on camera and shared to the world making us all look bad."

Mr. Doyle didn't reply.

"But I made my own bed and now must lay in it, right," Riley added.

Mr. Doyle nodded.

Nothing else was said.

11

The window shattered on the third kick, a sense of accomplishment racing through Stacy's system.

It didn't last.

Aside from the glass, which was now broken and in pieces all over the bed, nothing had changed. The sounds of the outside were no clearer than they had been, and the air in the room didn't cool as the warmth escaped.

Something was blocking the window, something on the outside, something that her foot was able to hit but not really displace at all.

And then she heard the front door open.

Shifting herself so that she could stand once again, she listened.

Footsteps echoed.

Fuck!

Use a piece of glass!

Scooting back toward the window, she started fumbling around for a piece that could be used as a weapon, pain flowing through her fingers as small slivers pierced her flesh, the task of finding a piece large enough to use as a knife seemingly impossible until...

She found one, her fingers somehow closing around the long thin piece without further injury.

Holding it, however, was going to be problematic, thanks to the razor edge and the oozing blood that slickened the surface.

The tape she had ripped free!

Could she make a handle?

Moving quickly, she headed to the corner, feet kicking around, trying to find the discarded strands.

While doing this, she heard the steps coming toward the door and realized she didn't have time to make some half-assed handle. Instead, she put herself next to the door, body positioned in such a way as to be able to thrust her entire body into whoever came through, her hands held at her side as far forward as they could reach, glass shard pointed outward. She would have to collide into the person to stab them, all without being able to see what she was doing, which would be difficult yet was really her only chance.

12

"So your friend's suspicion grew out of the fact that Kristi Woodman wouldn't talk to her or show her houses, despite her posing as an interested buyer, which fueled her to do some research on the girls displayed on the website, who she found out had prostitution records and were not old enough to be working as licensed real estate agents?"

"Yes," Alan said with a nod. "That's what she told me."

"And she told you all this the night you two got together after not having seen each other for five years?"

"Yes, following the attack by the intruder who was waiting for her."

Detective Robbins nodded. "The man you fought off but were unable to apprehend?"

"Well, I just reacted to the moment, my goal being to get him off of her and remove the threat. Once he fled the apartment, I didn't see any reason to pursue him, not without first checking to make sure Stacy was okay and assessing whether or not she needed medical attention."

"And last night?" Detective Robbins asked. "Shooting the man who was in your friend's room, was that just you reacting to the moment as well?"

Alan looked at him for several seconds, frustration building since they had already gone over this a dozen times during the early morning hours, and gave a simple, "Yes."

"Must have been quite the moment, your friend in trouble, Trooper Woodman fumbling his gun on the stairs, you picking it up, Trooper Woodman opening the door, you stepping in and seeing the bloody man with the knife..." He shook his head. "What was going through your head?"

"Nothing was. I just wanted to help Amanda."

"You had no idea that she was already dead?"

What are we doing here? Alan silently asked. *Why are we going over everything again?* "No," he said.

"Must have been quite a shock, shooting a man dead, adding a round to the head for good measure, and then finding your friend with her throat cut, and coming to the realization that the attacker had been fucking her while she bled out." He shook his head again. "I mean, seriously, how does one process something like that?"

Alan didn't reply.

"Then again, I'm sure you saw horrible things while overseas, yet still, hard to fathom such a scene, especially in a suburban home that your friend lives in."

Alan stayed quiet, mind trying to figure out what the detective was trying to achieve since he obviously hadn't called him down to go over the same things they had discussed this morning. He also didn't seem too interested in learning about Stacy's disappearance and figuring out what might have happened to her.

Detective Robbins went quiet as well and then started going through his notes as if he were looking for something. After doing that for several seconds, he looked at Alan and asked, "How long had you known Amanda?"

"What do you mean?"

"We keep referring to her as your friend, yet we never established how you two met and became friends. Did you know her before you and Stacy reunited last week?"

"Yeah," Alan said. "We shared a class together at COD."

"Ah, okay," Detective Robbins said, hand scribbling a note. "And, coincidently, your friend Stacy asked you to help her look into Kristi Woodman's real estate company, which is when you realized your friend Amanda actually worked there and that you already had an in."

"Something like that," Alan said.

"Your friend Stacy—"

"Who is missing," Alan interrupted.

"Sorry?"

"Stacy is missing, and all the time we're spending here going over things that we went over last night is time that could be spent trying to find her."

"When you say 'missing,' you actually mean 'not home and not replying to you,'" Detective Robbins noted.

"What?"

"You said earlier that you left her a message and that she

wasn't home and that her car was gone, correct?"

"Yes."

"Well, that doesn't sound like she's missing. She simply hasn't had the chance to reply to you, probably because she's on the road and doesn't want to text and drive."

Alan wasn't sure why, but the statement flipped a switch within him, one that opened the floodgate that had been holding his frustration at bay. "Look, I didn't come here to repeat answers I gave this morning at Amanda's, so unless you have something new you need to ask me, or are going to make an effort toward finding my friend who *IS missing*, then I think I'm going to call it a day and head home."

"You're just going to leave?" Detective Robbins asked, crossing his arms.

"Yeah. Do you have a problem with that?"

"Well," the detective said, spreading his hands, "it simply doesn't look good, refusing to cooperate in a police investigation into a double homicide."

"And exactly how am I refusing to cooperate?" Alan asked. He leaned back a bit and crossed his own arms.

"By walking out in the middle of an interview. Do I really have to explain it to you?"

"You could explain to me how this interview is helping you since we keep going over things you already know."

"Given the complexities of this investigation, going over things repeatedly is necessary, and given that you stood over a man and executed him in cold blood, I'd think you'd be a bit more tolerant of the process."

"Executed in cold blood?" Alan asked, anger appearing. "I was eliminating a threat, one that obviously would have killed me without thought, given what he had just done to Amanda."

"Being able to kill without thought seems to have been a

common trait last night."

Alan sighed, a growing desire to get up and leave hard to resist.

13

Heart racing, Stacy waited for the door to open, the sounds of the footsteps drawing closer and closer with each passing second.

And then he was outside the door, listening.

Stacy held her breath, all while her eyes desperately tried to glean some sense of her surrounding, pain appearing as she tightened her grip on the shard of glass, arms struggling to maintain the reach she had achieved around the right side of her body.

A key went into the lock, a *click* echoing.

The door opened

Stacy could sense the presence as the person walked in, her mind visualizing him looking to the right toward where she had been left earlier in the day.

She attacked, throwing herself against him, hands thrusting the pointed piece of glass into where she hoped his vital organs would be, ears hearing a startled grunt as they collided.

The glass pierced flesh but didn't go in very deep, her fingers probably getting the worst of the damage as they slid down the edge.

And then a hand was grabbing her by the arms and throwing her across the room, her legs fighting to maintain her balance as she blindly headed toward where the wall was, the edge of something catching her side and causing a cry to become muffled against the tape.

She didn't fall, body eventually meeting the wall.

She twisted, hands back behind her body, blood dripping from her fingers, her nostrils sucking in air while her ears tried to picture where the man was, mind wondering what kind of damage she had inflicted—hoping it was severe.

Without warning, he punched her in the stomach, hard, her body toppling from the impact.

Fingers were then pinching her nostrils shut.

Panic appeared.

Something was said, but it didn't register, her only focus being on trying to breathe, her body bucking against the floor, legs kicking, fingers digging into the carpet.

Spots appeared in the darkness behind her eyelids.

He's not letting go!

He's going to—

Something chimed throughout the house.

The fingers disappeared.

Her nostrils opened with what felt like a pop, air flowing in, her lungs demanding all she could get to the point where she was nearly snorting it like a coke addict with a fresh gram.

And then a hand grabbed her by the hair and pulled.

Pain was all that registered, her scalp feeling as if it would peel from her skull.

Something scrunched up beneath her as she was dragged into what she guessed was the closet, the door quickly shutting, its wooden surface smashing her knee before being secured within its frame.

A few seconds later, she heard the door to the room slam shut.

The chiming sound echoed again.

Doorbell, she realized.

Make some noise.

She waited a few seconds to give him time to open the door and then began kicking the wall as hard as she could, only to switch to kicking the door after three strikes since that would then rattle in the frame as well. Plus, if she were lucky, she might actually knock it from its frame, the sound of it splintering helping to snag the attention of whomever it was that had come calling.

14

Though he had witnessed it many times, Riley was still blown away by how quickly things could change when heading into the more run-down neighborhoods of Chicago, the thirty-five minute drive from the Naperville suburbs to the ruined blocks of the southwest side making it seem as if he had somehow teleported himself to a third world country. Even more shocking was how the areas could bounce back, the hollowed-out wheelless car shells that seemed at home in one block looking completely out of place in the next. It was surreal.

Mr. Right was in a townhouse of a run-down neighborhood that sat between an even more run-down business district and a series of old warehouse-like buildings that were constantly being assessed by various city agencies and independent contractors who would initially feel that with the proper renovation, the buildings could be turned into lofts that would attract a better type of resident than those of the surrounding areas, who would somehow uplift the neighborhood spirit. Of course, nothing ever moved beyond the assessment state, especially once the cost of such a task was presented. The history of failures in similar endeavors all across the city didn't help either, failures that, rightly so, spoke of how updating and brightening the appearance of an area wasn't enough to change it, not when it did nothing to address the heart of the problem. Instead, such projects were like putting a Band-Aid on an infected wound. Sure, it looked better, but the infection was still present and would simply worsen if not properly addressed.

Though it probably would be okay during the day, Riley felt a bit apprehensive about leaving his car parked on the side of the road simply because one never really knew what could happen. Beyond the radio, nothing of value was on display within, but that didn't mean an investigative smash-and-grab wouldn't take place. Unfortunately, without leaving it, he could not confront Mr. Right, and without confronting Mr. Right, he had no real reason for being out this way.

You don't really have a reason anyway.

Yes I do.

He had to find out what it was Sam and Kristi were up to, which meant he had to confront Mr. Right.

You're not going to like what you find.

Maybe it won't be as bad as it seems…

With this thought came the possibility that only Kristi had been visiting Mr. Right and that Walter Doyle had just assumed his brother was a part of it due to his knowledge that the two were running things.

You should have pressed him for more details.

You should have found out if he actually witnessed Sam interacting with the notorious pervert who exploits children on a regular basis yet never seems to be caught and prosecuted.

Except by us.

Memories of watching Sam shatter the guy's knee came back to him, memories that once again made him question the possibility that Sam would make a deal with such a person. Or that such a person would make a deal with him.

People like this didn't just forgive and forget.

Something else was going on, something that he was unaware of at this point.

But I will find out.

And if Sam isn't involved, and it's just Kristi, maybe I can finally pry him away from her once and for all.

And if you can get him away from Kristi…

One thing at a time, his mind instructed, a hand instinctively checking his sidearm as he walked down the cracked sidewalk toward the broken gate that would allow him access to the busted front door that would open upon a hallway giving him a choice of two townhouse doors: the one to the left being the one that belonged to Mr. Right, the one on the right an abandoned townhouse that was often home to vagrants and people who had shot up their smack within rather than going home with it, the drug causing them to pass out on one of the soiled mattresses or cushionless couches that had been brought in from the streets.

Sometimes they didn't wake up, their bodies left to rot away while others continued to use the space, their battered minds unable to focus on anything but getting the dope into their bloodstream.

Will there be any bodies today?

You'll know soon enough, he said to himself, eyes watching as a young high-school-aged kid approached, one who was a lookout for a dope house that sat on the opposite corner. In addition to being a lookout, his job was to assess and guide suburban buyers to the right place, this area being one that suburban users would venture to during the daylight hours yet stay away from at night. Of course, this wasn't to say business slowed as the sun set. Instead, the customers simply changed into ones who were more desperate and unpredictable, ones whose addictions overshadowed the threat of violence that could erupt upon the sidewalks at any moment, ones who were often victimized by young gang recruits trying to build up street cred—or simply by individuals who seemed to thrive on conflict and could be set off by the slightest misperception of disrespect. Such was the way of the streets in these areas, areas that had been around for as long as cities had been lived in.

No suggestion was made by the youth on where to go, which probably meant his assessment was not favorable. In fact, the kid could probably sense that he was a police officer, word of which would spread fairly quickly throughout the area. How these kids knew was always a mystery, but he had experienced it enough to know that it was no coincidence. He also knew that, unlike the movies and TV shows, no shout of "Five-O" would go out, not when such an act would alert the authorities to who the lookouts were. Instead, he would silently pass and utter the word "cop" to another lookout who would have been watching everything as well, who would then quickly report it to another, who would then go into the house and report it to the sellers, all while eyes were kept upon him. It was a crude yet effective setup.

As expected, the gate in front of the townhouse was broken, as was the front door, the owners of the building having learned long ago that it was pointless to fix it when it would be broken within a week. The same was true of the streetlights.

Sensing the various lookout eyes upon him, Riley walked into the building, the smell of something rotting from the abandoned townhouse on the right hitting him, rot which, thankfully, didn't seem overwhelming enough to be human. Most likely, it was a rat that had been somehow killed, one that nobody felt responsible for and thus didn't toss out. Mixed in with that was the smell of unwashed humanity, a peek through the cracked door confirming that several people were in there, sleeping off whatever they had shot up earlier in the day.

Confident that no one from that area would confront him, Riley moved over to Mr. Right's door and carefully tried the doorknob.

Locked.

Knowing he couldn't get through without someone on the other end opening it, not without a lock-release gun or, more likely, a battering ram, Riley knocked.

Footsteps echoed and then a girl asked who it was.

"I need to speak with Mr. Right," Riley said.

"Why?" the girl asked.

"Business."

The girl hesitated and then said, "He isn't here."

"Where is he?" Riley asked.

"Not here."

"When will he be back?"

"Later."

"Did he leave himself or did someone come get him?"

"Himself."

"But his van it still out front."

The girl hesitated again.

"What type of business do you want to speak with him about?" she asked.

"Girls," he said, mind suddenly wondering if this was going to get him anywhere. Last time he had been here, a simple knock and an expression of interest in spending time with a girl had gotten them through the door. Now, well, it seemed they were being more cautious, probably due to what Sam had done.

"Your name?" she asked.

"John."

More hesitation, then, "One moment, please."

Listening close, Riley heard the footsteps as the girl went into the back room. Not long after that, she returned, her heels clicking away, and opened the door.

15

"What can you tell me about Mr. Woodman?" Detective Robbins asked. "Samuel Woodman, that is."

"Not much really," Alan said after a moment.

"Did you know he used to be a police officer?"

"Yeah, I knew that," Alan confirmed. "With the city."

"And that he worked with the sex crimes division and spent quite a bit of time undercover."

"Yeah."

"So when you said 'not much,' you really meant nothing you really wanted to share with me at this moment."

"Seems you already knew everything I do," Alan replied.

"That's all you know?"

Alan shrugged.

"See, again, for someone who could easily have charges leveled against him, you're not being very cooperative."

"Ask me a question and I'll let you know if I can answer it," Alan said, voice firm.

"Okay," the detective said. "Did you know that he was forced to retire early with only part of his pension, due to things that unfolded when he was working undercover?"

"I'd heard something about that, though didn't really look into it myself, and if Stacy had uncovered anything in that area, she didn't share it with me."

"Well, I've put in requests for information but so far haven't been able to learn much in this short bit of time. One thing I do know, he nearly killed a man—a pimp who was peddling teenage girls to perverts—to the point where the man will spend the rest of his life eating through a straw."

"Sounds to me like he should have gotten a commendation for such a thing, not fired."

"Couldn't agree more," Detective Robbins said. "And it seems many others felt the same way, given that they allowed him to retire early rather than be fired, or..."

"Or what?" Alan asked.

"Or someone didn't want a pubic relations nightmare."

"Didn't they risk that already by letting him retire rather than firing him?"

"For beating up a pimp who peddles underage girls? No, no one would dare question the decision on letting him retire early after that. After all, who is going to stand up for the rights of such a person, even if technically he does have rights and shouldn't have been beaten to within an inch of his life by an undercover officer? However, what strikes me as odd about this entire thing is how quickly it was all settled, almost as if Samuel Woodman didn't want to put up any type of fight whatsoever."

"Maybe because he knew he had a good thing offered to him and didn't want to risk losing that," Alan said.

"That's one possibility," the detective confirmed.

"The other?"

"That he knew there was way more to the situation and didn't want any type of investigation unfolding."

"But wouldn't an investigation have unfolded anyway, given that he was working undercover for the city and would have been providing them information to help make arrests?"

"You would think so, but it doesn't seem like much was done following the incident with the pimp. Sure, there were a handful of arrests made, and prior to this Samuel Woodman was responsible for many arrests within the area he worked, one of those arrests involving the man you killed last night, but within that specific investigation where he lived and breathed the underground sex trade for nearly a year, nothing but a few small-time Craigslist pimps, which surely was not the focus for his immersion into that world. No. It's almost as if everyone involved wanted to simply move on."

Alan waited, unsure why the detective was focusing so much on this but knowing there had to be a reason.

"During your time with her, did Amanda ever talk to you about who her roommates were?"

"Um…not really," Alan said, the shift in question direction catching him off guard.

"Did you ever meet any of her roommates?"

"No, just saw one of them from a distance."

"How old would you say she was?"

"College age, just like Amanda."

"So you never met any of the younger girls that lived with Amanda?"

Alan hesitated and then said, "I did once see Mrs. Woodman with a girl that seemed fairly young. They were at the college talking with a man who left with the girl." *And Stacy followed them to the place in Joliet where she was held captive and raped.*

"Yet you never felt the need to contact the police about this?" he asked.

"I didn't witness anything illegal unfolding," Alan said.

"But you had suspicions on what it was that Amanda and her roommates were involved in."

"Yes," Alan said, "but no real proof."

"I see." The detective paused, then asked, "Do you think Samuel Woodman and his wife are engaged in the trafficking of underage girls?"

"Honestly, I don't know."

"But you do know they are involved in prostitution."

"Yes."

"Very well, one last question and then you can go...for now."

Alan waited.

"Do you think, if your reporter friend Stacy uncovered information and evidence that Samuel and Kristi Woodman were involved in the prostitution of underage girls, would she have said anything, or kept it to herself so that she could continue working her story?"

"Honestly, I don't know," Alan lied.

"Very well. Please stay in easy reach in case I have any more questions, and if you are finally able to get in touch with your friend, have her call me right away."

Alan nodded.

16

Horror and disgust slithered through Riley's system as he looked upon the glammed-up teen girl, his mind quickly envisioning a scene where a sweaty, beer-bellied man handed over money so he could take her by the hand into one of the upstairs rooms, his perverted sexual desires helping to whittle away whatever innocence she still carried within her abused body. Making it worse, she was not the only child there. Two more were sitting on the couch in the front room, tiny hands holding controls for some gaming system that was plugged into the TV, the screen split into two halves. Neither looked at him as he stepped inside, their eyes completely focused on the game.

"Fifty dollars," the girl who had opened the door said, hand out.

"What?" Riley asked, eyes going back to her.

"Fifty," she repeated. "Seventy-five for bareback. Twenty-five if you just want a knob-job."

"I want to talk to Mr. Right," Riley said.

"What for? He already said you could have one of us." She shifted her glazed gaze over toward the TV area and said, "Hey, get your asses over here."

A frustrated grumble echoed as the two girls paused the game and stood up, the one on the far side of the couch smoothing out her skirt before starting to walk over, the act looking as if it was meant to stall things a bit rather than fix her presentation.

"No, it's okay," Riley said, holding up a hand. "I'm just here to talk to Mr. Right. You two can keep playing."

The two girls looked at him for a moment, then at each other, and then at the girl who seemed to be momentarily in charge, confusion present.

"He back that way?" Riley asked, thumb angling toward the door at the end of the hallway.

She nodded. "But—"

"Great, thanks." Riley stepped into the hallway and started toward the back room, one that he knew from the first visit acted as the main office of this disgusting establishment.

Behind him, he heard the sounds of the game begin again, sounds that seemed to be missing an element, due to the lack of gleeful expressions from the two who were playing.

And then he was at the office door, a momentary pause to refocus his mind unfolding before he reached down to open it.

Deep breath.

He turned the knob and stepped into the room.

"Hey—" Mr. Right began from the couch, his frustration over being interrupted during a *Judge Judy* ruling obvious, but then stopped, recognition appearing on his face as he looked upon Riley. "What the fuck do you want?"

"To..." *Talk* was going to be his reply, but he stopped when he realized that both of Mr. Right's hands were unscathed and that his knee was no longer in a cast as Sam had said, but in a brace.

"To...?" Mr. Right pressed, face failing to mask a wince as he twisted around into a sitting position, his right hand killing the TV before setting the clicker aside.

"I hear my brother has been paying you some visits," Riley said.

"Yeah..." Mr. Right stared at him. "What about it?"

"What did he want?"

"My help."

Riley pulled his gun and pointed it at him. "I'm not in the mood for games."

"Fuck, man, I swear," he said, hands raised.

"My brother came to you for help?" Riley said, gun still pointed, voice making it clear he thought this was bullshit.

"Yeah, well, sort of."

"Sort of?" Riley asked. "You better start making sense, or I'll make it so you and those crutches become lifelong buddies." He cocked the hammer back on the pink pistol. "Or maybe I'll aim a bit higher and make it so you can never deflower a thirteen-year-old girl again. How about that?"

"You want to protect little girls, maybe you should start by castrating your brother!" he snapped.

Anger flared through Riley and before he could stop himself, he backhanded Mr. Right with the pistol.

Blood oozed from his mouth, followed by a tooth that he spit out into his hand. "Mudderfucker," he voiced, word heavy as he tried not to move his lips too much.

"My brother does not fuck little girls," Riley said, gun an inch away from the man's face.

Mr. Right spit out more blood, clearing his mouth. "Yeah? Then I guess the guy in the video just looks like him."

"What video?"

"The one that ruined his career," he said, spitting again, the blood considerably less this time around. "Why'd you think he was forced to leave the police force?"

"Because he beat the living shit out of a pervert like you after the guy killed a girl he had gotten close to and was trying to help."

"You actually believe that bullshit?" Mr. Right asked. "Dude, your brother killed that girl himself because she knew he was a cop and was going to rat him out to everyone, and then he beat the shit out of the guy that was running her to get the videos he had of them and the other girls he had been with."

Riley didn't reply, *couldn't reply*, not when every ounce of self-control was keeping him from pulling the trigger.

Lower the gun, he said to himself.

He did as his mind suggested, thumb easing the hammer back in place.

Then, "Okay, I'm listening."

"Did you ever wonder why your brother strived so hard to work sex crimes?" Mr. Right asked.

Riley didn't reply.

"It was so he could know where all the investigations were taking place and keep himself safe in his own pursuits."

"You're full of shit," Riley said.

"You think so?" Mr. Right asked. "You want to see a video of your brother with a little girl?"

"You have one?"

"Yeah."

"Why?"

"Why what?"

"Why do you have footage of something like that?"

"Like I said, your brother wanted my help."

"Help with what?"

"With finding out who it was that was trying to blackmail him with such footage." He grinned. "It's funny, all the knowledge your brother had about the sex trade, yet he failed to realize that blackmail is one of the biggest elements. We all film the guys that fuck our girls, mostly to sell it to the kiddie-porn freaks, but also to use just in case the pervs decide to get foolish and demand free action for not ratting us out to the police. Amazing how often something like that happens."

"You're telling me my brother used to fuck your girls and you filmed it?"

"No, your brother never fucked any of my girls," Mr. Right said. "But he fucked someone's girls, someone who had footage of it and decided to use it against him."

Something clicked. "Wouldn't my brother know who it was that was trying to blackmail him, based on the girl he was with in the footage?"

"This is the footage that he killed the girl and paralyzed her pimp over, footage that he thought he had completely destroyed. But like I said, footage like this is often sold to kiddie-porn freaks, ones who then copy it and sell it themselves. He shrugged. "At some point someone put two and two together and is now trying to fuck your brother."

"And he came to you to figure out who it was?"

"Well, I think he thought I was the one that was blackmailing him, given the recent unpleasantness that occurred." He pointed to his knee.

Riley thought about this.

"You want to see the video?"

He didn't but also knew he had to. If what Mr. Right was saying was true, he had to see it with his own eyes so there would be no room for doubt.

"Show me," he said.

Mr. Right nodded and hobbled over to his desk where a laptop sat, his hand taking hold of the mouse.

Several clicks followed and then he turned the laptop so Riley could see the screen.

Riley stepped forward to get a better view and then watched as a scene unfolded with his brother and a little girl, one who was wearing a sailor suit. Neither one ever looked at the camera, which had obviously been hidden for the sole purpose of watching men as they got into bed with whatever girl had been chosen.

"Okay, enough," Riley said about twenty seconds in. Seeing his brother with a girl of legal age would have been bad enough, but this...he couldn't even begin to process it.

"Don't you want to see it all? This beginning stuff is nothing. Once he gets going, he really pounds the shit out of her."

"I said enough," Riley snapped, a strong desire to pull the gun again unfolding.

"Okay, okay, okay," Mr. Right said, twisting the computer back around so he could shut it off. After that, he looked up and asked, "So…any questions?"

Riley shook his head, momentarily unable to speak. Then, "When was this sent to my brother?"

Mr. Right shrugged. "Couple weeks ago."

"And my brother came to you for help?" That still didn't make sense.

"Well, at first he thought I was the one behind it and was going to go all Rodney King on my ass, but then, once I made him realize differently and convinced him that I could help, we were able to strike up a deal."

"What deal?"

"One that is mutually beneficial to both of us. I get him young girls and point clients his way, and he gives me a percentage of the profits and videos to sell."

"And if you can't figure out who it is that is blackmailing him?"

"No worries there, I already know who it is."

"You do?"

"Yep?"

"And why haven't you told my brother?"

"Because I struck a deal with her as well."

"Her?" Riley asked, his mind momentarily drawing a blank before a realization arrived. "Kristi?" he blurted out.

"You got it."

"And you made a deal with her as well?" Riley asked, completely confused.

"Yep," he opened a desk drawer. "One that I'm about to fulfill."

Riley saw the gun being pulled from within the desk seconds before it actually was, his intuition warning him so that he could pull his own while dropping down into a protective crouch, trigger finger squeezing off several rounds without any thought.

Screams echoed from the front room as the girls panicked, the sounds of something shattering on the floor reaching his ears, all while Mr. Right slowly slumped over, a startled look on his face, which stared back at Riley for several seconds before the force of gravity did its thing.

Heart racing, Riley hurried over to the desk, eyes needing to see the gun, mind needing confirmation that it was there so doubt of himself wouldn't spring up.

It was there, Mr. Right's fingers actually managing to maintain a hold upon the grip, right hand and pistol dangling at his side.

Kristi wanted him to kill me.

And Sam was fucking—

A gunshot echoed, followed by an odd *thump* on his left arm, one that seemed to vibrate up to his shoulder, almost as if his funny bone had been struck.

Pain followed.

He turned, his own actions noticeably slow.

A second and third gunshot followed, the bullets hitting the wall behind him, the smell of burnt cordite strong and stinging his eyes, his ears ringing from the blasts, the pain in his arm growing more and more intense as the defensive adrenaline that raced through his bloodstream subsided.

Terror was the first thing he recognized on her face, followed by panic, which was evidenced by her shaking hands, the pistol sweeping back and forth across the room.

Unable to raise his left hand in a calming gesture, and not

wanting to raise the one with the gun for fear that it would cause her to pull the trigger, Riley carefully said, "Everything's okay. Just put the gun down."

"Y-y-you s-shot him," she said.

"Yes, but only because he was going to shoot me," Riley said, calmness threatened by the pain in his arm. He also felt a horrible wooziness come over him, one that he managed to fight off. "I'm here to help you, so please, just put the gun down."

She didn't reply, the gun still waving back and forth in her trembling hands.

"I promise, I won't—"

He felt the bullet punching through his chest before he heard the blast, followed by a horrible sucking sensation that made it difficult to catch his breath.

His legs disappeared, body crumpling to the floor.

Several more gunshots echoed, all the bullets passing overhead and hitting the wall behind him.

Nothing else registered with him after that, the sensation that he was sucking air in through a tiny straw making it difficult to focus upon anything but his attempts at breathing, the only exception to this being the sound of a voice at one point, the words unknown to him, followed by a realization that his body was being lifted. After that, he was gone.

17

"You know they couldn't hear you all the way up there by the door, especially not with their masks muffling everything," Sam said once he was back in the room, talking through the closet door. "And even if they could, I would have simply told them you were sound effects for the scary party I'm hosting tonight or something."

Masks? Stacy wondered, suddenly remembering it was Halloween. *And if people are already trick-or-treating...*

It must have been later in the day than she thought.

Sam didn't say anything else after that, his body moving to another area of the house.

Bathroom, she noted after she heard a toilet flush.

The sound of running water followed.

And then he was back, closet door opened, his hands pulling her from within.

The sound of a plastic bag crinkling reached her ears, followed by the smell of latex as he roughly pulled something over her face.

"Oooh, creepy," he said. Then, "Shit."

Whatever was pulled over her head was pulled off, followed by a cloak of some kind being put over her, the thin fabric snagging against her bloodied fingers as it settled in place.

The latex returned, the sounds of her breathing against it echoing.

"Much better," he said.

He put a Halloween mask on me, and some kind of costume cloak. Why?

"Kristi, it's me," he said without warning. "Heading to the city to make the delivery. Be back in like an hour, maybe two, depending on traffic. Love you, bye."

A hand gripped her arm beneath the cloak.

"Let's go," he said. "Walk where I guide you or else you'll hit a wall."

She did as instructed, her plan being to make a run for it once she was led outside, if she was going to be led outside.

And then what? she asked herself. *Scream for help?*

The tape over her mouth wouldn't let any sound out, and the mask would just make it look like she was some crazy fool making an ass of herself, one that would trigger warnings within the overprotective parents who were probably already in a state of heightened alert. In fact, such people would probably pull away from her rather than try to help, which then would allow Sam to recapture her.

They didn't even go outside. Instead, he led her into the garage, which was attached to the house, and around to the backseat of the car, where he managed to get her seated, a comment about watching her head leaving his lips, his hands quickly buckling her in place.

I look like a costumed kid on their way to a party, she realized, only the party would be one where she was the favor.

Fear tickled her spine.

She had to get free.

But how?

Just moving her fingers brought pain, so actually trying to use them to achieve freedom…it didn't seem possible.

But you have to.

This car ride is your last chance.

"So, what kind of music do you like?" Sam asked. "I tried figuring it out when driving your car last night, but everything in there is fucked up. And your *check engine* light is on, though I guess that doesn't really matter since it's unlikely anyone will ever be driving it again from this point on."

Beneath them, the car bounced as it hit the curb and backed into the street.

"Man, look at them all," he said while braking and shifting to drive. "They don't even wait for it to get dark out anymore. When I was a kid, me and Riley would start just before sunset and wouldn't stop until like nine at night. It was great. We'd get enough candy to last for months. Afterward, we'd watch horror movies on channel eight that would terrify us to the point of not being able to sleep until Thanksgiving." He sighed. "Now, everyone does their trick-or-treating during the daylight hours and heads home when it gets dark. What's the point of that?"

Probably because parents worry that people like you and Rusty are on the prowl, ready to snatch up their kids and sell their bodies.

All went quiet for a moment, and then he began playing with the radio, searching for something to listen to while driving.

Stacy tested her fingers a bit while he did this, trying to see if she could endure the pain that would arrive as she disengaged the seatbelt.

All you have to do is press it, she noted to herself once she had located it within the darkness. *And then open the door...*

This second part would be tricky, her mind unable to pinpoint the location of the handle. She also couldn't really reach around and search for it prior to her release, the seatbelt and the way her hands were bound behind her making such exploratory movements impossible.

And then what?

Anyone that sees you will just think you're some kind of masked lunatic, one who will probably get hit by a car while running through the street.

Still, she had to try.

Plus, if she did get hit by a car, the person driving would probably stop and get out to see if she was okay, at which point Sam would have no choice but to flee.

Do it.

Not until we stop.

Music echoing, Stacy waited, knowing the car would have to come to a halt at some point prior to getting on the expressway.

About a minute later, it happened.

Stacy popped the seatbelt and twisted, her bound hands searching the door through the fabric of her cloak.

Find it!

She did, only it didn't open, pain echoing as she yanked at it several times.

Nothing.

"Child locks," Sam said from the front, turn signal echoing as he pulled the car to a halt on the side of the road. "After what you did in the back bedroom, and after hearing how you escaped from that guy's place in Joliet, I wasn't taking any chances." With that, he got out of the car and came around to her side to buckle her seatbelt once again. "I have a feeling they're going to love you at Mr. Sullivan's place. They like feisty girls there."

The door closed.

A couple seconds passed and then the driver side door opened.

"By the way, I found the guy at your place. Rusty, I believe. Talk about a freak. He was trying to get free when I went back over there and was maybe halfway through the tape when I walked in. Scared the shit out of me. And the number you did upon him, Jesus fucking Christ! Crushing his balls! The guy really has it in for you now, which is great because I made a deal where I would give you to him if he helped us by killing your boyfriend."

Rusty's going after Alan!

"Of course, we aren't really going to give you to him, and if he makes a fuss I'll just put a bullet through his head, so..." His voice faded without finishing the statement. "Now let's just hope he is able to do the job. Your boyfriend's pretty tough seems to react pretty quickly without having to think. Thankfully, with it being Halloween, I doubt he will be on the defensive when answering the door."

Stacy listened to all this while leaning against the window, the latex mask keeping her from being chilled by the glass, mind wishing she could somehow warn Alan about Rusty.

And then her mind shifted to contemplating what was in store for her, fear of what was going to happen in the days to come chilling her far worse than the cold glass ever could have.

You escaped from Robert at Rusty's place, and maybe you'll be able to escape again once you get where you're going.

Never give up. Never surrender.

The sound of something buzzing reached her ears.

"Yeah?" Sam asked, voice loud.

"Something's wrong at the place on Hoffman," a female voice, probably Kristi's, echoed from a speaker. *"There's police tape all over the door!"*

"What happened?" Sam asked.

"How the fuck should I know?"

"Okay, I'll look into it when I get back."

"Fine. And Vicky and Crystal will be here since I obviously couldn't leave them there."

"Okay. No problem. I'll be back in like an hour."

"Fine. I'll—" DONG! *"Jesus Christ."*

"What happened?" Sam asked.

"Fucking trick-or-treaters. I put a sign up saying NO CANDY, but they're still ringing the bell every five minutes."

"But there is candy. I put a big bowl of it by the door."

"Yeah, and when you get back YOU can hand it out. Until then—
"

"Sweetheart, if you don't give them candy, they're going to egg the house again. It's only one night."

The call ended without a reply.

"Kristi's not a fan of Halloween," he said as if that hadn't already been obvious.

Stacy didn't care about his wife's dislike of the holiday. She was, however, curious about what had happened at the house where the girls lived, the statement about police tape having totally snagged her attention. Unfortunately, she wasn't able to ask anything about it, and even if she could, she doubted he really would have been able to share anything with her.

18

Though it wasn't on the way back home, and though he knew she wouldn't be there, Alan felt compelled to stop by Stacy's place. As expected, she was not home, car still gone. Unsure what to do, he tried to call her again, but like before it went to voicemail. He then sent a text, one that briefly described everything that had happened last night and today. Once that was complete, he tried calling Walter Doyle, which also went to voicemail. Alan didn't leave a message.

Now what?

You still have the phone.

Looking through it once more, maybe he would be able to figure something out, something that had eluded him earlier.

But what?

How did one find something when he didn't know what he was looking for? And how would that something help in figuring out what had happened to Stacy, which, honestly, was the only important thing at the moment?

You should give the phone to the police.

He had no doubt that they would come looking for it eventually, and if they found it in his possession, there would be hell to pay.

Plus, there's really nothing more for you to investigate within the prostitution operation. Amanda is dead and the Woodman family knows who you are. It's over.

No, it wasn't over.

Stacy was missing, and if the police weren't going to take that aspect seriously, then he was going to find her himself.

How?

Nothing followed.

Beyond confronting Kristi Woodman and her husband, he

really had no idea what he could do. And confronting them didn't seem like a good idea, not when he didn't really have anything to back up his claim that they were responsible.

What about Riley Woodman?

Though he was obviously a part of the prostitution operation, Alan had gotten a sense that he was a good person who simply wanted what was best for the girls in his care. But would that carry over in the Stacy situation, especially considering that her goals completely conflicted with his? Was he the type who would try to do the right thing in every situation, or did he pick and choose which situations it was required for?

Alan didn't know—couldn't know—after only having met him once.

Plus, you did have a gun on him in the beginning, one that he saw you use, so...

Still, the impression he had gotten was a favorable one, and since he didn't really know what else to do, he might as well try to find out if he could help.

Only you don't know how to get in contact with him.

Maybe Walter Doyle could help—if he would answer the phone.

He was stuck.

Feeling helpless, he looked around the alleyway parking area that he was standing in.

A yawn followed.

Go home, scare the trick-or-treaters, watch some horror movies, and get some rest.

You're no good to Stacy as a clumsy, sleep-deprived fool.

A year ago, he could have endured and pushed through, and while his mind wouldn't have been as sharp as it could have been when at one hundred percent, he still would have had an edge over those who weren't used to pushing it for days at a time. Now, however, given how hard his body worked just to keep his disease at bay, and how little nutrients he got from the lack of digestion that took place within his damaged intestinal track, he just couldn't continue onward like he had back then. It wasn't a matter of willpower, but one of his body simply being unable to do it. He needed to call it a day and get the rest he had promised himself when deciding to skip class that morning.

On cue, another yawn followed, one that seemed to sap all the remaining strength from his body.

Keys in hand, he returned to his car, a serious sense of defeat and disappointment unfolding.

Nothing you can do.

Guilt followed, the fact that he had been unable to save Amanda weighing heavy on him.

Should have known someone else was in that house.

Should have told her the truth earlier.

Should've, would've, could've… The thoughts reminded him of the sleepless nights he had suffered once he was home after his first tour in Iraq. The memories didn't haunt him, but they did weigh heavy on him from time to time, mostly because there always was the chance that a different outcome could have been brought about if different actions had been taken.

Unable to keep the thoughts at bay, Alan drove home and, after having a cup of tea, started to get everything ready so that he could scare the kids once the sun finally set.

19

"Holy shit," Sam said, his hand cutting off the radio, which had been pummeling Stacy's ears with crap for at least twenty-five minutes. "Fuck."

Whatever had happened, Sam was not sharing the details with her, but given his surprised reaction to whatever it was, and the fact that they were soon on the expressway once again, Stacy knew it had something to do with the place he had been taking her to.

And then they hit traffic, the radio being turned back on to check the travel times, Sam growing more and more agitated as he was made to wait for the information he wanted, even though it seemed like he already knew what those times would be, statements of how fucked up I-88 became during the evening rush hour echoing throughout the car.

Do something!

What?

Find a way to get the attention of other drivers.

They'll just think I'm a kid in a costume.

So what? Do something.

All she managed was the release of her seatbelt once again, something that Sam didn't seem to notice. With that free, she tried the door once more, but it was still secure, as she knew it would be, as were the windows, which she could not roll down at all.

Frustrated, she waited as they slugged along with the rush-hour traffic, the positive thoughts on how she had been given a reprieve from entering into Mr. Sullivan's world doing little to bolster her spirits.

20

Alan heard the crunch of leaves as he was plugging in the extension cord for the tape player that he would have sitting beneath the chair echoing ghastly sounds, and he started to come back around toward the front of the house, extension cord uncoiling with each step. Originally, he had planned on plugging the tape player in with an extension cord stretched to his seat from the garage, but then he vetoed that idea, given the potential for it to become a trip wire as the kids fled the terror he was going to unleash upon them as they made their way to the candy bowl. Scaring them was one thing, making it so they fell and broke their faces another. A lawsuit at this point in his life was not something he wanted, especially not with all the shit he was already facing, thanks to the unexpected "long time, no talk" email Stacy had sent a week earlier.

"Trick or treat!" a group of costumed kids cried as his mother answered the door, Alan stepping up behind them as he came around the front corner of the house, body slowly but surely making its way between all the strands of spiderweb he had stretched out over the bushes and the low-hanging twisted branches of the crab apple tree.

If I had my mask, I could really scare the crap out of them as they turned...

Even without it, one of the kids jumped when he turned and saw him simply standing there watching them, an air of caution present as they returned to the driveway and started toward the front yard to head to the neighbors' house, all of them stopping when they saw the tombstones and the arms coming out of the ground. Without a word, they decided against cutting through the yard and instead headed down to the sidewalk.

Alan smiled.

"You better hurry," his mother said. "You've missed five groups already."

"I'm waiting for it to get dark so I can plug in the strobe light."

"I don't know if you'll get that many once it's dark. The last couple years, we've only gotten a few once the sun sets."

Alan thought about that and then said, "Well, the ones that do come around are going to get quite a surprise."

She smiled.

"Can you take this and put it under the chair while I plug in the strobe light?" He was going to put it in the tree facing upward against the dome of spiderwebs he had created. Fake body parts and rubber rats were tangled within the web, making it quite morbid, and with the strobe light going, it would look really creepy.

"Sure." She stepped forward and took the cord while he walked back to the outlet for the second extension cord and unwound it as he followed the first cord.

"And can you hand me the—" He felt his phone buzz.

"Hand you—" she started to ask but stopped when she saw him pull out the cell phone.

It was Walter Doyle.

"Hello?" Alan asked.

"Mr. Miller," Walter Doyle said. "I just got your message."

"Ah yes," Alan said, eyes noting a group of kids heading this way. He started walking to the other side of the yard, not wanting the kids to feel awkward about stepping up to the door while he was there with the phone. "I was wondering, would you be able to help me locate the contact information for someone?"

"Well, that depends on who it is and whether or not their information is in the public record."

"It's for a man named Riley Woodman," Alan said. "He's the brother of Samuel Woodman, who we talked about the other day—the one that is running the prostitution thing with his wife. Riley Woodman and I met each other last night, but we never exchanged contact information."

"Ah, I see," Mr. Doyle said. "Unfortunately, I would not be able to give you the contact information of a police officer."

Alan was about to reply with a "thanks anyway" comment, but then he realized something and asked, "How'd you know he was a police officer?"

Mr. Doyle went silent.

"Are you still looking into all this?"

"A bit," Mr. Doyle said.

"Why?"

"Like I said the other day, I'm curious. It isn't every day you run into a fellow Special Forces veteran working a suburban prostitution case in your own backyard."

"Well then, during this curiosity, did you happen to come across the information I'm asking for? It sounds like you did."

"I have it, yes."

"Can you give it to me, please? A girl was killed last night and my friend is missing, and I think Riley Woodman should know that I think his brother and his wife probably have information on what happened to my friend."

"How about this? I will contact Mr. Woodman and let him know that he needs to contact you," Mr. Doyle said. "That way no ethical lines are crossed."

"If no ethical lines were crossed, how did you obtain Riley Woodman's information yourself?"

"It came up during my initial investigation."

Though Alan wanted to call bullshit on that, he knew the possibility of it being true was there; thus he didn't lash out. Instead he simply said, "Well, if you could please have him give me a call, it could be a matter of life and death."

"I will."

"Thanks."

With that, the call ended, Alan contemplating and trying to wrap his mind around Walter Doyle and his involvement. Was he truly just a curious private eye, or was there more at stake here? Could he actually be a part of it all? Was he a customer of the Woodmans who, given his talents as a private investigator, had noticed Alan watching things one day and wanted to find out what he was up to?

You'll know soon enough, he decided and headed inside to gather up the rest of the items he needed for the display, his hand grabbing a mini Twix bar from the candy bowl while doing this.

Not long after that, he had everything ready to go and now just had to wait for it to get a bit darker before sitting in the chair next to the candy bowl, his lifeless dummy-like body ready to spring up and scare everyone who came to the door.

21

"I don't know," Sam said, voice raised. "When we pulled up, the place was swarming with police and bystanders, and a CBS news van was arriving just as we did."

"Maybe it was just a drive-by?" Kristi said.

"Police were coming in and out of Mr. Right's place. Whatever happened, it involved him."

"Still could have been a drive-by."

"Maybe."

"Have you tried calling him?" Kristi asked.

"With the police there?" Sam demanded, voice carrying an "are you crazy?" tone. "That'd be like waving a flag at them and shouting 'over here, look over here, we're involved too.'"

Kristi didn't reply to that and instead said, "So what do we do now?"

"Now? We step back a bit and wait to see what unfolds."

"And if the police come by?"

"We answer their questions as best we can. Don't get aggressive or defensive with them, and if they bring up anything to do with prostitution and the girls, we stick with the cover story about giving them a fresh start. Riley's idea about making them go to school will finally pay off since it will help support that image."

"Have you spoken to him?" she asked.

"I tried, but he isn't answering his phone."

"He's going to fuck everything up. I know it."

"He'll be fine. The last thing he wants is to end up in jail, and if all this blows up, that's exactly where he'll be, so don't worry."

"You should never have brought him into this," Kristi said.

"We needed his money."

"You could have gotten all the money we needed yourself from a dope house."

"Yeah, but not access to the police databases."

Kristi didn't reply to this.

DONG!

"GO AWAY!" Kristi shouted.

"Easy," Sam snapped. "I'll go take care of them."

Several seconds passed, a sound of kids crying, *"Trick or treat!"* reaching Stacy's ears as she sat on the couch, face still taped and masked, body cloaked, wrists handcuffed.

"Did you know Vicky and Crystal actually threw a fit about not getting to go trick-or-treating?" Kristi said as Sam walked back in. "I guess Amanda promised them she would take them."

"Why'd she do that?" Sam asked.

"I don't know, but it led to Vicky throwing a tantrum while I was driving, one that only got worse when she saw other kids trick-or-treating." She paused. "And then I couldn't even drop them off because the house had police tape on it, and I tried calling Stuart to see if he wanted to keep them overnight—a freebie just to get them out of my hair, but he isn't answering his phone. And you said *she* killed Robert, which explains why he hasn't been returning our calls, so I couldn't let him have them either."

She is me, Stacy said to herself, her growing question on if they remembered that she was there sitting on the couch, listening, finally answered.

DONG! DONG!

"I swear, I'm going to start poisoning some candy if they don't stop soon!"

"Jesus Christ, just relax," Sam urged.

Sounds of him greeting the kids, commenting on their costumes—a witch, a pumpkin, and a ghost—and handing out candy followed. After that, he must have waited in the doorway, because he was soon talking to another group of kids, the doorbell having never even DONGED.

The door closed.

His footsteps back into the room echoed.

"Where are Vicky and Crystal?" he asked.

"They're being punished," Kristi said.

"Punished?" Sam asked, voice weary. "How?"

"Don't worry. By this time tomorrow, they're going to know we don't tolerate that kind of behavior." Before he could respond to that, she asked, "What're we going to do about her?"

"I don't know. We can't keep her here in case the police do show up to talk with us at some point, but without Mr. Right, we have no way of contacting Mr. Sullivan, so…"

DONG!

Nothing was said, the sounds of him attending to these trick-or-treaters unfolding.

"Here's what we do. I'm going to go see if I can get in touch with Riley and find out if he knows anything about what's going on at the house on Hoffman and at Mr. Right's place. While I do that, you take her to wherever it is you have stashed Vicky and Crystal. That way no one is here if the police should show up. I will then meet up with you after I finish talking with him, and we can figure out what to do."

"What if he refuses to help us?"

"He doesn't really have a choice, and he knows that. If we fail, he fails. The most important thing right now is simply keeping our heads and not flying off the handle."

"This isn't my fault!" she snapped.

"Did I say it was?" Sam asked.

"You think that. She knew what was going on and would have kept harassing us!"

Me again? Stacy wondered, mind noting that these two had obviously fought about this before, given how quickly Kristi launched into a defensive position.

"We're not going to do this, not right now!" Sam snapped.

DONG!

"Understand?" Sam demanded, this time ignoring the bell.

Kristi huffed.

DONG! DONG!

Sam went to the door and silently tended to the trick-or-treaters. Upon his return, he asked, "By the way, where are Vicky and Crystal?"

"The house on Walnut Avenue."

"Why there?"

"Because it was close."

"What did you do to them?"

Kristi didn't reply.

"I'm serious, what did you do?"

"They'll live."

Sam sighed and said, "Fine, whatever. Let's get her over there as well so that this place is clean."

"What about her friend?" Stacy asked.

"No worries, I got that covered. After tonight we'll no longer have to worry about him fucking things up."

Stacy rattled the handcuffs upon hearing that, her wrists uselessly trying to free herself.

"Aww, don't worry, my dear," Kristi said. "You'll have plenty more fuck buddies where you're going. In fact, if we have to keep you through tomorrow and the weekend, maybe we'll bring a few of our clients over to have their way with you." Kristi came around behind her and cupped her breasts through the cloak. "I have a feeling some will pay a handsome fee for the opportunity to enjoy your flesh. What do you think, Sam, would Mr. Sullivan mind if we let some of our clients have their way with her before we hand her over—a parting gift, so to speak?"

Vocally, Sam didn't reply.

DONG!

Kristi didn't seem fazed by the doorbell this time, her hands still on Stacy's breasts, and then, while Sam was tending to the trick-or-treaters, she whispered, "My husband has a boner right now from me touching you, which is interesting since he can never get it up when we are together." She squeezed, causing Stacy to wince. "I was starting to think it was just little girls that got him off these days after I saw the videos of him with them, but maybe he's just not into me anymore."

Stacy wanted to reply to that but couldn't.

"I may try something with you later once he's at the house," Kristi said and released her breasts.

"Older kids are out now," Sam said while walking back into the room. "We're totally going to get egged once we're gone and have no candy to hand out."

"Oh well," Kristi said. "Nothing we can do. Help me get her into the car?"

"Okay."

Once again, Sam marched her toward the garage, only this time, after a protest from Kristi, she was put in the trunk rather than the backseat, a statement on how no one would see her being pulled out of the trunk once she was in the garage of the other house being made.

Maybe I can kick out the taillight, Stacy said to herself, memories of writing an article on how to escape a kidnapping unfolding.

Frustration at not trying that the night before when she had been put in the trunk followed, though it was short-lived, as her determination to put right that mistake arrived. First things first, however, she had to wait until they started moving, the last thing she wanted being the successful kicking out of the taillight in plain sight of Kristi and Sam.

22

Alan heard the crunch of leaves as a group approached the house and stilled himself as he leaned back in the chair, body slumped as if ready to fall over at any point, head resting at an awkward angle against the bottom of the wall-mounted mailbox.

Within the mask, his breathing seemed really loud, almost like that of Michael Myers in *Halloween*. Thankfully, the horrific sounds of people being dismembered by chainsaws followed by spooky music that echoed from beneath his chair would keep them from noticing whatever sounds he was making. The gentle rise and fall of his chest as his lungs continued to function was also masked, not by the sounds beneath him but by the flashing lights of the strobe he had put in the tree.

Closer and closer they came, the dry brittle leaves he had scattered all around the front making it impossible for anyone to approach unnoticed.

"Oh my," someone said as they finally came upon the scene. "This is spooky."

With his head angled the way it was, he could just barely make out the group as it stood near the opening between the garage and the bushes, though he did see enough to realize this was not a group of kids, but a group of adults who had a kid with them, one who looked to be about seven and was dressed as a witch.

"See that, Gabby," another said. "The sign says take one."

Thinking it would add to the illusion that he wasn't real and that no one inside wanted to be disturbed, Alan had put a sign above the candy bowl that read PLEASE TAKE ONE. The bowl itself was sitting on a table in the corner, which required the trick-or-treaters to walk by his lifeless dummy-like body, one that didn't appear to have legs, given the flat three-by-three piece of plywood he had set on top of his knees, the edge plainly visible beneath the blanket that was draped over it. The fake rubber hands that were sticking from his sleeves added to everything, and for those who were really detail oriented, he had switched up the right and left so that the thumbs were sticking out on the wrong sides. Such details could easily snag the mind, making it less likely they would notice other elements that would give him away.

Gabby did not move toward the candy bowl, her own bag clutched tightly to her chest.

"It's okay, he's not real," an adult female, maybe the mother, said. "Go on and get a piece of candy."

Gabby shook her head.

"It's just pretend," she continued.

Gabby shook her head again.

"And look, I think I see your favorite in there, but you have to be a big girl and get it yourself."

The sounds of a person screaming as they were hacked to pieces echoed.

"Maggie, maybe you should get it for her," an adult male said. "It's a bit intense."

"How about we go up together?" Maggie said.

Gabby still wouldn't budge.

"Okay, watch me," Maggie said and walked over to the bowl.

Alan didn't budge.

"See, he's not real."

"I don't want to," Gabby said, her witch's hat almost being knocked free as she pressed her face into Maggie's side.

"Okay, Daddy will get you one. What kind do you want?"

Gabby didn't reply, face still buried.

"Can you get a Twix?" Maggie said.

The dad nodded and headed to the bowl.

Alan shouted while reaching for him.

Screams echoed from both the mother and father, and Gabby took off running into the yard.

"Oh my god," the dad said over and over again, a hand to his chest. It was all he could say, his head shaking as he looked down at Alan.

Alan took off the mask, face unable to hide a huge smile.

"That was good," the dad finally said. "Jesus." He took a deep breath. "Wow."

"Here," Alan said, grabbing a handful of candy. "I think she deserves a few extra pieces."

"Thanks," the dad said, one hand still holding his chest. He sighed and then turned to find his wife and daughter.

Alan watched them go, satisfaction spreading throughout his body. Now if he could just get a dozen more people to come up to the door, it would all be worth it.

23

Stacy kicked and kicked but was unable to dislodge anything from within the trunk, her only accomplishment being to send a bolt of pain shooting up through her leg into her spine.

And then they were bouncing over some railroad tracks, ones that likely belonged to the set that bisected the cities of Wheaton, Glen Ellyn, and Lombard.

Then again, her mind could have fucked everything up, and they could easily be heading south into Naperville somewhere, or east toward the city, the only thing she knew for certain being that they had gone over some railroad tracks.

Keep kicking!

What's the point?

Rather than answer that, her legs did as instructed and continued to pound away at where she thought the taillight was, all to no avail.

And then they were coming to a stop, the sounds of a garage door closing behind them echoing.

Stacy shifted, a new idea appearing, one that she mentally labeled: *Kick the bitch!*

Kristi popped the trunk, the lid springing open and then gently lowering back into place without latching.

Will she be centered when she lifts the lid or to the right a bit since she's coming around from that side?

Stacy had no way of knowing but figured that a kick to the center was probably her best choice.

The sound of heels on cement echoed for a moment and then stopped.

A slight creak of the trunk hinges appeared.

Stacy kicked, her heel connecting with nothing but air.

And then something cracked down upon her shin, the pain nearly unbearable, a cry echoing within her head, parts of it breaking beyond the gag and mask.

Tears appeared, her eyes unable to keep them at bay, their wetness soaking into the tape that still clung to her face, though, thankfully, it had loosened its hold upon her eyelids during the day, the stickiness slowly but surely losing its effectiveness as the hours progressed.

The sound of something heavy hitting the ground followed, whatever object Kristi had held now tossed aside while she grabbed Stacy and pulled her from the trunk.

Stacy could not stand; the pain in her right leg too much.

"Don't want to walk, do you?" Kristi said. "Fine."

Without warning, something was slipped over her throat

and tightened.

"I'm going to drag you like a dog on a leash, and if you don't keep up with me, you're going to get choked." With that, Kristi started pulling, Stacy trying to stand but unable to get to her feet, which caused the loop around her throat to tighten to the point where she could barely breathe.

"Come on," Kristi demanded, kicking her with the point of her heel. "Get on your knees and shuffle if you have to, but you better be able to stand once we get to the stairs or else I'm pushing you down them."

Stacy tried to do as instructed but couldn't get herself onto her knees. It wasn't the pain, which, thankfully, was dulling out, but her inability to shift herself into a position where she could push herself up.

"Come on," Kristi repeated, yanking at the leash. "I didn't hit you that hard!" She kicked her again.

Stacy didn't get up.

"Wow, you're pathetic," Kristi said. She delivered another kick, this one right into Stacy's hipbone, the pain and anger mixing together in a way that would have probably resulted in Kristi's death if Stacy had been able to get the better of her. Instead, given her position, she simply curled herself into a ball on the cold cement, crying, not caring if Kristi strangled her with the leash.

Several seconds passed.

"You're never going to last with Mr. Sullivan if you don't buck up a bit." With that, she grabbed Stacy by the shoulders and dragged her to the doorway of the garage, several grunts leaving her lips as she fought to get her body up and over the step. From there, she dragged her across a smooth surface into a room where she wrapped the leash around something. "We'll just wait here until you're ready to stand and can walk down into the basement."

24

"How's it going?" Alan's mother asked, door barely opened, entryway still dark just in case she had to close it quickly at the approach of a group of trick-or-treaters.

"Pretty good," he said through the mask, voice loud to overcome the soundtrack beneath him. "I've gotten like eight groups so far and freaked them all out."

"I've heard the screams," she said with a laugh.

"One person even poked me with a stick trying to see if I was real, but I never flinched so he finally went to the bowl."

"When're you coming in?" she asked.

"I'm going to give it another half hour and see if we get any more kids. Doesn't seem like many are out, but I did hear what sounded like a group laughing down the street a while ago." He wasn't sure which direction they were going, but if they were coming this way, they surely would be here soon.

"Okay, well, I'll head back inside. Once you're done we should watch *Halloween*."

"For sure," he said.

The door closed.

Another echo of laugher erupted, though it sounded no closer than it had earlier, which made him wonder if it was really trick-or-treaters or just a group causing mischief.

Egging a house, or maybe decorating it with toilet paper?

Alan almost got up to go look, when he heard the sound of leaves crunching, his body quickly taking on the awkward "balanced against the mailbox and wall" look once again.

A lone trick-or-treater appeared, one that looked to be a big kid or even an adult, the costume a ski mask, one that chilled Alan to the core because he looked like a member of an Iraqi death squad, the only thing missing being the iconic AK-47 they had always possessed.

The man stopped, eyes taking in the display before shifting to Alan.

Alan waited, an odd certainty that this person was up to no good flowing through him, his own eyes trying to collect as many details as he could about the man in the midst of the strobe-light flashes.

More leaves crunched, the sound of kids approaching from the opposite direction echoing.

The man backed away and waited by a tree in the side yard, something that confirmed to Alan that he truly was up to no good, and for some reason his house was the target.

Or am I the target?

Is it someone from the prostitution setup?

Someone who wants to put an end to my involvement in all this?

Someone who would know where Stacy is?

The group of kids came into view, all of them stopping when they saw Alan's body, hesitation gripping them.

One of them then came forward, eyes never leaving Alan, body slowly making it to the candy bowl.

Alan didn't move.

Seeing their brave companion make it to the bowl without incident, the rest of the group came in and, ignoring the sign, filled their bags with handfuls of candy before moving to the next house.

By the tree, the man waited, Alan just barely able to make him out in the shadows.

A minute came and went, then two, the man obviously waiting for the group to get several houses away before he came back.

25

"Isabella, calm down," Kristi said, voice elevated. "What do you mean the police were there?"

Silence followed as Kristi listened, Stacy wishing the phone were set to speaker mode so she too could hear what was going on.

"About Amanda?" Kristi asked.

More silence.

"Okay, no, I have no idea what they're talking about, but...no, Isabella...ISABELLA, calm down!"

Stacy heard a frantic voice echo from the phone but could not make out the words.

"No, you're not in trouble for talking to them. You had no choice." Kristi paused. "Take a deep breath." Another pause. "Okay, now, tell me what it was they were asking you and what you told them."

26

The screams of a female victim pleading for mercy before being hacked to pieces echoed from beneath Alan's chair as the ski-masked man returned to the front door, his eyes once again taking a moment to look at Alan's dummy-like body.

Several seconds passed.

Alan waited, mind and body obtaining an odd calmness that reminded him of being in the mountains of Afghanistan, concealed within the pine trees, waiting for the Taliban convoy to make its pass from Pakistan into Afghanistan.

The man pulled out a gun and pointed it at Alan.

Alan didn't move.

The man held the gun on him for several seconds, all while the sounds of a chainsaw coming to life filled the air.

The man stepped forward, gun still trained on Alan, and reached out his left hand toward Alan's chest, his fingers poking into him, the pillow Alan had put beneath his dark cloak to give himself a puffy stuffed-dummy look absorbing the fingers.

"Huh," the man mumbled and turned toward the front door, left hand now extending toward the doorbell, which he pressed. Alan heard the chime within the house.

She'll answer it!

Now!

Alan sprang up from the chair, wooden board tossed from his knees.

Startled, the man twisted just as Alan grabbed hold of him, arms locking around his body in an attempt to pin his arms and neutralize the gun.

The light in the entryway flickered on, his mother coming to the door.

Twisting around, the man managed to get himself angled in a way that allowed him to slam himself against the brick wall, crushing Alan between him and it, which hurt.

Alan did not release him, however, the pain of the impact pushed from his mind.

"Alan!" his mother cried as she opened the door and saw the struggle.

The man twisted again, this time bringing the gun hand around so that it pointed toward his mother, his finger pulling the trigger.

A gunshot echoed, followed by the mirror in the entryway shattering.

Stunned, his mother froze in place.

Another round went off as Alan tried to grab the gun.

His mother made a "humph" sound and crumpled to the ground.

"*NO!*" Alan cried, foot managing to plant itself against the wall so that he could push against it, the force causing the two to go across the small front porch and into the candy table, the edge catching the man in the hip before flipping over, candy spilling everywhere.

Alan then threw him to the left, straight into the chair he

had been sitting on, the man toppling over it and falling to the ground.

Another gunshot echoed, the bullet hitting the brick wall and bouncing off into the night somewhere.

Alan charged toward the man, only to slip as his foot came down onto the blanket-covered piece of plywood, which slid right out from under him.

He fell on the man, his mask shifting in such a way that he could no longer see, his hands fumbling in the darkness to grab the man so he could keep him from getting back to his feet.

The man hit him with an elbow, though thankfully he didn't have enough room to really drive it into him. Alan ignored the blow and grabbed onto the man's face, fingers going toward where his eyes should be, finding his nose instead and shoving up into it.

A blast echoed, the explosion knocking Alan to the side, his head feeling as if it had been smashed with a brick, yellow sparks erupting all over the place within his mind before darkness settled.

27

"I have no idea where he is," Sam said, having arrived at the house a few minutes earlier. "He isn't home, and I couldn't find anything at his place that shows where he might have gone."

"What does that mean?" Kristi asked, concern evident.

"Fucked if I know, but—" He stopped.

"Who's that?" Kristi asked.

Sam didn't answer the question and instead simply said, "Okay, great. We'll bring her over in the morning as promised." A pause. "Tonight? No, we really can't do that. Too risky, what with all the authorities out and about, given the holiday." Another pause. "Yeah, first thing in the morning." Another pause. "Okay, we can do that too." Another pause. "Yep, okay, have a good night and we'll see you in the morning."

"What was that all about?" Kristi asked.

"Alan Miller is dead," Sam said.

Hearing this, Stacy's heart sank.

Friday

November 1, 2013

1

Alan saw nothing but darkness when he opened his eyes, a darkness that eventually yielded to reveal a room where the lights had been switched off, the only illumination slithering in beneath the door.

Not my room, he noted to himself.

Not the back of an Iraqi used car lot either.

Memories of finding the camera setup with the dark curtain and the bloodstained floor filtered in, as well as all the tapes of beheadings that had taken place, the raid having been conducted after information from a detainee had pinpointed the location as one the insurgents used.

He pushed the memories away and focused on the room, the realization that it was a hospital room arriving less than a minute later.

Call button.

He pressed it.

About thirty seconds passed before a nurse walked in. She didn't turn on the light within the room, but she did open the door enough for the hallway light to spill in.

"Where am I?" Alan asked.

"Edwards Hospital," she said.

"What happened? Was I shot?"

"You just have a bump on the head and are going to be

okay. Why don't you go back to sleep? In the morning the doctor will talk to you."

"Okay," Alan said, then, "Wait, my mom?"

"She's okay. She went home to get some rest and will be back in the morning. Now go back to sleep."

Alan did, the statement about his mother being okay replacing the visual of her falling down in the entryway after the gunshot. Questions about that and what happened were still present, but they did not hold back the sleep that wanted to return. The same could not be said of the diarrhea that came a few hours later, but by then light was beginning to appear in the window, which meant the sun was rising and he would have been waking up anyway.

2

Even though quite a bit of tape had come unglued from her face due to tears and sweat, enough was still stuck in place to make the act of ripping it free incredibly painful, a scream echoing from her lips once her mouth was finally useable.

Water followed, Sam insisting that she drink an entire bottle to combat the dehydration that was present, an earlier argument with Kristi about needing to give her fluids having been won. He also had made her take Vicky and Crystal down, Kristi having hung the two from their wrists in the basement as punishment for throwing the temper tantrum, something that she also wanted to do to Stacy while they waited to make contact with Mr. Right. Thankfully, Sam had vetoed the idea.

"Are you serious?" Kristi demanded after his next instruction was given.

"Yes," Sam said. "I don't want her smelling like piss and shit when we deliver her."

"But—"

Sam grabbed her by the arm and squeezed, startling Stacy,

who was sitting on the floor by the stairs, and causing Kristi to cry out. "I'm not going to argue with you!" he snapped. "Just do what I say."

Tears appeared in Kristi's eyes, ones that looked rage induced.

Nothing else was said after that, Kristi grabbing her things so she could go get the bathing supplies from Walgreens.

Following Kristi's departure, Sam went over to Vicky and Crystal, both of whom were sitting against the wall, frightened, bodies obviously in pain from the ordeal Kristi had put them through.

3

"The gun was so close to your head when it went off that it knocked your equilibrium out of whack, which is why you kept throwing up while in the ambulance," Dr. McCoy said.

"I don't even really remember that," Alan said.

"The gunshot?" the doctor asked.

"No, the ambulance ride."

"Ah, well, your mind was pretty scrambled afterward. According to the first responders, you were speaking what sounded like a foreign language when they asked you questions."

Alan didn't reply to that but then realized there was a bit of a question wrapped up in the statement. "I probably thought I was back in Iraq."

Dr. McCoy nodded. "While in Iraq you suffered roadside bomb blasts?"

"Yes."

"Then it's not surprising this triggered a flashback-like situation where you thought you were there once again."

Alan didn't reply to that.

"I take it you're aware of the impact repeated blasts can have on the brain?"

"Yes." Even if he had not been given detailed information on such things by the military, all the recent media coverage about football players who had suffered extensive brain damage after being hit over and over again during their careers would have given him a pretty good idea of what the repeated blasts had done. "Did the gunshot last night cause my brain to bounce too?"

"No, that was more of a shock to your system, one that didn't even cause a concussion. And since you were wearing a mask at the time, you didn't suffer any burns from it. Now, had the gun been shifted a few inches—"

"We wouldn't be talking right now," Alan said.

"Exactly."

"So now what?"

"You stay here for the day, probably overnight again, so that we can observe you, which even though you didn't suffer severe injury, is highly recommended following something like this, especially after what you went through in Iraq. And then you go home and take it easy for a few days."

"And if I wanted to leave right now?" Alan asked.

"I would not recommend that."

"I know you wouldn't, and believe me, I'm not about to get up and walk out of here a minute after you leave, but I just want to make sure that if I wanted to, I could."

"The answer to that is yes."

"Okay, good."

"You can also speak with the police if they decide to come ask you questions, which I'm sure they will do now that you're awake and aware."

"Have they been by?"

"I do believe an officer was here last night to take down some basic info—medical stuff on what happened—but nothing as far as inquiries into the shooting and who it was that perpetrated it."

"Okay." Then after a few seconds, "Is there any way for me to call my mom?"

"Of course," the doctor said while motioning to the bedside phone. "Just dial nine for an outside line."

"Okay, thanks."

With that, the doctor left, Alan shifting over to use the phone as he disappeared down the hall.

4

Kristi made Stacy and Vicky shower together, the handcuffs, which had been removed so she could undress, reattached once she was naked, this time in front of her body so she could maneuver around in the shower without losing her balance and scrub herself clean with the new Ocean Breeze body wash and loofa that Kristi had purchased.

It was a humiliating experience, one that had a bit of horror to it as well once she caught sight of the scars on Vicky's butt and upper thighs.

"Did they do that to you?" Stacy asked once the water was running, water that she actually relished as it hit her body, despite the disgust she felt at being naked with the teenage girl.

"No," Vicky said. "That's from before."

"Before?" Stacy asked.

Vicky hesitated. "Kristi said we're not supposed to talk to you."

"It's okay. She can't hear us in here," Stacy said. "And I won't tell."

Vicky rubbed at her wrists, the marks from the ropes that had held her to the ceiling still present, some areas of her flesh actually torn open while others were simply bruised from the pressure and strain.

"My mom's boyfriend did that if I didn't behave."

"And Sam took you from him?"

"Yes, him and his brother, but now they are going to give me back."

"Why?" Stacy asked, her hands doing nothing to clean herself as instructed, body simply enjoying the hot water.

"Crystal says they're partners now, even though Sam hurt him really bad when they came to get me."

"Partners?" Stacy asked.

"Yeah. So that they can sell lots of videos of us and make even more money, and so the people in the city with kids can use the houses that Kristi and Sam have for scenes with people out here." She paused. "Can I get the water?"

Stacy nodded and shifted so Vicky could stand beneath the spray, gooseflesh instantly springing up on her own arms as the warmth from the water left her body.

Vicky started soaping herself and then asked, "Can you do my back?"

"Um…sure," Stacy said, handcuffed hands circling the loofa against her skin.

Nothing else was said after that, Vicky seeming to lose interest in talking as the shower progressed. And honestly, Stacy wasn't really sure what the point of asking her questions was. Alan was dead, and she was going to be delivered to this Mr. Sullivan at some point. The story didn't matter anymore; all she needed to do was figure out a way to prevent what was going to unfold in the near future.

The shower rod, she said to herself as the shower came to an end, Kristi having shouted at them to wrap it up through the door. *Pull it down and use it as a weapon!*

Best of all, Sam wasn't even there, having left to go see if his brother had finally returned, who, if what she had overhead was correct, still hadn't replied to any of the messages they had left, which meant all she had to do was subdue the bitch and she would be free.

"What're you doing?" Vicky asked as Stacy reached up to the rod with her cuffed hands.

"I just want to see something," Stacy said, giving the shower rod a yank.

As expected, it was not attached to the walls with anything, just braced between them, the rod similar to the one in her apartment, only with better springs that were not all fucked up and actually kept the pressure going outward when between the two walls.

"You broke it," Vicky said and then at the top of her lungs, *"Kristi, she broke the shower!"*

"Bitch," Stacy snapped.

Vicky grabbed the rod.

"Let go!"

Given the handcuffs, Stacy was unable to reach for Vicky while holding the rod, so instead she shifted toward Vicky as if swinging it into her gut.

Startled, Vicky lost her balance on the soapy floor and fell, head cracking against the tub edge with a sickening *thunk!*

Blood appeared and oozed toward the drain with the remaining suds.

The bathroom door opened.

Stacy stepped from the tub and thrust the rod at the small bathroom window, the sound of glass shattering echoing within the tiny room just as the sounds of something being sprayed appeared.

Crying for help became hopeless, her face and body engulfed in something that made it impossible to breathe, snot running from her nose while tears blinded her eyes.

She swung the rod, hoping to hit Kristi, but only managed to smash the mirror, pieces of it falling to the sink and floor.

And then something cracked her on the head, knocking all

sense from her, the only thing she could understand being the pain, followed by the sudden inability to stand.

The sound of Kristi gagging came a few seconds later, as did a horrific pain in her wrists as Kristi grabbed her by the handcuffs and dragged her from the bathroom.

5

"Absolutely not," his mother said. "You're staying here like the doctor wants until they're sure you're okay."

"Mom, I'm fine," Alan insisted, his frustration hard to control. "And I need to go home."

"No, you need to stay here like the doctor said."

"In Iraq, I was knocked around way worse—"

"You're not in Iraq right now, and as long as they want you to stay here, I won't drive you home."

"But—"

"Let's not argue," his mother urged. "One day. It's not the end of the world."

Alan waited a moment and then said, "But what if that guy comes back while I'm gone?"

"If he does, I'll put a bullet through his head just like you would, something that I think he can appreciate after I shot at him last night."

Alan was still surprised by that, the image of his mother shooting a gun, let alone shooting at another person, something he couldn't visualize at all, yet apparently she had done just that.

Now if only she had hit the guy in such a way that he had been unable to get away, that would have been perfect. But, alas, shooting a person, even from a couple feet away, was not easy, especially if one wasn't experienced with using a firearm.

THUNK! THUNK!

Alan and his mother looked toward the door.

"Excuse me," a nurse said. "There's a Detective Robbins here to see you. Are you feeling up to speaking with him?"

Alan looked toward his mother, then back at the nurse, and said, "Yeah, I suppose." To his mother, "I have a feeling he'll want to talk to me alone."

She nodded and said, "I'll be back later tonight."

"Okay."

"Do you need me to bring anything?" she asked, right arm finding the sleeve of her jacket. "Tea, your book, anything?"

"Just my book, I guess," he said. Guilt followed since he had no intention of staying here, which meant asking for his book was a type of lie.

"Okay. Give me a call if you think of anything else you might need. I gave you your cell phone, right?"

"Yep." He nodded toward his bed tray. "Got it right there."

"Okay, hang in there," she said, followed by an "I love you" and "will see you later" statement.

Not long after that, Detective Robbins was walking into the room, his coat in his hands, eyes looking around for the best place to sit.

6

"Sam, she killed Vicky!" Kristi snapped into the phone, her voice wet sounding from the irritants that she had walked into when entering the bathroom to grab Stacy's wrists. "And she attacked me with the shower rod."

Once again, the phone was not set to speaker mode, so Stacy could not catch Sam's side of the conversation. Whatever it was, however, it didn't help ease Kristi's anger.

"I don't care about finding your brother. Get the information for Mr. Sullivan and get her to him. I don't even care if he pays us anymore. I just want to know she's there and is suffering."

Stacy shifted herself while listening to this, her wet naked body starting to shiver as she curled herself up on the hardwood floor of the bedroom that Kristi had dragged her into, the irritants from the spray she had been hit with still wreaking havoc upon her eyes, nose, and throat.

"Let me put it this way, if you're not back here in twenty minutes, I'm going to kill her, and then you can have fun trying to figure out how to dispose of her body. Got it?"

With that, the call ended, Kristi coming forward and kicking her in the leg.

"Stupid bitch," Kristi said, her voice a bit calmer than it had been on the phone. "I hope they keep you alive for a long time and really fuck you up between the fight nights."

A second kick landed, this one right in the spot where Kristi had struck her the night before while she was in the trunk, the pain bringing fresh tears to her eyes as well as a snot-filled cry.

"Who knows, maybe they'll let me come see a fight one night, or maybe some other event where they let men have their way with you." She nudged Stacy's naked genital region with the point of her heel. "What do you think, could you survive a night where hundreds of men fucked that pussy?"

Stacy grabbed the foot and tried to twist it, but Kristi must have been ready for the attack, because she pulled her foot away without a problem and then planted another solid kick, this one right between her legs. The pain was intense and, if the laugh from Kristi was any indication, amusing.

7

"They were able to recover two slugs from inside your house, but whether or not those will match up to anything within the system remains to be seen," Detective Robbins told him. "As far as the man you killed the other night, we've been able to connect him to a man named Jeremiah Right, who is a pretty significant figure in the sex trade. Slick too, it seems, since he has never been arrested for anything, yet he constantly pops up on the radar when looking into such things via word of mouth. His involvement in all this, and the fact that he was killed yesterday by Riley Woodman, who was also shot and killed, has really caused things to explode. Just about every agency you can think of is now involved, and more will probably join in since one of the young girls he had living in a room on the second floor was from eastern Europe." He shook his head. "And now you're tangled into all of it because you decided to help a friend with a freelance news story she wanted to write."

Alan thought about that, unsure what to say, and then shifted things by asking, "Have you located her yet?"

"No, but if the Woodmans are holding her somewhere like you suspect, it is only a matter of time before she is located. I have a request in right now for information on all the properties the Woodmans own, as well as requests for information on Samuel Woodman's activities while he was undercover, just in case that could bring up information on contacts he may have within the sex trade."

"But…" Alan asked, sensing a downside.

"But the chance that I'm going to be able to keep hold of this case is pretty much nonexistent, given everything that has unfolded. As you can imagine, this thing is going to turn into a jurisdictional nightmare, one that my superiors don't want to get tangled up in."

"So why come talk to me?" Alan asked.

"Because the two homicides that I was called in for are still mine at the moment, and even though I have nowhere to go with them and see no cause to charge you with anything at this point, I wanted to give you a heads-up on what to expect."

"Thanks, I guess," Alan said.

"Also, it would probably be in your best interest to step

back from this little amateur investigation you've got going, especially now that all these different agencies are looking into things. Hell, given your history, I wouldn't be surprised if the military gets involved too, just so they can be informed of any potential embarrassments that might come their way."

He's probably right about the military. Out loud, he said, "My friend is still missing."

"Yes, but she is more likely to be found alive if you let the professionals handle this."

"You mean the ones who have been unable to nail a well-known sex trafficker and had no idea there was a suburban prostitution enterprise disguised as a real estate business operating right under their noses? Those professionals?"

Detective Robbins didn't reply to that.

"Seems to me Stacy and I uncovered more about this thing in a week than anyone else did in all the months it's been operating, and because of our actions, events have unfolded that have resulted in the death of a major figure in the sex trade, a death that created a breach that can now be exploited by law enforcement."

"And if you and Stacy had simply gone to the authorities with your information—"

"They would have made a few small-time arrests and never drawn a connection to the bigger issue," he said, cutting off the detective. "And once all was said and done, all the girls that were 'rescued' would have been tossed back onto the streets to find new pimps and suffer more injustices."

Once again, Detective Robbins didn't reply, a look of serious contemplation appearing upon his face.

Alan waited.

Nothing was said for nearly a minute, and then, to Alan's surprise, the detective slapped his knee and stood up, a statement on needing to get back to work leaving his lips.

"Oh, by the way," Detective Robbins said, his exit halted in the doorway. "No one has been able to locate the cell phone belonging to the man you killed, which seems odd. Do you know anything about that?"

"No," Alan said.

"Hmm…okay, well, if you should hear anything about the phone, or anything that might help in this investigation, please feel free to pass it on to me."

"I thought you were going to lose this case," Alan said.

"I am, but I can still pass on information if it comes my way, thereby ensuring it gets to the proper place without delay."

Alan nodded and then, when nothing else was said, watched the detective return the nod and walk through the doorway, his steps quickly fading as he headed toward the elevators.

Maybe he's right.

Maybe I should just sit back and let things unfold as they may.

And leave Stacy to suffer whatever fate they decide for her?

He couldn't do that, especially after failing Amanda. No. He had to find her. He had to get to her before the authorities closed in on things, which would probably result in her being killed.

Grabbing his phone, he started to pull up cab companies but then realized his mother had not brought his wallet, which meant he would have to find out if they accepted payment upon arrival.

They probably do.

Even so, he decided to try a different route, his finger pulling up his call history and once he was hovered over the last call he had made to Walter Doyle, hitting send, his hope being he would answer this time around.

8

Though she had no way of telling time, Stacy was pretty sure more than twenty minutes had passed since Kristi's call to Sam, which meant that Kristi's threat to kill her should Sam take longer than the given time frame had been a bluff.

During that time, her eyes also started to clear, allowing her to keep them open long enough to process her surroundings. This wasn't to say the pain had faded completely, because that wasn't the case, but the feeling of suffocation and that her eyes were on fire had dissipated.

And then Sam was back, shouts of *"why did you have her shower with Vicky?"* and *"you told me to get her clean"* being thrown back and forth, which then turned into a shouting match about whose fault all this was, statements about him fucking kids and pissing off pimps being made, which then led to what sounded like a slap. After that, nothing more was said, the only sound being that of Kristi crying.

9

Discharging himself from the hospital was easier than Alan thought it would be, all of it simply amounting to the signing of forms and an assurance from him that he would call in with his insurance information.

Walter didn't say anything while he did this, his eyes simply looking around the hospital, a statement about how he used to come here a lot with his wife while she was sick being made during their walk to the parking garage.

"That was back when all those painted dragons were everywhere," Walter said.

Painted dragons? Alan asked himself, having no idea what Walter was talking about. *Must've been when I was overseas.*

Nothing else was said as they headed to the car, Alan trying not to show how difficult the walk was, his head not enjoying the journey at all.

"So where to?" Walter asked once they were in the car, Alan

forced to move several files that had been left on the seat. "Your house?"

"Yeah."

"Okay."

Silence settled, Alan watching as they made their way from the parking garage to the side road and eventually onto Washington, which would take them through the downtown Naperville area toward Ogden Avenue.

"Why did you agree to come pick me up?" Alan asked.

"You asked me to," Walter said.

"Yeah, I got that part down solid. What I'm wondering is why did you say yes when I asked?"

Walter shrugged.

Something wasn't right about all this, but he wasn't sure what, and since it didn't seem sinister, he decided not to press.

RILEY WOODMAN.

The name was written on the header of a file that sat on top of the stack of files that he had moved to his lap when getting into the car.

Beneath that was one that said SAMUEL WOODMAN and beneath that KRISTI WOODMAN.

His own file, which he had already looked through, was the fourth one, and beneath that was one that was simply labeled GIRLS.

Alan caught Walter's glance toward the files and asked, "Was all this part of your investigation when hired by that guy's wife?"

"No...well...it all started with that, but like I told you the other day, I got curious about what was going on and continued to look into things." He signaled for a turn. "Of course, I had no idea it would get so crazy."

"That makes two of us." Then, nodding down toward the

file, he asked, "Mind if I take a look inside?"

"Figured you'd want to, which is why I left them on the seat." He made the turn. "By the way, Riley Woodman's dead."

"I know," Alan said.

"Really?" Walter asked, his surprise seeming genuine.

"Yeah, a detective paid me a visit in the hospital." He stopped there, deciding that since Walter had not been as forthcoming as he could have been with information the other day, he would not be either, not unless Walter gave him something that would help in learning where Stacy might be held.

"And did he give you any details about where it was that he was killed and what he was doing?" Walter asked.

"Yeah."

Walter looked over at him for a moment and then said, "Then you're aware that this thing is much bigger than you initially thought—bigger than I thought—and that there are some serious players involved."

"It would appear that way."

Alan looked through the file but didn't absorb much, the issues with his equilibrium making it impossible for him to read while they were moving without feeling as if he was going to get carsick.

"So, what are your plans?" Walter asked.

"My plans?" Alan said. "What makes you think I have any plans?"

"Because I know your type. Hell, I'm your type. And after everything that has happened, especially after last night, I don't see you backing down."

Alan smiled. "You think I'm going to go all Rambo on them."

"Rambo," Walter said with a sigh.

Alan regretted the comment, given that Walter might view the John Rambo character in a much different light than he did since it was his era of Special Forces soldier that had been portrayed in the novel and movie, the former having done a much better job of portraying what those soldiers had gone through than the latter had.

"My friend, Stacy Collins, is still missing," Alan said. "And if this thing is as big as everyone now thinks it is, there is a good chance that she will disappear into the underworld soon, which means I have to find her while she is still within reach."

"You think she's still alive?"

"I do."

"How come?"

"Because in a system like this, even though it seems like they have an abundance of females they can choose from, I don't think they will simply turn away one that they have within their possession."

"But what if they want to make an example of her?" Walter asked as they turned left onto Naperville Road from Ogden Avenue.

"An example for whom?" Alan asked. "Other reporters? That would just bring more attention to themselves, which is something I doubt they want. And as far as the girls they already have, how would making an example of a reporter serve to keep them in line? By displaying how harsh they can be? They probably already know all about that, and even if some don't, why waste a perfectly good, young, attractive female to display such a thing when they probably have someone else within their ranks who will cross the line and be a better example, given the connection she already shares with the other girls?"

Walter nodded. "And you think she is still within reach, maybe a prisoner of Samuel and Kristi Woodman?"

"Yes, at least I'm hoping she still is," he said. "And any information you have that I don't yet know that may help in finding out if this is true would be greatly appreciated."

"I will tell you what I know thus far, but I'm going to be

honest with you, it isn't much." He signaled for a right turn as they neared Butterfield. "The only link they had with the underworld that I knew about was with this guy Mr. Right, who, as you know, was killed in whatever it was that unfolded between him and Riley Woodman."

"And getting information about that is probably beyond our capabilities at this point, right?" Alan asked.

"The sex crimes people will be all over that place, and the state police will probably be working with them to see what type of link Riley Woodman had with them, which means they will soon be all over Samuel and Kristi Woodman as well."

"But that will take time as they decide who gets to do what, correct?"

"It's possible, but it won't be in the form of bickering and jurisdiction grabs as the movies would have you believe. More of a sorting things out and seeing what types of links they can make now that a lot of information will be available, information that is scattered about different jurisdictions and departments."

Alan thought about that.

"One thing is certain, though," Walter added.

"What?" Alan asked when he didn't continue right away.

"Samuel and Kristi Woodman are not going to survive this. They are way too exposed, so either they will be arrested or they will be killed, the latter depending on if there are other connections to the underworld, ones that will need to be severed before they too are exposed to law enforcement." He turned onto Butterfield. "And in that regard, knowing that time may be against them, there is a chance that your friend could be killed simply because they want to sever all the links."

10

An odd type of silence settled over the house after the slap Sam had delivered to his wife, a silence that felt very uncomfortable and awkward, yet also somewhat positive because Stacy had a feeling that neither of them knew what to do. This Mr. Right, whoever he was, was not returning Sam's calls, and given what Sam had seen when driving her to his place last night, it seemed likely that something had unfolded that had pretty much severed the connection Sam and Kristi had to Mr. Sullivan, thus ruining their plans. Less clear to her, but obviously causing problems for the two, was something that had unfolded with their girls at one of the houses, something that had gotten the attention of the police.

Something that led them to kill Alan.

Or maybe they had been planning to do that anyway?

She pushed the thoughts of Alan from her mind and turned her focus back on the room she was in, thoughts of attempting to escape once again entering into her mind.

Footsteps.

Fuck!

A few seconds later Sam was in the room, arms crossed.

Though she wasn't gagged, hadn't been since the shower, Stacy didn't say anything.

Sam studied her, eyes seeming to take in every inch of her naked body before saying anything. She didn't try to cover up, given that she felt it would show weakness. "You've turned out to be quite the troublemaker."

Stacy didn't reply.

"You and that boyfriend of yours," he added. "If it wasn't for him, this would have all been settled last week, but...well..." He put his hands up in a "what can you do?" gesture.

"It was you waiting in my apartment," Stacy said.

"It was."

"You weren't there to kill me."

He seemed surprised by this. "I wasn't?"

"No. If you had been, you wouldn't have told me to back off when punching me in the stomach. You would have just killed me and been done with it."

This time it was Sam who did not reply.

"And you know what? It was because of your attack that night that Alan and I started to investigate. Up until then, I wasn't sure if I really had a story or if it was all in my head, but after that, I knew I was onto something big. So you can thank yourself for getting everything all fucked up."

"Cute," Sam said with a nod.

Stacy wasn't sure what was "cute" about what she had just said, but decided to let it stand without comment.

"Anyway, I came up here to let you know that if we're unable to figure out a way to get you to Mr. Sullivan, we're going to hand you over to Rusty." He smiled. "So we'll wait and see what unfolds during the next several hours, and if things are still quiet on that front, we'll call Rusty. Who knows, my initial thoughts on him might be incorrect, and maybe he will be a valuable partner now that Mr. Right seems to be finished."

He waited, but she didn't reply.

"So enjoy the next couple hours in here because one way or another, things are going to get really nasty for you."

He smiled and then twitched as his phone buzzed.

"Oh, what do you know? It's Rusty again. He's been calling quite a bit these last few hours." With that, he accepted the call and said, "Hey, Rusty, still trying to fix some things on this end, but it shouldn't be much—"

"Rusty!" Stacy shouted. *"They're lying to you and not going to give me to you!"*

Startled, Sam tried to cover the phone while backing from the room and then, within the hallway, started to say something.

"They're giving me to Mr. Sullivan!" she shouted, hoping the

name would trigger something within Rusty's limited mind so that he would know she was telling the truth. After all, why would she know the name if what she shouted wasn't true?

Whatever Sam said to try to counter her statements, she did not hear it, his feet quickly taking him away from the bedroom they had put her in so that she couldn't say anything else.

Several minutes came and went, Stacy once again trying to wrap herself up into a ball to keep warm in the cool room, the movement needed difficult, given that her wrists were attached to the end of the bed frame in such a way that forced her to sit on the floor at an angle. While doing this, she asked herself why she had shouted, though only because she was starting to question what good it would do. Would Rusty actually race out to this area to try to secure what he had been promised, fucking things up for Sam and Kristi? If so, would he know where to look? Did he know about this place? Did he know about any of the houses, or even where Sam and Kristi lived when they weren't trying to avoid being confronted by the authorities for whatever it was that had happened at one of their other houses? Were the authorities even trying to contact them?

These thoughts led to ones about Alan and what type of investigation was unfolding with that.

Sadness followed.

Sam returned.

Silence engulfed them for nearly two minutes, then, "If you do one more thing like that, I'm going to drag Vicky's body in here and handcuff you to it for the rest of the day."

Stacy didn't reply.

"Or I could fuck Crystal right in front of you and then make you lick my cum from her pussy."

"That'll probably piss off your wife more than it upsets me," Stacy said, though, honestly, the thought of being forced to do something like that was so horrific that she was actually going to comply with his demand.

Unless I get the chance to escape.

No matter the threats, if an opportunity arose that seemed promising, she would take it.

"Keep it up, and you'll get to find out how pissed off it will make her, and how I deal with her little temper tantrums when they arise."

Yeah, by caving in.

Or does he?

Her thoughts on how their marriage worked were not solid, her earlier impression that Kristi was in control of everything having been shaken by recent actions and arguments she had witnessed while in their captivity.

11

Crime scene tape had been stretched around the front porch area of the house, yet it didn't seem out of place, given that it could easily be part of the Halloween display he had created. In fact, Walter apparently thought it was the display as they pulled up, but then realized differently when Alan asked him how long something like that would need to stay in place.

"It all depends," he said. "I can't imagine they have anything more to do here, not without someone having been killed, so you could probably take it down yourself since they won't come back to do it."

"You sure?" Alan asked.

Walter shrugged. "Well, maybe wait another day to be on the safe side."

Alan nodded, then, "Let's go inside and figure out what to do next."

Walter shook his head. "Sorry, I've dirtied my hands

enough with this thing and would much rather head home. These files are for you. I made copies, knowing you would want the information."

Alan stared at him for several seconds, something clicking. "You were never hired to investigate someone's husband, were you?"

"I was," he said, a very matter-of-fact tone present.

"But after that you…" Alan started, his mind pausing to let Walter fill in the blank.

"What can I say?" Walter said with a sigh. "I've been lonely since my wife died and am not exactly one who can easily get women to bed me, especially when not looking for anything more than a physical encounter."

Alan nodded.

"How did you know?" Walter asked.

"It just clicked," Alan said and then hesitated for a moment. "And I'm not judging you, but I do want to understand your motivation in all this. Did you really observe me while you were observing them for a client? Or did you observe me while going to visit one of the girls and wanted to find out what I was up to?"

"I observed you while observing the girls," Walter admitted. "I wanted to learn more about them, and the setup, before I took the plunge and voiced my interest in becoming a customer to Kristi Woodman."

"And then what, you started investigating me?"

He nodded.

Alan waited and when nothing else was said, asked, "Why?"

"Because I wanted to find out if you were an undercover officer that was part of an investigation." He shrugged. "You weren't, but in the end, I still decided it was in my best interest not to hire the services offered by Kristi Woodman."

Alan thought about that and then asked, "So why not help me? It's not as if your name is going to get smeared once everything is made public."

"Even if I had hired one of the girls, it wouldn't matter if my name came to light." He smiled. "Benefit of being my own boss."

Alan waited.

"But, alas, I cannot help you any more than I already have."

"Why?"

"Because the only work that remains is physical, and I'd be at a great disadvantage, as well as a burden to you."

"You really think so?" Alan asked.

"I know so," Walter replied.

Alan didn't know what to say to that.

Walter went silent as well.

"Are there addresses in here?" Alan asked. "For the houses?"

"Some."

"And the Woodmans'?"

"Yes."

"Okay."

Walter waited and then said, "If you have questions on how to proceed and want to run something by me, feel free to give me a call—unless it involves breaking into a house, in which case my answer will always be *don't do it*."

"Okay, I will," Alan said and then stepped from the car, a moment of hesitation appearing as he neared the police tape, followed by a mental "fuck it" as he pulled it down and went inside.

12

Time dragged as Stacy stayed curled in the bedroom, her naked body barely able to contain any warmth as the sun passed beyond the window, the natural darkness of the room returning.

Downstairs, silence seemed to rule, and if it hadn't been for the occasional sounds of movement, she would have started to wonder if they had left.

You would have heard the garage door.

Not if they simply went in Sam's car.

Thoughts like this came and went without leaving much of an imprint within her mind, the only constant being the cold and her frequent attempts at trying to shift her wrists into a more comfortable position. Nothing she did seemed to alleviate the pressure that the handcuff edges produced against her flesh, the only solution being to try to hold her arms up above their reach, which she couldn't do for more than a couple of minutes at a time.

And it will only get worse.

Footsteps.

Or just the house creaking?

No one came to the room, but that didn't mean one of them hadn't started up the steps.

Did they get in touch with Mr. Sullivan?

Though terrified of the prospect of being given to him, especially after what the girls had told her, she almost felt that was preferable to being given back to Rusty. Both would be horrible, but with Rusty, she somehow felt it would be worse simply because of what she had done to him. His lust for revenge, coupled with his insanity, would add horror and humiliation that was uncalculated; whereas someone like Mr. Sullivan, who would have her as part of his business, would be a bit more calculating and skilled.

It will still be horrific.

This thought stuck in her mind longer than the others had, as did the sense that someone had crept up the stairs.

What are they doing?

No answer arrived, at least not in the form of someone coming in and presenting themselves, so after several seconds, she shouted.

No response.

What if no one is there?

What if they're still downstairs and can hear you acting like a crazy woman who is imagining things?

Though she didn't know why, this thought scared her more than the idea of them standing outside the door. The thought that they might think she had broken to the point of hallucination…that was something she didn't want. Especially if it was true.

13

Alan's mother was not happy that he had come home from the hospital, but she also seemed to understand that arguing about it would be no use since there was nothing she could do to make him go back. In fact, given that he had gone through the process of being discharged, going back would have probably been quite the hassle, though he was sure they did have procedures in place for such things.

"Where's the gun?" Alan asked.

"They took it."

"Who? The police?"

"Yeah."

Fuck.

He had been counting on having access to a firearm while looking for Stacy, one that he would be able to use if needed.

Then again, with all the police involved, the chances that he might be confronted by an officer were high; therefore not having possession of a firearm might be for the best.

"They said they would be doing patrols around this area in case the guy came back," she added.

"That's comforting," Alan said. *"We know someone tried to kill you, but we can't leave the gun, because, well, it's a gun, so we'll breeze by the house every now and then to make sure everything is okay. We might even glance this way while breezing by."*

"They said it's highly unlikely that the guy will come back, and that we're probably better off not having the gun here since statistics show that people are often killed by their own gun."

Alan shook his head, wondering why the guy from last night would need to use their gun when he obviously had access to one of his own. He also was of the opinion that when people were killed with their own gun, it was because it had been used by a loved one during a domestic dispute rather than by someone who came into the home with the intent of causing harm. Whether or not this was truly the case, he didn't know, but it made sense.

You were planning to take it anyway, so don't feel all "they're leaving my mother helpless" about it. Following that, he told himself to quit dillydallying and figure out what his next move was going to be, a statement on how he needed to do some work leaving his lips.

"What work?" she asked, arms crossed.

He held up the files. "Stacy is missing, and I need to figure out where they're keeping her."

"Alan, let the police handle it."

"I can't," he said.

"Why?"

"Because…" Nothing followed, his mind drawing a blank.

She stared at him, a mix of fear and anger appearing on her face. "Someone tried to kill you last night because of her."

"I know."

"So don't you realize that means you should stop? You survived two wars, were in countless firefights and were hit by several roadside bombs, and then survived an illness that almost killed you—after all that, do you really want to risk getting killed at home?"

"We risk getting killed every day by just going outside,"

Alan said.

"Yeah, so why add more risk by going into a situation where people are trying to kill you?"

"Because if I don't and I later find out I could have done something to prevent Stacy from being killed, then I might as well not have survived everything that I have."

She didn't reply.

"And even if I don't end up helping her, knowing I tried, that..." He shrugged, the words he wanted failing to appear. "I don't know, but I have to try."

Again, she didn't reply.

Files in hand, Alan headed into his room to start going over them, but then, before he even got started, headed back out, realizing that he needed to make sure his body was in good condition so he could actually provide help. Two bananas later, with a mug of tea in hand, he returned to his room, eyes ready to scan the files to see if anything important jumped out at him.

It didn't take long to find what he needed: a list of addresses for the houses they owned, one of which was the actual home of Samuel and Kristi Woodman.

But do they really have her at one of them?

Only one way to find out.

First things first, he donned clothing that would be more suitable for prowling around neighborhood houses and then grabbed a knife, one that unfortunately added to the earlier Rambo comparison, even though he would not be going in with it as his primary weapon. Nope. The knife was just a tool, one that would be a weapon of last resort.

One that you have killed with in the past.

He thought about that for a moment, gooseflesh popping up along his spine as he recalled the sound of air rushing from the young man's throat.

Thoughts of Amanda followed, anger and a desire for revenge unfolding.

You already killed the one responsible.

But not the ones that created the situation that allowed it to become a reality.

Thinking about this, he grabbed the phone from the man that he had killed, a realization that it might come in handy at some point arriving within his mind, and headed out to his car. Once inside, he thumbed in the password to see if anything had arrived while he had been away and, much to his surprise, discovered several messages were waiting to be read, most from someone with the contact name of KW, the others from SW.

Kristi and Sam Woodman?

Who else could they be?

Not wanting to stick around in the driveway where his mom could see him, but also wanting to read the messages before he made his move, Alan pulled away from the house and headed down the road, guiding the car to the parking area of the lake, which was empty. There, he began to read the messages.

They don't know he's dead.

You could reply as him and see if they reply.

Hesitation hit.

Replying to the messages could help him learn where Stacy was, or it could spook her captors to the point of doing something drastic, the latter of which would haunt him forever.

Wasting time here, his mind chided as the indecision continued.

Making things worse, one of the messages pretty much confirmed that they had Stacy, the text stating: WE TRIED BRINGING LOIS LANE TO YOUR BOSS SO HE COULD MAKE THE TRADE, BUT SOMETHING HAPPENED. DO YOU KNOW WHAT?

Later, a question asking if he would be able to put them in

contact with someone named Mr. Sullivan so they could deliver Lois Lane to him as promised arrived, followed by an ARE YOU OKAY? inquiry a few hours later.

An idea arrived.

Rather than reply from the phone, he could call them as if he was this Mr. Sullivan himself and find out where he could pick up Stacy.

Best of all, if they were expecting contact from someone that they didn't know themselves, chances were good that they would pick up, even if the call was blocked. The question was, how did he block his own phone number?

Two minutes later, after searching Google for the answer, he placed a call.

No answer.

Good sign, he said to himself while dialing the number for a second time, this time without blocking his name, knowing that if his name had been attached during the first call, it would have been picked up.

"Alan?" his mother asked.

"Yep. Hey, did you get a call a few seconds ago that was blocked?"

"Yeah."

"Okay, good. That was me. I just wanted to test it out before I placed a call."

"Oh, who're you calling?" she asked.

"I'll tell you later once everything is all said and done. Right now I really need to get moving." With that, he ended the call and, using the number he saw within Stuart's contact list for guidance, called Kristi Woodman.

14

"What're you doing up here?" Sam asked, voice carrying into the room from the hallway.

"Nothing," a tiny voice said, barely audible. It seemed the footsteps earlier had been real. Then, "Why did she hurt Vicky?"

"Because she's trying to hurt us all and knew that hurting Vicky would make us all upset."

"I hate her."

"Well, don't worry. She'll be punished by Mr. Sullivan."

"Will he let me watch?"

"I don't think so, but you remember the worst thing that happened to you when you were bad?"

"You mean like being hung last night?"

"Is that the worst thing that ever happened?"

"Yes."

"Well then, think about what that was like and then how it would be for years, because that is what he is going to do to her, and not just hanging her, but he is going to hurt her and have others hurt her too."

"Good…I wish I could see."

He didn't reply right away, several seconds passing, and then asked, "Do you know what would hurt her a lot?"

"What?"

"If she has to watch you showing me how much you love me."

"Why?"

"Because that would really upset her and that is why she hurt Vicky, because you and her really love me and she doesn't like that."

"Oh."

"So do you want to hurt her like that?"

"Um…even with Mrs. W here?"

"Don't worry about her. I'm in charge, and she listens to me."

"Okay."

Nothing else was said as the two entered the room, Crystal wearing a simple dress that looked a bit rumpled, given that she had been wearing it for two days, Sam sporting what could only be a huge erection beneath his pants. The two were holding hands.

A horrible smile appeared.

He knew she had heard everything.

"He doesn't really love you," Stacy said. "He's just using you like everyone else has, and he'll throw you away once you're no longer worth anything to him."

"You're just jealous," Crystal said, tiny fingers proceeding to unzip Sam's pants and pull his erection free.

Stacy looked away.

"Look at me," Sam said.

"What?" Crystal said, startled.

"Not you, honey, I was talking to Stacy," he said. "I want her to watch."

"Oh."

Stacy continued to look away.

"Sam!" Kristi called.

Footsteps on the stairs followed.

"Fuck," Sam said, zipping up his pants. "Yeah?" he asked as she entered the room.

Kristi didn't answer right away, a questioning look going from him to Crystal to Stacy.

"What is it?" he urged.

"Um...I just got a call from Mr. Sullivan, who says he wants to meet up with us. He says that Mr. Right was killed last night and that he has been trying to figure out how to get in touch."

"Did he say what happened to Mr. Right?"

"I didn't ask."

"Okay, doesn't matter. Where does he want us to meet?"

"Here."

"Here?" He hesitated. "You gave him the address?"

"Yeah."

Sam didn't say anything.

"What?" Kristi asked.

Sam gave a dismissive wave and said, "Let's get her ready. You brought extra clothes, right?"

"No, just what she was wearing," Kristi said.

"No, clothes you brought for yourself. You brought extra, right?"

"I don't want to give her my—"

"Kristi!" Sam snapped. "We can't give her to him naked, and the clothes she was wearing are full of piss. Just give me some of your fucking clothes!"

She glared at him and then left the room, footsteps heavy as her heels tried to punch holes into the hardwood floor.

Stacy stared at Sam.

"What?" he asked, glaring back.

"Rusty's not going to be happy," she said.

"Why the fuck would I care about that?"

"Because he's crazy and probably knows more about your little sex ring than you realize."

"Let him try to fuck with us, I'll put a bullet through his brain."

"Maybe," Stacy said with a shrug.

Kristi returned with a skirt and shirt and threw them toward Stacy. "There," she said while turning back toward Sam. "Happy?"

"Yeah, now unlock her please," Sam said and handed over the key.

Kristi snatched it from him and walked over to Stacy, anger and hatred oozing, and proceeded to unlock the cuffs.

Stacy instantly rubbed at her wrists, an inaudible sigh escaping her lips.

"I don't have shoes for her, so I hope barefoot is—" Kristi stopped.

Stacy looked up to see what had happened and, much to her surprise, saw that Sam was holding a pistol on his wife.

"Honey, what are you—"

"Shut up and lock your wrists behind your back," Sam snapped. Then to Crystal, "Go downstairs and get the duct tape and the other pair of handcuffs."

"O-okay."

"Sam, what the fuck are—"

"I said shut the fuck up!" he snapped, finger cocking back the hammer on the pistol. "Put the handcuffs on."

Kristi did as instructed, the sound of the handcuffs clicking shut echoing in the room.

He turned to Stacy, gun still leveled on his wife. "Get dressed."

She did as instructed, her torn fingers thankful that Kristi had given her a shirt that she could simply pull over herself rather than one that needed to be buttoned up.

Crystal returned with the handcuffs and duct tape.

"Go lock Stacy's wrists behind her back," Sam instructed. "And then tape both their mouths shut and their legs together."

Crystal did as instructed, Stacy momentarily thinking she would grab the girl and use her as a shield, but then hesitating when she realized that Sam was really on edge.

"You didn't think I knew you were the one that was black-mailing me?" Sam asked, words directed toward Kristi, who shook her head and made a noise against the tape. "Crystal here overheard Mr. Right talking about it on the phone before I picked her up, and Amanda was pretty adamant about you having set up that scene where Emily was killed, so I took a look at your phone one day and wow, you've been a busy little bee." He grinned and turned to Stacy. "Hope you don't mind, but I'm going to send her along with you to Mr. Sullivan. Who knows, maybe one day I will get to see the two of you fighting each other for one of his events." He turned back to Kristi. "No offense, my dear, but I think she's going to beat the shit out of you if that happens."

Stacy, still startled by what had just unfolded, took a look at Kristi. Tears were running down her face. Anger was present as well.

"Now, Crystal, remember how we were going to hurt Stacy here a little while ago?"

"Yes," Crystal said.

"Well, seeing what we do together will also hurt Kristi, and I'm sure you're still mad at her for what she did to you last night, right?"

"Yeah, and for not letting us go trick-or-treating."

"Well then, since I'm sure we have a bit of time, let's hurt them both before Mr. Sullivan shows up."

"Okay," Crystal said, smiling, her hand once again unzipping Sam's pants.

15

Now what? Alan asked himself as he drove by the house on Walnut Avenue, his mind still surprised by how easy that call had been. *They aren't going to let you walk inside and free her.*

Call the police?

Though he knew that was what he should do, fear that they would surround the area and cause a hostage crisis that could go bad kept him from making such a call. Instead, he felt he had the element of surprise on his hands, and if he could simply work it to his advantage, he could rescue Stacy while subduing her captors.

Are they both there?

What if it's just Kristi Woodman?

One or two, he was going to have to go in hard and fast, the knowledge that they would have at least one firearm of some kind making it so that he had to get the upper hand in the first few moments. If he didn't, it wasn't an automatic defeat, especially if the gunshot drew the authorities, but the risk to Stacy would increase quite a bit, which was something he wanted to minimize.

Make noise at the front and then try to go in the back?

It had worked the other night with Riley Woodman, though only because the door had been unlocked and Riley had been trying to flee unnoticed.

Such carelessness probably wasn't the case here, not if they had someone captive, so…

Maybe you could get them to open the garage door and put her in the trunk, all without revealing yourself to them.

Anonymity was probably important to people within this world, and if what he had gathered from the messages and the call was true, Kristi and Sam had never met Mr. Sullivan.

But Kristi knows you, and if she catches sight of you, it's all going to blow up.

Indecision gripped him.

Call the police.

No.

After that, he considered calling Walter to have him ring the doorbell as if he were interested in the house, which would give Alan the chance to try to get in through the back, but then he figured Walter would not want to get involved.

The only other person he could think of to do such a thing was his mother, but there was no way in hell he was going to let her risk being anywhere near this situation.

You're on your own.

So…

He had no idea.

16

Though she wasn't watching, Stacy could still hear the sloppy gagging sounds of the blowjob, disgust flowing through her. Questions of how a grown man could indulge in such a thing followed, her mind demanding to know what would produce a sexual attraction toward someone so young.

Not wanting to see what was unfolding, but wanting to see what Kristi's reaction was, Stacy risked a glance back toward her and, to her surprise, saw that Kristi was staring intently at the two as they engaged in the act, a hot glare escaping her face. She was pissed.

More than pissed.

She's homicidal.

Do something.

Now was her chance.

Unfortunately, the handcuffs and the tape made it impossible for her to stand, and scooting herself over to them would be noticed long before she could get herself into a position to do harm.

DING-DONG!

The sounds of the blowjob stopped, Crystal looking up at Sam, who had turned toward the front of the house, a puzzled look on his face.

"Did Mr. Sullivan say he was in the area?" Sam asked.

His wife just glared back.

Without warning, he grabbed her by the throat, his wet erect penis flopping back and forth, flinging strands of saliva everywhere, and shouted at her to answer him.

She shook her head.

Sam released her and then went to the window.

DING-DONG!

"Fuck, I can't see anything from here." He turned to Crystal. "Keep an eye on them, okay?"

She nodded.

With that, Sam left the room.

17

Having been unable to decide on a plan, Alan decided to go through the front door, a pair of sunglasses that he never wore along with an old Cubs baseball hat that had been in his backseat put in place to help distort his face a bit, should Kristi be the one to answer. He also turned his back to the door, thereby making it so the peephole and window were both ineffective if they tried to look upon him from within, his hands behind his back in a relaxed folded gesture.

Having to ring the bell for a second time worried him.

Hard and fast!

The door opened inward, which meant once unlatched and partially open, he could throw himself against it with all his weight, hopefully knocking whoever opened it off-balance, allowing him to get the upper hand.

If that doesn't work.

All would not be lost, but things could get dicey, so hopefully the surprise of his forceful entry would catch them off guard and give him an advantage. If not and it all went to hell, he would retreat and call the police, all while quickly positioning his car to block the end of the driveway, making it so they could not use any of the cars that were parked in it—Amanda's, which had been left behind the other night, being one of them, while a second sat behind it. Whether or not one was in the garage, he did not know.

The door opened as a voice from within asked who it was.

Rather than answer, Alan threw himself against the door as hard as he could, a startled grunt echoing from the man within as the edge caught him in the chest, Alan's own body shocked by the sudden *thump* that echoed back as he hit the door.

And then he was inside, his body managing to squeeze between the door and the frame before the man regained his composure and threw his weight back against it.

18

Stacy heard the commotion downstairs and watched as Crystal twisted around to look out the door, her arm constantly wiping at her mouth as if saliva and pre-cum still clung to it.

Kristi shifted.

Stacy twisted her head back and looked at her.

Her hands are free!

She still has a key!

Crystal turned back toward them as the sound of tape being ripped free echoed, confusion followed by horror appearing on her face.

"SAM!" she cried.

19

Fuck, he's huge! Alan noted once he was in the entryway, mind and body readying himself to attack.

Though caught off guard from the door, the man seemed to regain himself quickly and therefore managed to shift a bit as Alan threw himself at him, his right arm bent in such a way as to hit him in the face with a swinging elbow, the blow catching the man's uplifted shoulder rather than his face.

Hands grabbed him, the grip solid, and slammed him into the wall, his head turning at the last second to avoid smashing face-first into the wall.

Yellow sparks flashed and his legs felt useless as the floor started to ripple.

Something hit him square in the kidney.

And then a second time.

The pain was unlike anything he had felt in a long time, and then, without warning, he felt his bladder filling as if he had to take the world's heaviest piss.

Push through it!

In reply, he swung his elbow back and hit the man in the chest, hearing a satisfying crunch as a rib broke.

The man groaned and then let go of him.

Alan hit him again, though with less force this time, and then turned.

"SAM!"

The man, who was clutching his chest, shifted a bit at the sound of his name and then tried to block the next elbow attack Alan delivered. His reflexes were not quick enough this time, however, and Alan felt a satisfying crunch as he broke the man's nose.

Blood squirted down.

"HELP!" the girl cried. "SHE'S FREE!"

Sam wasn't able to get distracted this time, mostly because Alan punched him in the broken nose just as the girl called for help, and then hit him again as he backed himself up into the wall of the hallway, this time with his left fist.

Gun! Alan shouted to himself as Sam dropped to his knees and pulled it, his hand grabbing the man's wrist before the thought even had time to be processed.

He twisted the wrist.

The gun fell to the floor.

Alan then swung a knee up and hit Sam in the face again, this time knocking him unconscious.

Movement!

Kristi!

She came toward him from the stairway, something in her hand, the spray coming at his face as he turned to confront her, his eyes, nose, and mouth all instantly inflamed by the pepper irritant that nailed him.

20

Thought difficult, Stacy managed to get the discarded handcuff key into a lock on one of the handcuff links but then couldn't seem to twist it, her fingers unable to shift themselves into the proper direction, given the angle they had to bend at just to hold the key in the lock hole.

Frustrated, she glanced at Crystal, who was still twisting in pain on the ground, Kristi having shot her in the face with a burst of pepper spray from a canister that had been in her pocket, tears and snot oozing from between her fingers.

Gritting her teeth against the pain from her torn fingers, Stacy did everything she could to twist the key, her mind not even acknowledging the sudden freedom of her left wrist as the link popped open until she used that hand to wipe at a bit of irritation that had developed in her eyes from the lingering pepper spray.

Realizing her freedom, she quickly sprang to her feet, left hand freeing her right wrists, and then took a moment to balance herself against the bed as the room swayed.

Once settled, she headed into the hallway and started for the stairs, ears guiding her toward where the commotion was, mind knowing that she needed to be careful because whoever it was that was causing the trouble after having rung the doorbell might not be there to help her.

21

Having been exposed to tear gas several times while training in the military, Alan was able to fight his way through the panic that initially set in and now was struggling with Kristi Woodman, his goal being to simply hold on to her long enough for his eyes to clear so that he could subdue her.

Unfortunately, she did not consent to his actions and did everything she could to try to break his hold on her, the nails of her fingers digging furrows in his flesh every chance they could get.

A finger went up his nose.

Whether or not she had consciously directed her attack toward the nostril, he did not know, but the pain as her nail went in, especially with the pepper spray irritants still caught within the tiny hairs, was intense.

And then she managed to knee him between the legs, and while the blow wasn't solid, it still jolted him to the point of letting go.

She squirmed from his grasp, Alan's hands catching hold but failing to keep one of her ankles, his own nails feeling her stocking ripping beneath them.

"Bitch!" someone said.

The sound of someone being hit, hard, reached his ears, followed by what could only be that of a body collapsing on the floor.

Alan tried to see what had happened, his teary eyes managing to glimpse several shapes.

"Alan?" a hoarse yet familiar voice asked.

"Yeah," he replied, his own voice wretched, thanks to the pepper spray.

"Oh my god, they said you were dead!"

"No," he said and then, with her help, got up to his feet, the adrenaline from the last several minutes starting to fade, which in turn allowed his jolted equilibrium to fuck with him once again, the bananas and tea he had consumed earlier ending up on the floor.

22

The shock of seeing Alan alive was impossible to describe, as was the knowledge that she had survived this harrowing experience.

Tears were the only way to express it, ones that Stacy wasn't embarrassed to shed as Alan held her in the kitchen, his own eyes brimming with tears as well, though his were obviously from the pepper spray he had been hit with.

Maybe not though, Stacy said to herself, face still buried in his chest. *Emotion could be playing a part.*

A groan echoed from the hallway.

Stacy pulled her face away and said, "We better do something with them before they both come to."

"Yeah," Alan agreed and started pulling his phone. "I'll call the police, and we can watch them until they get here."

Stacy nodded but then said, "Wait, we need to secure them first."

With that, she hurried up the stairs for the handcuffs that had been discarded, a momentary question about Crystal filling her head as she came upon the girl sitting in the corner of the bedroom, eyes red, tears and snot everywhere.

"Stay right there or I'll kill you," Stacy said.

Crystal simply nodded.

A second later, Stacy was back with Alan, handcuffs in hand, the key in her pocket.

23

They handcuffed the two to the stairway railings, forcing both of them up onto their tiptoes so that they wouldn't have any leverage to break the railings, Kristi coming to during the process and trying to struggle a bit until Stacy delivered a backhanded blow to her face and then sealed her lips with duct tape.

Sam, who was still unconscious and wheezing through a busted nose, never came to, the only difficulty with him being his size, which required the aid of a chair so Alan could hold his wrists in place while Stacy cuffed them from the stairs. Once that was done, his body slumped down against the cuffs, the railing groaning as the wood took his body weight.

"Think it will hold?" Alan asked.

"Long enough for us to get away and them to be found," Stacy said, her hand retrieving a phone from Sam's pocket.

"What're you doing?" Alan asked as she scrolled through the message file on his own phone.

"Calling the police," she said. "Can you go get Crystal? We can drop her off at one of the girls' houses."

"Shouldn't we wait here for the police?" Alan asked.

"Spending the rest of my day answering questions is the last thing I want to do." Her finger hit a button and she put the phone to her ear. "Go," she urged while nodding up the stairs.

Alan did, ears overhearing Stacy giving the address of the house while he got Crystal, a description of a yard with a For Sale sign in it being voiced.

"They're on their way," Stacy said once the two were back downstairs, Crystal and Stacy exchanging a look with each other that was less than pleasant.

At the stairway, Kristi was struggling to get free, her wrists already bloodied with the effort of pulling at the cuffs, tears flowing.

"Let's go," Stacy said.

"Okay," Alan said, eyes still looking at Kristi, who was looking back at him, pleading, tape muffling whatever she was trying to say.

"Alan!" Stacy snapped.

Kristi made one last plea toward him and then shook her head while kicking at the wall and pulling against the handcuffs.

Alan gave her a somber look and turned.

A muffled cry reached his ears.

Ignoring it, he stepped through the front door and pulled it closed.

"You didn't lock it, did you?" Stacy asked.

"Um…no," Alan said.

"Okay, good."

Somewhat puzzled, Alan followed her to his car, where she got in the backseat with Crystal, demanding to know where the other girls' house was located.

"I don't know," Crystal said, voice soft.

"Maybe we should just wait here and let the police take custody of her," Alan said.

"No," Stacy snapped. Then a bit more subdued, "I just want to go home and recover from all this." Her lip quivered. "Please."

"Okay," Alan said and pulled out of the driveway, his eyes taking one last glance at the house, mind amazed at how, given the quiet, peaceful look it presented, it could have hidden such horror.

24

"Hello?" Alan asked, a hand rubbing the sleep from his eyes.

"Mr. Miller, Detective Robbins. How're you doing?"

"Oh, hey, I'm fine." He yawned. "Sorry, I meant to call you earlier to see how everything was going with the Woodmans, but I fell asleep."

"Well, we're still compiling a list of addresses for the properties they own and putting together a list of contacts they may have made through Samuel Woodman when he was working undercover, so it's really only a matter of time before we locate them."

Locate them?

But…

An uneasy feeling appeared.

"Which brings me to why I'm calling. Earlier, you mentioned that you would give me a list of addresses, but I haven't yet seen one in my email."

After making the call this morning, Stacy was eager to leave and didn't want to wait around for the police…

Was it really the police she feared?

Who did she call?

"Mr. Miller?"

"Yeah, I'm here, sorry. Like I said, I meant to call you earlier but then fell asleep. I'll get my computer started and send that to you in a few minutes."

"Okay, great. And once again, any other information you can think of, even if it seems useless to you, might be just what we need on this end, so don't hesitate to pass it along."

"I won't."

"Great, thanks."

"Yep."

With that, the call ended.

Phone in hand, Alan headed downstairs to his room to send the promised email but then hesitated.

Call her!

Stacy's phone went right to voicemail.

"Fuck!"

He signed onto Facebook and looked to see if she was online. She wasn't. He sent a message anyway, one that asked if she was okay. Following that, he headed out to his car, exhaustion gone, and drove to the house on Walnut Avenue.

Nothing had changed.

No police tape was present, and the cars that had been parked in the driveway earlier were still there.

Who did she call?

He looked at his phone, hesitation arriving.

Nothing.

Taking a deep breath, Alan stepped out of his car and walked up to the front door, fear unfolding about what he might find within and what it would mean.

He opened the door.

Death!

No rotting had taken place yet, the smell being that of a body that had simply released its bowels and bladder. It was coming from Sam, who was hanging lifeless by the handcuffs, the side of his head where the bullet had exited a mess of chewed-up bone, blood, hair, and brain, some of which had splattered the hallway floor and wall.

Kristi was gone.

His phone buzzed.

Facebook message.

It was from Stacy.

I'm fine, just resting, you?

Alan looked at that for several seconds, questioning who, if not the police, she had called. No answers arrived, nor did a question about it go out to her, not when he knew asking it would document what she had done and cause questions to be raised.

Instead, he spent some time wiping down the surfaces that he had touched and then headed back home, an email with the addresses he knew about put together and sent. At the top of the list was the house on Walnut Avenue.

Sunday, November 10, 2013

"LONG TIME, NO TALK" (II)

As some of you may know from my last post, Walter Doyle offered me a job working as his assistant, a position he says I could hold until I've taken all the necessary steps toward becoming a licensed private investigator. As of now, I'm not sure if becoming a full-blown PI is what I want, but I have agreed to be his assistant while I decide. The only stipulation I have is that my time working for him does not interfere with my school studies since I would like to earn my associate's degree. After that, I will make a decision on what type of education I want to pursue.

As for my friend Stacy, we haven't really spoken much or gotten to see each other since everything broke, the police and media taking up most of her time, given their interest in hearing the details of her investigation, kidnapping, and escape—one that would play out nicely on the big screen, should anyone ever want to dramatize what occurred. (With all the twists and turns, and that hair-raising moment where she picks the lock on the handcuffs as Kristi Woodman comes up the stairs, I'm sure many offers are going to come her way.) Adding to the drama is the mystery that still remains surrounding the murder of Samuel Woodman and the disappearance of his wife, Kristi Woodman. Though asked many times about this, Stacy has been unwilling to speculate on what might have unfolded after her escape, her only knowledge of the situation being that

Samuel had left the house to find out what happened with his brother, leaving Kristi alone, which allowed Stacy the opportunity to fight her way out of the house, Kristi knocked unconscious at one point and handcuffed in an upstairs bedroom. Following that, Kristi disappeared without a trace, and someone murdered Samuel Woodman, someone who used a gun with the same ballistic signature that was found on the bullets recovered from my front porch Halloween night.